Knightraven Studi

TM

More Than Mortal

More Than Mortal is an epic adventure spanning two centuries in time and linking the incredible lives of history's most popular Victorian Age adventurers of the 1800's with the greatest action heroes of the Pulp Era and an assortment of well-known, real-life figures.

In this completely original action-adventure story, four champions of justice, Doc Titan, the Darkness, the Guardian, and the Scorpion, are brought together for the first time to battle a deadly threat and save the Earth and mankind from absolute destruction.

*Although **More Than Mortal** is a self-contained story, painted in bold sweeping strokes, **Pulp Heroes - The Khan Dynasty** and **Pulp Heroes - Sanctuary Falls** continues and concludes this massive three-part trilogy.*

Written and Illustrated by **Wayne Reinagel**

International Standard Book Number: 978-0-9815312-0-5
Library of Congress Catalog number:

Manufactured in the United States of America
Printed in St. Louis, Missouri
Published by Knightraven Studios
(A subsidiary of Knightraven Enterprises & Knightraven Books)

Cataloging in Publication Data
Reinagel, Wayne
Pulp Heroes - A Gathering of Titans.
P. Cm.
1.
2.
3.
4.
1.
II Title: Pulp Heroes.
III Title: More Than Mortal.

ISBN 978-0-9815312-0-5 $19.95 Softcover

This story about fathers
and their sons is dedicated
to my own father,

Donald Joseph Reinagel.

He has done a wonderful
job of raising four sons.

We love you, Dad!

An Introduction to Book One of the Pulp Heroes Trilogy

More Than Mortal

The aircraft was lined up in the crosshairs and Gibson's finger pulled back on the trigger. An iron-hard fist hit the side of his head, knocking him to the concrete sidewalk. Simon Blake, the Guardian, stood over his prone form.

"My people are on that plane!" Guardian stated through clinched teeth.

Before another word could be said, Darkness moved. He seemed impossibly fast as he flowed toward the white-faced man. Guardian's back slammed hard against the brick wall and his arms were pinned by an inhuman force hidden within the depths of the dark cloak. Darkness' face, a terrible, grimacing mask, was inches away from Blake's, and his eyes seemed to glow with crimson fire. Blake could feel the cold, hard barrel of a .45 caliber automatic pressed against the soft skin of his exposed neck.

Darkness spit angry words at him through tightly clinched teeth. "We're fighting a war here. In war, there are casualties."

"Those people in that plane aren't casualties, they are my friends!" Blake's emotionless face showed no signs of concern for his own safety. He continued. "Is this what it will come to?! Friend against friend?! Killing each other?! Damn it, we're on the same side! Doc's right, Gibson, you're out of control!"

Darkness slowly released his grip and Blake dropped to the ground. Darkness' face was completely hidden in the dim illumination of the alleyway. Only his blazing red eyes burned through the shadows. There was a moment of silence between the two old friends.

Darkness finally spoke. "You and I fight crime in very different ways, Blake. I do not believe in allowing dangerous criminals to escape. I will continue this battle on my own terms. Do not interfere again." Darkness backed away and the shadows seemed to embrace his form.

Blake started to reply and realized he was standing alone in the filthy alleyway. Darkness had vanished from sight. There was no laughter or prophetic announcement about crime. The bodies of two dozen men lay scattered in the streets or consumed in the fiery blaze of the burning vehicles. Perhaps Darkness was correct about this being a war.

Scorpion was casually strolling through the carnage, placing his scorpion emblem on the foreheads of every dead gangster he could find, whether he had shot them or not. Finally, he calmly walked up to Simon Blake.

Scorpion smiled. "God, I love this job." Realizing Blake was disturbed about his recent confrontation with Darkness, he continued. "Don't be concerned, we're probably better off without him."

"Perhaps, but I have a feeling before this is all over, we'll wish he was with us." Blake stated ominously.

Who is Doc Titan?

A mentally brilliant and physically superior modern marvel, **John 'Doc'
Titan** was raised from infancy to achieve the vertex of human development.
More than more than merely a 'renaissance man.' To become what his father
coined 'the ultimate man.' A super man.

After his father's death, Doc Titan dedicated his life to traveling the
world, battling evil-doers and helping those in need. With the aid of his five
friends, Doc lives a life of breathtaking action, deadly peril and incredible
adventure. This novel recounts one of his greatest and most exciting, fantastic
exploits.

Henry Marmaduke 'Kong' Larson - Despite his brutish, apelike
appearance, Kong is one of Doc's most valuable aides. Possessing a nearly
photographic memory, he can commit to memory any professional journal,
design specification, or technical research and recall every detail. He can
memorize the layout of any city at a glance or learn any written language in less
than an hour.

Bartholomew 'Bart' J. Blackwell - One of America's leading
mathematicians and cryptologists, Bart assisted the Allies in deciphering the
supposedly unbreakable secret codes of the Axis Forces and in creating the
'Windtalkers' code with the assistance of the American Navajo Indians.

Randolph Garnett 'Big Tom' Thompson - At six feet four and 280 pounds,
Thompson is what the pulps referred to as a two-fisted brawler. A giant of solid
sinew and muscle, Big Tom resembles an immovable granite wall, and he never
backs down from a fight. He is also one of the world's greatest aviators.

Kenneth Xavier 'Percy' Percival Pierce - Treasure hunter. Tomb raider.
From the perilous mountaintops of Tibet to the savage jungles of South
America, from sunken cities to lost civilizations - no ocean is too deep, no
mountain is too high for this man who fearlessly delves into the mysteries of
the ancient past.

Gilbert 'Gibs' Elliot Maddox - Barely four feet tall, this tiny man possesses
a giant intellect, especially in his field of expertise - electricity. Like Edison and
Tesla before him, Gibs has an affinity for what he refers to as 'the juice.'

And last, but certainly not least:

Pamela 'Pam' Titan - Doc's only known living relative. She is extraordinarily beautiful, described by some as a firebrand, a hellcat and an Amazon
woman - all rolled into one. Six feet tall and well-rounded, her one true love is
the siren call of danger and excitement. Whenever possible, she follows Doc
around the globe and into mortal peril, whether he wants her to or not.

Who is the Darkness?

The **Darkness** is the Master of Shadows, a mysterious, haunting avenger of destruction. This merciless creature of the night appears to be able to travel from shadow to shadow, across great distances. Using an invisible network of dedicated undercover agents, as his eyes and ears in the underworld of crime, Darkness attacks ruthlessly and vanishes back into the shadows. A faceless apparition, visible only as two terrible and unearthly crimson eyes, his very name strikes terror in even the bravest of evildoers. His hellish stare unlocks their deepest, most hidden secrets. His mocking laughter bores through their craven souls. His blazing twin .45's stops their evil plans forever. Beware, the **Darkness** comes …

Luthor Gibson - Millionaire, philanthropist, amateur criminologist and civilian disguise for the creature known as Darkness. Gibson wears dark-lensed glasses to hide the scars burned into his flesh, marking where his eyes used to be. Although completely blind, he appears to find hidden clues that the police have overlooked.

Max Grant - World War I master aviator, adventurer, explorer, a haunted man. After the war ended, Grant aimlessly traveled the outskirts of civilization, isolating himself from the seemingly indifferent world around him. Mongolia, Russia, Turkey, India, he became a man searching for the one thing he felt he lost during the war, his soul.

Megan Meriwether - a funny, intelligent, quick-witted young woman. Luthor Gibson recognized her talent for blending in with high society and the fast paced nightclub set. She is his eyes and ears, socializing and becoming friendly both sides of the law. Megan is his only confidante in a very dangerous and lonely profession.

James Chan - a simple, pleasant-appearing young man of Asian descent. Like Megan, James uses this boyish charm to infiltrate, and become friendly with, the upholders of law and the underworld of crime.

Sylvester 'Sly' Montgomery - A large, heavy-set black man, rarely seen outside of his limousine. An ex-cab driver, he knows every street, short cut and back alley. He manages the Montgomery Limousine Service, but the town-cars and the company are actually owned by Luthor Gibson.

Nick Drago - Tough, no-nonsense lone wolf of the underworld. Big, tough, with hard, chiseled features, Nick is the Darkness' spy in the badlands. He has a reputation as a deadly hired gun and a ruthless killer.

Valentine - One of the Darkness' first and most mysterious agents. Or is he simply another alias of the man known as Darkness? Except his single name, very little else is known about him.

Who is the Guardian?

Big game hunter, adventurer, mercenary, **Simon Blake** had finally decided to leave this dangerous lifestyle behind him. But this was not to be his destiny. The accident in New Salem was the worst in aviation history. Nobody should have survived the horrendous explosion. And yet, Blake miraculously staggered away from the devastation without a single scratch or burn.

Aided by six new friends, his travels have taken him from the familiar streets of New York to mysterious realms and distant worlds far beyond our imagination. He has crossed swords with crime rings, crooked politicians and madmen. He has boldly battled with supernatural forces - ghosts, mummies, necromancers, vampires, and dark cults. To help others in need, he founded the new organization called Unsolved Mysteries, Inc.

To the world at large, Simon Blake is a force of justice, a mystic debunker, a ghost-buster, a strange, pale vision, and an apparition. To the underworld of crime and the secret orders of dark magic, he is simply called … the **Guardian**.

Conall 'Mick' McGrath - Biochemist and pharmacologist, this solemn Irish-Scot lost his family, his wife and daughter, in an automobile accident only months before meeting Blake. Mick is Simon Blake's closest friend. In a fight, his fists become like bony mallets, the perfect weapons for dispensing justice to hooligans. But there is a mystery in his past that even Blake is unaware of and discovering it could destroy Unsolved Mysteries.

Barnaby Cornelius Roland 'Wall' Walker - Over seven feet tall and nearly four hundred pounds, sixty inches around the chest and a twenty-two inch neck, Wall might be the world's largest human. The living embodiment of a bearded, Viking warrior, the life of adventure called to the giant Norwegian.

Cassandra 'Cassie' Allison Greyson - An amateur archaeologist, this beautiful, delicate-looking is also a deadly expert with guns, knives, whips and many other weapons. More than one criminal had attacked the dainty girl and quickly discovered that dynamite comes in small packages.

Gabriel 'Gabe' Elias Robinson and Isabelle 'Bell' Robinson - An African-American couple who run the offices and warehouses of Unsolved Mysteries and Praetorian Securities. Gabe and Bell are brave, intelligent people of good character and keen intellects. They have worked with Simon Blake for the last six years.

Andrew Carter - The last member to join Unsolved Mysteries, Inc. Carter originally joined to write about Blake's life and sell the story to Hollywood. He soon became addicted to the action and adventure. A British Shakespearean-trained actor with a flare for the dramatic, he is constantly being accused of suffering from a Robin Hood complex.

Who is the Scorpion?

Crime has an enemy. Unstoppable. Relentless. Bringing death and destruction to those who prey on society. A ruthless creature of the night, dispensing justice with his twin pistols. He leaves his scarlet mark, the deadly scorpion, on the foreheads of those he has stopped. He is the scourge of crime and the defender of the innocent. Evil beware of … the **Scorpion!**

Preston Stockbridge II - A man shrouded in mystery. Men told of his courageous deeds during the Great War, but his life before that time has been lost in the distant past. He came to New York City with his faithful mute friend, Rav Chandra, and an enormous fortune. Preston played the part of the millionaire playboy philanthropist until he met the wealthy debutante, Whitney Van Pelt. She stole his heart and discovered his greatest secret. Stockbridge is the deadly Scorpion!

Whitney Van Pelt - Preston Stockbridge's fiancé and closest confidant. Fearlessly addicted to mortal danger and breathtaking action, Whitney is an important ally against the forces of evil. She has even donned the Scorpion outfit to assist him with his battle against crime.

Adam Coleman - An ex-soldier of fortune and a deadly marksman, Adam fought beside Preston during the Great War and several other conflicts afterwards. To throw Police Commissioner Jack Lockhart off the trail, the quick-thinking Coleman has donned the Scorpion outfit several times and even faked his own death.

'Rav Chandra' - After the Great War, a haunted Preston Stockbridge wandered aimlessly through Europe and upper Africa. At the border of Afghanistan, he was witness to a silent warrior single-handedly battling seven armed men. Christened Ghoshdashtidar Raviprakash Chandramouleeswaran Dakkar, this proud giant was forever banished from his native homeland. Upon returning to the United States, Stockbridge revealed to Rav his plan to pursue justice as the masked vigilante, the Scorpion. The faithful mute swore his allegiance to his friend and master.

Police Commissioner Jack Lockhart - A no-nonsense law enforcement officer and leader of the task force - Project Scorpion. His assignment is simple, arrest Scorpion on sight for dispensing vigilante justice. Or, failing that, stop him by whatever other means deemed necessary. The problem is, Lockhart believes that Scorpion could be the son of his late wife. His stepson. If he ever proves that Stockbridge is the Scorpion, how can he bring himself to arrest the greatest force of justice ever known?

Friends and comrades, willing to sacrifice nearly everything in their lives, to see justice done.

More Than Mortal

Act I: New York City

Chapter One .... Satan's Last Stand
Chapter Two .... Funeral for a Friend
Chapter Three .... Fallen Angel
Chapter Four .... Doc Titan - Man and Superman
Chapter Five .... Simon Blake - The Guardian
Chapter Six .... The Culling Begins
Chapter Seven .... It's a Salon!
Chapter Eight .... What Lies Beneath (The Chromium Club Gallery)
Chapter Nine .... The Robinsons are Taken for a Ride
Chapter Ten .... Totenkopf's Deaths-Head Squad
Chapter Eleven .... A Kidnapping Gone Wrong at the Stockbridge Mansion
Chapter Twelve .... Beware of the Black Skull
Chapter Thirteen .... The Doc Titan Trap
Chapter Fourteen .... The Death of Police Commissioner Jack Lockhart
Chapter Fifteen .... Killers at Work
Chapter Sixteen .... Death in the Air
Chapter Seventeen .... Death Deals Double
Chapter Eighteen .... A Farewell to Unsolved Mysteries
Chapter Nineteen .... Kong Gets a Bite
Chapter Twenty .... Coffin Nails
Chapter Twenty-One .... Detective Work
Chapter Twenty-Two .... Harold Bekker and the Mysterious Medallion
Chapter Twenty-Three .... The Dangerous Life
Chapter Twenty-Four .... The Battle at the Praetorian Securities Warehouse
Chapter Twenty-Five .... Bart Solves a Mystery
Chapter Twenty-Six .... Out of the Frying Pan
Chapter Twenty-Seven .... Kiss Kiss, Bang Bang
Chapter Twenty-Eight .... Victor Kaine's Secret Plan
Chapter Twenty-Nine .... Born Better

Chapter Thirty .... Calling in a Favor
Chapter Thirty-One .... The Strange Prisoner
Chapter Thirty-Two .... (How Many) Bullet Holes
Chapter Thirty-Three .... Captain Hazzard and The Pamela

Act II: To the North Pole

Chapter Thirty-Four .... The Invitation
Chapter Thirty-Five .... Flashback to 1916 - Grant and Rasputin
Chapter Thirty-Six .... Flashback to 1916 - The Secret
Chapter Thirty-Seven .... Flashback to 1919 - Too Many Degrees?
Chapter Thirty-Eight .... The Man of a 1000 Faces
Chapter Thirty-Nine .... The Titan Rehabilitation Institute and Clinic
Chapter Forty .... The World of Man
Chapter Forty-One .... Allied Intelligence
Chapter Forty-Two .... The Mystery at the North Pole
Chapter Forty-Three .... The Island at the Top of the World
Chapter Forty-Four .... Sanctuary Discovered
Chapter Forty-Five .... The Museum - Secrets Revealed
Chapter Forty-Six .... Flashback to 1918 – The Reunion of Titans
Chapter Forty-Seven .... Flashback to 1888 - Grey Eyes
Chapter Forty-Eight .... The Missing Page
Chapter Forty-Nine .... Flashback to 1888 - The Last Stand of Saucey Jack
Chapter Fifty .... Death Most Singular (The Death of Gabe Robinson)
Chapter Fifty-One .... Flashback to 1899 - Wilder and the Savage
Chapter Fifty-Two .... Return to the Hidden Acropolis
Chapter Fifty-Three .... Flashback to 1899 - The Titanic Choice
Chapter Fifty-Four .... The Illuminati
Chapter Fifty-Five .... Flashback to 1938 - The Guardian's Secret Revealed
Chapter Fifty-Six .... New Blood
Chapter Fifty-Seven .... Conspiracy Theories

Act III: The Battle

Chapter Fifty-Eight .... The Calm Before the Storm
Chapter Fifty-Nine .... Rendezvous Trap and Peril's Stowaways
Chapter Sixty .... The Plunge of the Seablade
Chapter Sixty-One .... War Clouds
Chapter Sixty-Two .... Attack on Skull Island
Chapter Sixty-Three .... Final Reckoning (Project Gladiator Revealed)
Chapter Sixty-Four .... Shadow and Sunlight

Act IV: The Finale

Chapter Sixty-Five .... Destination Known (The Departure)
Chapter Sixty-Six .... Epilogue

Act I: New York City

Chapter One
Satan's Last Stand

April 1, 1945   4 pm

Lewis Afar glanced over his evening newspaper and acknowledged the presence of the second man on the opposite corner of the street with a slight nod of his head. The first man had an air of scholarly intelligence about him, hence the nickname Prof, short for Professor. Ape was the man who had just walked up and stood near Prof. As his name implied, he was a muscular man, sporting a bulbous, shiny nose. Lewis turned his gaze toward the two men directly across the street from him. These two were Shyster and Sad Sack. Shyster, a handsomely dressed fellow with a waxy moustache, was having his shoes polished by a young boy in short pants. Sad Sack was Shyster's exact opposite. His worn, dingy clothes were disheveled and his face was rather homely in appearance.

Lewis was the only man who knew the true names of these fellows, and they all preferred it this way. All of the members of Lewis' unique crime fighting league were reformed gangsters and each had spent time behind prison bars.

Two blocks away, the engine slowly idled in a common, inconspicuous, hard-top sedan. A greasy-looking man, in the back seat of the black car, leaned forward and held five photographs close to the driver's face. Names were written at the bottom of each with a clean, legible script. The names and pictures matched Lewis Afar and the four other men. He tapped the photographs and pointed at the five men on the sidewalk. "That's them. That detective was right on the money."

Several years ago, Afar had mimicked such famous crimefighters as Doc Titan and the Scorpion. Like them, Lewis was also quite wealthy, although not in the same class as members of the Chromium Club. He was a handsome man, sleek-haired, always impeccably dressed, with bright gray eyes. He fought crime on the streets and gathered around him assistants who would help carry the burden. They were a small group of vigilantes, going places the police wouldn't, or couldn't, go. They donated most of the ill-gotten profits, stolen from the various mob bosses, to the poor, keeping only enough to pay their expenses.

Like the Scorpion, Afar left his own unique mark at the scenes of the crimes. His calling card was a devilish figure, projected onto the wall over his pummeled victims, using a flashlight with a scarlet satanic symbol taped over the lens. The newspapers had nicknamed him Captain Lucifer. He called his secret cadre of crimefighters, Satan's Angels.

Captain Lucifer and Lank, his chief lieutenant, knew the real names of everyone in the group, but the members themselves only knew each other by code names like Ape, Irish and Shyster. A few had useful skills in medicine or pick-pocketry but most were just tough guys, following their chief. Lewis Afar had waged an unceasing war against crime in the guise of the seemingly super-human Captain Lucifer, along with his reformed gangster pals, for several years. They battled murderers, mob bosses, racketeers, and common street thugs. They kept shipments of illegal drugs and guns off of the streets of Manhattan.

The members of Lucifer's crew showed a normal amount of apprehension or greed in the situations they got into and often one of the crew would get killed during the course of an adventure. This group of young hooligans was neither invincible nor charmed, and it seemed foolish to continue attracting the attention of the police and the district attorney. So Captain Lucifer and his band of misfits became undercover agents of street justice. They would still battle crime but nobody knew exactly who they were. They would set up random meetings in alternating locations to plan their next move. And nobody knew where or when Satan's Angels might strike next.

Two men stepped from a black and yellow cab, one was the passenger and the other was the driver. The fat, jolly-faced driver was Irish. He flipped the sign atop his cab to Off-Duty and locked the car. His passenger, a tall thin man, almost gaunt, was Captain Lucifer's chief lieutenant, Lank.

A slender man dropped a dime on the dirty, weather-beaten wood counter at the newsstand and picked up a copy of the pulp magazine, *The Apparition, Private Investigator*. He leafed through it as he walked past Lewis and leaned against the wall of the corner building, about eight feet away. He had a wiry little mustache that pointed up at the ends. This man was Johnny English. The last member of tonight's gathering, nicknamed Dusty, sauntered down the sidewalk, stopping to admire things in shop windows as he approached. They were all here.

Lewis Afar folded his newspaper and tucked it neatly under his arm, before starting across the street. He adjusted the cuff link of his right sleeve, a signal for the others to follow him. The cuff links were shaped like small, silver and red devils, holding pitchforks. He wore a matching tie-pin. His goal was the all-night diner two blocks down. The small group of men casually followed, in such a fashion that it attracted no attention from the other by-passers on the sidewalks. Lewis smiled slyly as he walked, happy in his group's ability to move inconspicuously around the busy streets of New York City. Little did Lewis suspect that he and his league of crime fighters had a rendezvous with death.

The greasy-looking man in the rear of the hardtop sedan leafed through the folder. It contained several photographs and various details on each of the nine men. Each photograph was labeled at the bottom with the names of Captain Lucifer or one of his agents. "That's the last two. Johnny English and Dusty are their names." He waved at the other two cars parked along the short boulevard.

The two black inconspicuous vehicles skulked slowly down the street, unnoticed by Lewis, until he spied a reflection in one of the shop windows. Like quicksilver, his smile vanished. He quickened his pace, hoping to reach the haven of a basement stairwell. Too late. The staccato rhythm of a Thompson machine gun filled the afternoon air, even as he leapt for safety. A slug gouged through his shoulder and another burled through the flesh of his bicep. The last bullet to hit him clipped the top half-inch off of his ear. By now there were at least three more machine guns filling the air with lead. The sound was deafening. Afar was able to see quite a bit from his secure, concrete foxhole. Much more than he ever wanted to. Innocent people were being mowed down by leaden death.

He watched helplessly as Ape, Prof, Sad Sack, and Johnny English were dropped to the ground by the machine guns before they could even react to the threat. Dusty was hit several times and fell face down in the street, a crimson puddle spreading beneath his body. Afar's guns literally sprang into his hands as he stood in the basement doorway and fired at the black touring cars. Savage spurts of orange and crimson speared from his automatics. One machine gun disappeared back into the car window, as its wielder was struck in the face by a bullet from his gun. Shyster had pulled a revolver from its shoulder holster and joined in the fray. A bullet left a small red mark on his forehead and he looked like a puppet with its strings cut, as he slowly dropped to his knees and fell over.

A little girl was crying on the curb of the street, where she had tripped. Irish, in a heroic gesture, scooped her up in his arms and started for the security of a brick-lined doorway. He didn't make it; a scarlet path of holes stitched its way across his wide back. At least he didn't die in vain; the little girl was safely tucked behind a heavy-gauge, blue steel mailbox. The man known only as Lank, stood in the middle of the street and exchanged bullets with the machine gunner in one of the cars. Brave and unflinching, he managed to shoot one man, but he dropped a moment later as another gunner peppered him from the second car. Afar had continued firing and hit the gas tank of the first car. The resulting explosion lifted the rear end of the heavy automobile several feet into the air, where it hung for a fraction of a second, before crashing back to the ground. Store windows on either side of the street had fractured and sprayed glass in all directions, littering the sidewalks. The second car turned onto a side street and the engine roared angrily as it sped away. One last hail of bullets came from the small, oval rear window; chipping brick fragments away from the building behind Lewis's head.

Lewis Afar, the man known as Captain Lucifer, was in shock. He felt as though he had been dropped into a war zone. Smoke and flames were everywhere. The eight members of Satan's Angels were all dead; lying like broken dolls on the dirty streets they had sworn to protect and defend. Lewis had trouble catching his breath. He could hear a faint, bubbling noise and glanced down. Three bullet holes had bored their way cleanly through his chest and abdomen. Both lungs had been punctured. He smiled as he noticed the splatter of blood on his white dress shirt appeared to take the form of a devil's scarlet silhouette. How appropriate.

His last thought was that at least he wouldn't have to attend another funeral for a friend. He had buried too many friends over the years. Captain Lucifer's war against crime was over.

Chapter Two
Funeral for a Friend

April 4, 1945   6 pm

The cemetery was quite old but very well maintained. The surrounding neighborhood was quiet at this time of night, especially with the slight drizzle of misty rain falling on the occasional pedestrian. Men walked with their coat collars pulled up around their necks and hats pulled down tight. Even though it was officially springtime, there was still a chill in the air. The haunting sound of a lonely violin drifted in the darkening skies. It played a morose melody known as *Adagio for Strings* and, even though it was not loud, the notes were carried a long distance on the night breeze. The tune continued, seeming to have no beginning or end.

The old man sat a short wall of stone, under the corner of a pavilion roof, where he could stay dry. His eyes were closed as his fingers drew the bow across the strings. He seemed lost in the sad melody. At first glance a passerby might think he was bent over the violin at a strange angle, however, it would soon become obvious that the poor, ragged fellow suffered from a physical handicap, a hunchback. His long, unkept gray and black hair fell in long strands from under his oversized slouch hat and cascaded across his shoulders. He wore tattered clothes that had seen too many winters.

Unfortunately, since the Depression had struck New York in 1929, there were too many of these 'lost men.' Men who had lost everything, almost overnight, and had taken a plunge from successful business men to homeless beggars. Even now, fifteen years after the Depression started, thousands of ruined men still lived on the streets of Manhattan. There was, however, one odd thing about this particular street musician. The antique violin he played so passionately was a priceless two hundred year-old Stradivarius.

At the end of the block, a large limousine pulled up to the curb. There was no movement for several minutes. Finally, a passenger emerged. The man was tall and extremely well-dressed. His tailored suit and coat spoke of great wealth. He wore an expensive hat and carried a blind man's walking cane. Strangely enough, he did not appear to need it, so confident were his movements. In New York City, unlike most parts of the nation, the extremely rich mingled with the destitute and poor on a daily basis. Even in this modest neighborhood, neither the man nor the limousine would draw a second glance from the average pedestrian.

Most of his face was covered, with his coat collar pulled up and his hat drawn down. He wore a pair of dark glasses that covered his eyes and most of the strange scarring visible at his brows and cheeks. For a full second, those sightless eyes turned toward the hunchbacked, violin player. His face was thin, his nose was long and straight, and his cheeks were high and well defined. To the average person he would be considered very handsome. On one finger was an extraordinary ring, a fire opal that blazed with an internal fire, despite the dusky skies.

He spoke to the chauffeur, asking him to wait in the car and then strolled into the ancient graveyard. As though he had been there before and knew exactly where he was going, he walked with an air of confidence. His cane tapped the stone path and the echo carried only a short distance. He passed within several yards of the hunchback, who was still playing his quiet, but passionate, music. Only a few hundred feet down the path, he stopped in front of a large, gray tombstone. The ground in front of the stone was freshly dug. Most folks would have thought this old graveyard had been filled long ago, however, someone had been buried here quite recently. The smell of freshly dug, wet dirt was pungent. The man stood silently, leaning against his cane, at the foot of the grave. While his blind eyes stared straight ahead, he breathed a sigh of sad regret. He had only met the occupant of this grave a few times but they were men cut from the same cloth. They had shared a common interest.

A creak of metal against metal drifted through the darkness. One of the great iron gates at a second entrance opened and another man entered the graveyard. This man was similarly dressed, with nicely tailored suit, coat, and hat but lacked the cane and the unique ring. He hesitated for a brief second, as he noted the tall man at the gravesite. As he walked toward the grave, however, the first man turned to leave. They took different paths through the full graveyard, littered with thousands of stones, some dating back hundreds of years. Large mausoleums bore the names and crests of prominent, well-respected New York families. Stone statues of angelic figures silently witnessed the night's mourners.

The tall, blind man almost passed by the violin player but stopped to drop money into the open violin case. The faded letters, embossed in the felt liner of the case read the name Guido Salvatore. The old fellow nodded his unseen appreciation at the contribution. He stopped playing long enough to hand the wealthy man a playbill for a future street concert. Sometimes local businesses would pay the hunchback a few dollars to pass out flyers to advertise their wares. The tall man continued back to his limousine and a minute later he was gone.

The second man now stood at the same grave as the first. He removed his hat and bowed his head. Coal black hair fell down and covered one eye. Several minutes passed; with the only sound coming from the violin, carried in the evening wind. The dark-haired man was in his mid-thirties and ruggedly handsome. His face showed no signs of emotion as he paid his silent respects to the inhabitant of the grave. Finally, he turned and walked in the same direction that the blind man had taken. He also stopped and contributed to the meager collection in the hunchback's violin case. In return, he also received a playbill. Seeming to be in no particular hurry, he strolled down the sidewalk and vanished into the night. Guido, the hunchback musician, lifted his gaze and suddenly noticed a third man was standing at the gravesite that the first two had visited. Guido had only glanced away for a second and had heard nothing!

This fellow was the largest of the three visitors tonight. He was well-proportioned enough that at first it wasn't obvious. But Guido had remembered that the tombstone was nearly the size of the first two men, shorter than the first man but about the same size as the second man. This third mourner stood a full head taller and seemed to dwarf the headstone. Certainly, the man was of gigantic proportions.

Guido glanced back to the street, as he watched a young couple strolling along the quiet sidewalk. They whispered and laughed at some private joke and then they were gone. Guido returned his attention back to the third man. He yelped in surprise and nearly dropped his violin. The giant man was standing only three feet away! He hadn't made a sound, as he left his position at the tombstone and approached Guido.

Bronzed skin covered the giant's face and hands, weathered from years of exposure to the elements. His face was very handsome, as though sculpted by a master stone-carver. He wore no hat and the mist did not seem to bother him in the least. His head was shaved smooth and he sported a thick mustache and goatee. He stood nearly seven feet tall by Guido's estimation. From his pocket, he removed a quarter and casually flipped it into the open violin case. Guido handed the giant a playbill from the stack. As the man turned away, Guido whispered under his breathe, "Cheapskate."

The large man stopped, smiled, and then continued on his way. Guido smiled broadly, exposing a crooked set of stained teeth.

The giant walked two blocks and noticed a woman walking slowly down the sidewalk. Her vision was poor and she groped along the building to make her way. Her clothes were ragged and she appeared destitute. The giant walked up to her and placed a card in the woman's open hand. It held the address of a hospital and the large man's name. It simply stated Doc Titan. When she arrived at the hospital, she would be fed and her eyes would be examined by experts. The blinding cataracts on her eyes would be removed and Doc Titan would pay the bill. If he was available, Doc would do the surgery himself. Doc Titan was a well-known philanthropist and a true humanitarian. He walked away and removed the playbill from his pocket. On the reverse side was a simple handwritten message.

Tomorrow night. Chromium Club. 8 p.m.

Doc read this, then crumpled the paper and tossed it into the street trash bin. He walked away and was soon out of sight. One minute passed. A second. Then a third. Faint footsteps approached and a tall, broad-shouldered man came into view. He wore a tan overcoat and a dark hat with a leather band. On the lapel of his coat was silver, decorative pin shaped like an angel. He stopped at the wastebasket and paused. Lighting a cigarette, he cautiously studied the street and sidewalks. Nobody was within view.

He reached into the trash receptacle and removed the message Doc had thrown away. He read the brief message and tucked it into his coat pocket. Three minutes later, he was in a sidewalk phone booth and feeding it several coins. A gruff voice answered and he read the information from the back of the paper to the voice on the phone. The man at the other end acknowledged the message and hung up.

The broad-shouldered man felt good. He was being very well paid for this information and he had completed a difficult assignment. For the last several days he had barely slept, hadn't even had time to read the newspaper. This had been a difficult stake-out. Now that the assignment was complete, his plan was to grab a newspaper, take a long, steaming shower and sleep for three days. He stopped at an all-night newspaper stand, glancing at the racks of pulps, comics, and newspapers. He smiled at the newest pulp covers of *Doc Titan* and *The Darkness*. However, *The Scorpion* had always been his favorite. It was a shame the publishers had stopped printing *The Scorpion* last year, due to war-time paper shortages. He had also liked the short live series *The Guardian*.

His eyes settled on a headline in large bold print. **APRIL FOOL'S DAY MASSACRE! TWELVE KILLED IN STREET SHOOTOUT!** As he read further his eyes grew larger. My God, what had he done? He dropped the paper and ran back to the graveyard. Five minutes earlier, Guido had packed up his violin and his meager earnings for the night and left the graveyard. When the broad-shouldered man arrived at the graveyard he quickly searched for the old man. He found himself standing in front of the recently dug grave that the three other men had visited.

The inscription carved into the headstone simply read, *Lewis Afar. Born April 1st, 1904. Died April 1st, 1945. He lived and died a hero. May he rest in peace.* Such a short eulogy for a mystery man. A man once known as Captain Lucifer. A crime fighter. A hero. Next to the engraved lettering was an embossed figure, an odd one for a gravestone. It was a simple outline of a figure ... of a devil holding a pitchfork.

Tears welled in his eyes as he read the inscription. What had he done? How could he fix this? He ran back to the street and hailed a taxi. Maybe it wasn't too late. Not if he hurried.

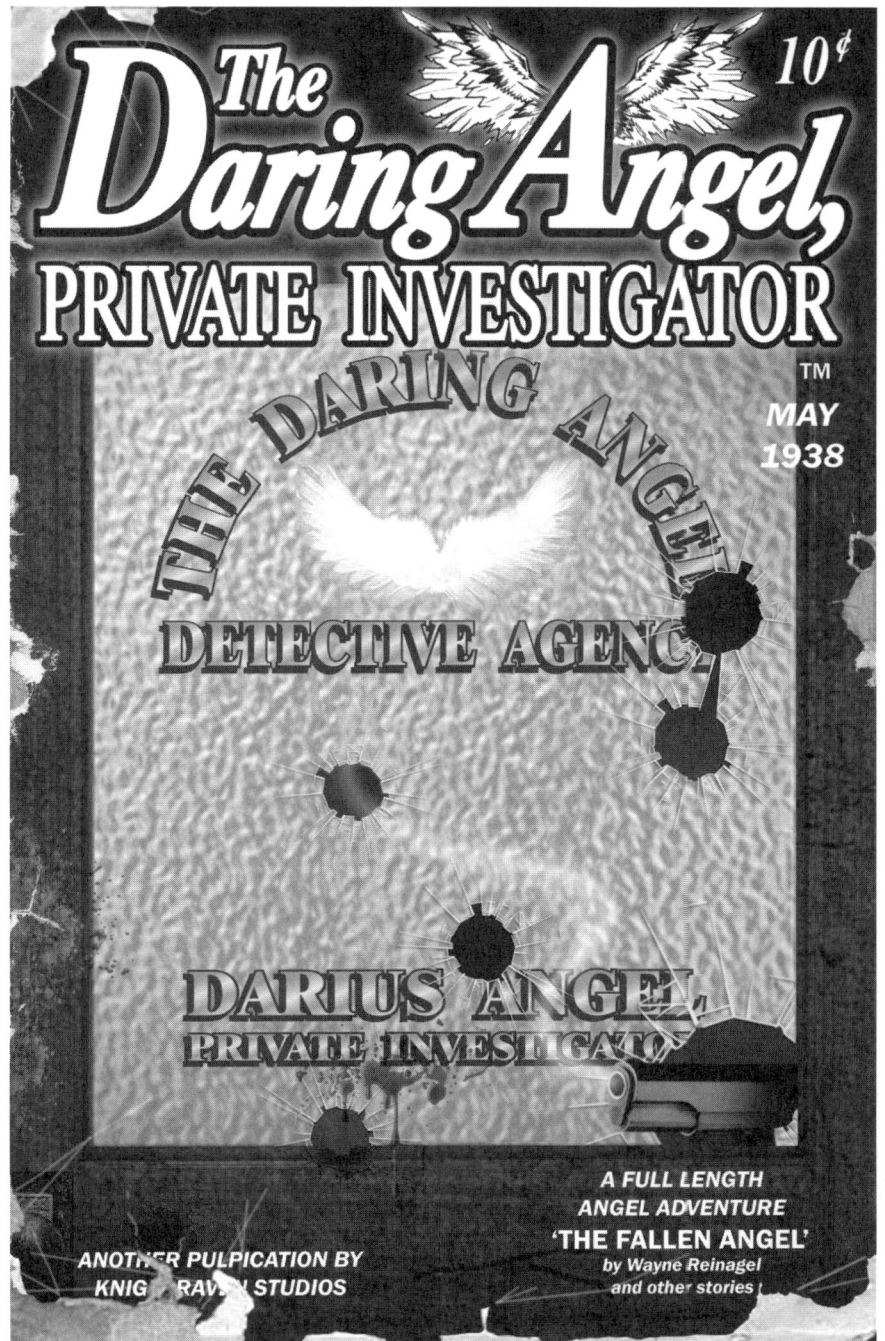

Chapter Three
Fallen Angel

April 4, 1945   8 pm

The tall, broad-shouldered man, stood over six feet in height. The angel pin on his coat lapel reflected silver from the streetlight, as he lifted the flap of the blue, steel mailbox and dropped in the thick manila envelope. It disappeared into the dark depths of the metal United States Postal box. "I'm doing the right thing." The man thought to himself. This started out as a simple surveillance job, but something was definitely wrong. Nine men, and several innocent civilians, had died because of the information that he had assembled and provided to one of his clients. He had been well paid for what appeared to be a simple assignment. Provide details of the daily habits of a list men and women. Where they went, what they did, the usual research. And that was his occupation, a private investigator.

The lean-waisted man pulled his tan overcoat closed and lowered his dark hat further down on his head. It would be better if he wasn't recognized. Even gangsters and felons rarely messed with government property, like USP mailboxes, but no reason to tempt fate. The package needed to reach the Chromium Club or more men could die. Important men. Men he had idolized as a young man. When he read the newspaper tonight and saw the list of names, he knew he had been a fool. He had been offered too much money for a simple stakeout. But he needed the cash and convinced himself the two men actually were who they claimed to be. Studio agents who were looking for a way to contact possible clients. Important clients.

But then he saw the list of names of the men who were killed … murdered. Shot down in the streets of New York City, in broad daylight. Lewis Afar and eight of his crew, the group known to a select few as Captain Lucifer and Satan's Angels. The same names and faces he had provided to his clients. And he had provided them with others. John Titan. Preston Stockbridge II. Luthor Gibson. Simon Blake. And all of their known associates. He had given the two men the information before reading about the gun battle. The two clients who wished to remain anonymous, insisting on being called Mr. Jones and Mr. Smith.

The detective crossed the vacant street and entered the front of his office building. The structure was old and mostly empty, but the rent was cheap and the landlord didn't care if he slept in his offices at night. The tiles on the entryway floor were old and worn. Some were even missing. He climbed the stairs to the third floor and walked down the long hallway. He fumbled with the key to the office door and it finally opened with a small creak. The gold lettering was old and faded. His name could barely be made out these days; only the name Angel was legible. However, the words Private Investigator could still be read clearly. And really, that was all his clients cared about. What he did, not who he was.

He swung the inner office door open and hesitated. The detective had been in the business long enough that his sixth sense was well-developed. Sixth sense or that little voice in the back of his head that warned him of impending danger. Didn't matter which it was. He felt for his .45 caliber automatic in his coat pocket, but then remembered that it was still under his desk. He had glued an old holster under the middle drawer of his desk and stored his gun there. Just in case he needed quick access to it in an emergency. Like now. Stupid. The desk light clicked on.

The man sitting behind his desk smiled politely, but it was obvious to Angel he was a crook. A gangster. He had an oily, snake-like presence about him. One gold tooth was displayed in that smile. Gentlemen didn't put gold in their mouth, they wore gold watches. This man was a street thug. He also sported one of those silly-looking, pencil-thin moustaches. In fact, he knew of the man, but by reputation only. The word on the streets was that he worked for Man-Mountain Marko. Goldie … something. The name slipped his mind, but for some reason the face looked vaguely familiar.

"What can I do for you, friend?" Darius Angel asked the slick crook.

Goldie's smile widened, showing off his prominent gold tooth. "Are you the private dick named …?"

Angel cut him off sharply. "Private investigator." He hated the slang word for detective, especially the way this hood used it as an insult. "And my name's on the door. What do you want? Why are you in my office?"

Goldie grunted and indicated the door with a nod of his head. "The door was unlocked, so I figured I'd wait for ya here, in your office." He leaned back in the leather chair, locked his hands behind his head and placed his feet on the desktop. He indicated the business card lying next to his shoe. "Darius Angel, the Daring Angel. That's a clever nickname for someone in your racket. I got stuck with the moniker of Goldie. You can probably guess why." He flashed another smile, showing off his namesake.

Angel could have argued the point about the door being unlocked, but right now it didn't matter. He gave the man a minute, rather than ask the question a third time. In this profession, you had to have patience. And nerve. He reached forward and pushed the man's feet roughly off of the desktop.

Goldie's eyes narrowed, his temper flared and showed on his features, but then he smiled again. Angel would have to watch this guy. Hot tempered, but smart enough not to lose control.

Goldie continued. "You have certain documents my boss … uhm … an associate of mine would like to purchase."

"Yeah? What's that, pal?" Angel walked around the heavy wooden desk, indicating to Goldie to vacate his chair.

Goldie stood up and walked toward the sofa. This is where Darius slept most nights. Better than his filthy apartment. Goldie turned to face Angel, but continued to stand. "You did some investigating for two men … movie producers or studio agents, I believe. Watched some famous people, wrote down their habits. Where they went. Who they met. That sort of thing."

Angel dropped into his chair, the leather still warm from its previous occupant. "And if I did? My clients pay me for my confidentiality and their privacy." Darius glanced at his desktop and saw the framed photograph of his Eskimo friend named Ghun-goosh, of the Kwakiutl tribe. And standing next to Ghun-goosh was Gabriel Wilder, the man Darius Angel use to be, in a previous lifetime. Between them was an eight-foot tall totem pole. In 1938, Gabriel and Totem had tracked down the four murderers of his father, Clinton Wilder. In the photo, Darius was wearing his tan trench coat and a white, silk domino mask. Years ago, Darius had tucked this picture in the back of the bottom, left-hand drawer of his desk. This oily gangster must have already started searching his desk drawers and discovered the old photograph. Darius must have interrupted him before he finished the search or he would have already found the files he was asking about.

"I would be willing to pay you a rather … large sum of money. Just think, you could be paid twice for the same work."

"I don't think so." Angel reached under his desk and felt for the holster. It was empty! Damn!

Goldie held up Angel's gun. "Looking for this? Bad move, pal. This could have gone differently. Egorov?" He said loudly.

At first, Angel wondered at the meaning of the word Goldie had spoken and then realized it was a name. A large, barrel shaped man with a mass of facial hair entered the room. When he spoke, his Russian accent was quite obvious. Darius Angel could tell from the look in this man's eyes, that he was not someone to be trifled with.

Konstantin Egorov ordered, "Please place your hands on top of the desk and make no sudden moves. Good. Now, we will ask you again. Where are your copies of the files Goldie mentioned?"

Darius considered for a moment. Double payment for the same job … not a bad deal. But something smelled rotten about this. And the names in the files were of men Angel respected.

"Sorry, but I don't know wha …!" Angel screamed, as much in shock, as he did in pain. The giant Russian had pulled out a large hunting knife, raised it overhead and drove the point through Angel's hand, pinning it to the wooden surface of the desk. The blade was so sharp, he didn't even feel pain for the first few seconds. He attempted to bluff his way through the agony and then thought, to hell with this.

Egorov leaned forward, his large, bearded face only inches from Angel's. "Now, I will ask you again. Where are the files?"

Darius gritted his bared teeth and spat the words, "The middle drawer on my right. Under a false bottom."

Goldie opened the drawer and pulled out several files. He leafed through them and grunted.

"Yeah, these are the ones." He acknowledged.

Without uttering another word, Egorov roughly pulled the knife blade from Angel's hand. Darius gingerly supported the damaged hand with his other. Egorov threw a small bundle of money on Darius' desk and strolled toward the door without looking back. Angel rose up from his chair and faced the retreating men.

Goldie turned in the doorway and smiled at Angel. "Hey, you don't remember me, do you?" Darius slowly nodded negatively. "Didn't think so. You use to wear a white, silk eye-mask. Called yourself the Avenging Angel Detective, didn't you?"

Darius waved his open hand dismissively. "That was a long time ago."

"Yeah, but I remember. You knocked out my front tooth and sent me to prison for two years. I never did properly thank you."

Before Angel could move, Goldie raised his gun and fired until the clip was empty. The deadly barrage of bullets perforated Darius' torso and the impact threw him backwards, out of the window and onto the streets below. As a pool of his blood darkened the street, his last living thought was, 'Belshazzar.'

The light, spring breeze blew in through the broken window, as Goldie walked back to Angel's desk. He casually tossed the spent automatic onto the desktop and picked up the small bundle of money Egorov had left behind. "This is yours … and I'll take this as mine." He looked out the shattered window and felt a wild exhilaration when he saw the detective lying dead and broken on the street below.

Goldie waved a salute out the window, sneered an ugly smile and walked away. "So long, Avenging Angel Detective. Sure clipped your wings, didn't I?" His laughter echoed in the small, empty detective's office.

Chapter Four
Doc Titan - Man and Superman

April 5, 1945   7:30 pm

The large, brass plaque over the front door read:

Pamela's Beauty Salon and Day Spa,
A subsidiary of Titan Investments, Incorporated
and the Hunter Island Holding Company.
Founding members:
Pamela Titan
Cassandra Greyson
Megan Meriwether
Whitney Van Pelt

The tall, muscular woman leaned over Cassie Greyson and spoke in a husky German accent.

"Ve haff vays to make you talk."

Cassie replied slowly. "I don't care … what you do to me, I'll never … talk."

Sweat beaded on her brow and it was obvious, just from her expression, that she was in agony. Cassandra 'Cassie' Allison Greyson was a petite-figured woman approaching her thirties, but still had the figure of a twenty-year old. She was often described as cute as a china doll, and appearing nearly as fragile. In her case, however, appearances were deceiving. She had learned JuJitsu as a child, among other defensive, unarmed battle techniques, and could toss full-grown men over her dainty shoulders. She had beautiful, shoulder-length, platinum-blonde hair and lovely light-gray eyes. She had a button of a nose and full lips. Barely over five feet tall and just under one hundred pounds, she was adorable.

Right this moment, however, she was doing her best not to break under the torture. Her arms were pinned back and her shoulders ached from the pressure. She couldn't take much more before she surrendered to her assailants. The other woman spoke in an exaggerated French accent.

"Giff up, leetle gurl."

Cassie bit her lip and smiled. "Never." She pushed with all of her might and the barbell was raised again. "That's thirty."

The large woman laughed and dropped her phony German accent. "Wow, never thought you would make it. You sure are a tough little vixen." Pamela Titan helped Cassie place the weight back on its stand. "If you ever leave Uncanny Mysteries, Incorporated, you can always come work for me at the beauty salon."

Cassie breathed a sigh of relief. "And rob rich New York clients like you do? No thanks. I'm quite happy as simply an investor in your business. And it's Unsolved Mysteries, Incorporated."

Pam flexed her muscular arms. "Robbery is such a vulgar term. I simply charge them astronomical fees to make them look gorgeous. And I cater to New York's social elite, because they can afford to pay my fees." Pam smiled and picture-framed her face with her hands, in a mock photo shoot. Her features were as stunning as Cassie's but her appearance differed greatly. Nobody would have compared Pam to a cute doll, however, she *was* breathtakingly beautiful.

She stood nearly six feet tall and while not thin, she had memorable, statuesque curves. She could wear an evening dress one night that would turn every head at a social event, male and female, and wear a denim shirt and jodhpur trousers the next and still turn heads. She had been raised as a tomboy in a Canadian lumber mill town. As a young girl, she could outfight any boy, and when she grew up, she could out drink them. Kong called her a pip, and Bart referred to her as a peach, both were compliments in their minds.

She was always ready to join Doc Titan and his crew on a wild, new adventure. The more dangerous, the better. Her cousin, however, felt it necessary to protect her. But the adventure lust that coursed through Doc's veins, was also in Pam's blood. She always found a way to sneak into the action. With a color scheme similar to her cousin's, Pam had attractive, brass-colored shoulder-length hair and copper-hued skin. Her eyes also had the rather unique deep brass color her cousin's possessed.

"You torture them with lifting weights and pushing balls and running in place, and they pay you for this?" The third woman, with the exaggerated French accent, asked.

Pam frowned jokingly. "They pay very handsomely, Megan. Very soon, I'm going to open a franchise of clubs. And if you think this is torture, wait until the massage. Hilda is from Yugoslavia. She can bend a horseshoe straight, using only her bare hands."

The woman named Megan 'hummpfted' in disbelief. "Seems like an awful lot of work to me." She tilted her wine glass up and swallowed the last of the golden elixir. "I'll just stick to drinking your expensive champagne." She wasn't a big drinker and felt a little tipsy from the two glasses she had sampled in the past hour.

Megan Meriwether was a lovely woman, also turning her share of heads at social events. And the city was her environment. Even though she enjoyed adventures, she preferred the simpler life. Hobnobbing with the rich and famous, champagne breakfasts and caviar lunches, tea rooms and beauty parlors. Her idea of roughing it was to wear high heels. She had a sharp mind and a quick wit, which often saved the day when she assisted the Darkness. She was certainly drawn to the mysterious man in black and his alter ego, Luthor Gibson. However, she understood this was also just another disguise. She had shoulder-length, black hair and deep, dark eyes. She was still dressed in a nicely tailored business skirt and jacket, having just finished a case with the Darkness. Gibson had Sly, his limousine driver, drop her off at Pam's place, while he headed to the Chromium Club.

Cassie was dressed in jogging pants and a sweat-shirt with her Alma Mater's name and emblem, Vassar University. She and Whitney Van Pelt had attended the renowned college at the same time. Even in these baggy, worn clothes she was a stunning beauty. She and Pam had been exercising for the past hour. She turned to Pam and asked. "Are you ready to hit the showers and join Megan, before she drinks your entire stock?"

For the next twenty minutes, the ladies enjoyed the cascading waters in the steamy shower. Many men would have paid extraordinarily large sums of money just to watch the bathing beauties. Afterwards, the three women, dressed in simple, ankle length cotton robes, relaxed in Pam's private room at the rear of the building. Megan, propped up on an enormous pillow, was slowly sipping on her third glass of champagne.

Megan hiccupped. "Pam, what was it like growing up around little Doc Titan?"

Pam shrugged her shoulders. "Actually, Megan, I didn't meet Doc until I was nineteen. I was born and raised in Canada. He had heard about my father, his uncle, Alex Titan, dying from a heart attack, brought on by a wolf attack. A werewolf attack, to be accurate." Cassie and Megan eyed Pam as though she had suddenly grown another head. "It was fake werewolf, of course."

Megan raised an eyebrow and said teasingly, "Of course. Real werewolves so rarely go to Canada." She tittered drunkenly.

"So, Pam, why did you ask us to meet you here tonight?" Cassie asked.

"It about what's happened since our island adventure last year. I'm not saying anything else until Whitney gets here. I have a surprise for you girls."

Megan's eyes grew large. "Oh, I haven't shown you girls my surprise. Remember that snake that tried to eat me on that island."

Cassie shivered, "How could I ever forget?"

"He didn't give his life in vain." Megan held up a lovely pair of snakeskin boots. "Now I have something to remember him forever."

"That snake was huge. All you got was a pair of boots?"

"Actually, I had twelve pairs of boots made. And a vest. And five belts. Oh, and you'll each get a nice snake-skin Christmas present." Megan said with a smile.

Pam shook her head and chuckled. "He really *was* a big snake, wasn't he?"

Cassie glanced at the wall clock with concern. "I wonder where Whitney is?"

John 'Doc' Titan stood like a bronzed statue, gazing over the cityscape far below. From the windows of his private suite of offices on the 116th floor of the Titan Building he could see the entire expanse of Manhattan Island. Several blocks to his right he could see the Empire State Building, a towering building resembling a colossal obelisk. For two short months, in 1931, the ESB was New York's tallest building, before the Titan Tower eclipsed it in height. The ESB was 85 stories tall with an additional sixteen-story art deco tower and a 102nd floor observatory. In contrast, Titan Tower was a full 124 stories tall. The top four floors were designed as a hanger to house gyrocopters, also known as autogyros, and small dirigibles. Unlike the ESB, the Titan building did not taper near the top of the structure, but the top four floors were cut off at a forty-five degree angle. A giant recess was designed into the 121st floor so a full-sized zeppelin or dirigible could be safely moored to the tall building.

Doc Titan and his father, Professor Clarke Titan, had designed and financed the building of the great monolith. Doc's father wanted a location where he and his son could study mankind from on high, like the mythical Titans, the children of the ancient Greek Gods. After his father's death in 1930, Doc became the sole owner of nearly completed Titan Tower. He used the top dozen floors for his own purposes, housing libraries, laboratories, and private suites. During the Great Depression, Doc had saved many companies from bankruptcy. These included lumber mills, airlines, cruise-ship lines and many more. Most of these companies leased entire floors of the Titan Building. The other floors were rented to New York City's most prestigious businesses.

John Titan was a unique individual and was involved in a very dangerous business. Righting wrongs and punishing evildoers. He had been trained for this unique occupation since he was barely a year old. His father had hired the finest men in every vocation to train his son.

And he had not neglected the physical acumen. Experts at boxing, wresting, savate, karate, and nearly every art of unarmed fighting. Tumblers, acrobats, jugglers and other circus performers taught him their unique skills. Then, men who used weapons, from guns, knives, swords, and many other lesser known weapons. By the time he was twelve, Doc Titan was certainly the most dangerous man alive. By the time he was sixteen, he knew more than most of his masters and instructors. Sixteen grueling hours a day, seven days a week, fifty-two weeks a year, Doc trained, practiced and studied. It was the only life he knew.

Now he was forty-five years old. He had been chasing and defeating villains, evil masterminds, crooks, and tyrants for the last fifteen years. He had witnessed sights that would have shocked the bravest of men, fought creatures high in the air and far beneath the oceans, from other planets, and even some that defied description. Several times he had fought with creatures long thought extinct. Doc had traveled to nearly every country, found lost civilizations and remote, uncharted islands. He had witnessed the effects of a multitude of horrible weapons of mass destruction, things that would forever replay in his mind.

Men bursting into flame on the streets of Manhattan, turning invisible, becoming mummies while onlookers stared in disbelief, or stripped to the bone in mere seconds. Buildings exploding, large chunks of granite propelled through the air by unseen forces, remote islands disappearing beneath the ocean waves or covered in volcanic ash, as forces from beneath the ground expelled molten lava. Things too incredible to be believed.

Doc truly loved the adventure. He enjoyed the company of his best friends, traveling to exotic lands, meeting people from other cultures, and discovering things lost to mankind for centuries. This was the life he was raised to live, and he wouldn't have traded it for any other profession. The only other vocation in which he felt truly 'gifted' was as a practicing physician. He enjoyed helping those less fortunate. But, at times, like now, he was … weary. Exhausted from the constant burdens he placed upon himself.

As Doc stood at the large window opening, he watched the lights of the city below. Standing in the massive, elaborate surroundings of the interior offices, Doc appeared to be an average, well-proportioned man. He wore a nicely tailored three-piece suit, including coat and vest, obviously tailored to his unique build. It wasn't until he stood next to a normal-sized person or object that his large size became apparent. Doc was nearly seven feet tall and weighed in at three hundred and fifty pounds. His movements were so smooth; he might have glided on ball bearings. The corded sinews on the backs of his hands and on his neck gave the appearance of bundled piano wire. His copper-hued face looked as though it had been carved from brass, possessing high, strong cheeks and a high forehead.

His scalp was shaved smooth and was the same hue as his weathered face. He wore a thick mustache and goatee, slightly darker than the color of his skin. It sported a fingertip width of white hair, starting at the edge of his left nostril and heading south. One of his most striking features were his deep, brass-colored eyes. The pupils appeared to be filled with a mercury-like liquid that alternately seemed to either reflect light or appear bottomless. Doc Titan was indeed a unique individual.

Kong scratched his bullet-shaped head. "Doc, are ya alright? Ya haven't said anything all night."

Doc turned slowly and stared from Kong to Bart to Gibs. The room was quiet and the men stopped what they were doing and focused on Doc.

"Do you guys feel it?"

Bart was polishing his slim, black cane with his handkerchief. "What exactly are you referring to, Doc?"

"That itch at the back of your neck, when you know something is out of place. A feeling or premonition of things about to happen. Like your subconscious mind is trying to warn you of …"

Kong chuckled. "Ah, Doc, ya just got the heebie jeebies."

Bart folded the silk cloth and arranged it neatly in his suit pocket. "Excuse me? In English, if you please."

Gibs sneered. "For Kong, that was English."

Kong frowned. "Aww, go play with your bug zapper, Gibs."

Gibs' smiled vanished, replaced by a scowl. "I'm stuck again. I'm missing something, but I can't figure out what it is."

Kong continued. "All I was saying is this; Doc just came back from the gravesite of a man in a similar profession to our own. So ya start getting this nervous feeling. Ya start asking yourself, could this happen to me? Is there a bullet out there with my name on it?"

Gibs scolded. "Gee thanks, Kong. For the last dozen years we've been lucky. Thinking like this will jinx it. Like the police officer who only has a week until retirement and he starts feeling a need to be overly cautious. And that's when he does something really stupid and gets himself killed. We've all faced Old Man Death and escaped him every time."

Bart removed a delicate, gold watch from his vest, wound it twice, and dropped it back into his pocket. "Yes, but all of us in this room have been at death's door, or beyond. More than once, only Doc's special skills as a great physician saved our hash."

Kong was still concerned about their leader. "Doc?"

Doc smiled, unconvincingly. "You gents might be correct, but I have a feeling something bad is about to occur. Watch your backs, brothers. I'm heading over to the Chromium Club to meet an old acquaintance. I should be back in a few hours."

Chapter Five
Simon Blake - The Guardian

April 5, 1945   7:30 pm

Megan refilled all three glasses with another round of champagne. "Okay, Cassie, you've been hanging around Unsolved Mysteries, Incorporated for six years now. Does Simon Blake still give you the willies, with those icy eyes and that ghastly white hair and skin?"

Cassie sipped slowly and responded. "Don't you remember? His hair and face are no longer white after that incident with that banshee creature. Besides, you should really get to know him, Megan. Simon is a very good man, who has had very bad things happen to him."

"Maybe so, but his eyes are still creepy." Megan said with a shiver.

"Do you love him?" Pam asked without warning.

Cassie simply smiled through her champagne glass and said nothing.

Simon Blake stared out the windows of his Barren Street offices. The settings of this simple office were much different than Doc Titan's palatal skyscraper apartments. His reception area had a simple, mild-patterned rug, and several rather non-descript tables and chairs. Nothing in the room stood out as ornate or elaborate. In fact, the only feature of the room that was note-worthy was the large window overlooking the street in front of his offices. Naturally, this window was bulletproof. Blake had been in this crime-fighting business a relatively short time but he had managed to make a long list of enemies.

This would explain why the entire block of buildings on Barren Street was actually reinforced, armored fortresses. Double layers of brick, bulletproof glass, concrete floors and ceilings were the standard construction. Additionally, Simon Blake had bought the entire block, to prevent criminals from attacking from next door. Or even allowing innocent bystanders, living near Unsolved Mysteries, Inc., to be in harms way. Most of the buildings were simply faux storefronts without actual businesses inside. Blake maintained some of the buildings as garages for his fleet of fortified vehicles. These ranged from simple roadsters, built for speed and endurance, to larger town cars with armor plating, bullet-proof glass and tires, and finally, a variety of delivery trucks, with the latest in electronic surveillance equipment. In the past, he kept two autogyros in one of the structures. With the aid of a several grateful US government officials, he had received special permits and moved his small fleet of aircraft into a waterfront structure, only blocks from Doc Titan's Global Navigator Consortium. This plain brick building had a simple plaque at the large doors that read Praetorian Securities.

As a young man, Simon Blake had traveled the world, seeking his fortune. Silver mines in the American Southwest, oil drilling in Alaska, amethyst ventures in Australia, diamond mining in Africa, engineering projects in Russia, and various expeditions to the darkest, most uninhabitable regions of Earth. He had often been hired as a soldier of fortune. Between travels, he accumulated a multitude of degrees from many universities in a variety of respectable vocations, including medicine, engineering, chemistry, and many others.

Even though he was still in his late twenties at the time, Blake had managed to amass a vast fortune. But he left the dangerous lifestyle as a big game hunter, adventurer, and mercenary behind him to settle down and begin a family. In 1937, he had decided to marry a beautiful young lady, Alicia, and within the year they were proud parents of a son, named Benjamin. Simon had a loving family and his life was a perfect picture. But this was not to be his destiny. In the blink of an eye, his perfect world was destroyed.

The accident was the worst in aviation history. The two airplanes collided in mid-air, killing over fifty people. (This occurred only a few months after the German zeppelin *Hindenburg* had crashed to the ground on May 6, 1937 and took the lifes of thirty-six passengers and crew.) Blake's wife and infant son were among the victims. Nobody could have survived the horrendous explosion. And yet, Blake miraculously staggered away from the devastation without a scratch or burn. He awoke a week later in a hospital ward and discovered his coal-black hair had become snow-white chromium, and his sun-tanned skin had bleached white, lacking any pigmentation. The muscles beneath his white face were completely paralyzed and lifeless, like a pale, emotionless mask from the grave.

After regaining consciousness, his mind snapped from the trauma and he was temporarily confined to the mental ward of a nearby hospital. He met Conall 'Mick' McGrath, the hospital's pharmacist, and soon discovered Mick had lost his own family, his wife and daughter, in an automobile accident earlier that year. Mick was a quiet, but likable, fellow and they quickly became close friends. After Blake's release from the hospital, he enlisted Mick's aid to investigate the plane crash.

They soon met Barnaby Cornelius Roland 'Wall' Walker and he was recruited to their noble cause. While investigating the accident, Blake discovered something odd that had been withheld from the newspapers. There were no other bodies found in the wreckage from either flight! The passengers and crews, including Blake's family, had completely vanished!

Who or what was responsible for the disappearance of the Blake's wife and son? Was it possible they were still alive? What happened to the other fifty passengers? How did he survive the explosion unharmed? Even now, years later, the answers to these questions eluded Blake.

Seemingly forged into something more than human, a figure of ice and steel, possessing superhuman strength, Blake became relentlessly obsessed, a machine of vengeance, an impersonal force, with the burning need to solve this mystery. Others soon joined their ranks. Aided by six new friends, his travels had taken him from the familiar streets of New York to mysterious realms and distant worlds far beyond our imagination. He had crossed swords with crime rings, crooked politicians and madmen. He had boldly battled with supernatural forces - ghosts, mummies, necromancers, vampires, dark cults, and even a cabal of arcane sorcerers. To help those in need, Blake founded the new organization called Unsolved Mysteries, Inc.

While in the hospital, Blake had discovered that he could now mold his lifeless features like putty and assume the appearance of anyone. He became known as the man of a thousand faces. But the single feature possessed by Simon Blake that shook villains to their core was his hypnotic eyes. Nearly colorless, his pale, icy-steel eyes seemed to stare through men, instead of at them. Blake dedicated his life to battling crime and injustice, while searching for his lost family. This deadly foe of the underworld had been nicknamed the Guardian.

In his battle against crime, Guardian was joined by six individuals who had also been victims of the criminal underworld. They soon became his most loyal friends. For the last six years they had battled side by side against evil villains, strange creatures, and mad scientists. Fortunately, Guardian had proven himself to be a scientific genius, with senses and physical strength far greater than average. His personal code was a simple one, refusing to take the lives of even the lowest crooks. Much too often and despite his warnings, the villains, motivated by greed or hate, destroyed themselves.

One year ago, another life-altering incident occurred. In an adventure his companions called the *Cry of the Banshee*, Blake battled a demonic doppelganger known as the Magus Wraith. The poltergeist had nearly killed him. Much to everyone's surprise, after quickly recovering from his injuries, he had regained the use of his paralyzed face muscles and his white hair returned to its original coal black color. His pale eyes, however, like ice in a polar dawn, still burned with the same intense flame.

Running his gloved hand through his thick shock of black hair, Blake appeared weary. On the best days this was a difficult lifestyle. And this had not been the best of days. Recently, one of the 'good guys' had fallen to some unknown group of … what? Crooks? Criminals? Evil masterminds? Megalomaniacs? After a while, you simply ran out of names to call these villains. Lewis Afar had been an old friend, dependable and true, and had assisted Blake several times in the past.

Blake's eyes were attracted to the corner building below him. The rest of the block housed offices, apartments, warehouses, and garages for his privately owned Unsolved Mysteries, Incorporated business. And the small sign on the main door of the offices read exactly that. *Unsolved Mysteries, Inc.* Small engraved letters on a discrete gray sign. And yet, for the people who truly needed his services to fight injustice, to go to places the police could not or would not go, it might have appeared as large as a billboard.

Simon Blake was still a young man, now in his late thirties. Since losing his polar-white hair and dead facial features, he was no longer a person who stood out in a crowd. This was fine with him. He had grown tired of friends, clients, even people on the streets, simply stopping to stare at him. Unlike his friend, Doc Titan, who inspired awe and wonder with his handsome appearance and superior physique, Simon Blake had simply been … a freak. A pale reflection of a complete human being.

He was glad when the creature, that had nearly killed him, changed him back to the man he had once been. Blake was no great muscular giant but he possessed an uncanny amount of strength, considering his size. Standing five feet eight inches and weighing around one hundred seventy pounds, Simon could now walk down a typical Manhattan sidewalk and not have a single person take notice of him. He had come to enjoy being anonymous, another face in the crowd.

Wall and Mick were standing outside the front door of Mick's corner laboratory. Merely two old friends, quietly talking to one another. Mick was puffing clouds of gray-white smoke from his weathered pipe and staring up at the evening skies. They had known each other for only six years, but in this profession of constant danger, six years was a lifetime. Like Blake, Cassie, Gabe and his wife Isabelle; Wall and Mick lived in apartments within the block. This gathering was more than just close friends and co-workers; they were Blake's family.

Wall's full name was a mouthful, Barnaby Cornelius Roland Walker, but nobody ever called him that. And 'Wall' fit him so well. When he first met Mick he had warned him. *"The name's Wall to my friends,"* he had said. *And then he added dangerously, "Most people try to be friends with me."* Of course, they soon discovered that the man-mountain was a big Teddy bear. Actually, a *huge* Teddy bear. He stood over seven feet tall and weighed nearly four hundred pounds, all tendon, sinew and muscle. His arms and legs were so massive they resembled tree trunks. He could bench press a car without breaking a sweat. He was often referred to as the most powerful man on Earth and one of the keenest minds in the field of electrical engineering.

Raised in a poor family, during the height of the Depression, he had to leave school after sixth grade but continued to read every book ever published on electricity. He was content with the simple life of a furniture mover and part-time bodyguard, until he met Simon Blake. Hailing from Gokstad, Norway and the living embodiment of a bearded, Viking warrior, the life of adventure called to the giant. Blake accidentally bumped into the good-natured, gargantuan man while investigating his family's disappearance and they quickly became close friends. Barnaby Cornelius Roland Walker became the third member of Unsolved Mysteries, Incorporated.

One month later, he met the woman who would forever change his life. Cassie Greyson was a cute, diminutive bundle of pertness that craved the life of danger and intrigue. Wall was love-struck at first sight. Unfortunately, it seemed that there was never an opportunity for the large man to voice his feelings toward her. Besides, at times, she seemed rather taken with Simon Blake.

The man he was talking to was Conall McGrath, or simply Mick, as he liked to be called by his closest associates. Mick was the Guardian's first and foremost aide, and Simon Blake's closest friend. Like Blake, McGrath had lost everything when his wife and daughter had died suddenly in an automobile accident. He had also suffered at the hands of criminals. When Mick was still a youngster, his father Dugan McGrath, had bravely opposed criminals attempting to extort 'insurance' money from his neighborhood. A 'membership in their protective association' is how they had phrased it. He physically tossed them into the streets. To make an example of him, they torched his drugstore. Mick's father and mother died in the blaze.

Mick stood over six feet tall, with coarse red hair and bitter, piercing blue eyes set into his freckle-splotched face. Long sideburns and temples were painted with white, showing he was no longer a young man. But he was never one to back down from a tussle, especially when he had his 'Irish up.' His massive hands, when doubled into fists, became deadly bone mallets. Perfectly designed for knocking some sense into a hooligan.

Ever the dour Scot, Mick was an excellent biochemist. Blake had purchased a run-down drugstore when he bought the entire block of buildings. He generously gave McGrath the deed to this structure on the corner of

Seminary and Eighth Avenue. It was much larger than it actually appeared and a doorway had been added between it and the next building.

Housed inside the corner building was a fully out-fitted biochemical and pharmaceutical laboratory, allowing Mick to work on his chemical experiments and devices to aid in their battle against crime. The attached building was an electrical engineer's paradise. Wall conducted experiments and developed the fantastical devices that Guardian and his aides used in their war on evil.

Neither of the buildings were accessible from the front entrances, which had been fortified to withstand anything short of an armored missile attack. A maze of adjoining doorways linked all of the buildings on this side of the street to one another. The only functioning entrance was in the middle of the block, at the main offices of Mysteries Unsolved, Inc.

Blake continued to observe his friends at the street corner. If he had been able to eavesdrop, he would have heard a most curious conversation.

"Zounds, lad. When are ye thinkin' of askin' her?" Mick queried, in his thick Scottish brogue.

Wall responded nervously, stroking his thick beard. "Tonight, when she gets back from Pam's Place."

Mick's face broke into a quick, broad smile as he patted the other man's wide back. "Congrats, my friend. I wish ye both the best."

"Thanks, Mick."

The gargantuan man turned his head and noticed Simon Blake watching from an upper window. Mick and Wall smiled and waved to their leader. He politely returned the gesture.

Glancing at his watch, Blake noticed it was nearly eight o'clock. Time to meet the others at the Chromium Club. Walking to the garage, he passed Andrew Carter's private quarters. Andrew was a handsome, young man and actually resembled Simon in several ways. A British Shakespearean-trained actor with a flare for the dramatic, the others had always teased Andrew of having a Robin Hood complex. He was the only member of Unsolved Mysteries, Inc. who had not suffered a loss at the hands of crime. He was in it for the thrill of the adventure. Simon was glad to have Carter join their merry band of misfits, and not simply because Andrew was the man who had saved Simon's life during the *Cry of the Banshee* case. Andrew carried scars of his own from the daring rescue but never mentioned them.

Andrew walked up to the open doorway and faced Simon. It was like looking in a mirror. An old mirror. Simon faced a white-haired, pale-faced individual in a light gray suit. "Hi, chief. I'm heading out to investigate a murder downtown. Some detective was shot and thrown through his office window. Fell four stories. Meeting a police inspector named Hannigan. You know of him?" Andrew finished applying the white makeup and adjusted the tight-fitting wig.

Blake thought for a second. "Yes. He's a good man. A bit headstrong. You'll have to stand up to him if he tries to brush you off. Met him three years ago, during that incident with the museum mummies running around Manhattan. We only met that one time, so he'll never suspect you aren't me. Good luck, Andrew." Simon started to walk away and turned back. "Be careful out there, this is a dangerous business."

"Heck, chief, danger is my middle name." Andrew smiled widely, as if he were having the time of his life.

Blake reminded Carter as he left. "Oh, and Andrew? The Guardian never smiles."

Simon Blake still had his moments of doubt about this whole thing. When Andrew Carter had come to him and asked if he could continue to play the part of the icy-faced man known as the Guardian, perhaps he should have declined the offer. Not all of the criminals he had met in the last few years believed that the Guardian had lost his white face and hair. They believed he disguised his true appearance with wigs and flesh-toned makeup. Let them believe whatever they wanted. Besides, Andrew Carter was able to defend himself. He had already proven himself time and again. Grimly, Simon continued toward the garages.

Chapter Six
The Culling Begins

April 5, 1945   7:45 pm

Totenkopf, code-named The Black Skull, stood looking out of the large opening at the pale moon's reflection off of the ocean's surface. Fryderyk Chopin's famous Piano Sonata No. 2, sometimes known as the Funeral March, was playing in the background. His grim, deathlike visage could have been carved from a dark, marbled stone. Even the eyes moved sparingly. A warm breeze caressed the silent, gaunt human statue. The man-made cavern opening was several stories tall and a couple hundred feet wide. After six long months of demolition, the construction of the hidden airplane hanger was finally near completion. With its natural camouflage of the mountainside above, a surveillance airplane would never suspect this island housed a massive aerial strike force. Strafing runs by enemy aircraft would be impossible.

Turning to his head scientist, Randolph Schmidt, Totenkopf questioned him. "Is all in readiness, Professor Schmidt?"

Randolph Schmidt was a middle-aged man with spectacles that hung on the tip of his nose and thinning, gray-white hair combed down the center of his head. Despite this, his hair always appeared disheveled. A pencil-thin mustache traced along his upper lip; otherwise he was always clean-shaven. Although sporting a bit of extra weight and a slight hunch to his back, doubtless from sitting at microscopes most of his life, Schmidt seemed in good health. He had a slight German accent, but not noticeably pronounced. He spoke clearly and directly to Totenkopf, never averting his eyes. The skull was only a simple, rubber mask but most men found it impossible to stare into its features for long. Totenkopf liked this about the elder man. He did not do his work from fear of what Totenkopf could do to him, but out of loyal dedication to the Black Skull and the Third Reich.

Professor Schmidt walked up and faced Black Skull. "Yes, Herr Totenkopf. Phase Three is ready and awaiting your word to proceed."

Totenkopf was pleased with this announcement. "Very good, Professor."

Dropping his voice, so nobody else could overhear, the professor questioned. "Herr, Totenkopf. Phase Four, the final phase, will be ready in eight days. Has Victor Kaine brought the sixth and final Danner notebook yet? That journal will be needed for the last injection."

Black Skull was glad he had someone with whom he could freely converse. "No, he still hesitates."

Schmidt lowered his voice further. "Excuse me for saying, sir, but I have doubts about Kaine's loyalty to our cause. Are you certain he can be trusted?"

Totenkopf confided with Schmidt. "Professor, I do not trust that man in the least. At some point I will request your assistance, when we are certain we have the complete set of notebooks. Can I rely on your support?"

Without hesitation, the professor replied, "Absolutely, Herr Totenkopf. You can count on my faithfulness."

"Very good." Totenkopf said and then added. "I will come to the labs shortly to witness the Third Phase."

Black Skull fingered the large Swastika on his collar and watched the professor walk away. Brave man. Men feared Hitler. Men feared Totenkopf. Men feared Victor Kaine. Hitler feared … every man. Quite simply put, he was a coward and a madman. Black Skull and Kaine did not fear each other; they simply did not trust one another. But this simple professor didn't appear to fear any of them. He was certainly the bravest man Totenkopf had ever met and for that reason he liked the elderly man. If only his own father had been such a respectable man, instead of a stupid, abusive drunkard.

Victor Kaine entered the massive hidden hanger. Dressed from head to foot in brilliant white, he was in total contrast to Black Skull's dark uniform. He strolled easily and quietly past the empty planes lined up along the tarmac. His shoulder-length, white hair moved lightly in the breeze from the ocean. Kaine was tall, over six and a half feet, but did not appear to be a powerful man. In fact, he looked rather pale and gaunt. But his movements professed great strength. His face was thin, the cheeks pronounced, and his eyes were slightly sunken. His light-colored eyes seemed to take in everything around him.

One of his most striking features were his hands. The fingers were incredibly long; being the length of a normal mans entire hand. Some said he had the face and demeanor of a poet, quiet and reserved. However, he had been convicted of strangling two men at the same time, one with each hand and sent to the Russian Gulag in Siberia.

His bodyguards, Hermia and Xena, walked along side him. The hulking ladies rarely left his side since first meeting him in Siberia. He entrusted his very life in their large hands. Bidding them to stop and watch from a distance, he walked up to Black Skull and frowned unintentionally. This obsidian skull mask was a little bizarre, pitch black in color with only two small openings at the eyes. Victor didn't care much for playing games, but he did understand fear and intimidation were powerful tools when it came to controlling men. As a true leader, he preferred controlling, rather than killing, the men in his charge. This included his enemies.

Kaine addressed the Nazi leader. "The cleansing has begun."

"Very good." Totenkopf rubbed his gloved hands together. "By this time tomorrow, these 'supermen' will be no more."

"You might find these men and their friends are a little harder to kill than you think." Victor warned.

Totenkopf spoke confidently. "Black Skull and the Third Reich will succeed where all others have failed."

Without saying another word, Kaine turned on his heel and walked back to his large lady comrades. "He's a madman, but for now he has his uses. Soon we will turn this operation to our advantage, but for now, we bide our time and you wait for my signal. Our forces in the United States are ready and we will succeed where Black Skull fails. Konstantin Egorov has gathered the information we required and will begin his assignment in fifteen minutes. Tomorrow, we begin our takeover of the world, and this time, not even Doc Titan will be able to stop us."

Chapter Seven
It's a Salon!

April 5, 1945   7:45 pm

Cassie was twirling a locket of blonde hair around her tiny finger. "Besides, talking about creepy, doesn't Darkness give you the heebie jeebies? We know he's actually Luthor Gibson, but they are like two completely different people. Luthor is a complete gentleman and Darkness is ..." Cassie shivered involuntarily. "And how does Luthor see, if he's really blind?"

"Oh, Darkness is harmless, once you get to know him. His bark is worse than his bite. Unless, of course, you commit a crime. And Luthor really is blind. Somehow, when he becomes Darkness, he can see again. It has something to do with the scars around his eyes, the ones he received when he was in India after the war. Something or someone blinded him. I saw him once without his shirt on. He has other scars on his chest and back, too. Like he was burned or branded. Weird looking hieroglyphic symbols. He's never really confided in me about that time of his life. Luthor's still such a mystery.

"Recently, however, Doc designed a pair of custom-made dark glasses that simulates nighttime and now Luthor can see while wearing them. Besides, this job has its perks. Ol' Lew has quite a nice tush. Occasionally, I drop my purse, just so he'll bend over ..." Megan started confessing, with a smirk on her lips.

Pam threw a small pillow at Megan. "Pervert. You ladies need to get ..." She stopped talking as a scarlet light blinked on the wall. She flipped a switch and a television screen hummed into life.

Megan frowned. "What's the red light mean?" Her words slurred slightly and she giggled.

Pam studied the screen intently. "Somebody just came into the building, in the main lobby."

Megan waved a small hand nonchalantly. "So?"

"I locked that door when the last of my girls left." Images showed up on the screen. Three men, one armed with a machine gun. Pam flipped another switch. The voices of the men could now be heard.

The tall man looked around the lobby and appeared uncomfortable. "What are we doing here, Eddie?"

Eddie, the short, angry man to his left, replied. "Boss said we'd find our targets here, at this address. Let's look around, Kirby." He cracked his knee on a bench and swore profusely. "Damn, its pitch black in here."

Kirby was the tall man. "In a beauty parlor?"

Pam talked to the man on the screen, even though he could not hear through the one-way speaker system. "It's a beauty *salon*."

The third man was extremely thin, so emaciated he made scarecrows look healthy. "This can't be the right place. It's a beauty parlor for God's sakes!"

Pam tapped the screen with her fingernail and repeated. "*It's a salon!*"

Cassie placed a small hand on Pam's shoulder. "I don't think they care, honey."

Kirby, the tall man, confessed. "Well, I don't cotton to the killing of women, Graves."

'Graves' Gladney was the name of the thin fellow. Everyone called him 'Graves', because he looked as though he belonged in one. He leaned his machine gun against a magazine rack. Looking around, he grabbed the *Darkness* pulp and stuffed it in his shirt. He liked *Scorpion* pulps more, but the *Darkness* pulps were nearly as good.

Graves admitted. "Me, neither. Boss didn't tell us about this being a beauty parlor."

Pam opened the door and yelled into the darkness, "It's a beauty SALON!"

On the television screen, the three men drew guns from their shoulder holsters and followed the sound of Pam's voice.

They approached the door, where light poured into the hallway from the overhead transom. Kirby stood on one side of the door opening and Eddie stood on the opposite. Graves leaned back and kicked the door hard with one foot. It swung open and the men entered quickly, guns leading the way. Pam stood quietly in the center of the room, dressed in only the simple, white cotton robe. Graves nervously licked his lips.

Kirby spoke finally. "Don't move lady." He glanced briefly around the room. Pam seemed to be here alone. "Guys, what if we just take her back with us? Let the big boss decide what to do with her."

Graves agreed and stuttered. "Y-y-yeah. M-m-may … maybe we should ... search her. F-f-for … you know … weapons."

Pam smiled. "Boys, do I *look* like I have any weapons on me?" She opened her robe and gave them an eyeful of her naked form.

Graves dropped his gun and didn't seem to notice as it bounced off of his foot and clattered onto the floor. Eddie's mouth hung open and his eyes widened. Kirby simply stared, seemingly turned to stone by the beautiful Medusa before him.

Cassie stepped from behind the dressing curtain. Kirby swung in her direction, but her foot caught him under the chin and lifted him off the ground. The back of his skull hit the floor with bone-jarring force. As Kirby was going down, Graves attempted to hit her on the head. She spun away from the glancing blow and struck Graves with an open palm to the chin. Her other fisted hand struck him in the stomach and as he bent double, her elbow drove down on the base of his skull. Pam stepped forward and knocked Eddie to the ground with a few well-placed punches. Cassie ripped the wiring from a lamp and hog-tied Kirby with the skill of a professional cattle wrangler. Graves groaned and Cassie punched him again.

"I hate being hit on the head." Cassie said as she turned and noticed Pam's robe was still hanging open. "Why don't you cover yourself up, before you poke out someone's eye?"

Megan raised her head above the desk and hiccupped loudly. "You guys done playing roughhouse?"

Cassie teasingly stuck out her tongue at Megan. "Society lush."

"That's Miss Society Lush, to you." Megan smiled and added. "I would have helped; but I just had my nails done today. Besides, playing a social lush is part of my undercover disguise." She played up the helpless woman role, but Cassie noticed as Megan slipped her small handgun back into her purse. Megan Meriwether had been ready for action.

Pam handcuffed the other two gangsters and stood up. "So, are these gentlemen friends of yours, Cassie?"

Cassie nodded. "No, I don't recognize them."

"Me, neither." Megan added, inspecting their features.

Pam threw a pan of water into the men's faces. They sputtered and glared daggers at the women.

"Who sent you guys here? Who is your boss?" Cassie grilled the prisoners.

Kirby smirked and spoke like a street-tough gangster. "You dames won't never get us to talk."

Pam smiled evilly. "Sounds like a personal challenge. Guess we'll just have to torture them."

Kirby boasted proudly. "You'll never get me to talk. I was once tortured by the Dent boys for five hours, and I never said a word to them." Kirby had a strong, Brooklyn accent. 'Word' was pronounced 'woid'.

Pam looked at Cassie and Megan. "This will only take about five minutes."

Pam Titan lifted the man off of the ground, tossed him over her shoulder, and carried him into the next room. The other two men glanced at one another nervously. "What's she going to do to him?"

Megan played up the part. "With Pam, you never know." Nodding to Cassie, she continued. "Remember the last guy she tortured?"

Cassie shivered violently, playing along with Megan. "It took two days to get the stains out of my carpet." She winked at Megan as the bound men exchanged apprehensive glances.

From the other room they could hear Kirby asking in a slightly worried voice. "Hey, lady, what are you doing?" There was no reply from Pam. Suddenly, the man screamed so loudly, Graves jumped three inches off of the floor.

Graves licked his lips. "Geez, what's she doing to him?" Seconds later, another scream followed the first, this one was much louder. Graves had never heard anything like this before and he had been witness to several beatings in his day. And it had only been one minute since Pam had dragged Kirby away.

Pam's pleasant voice could be heard in the next room. "I'll give you one last chance to speak."

Kirby's weakened voice could be overheard saying, "I'll ... never ... talk." Seconds later, a third, gut-wrenching scream was heard and then total silence. Footsteps came down the hallway and Pam stood at the door opening.

Pam braided her fingers together and cracked her knuckles loudly. "He's passed out already. Guess I'll need another one." Eddie and Graves looked at one another with worried expressions. From the sounds in the next room, she had nearly broken Kirby and had taken less than three minutes to do it. Eddie wet his lips and shivered in fear.

Graves broke first. "I'll tell you whatever you want to know."

Pam looked sternly at him and then at the other two women. "Maybe I ought to torture him a little, just to make sure he's not lying."

Graves eyes became larger. "I'll tell the truth, I swear."

Eddie elbowed Graves. "The boss will kill you."

Graves turned on his friend. "Fine, take him next."

Eddie's eyes quickly became large, round saucers, as he eyed Pam. "No! No! We'll talk! We'll talk!"

Graves began talking. "W-w-we work for Mike 'Iron Jaw' Johnson."

Megan leaned toward Cassie and quietly whispered, "How come we always fight against men who have quotation marks around their names? Iron Jaw?" She rolled her eyes in disbelief.

Graves continued, his stuttering becoming worse. "H-h-he agreed to pay us f-f-f-ive thousand dollars each to k-k-kill everyone in this building. We didn't know it was a b-b-b-eauty parlor."

Pam unexpectedly slapped him hard across the face, raising a hand-shaped welt on the tender skin. Graves was uncertain what offense he had committed until she said between clenched teeth. "It's a beauty SALON."

Cassie pushed him for more information. "That's it? That's all you know?"

Graves looked more nervous than before. "Y-y-yes. T-t-that's all."

Eddie looked around the room and volunteered. "Except there was suppose to be four people here when we arrived."

Megan added aloud what Pam and Cassie were thinking, "Whitney."

Pam grabbed both men by the collars and began dragging them down the hall. They saw the unconscious form of their comrade, Kirby, strapped to a chair. His eyes had been covered with a blindfold.

Graves was sweating profusely and ready to beg for his life. "We told you everything, lady. What did you do to Kirby?"

Pam dropped the two men and walked over to the chair, resembling one used by barbers or hair stylists. Its framework was sturdy enough that a man could be strapped to it and bound tightly. She lifted one of Kirby's pant legs and displayed his hairy legs. Several large rectangular areas were completely stripped bare of hair. Pam then grabbed Kirby's head and tilted the top of it in their direction. He sported a 'reverse Mohawk', a completely nude patch down the center of his head. She smiled at the bound men. "Men are such babies. Women come into my salon every day and have waxing done to more delicate areas than just their legs."

The men were bound and strapped to the other two chairs in the room. Pam made a phone call to men in Doc's employ, who would come and take the gangsters away. They locked the door to the room and, after dressing for action, headed for Pam's private garage.

Cassie laughed and confessed to Pam. "I honestly thought you were cutting off fingers or something worse, the way he was screaming. I can't believe you just tortured a man by waxing him. I'm impressed."

Megan smirked. "And the bald strip on his head? Nice touch."

Cassie became serious. "We need to find Whitney right away. Her life might be in danger."

Pam grabbed the keys to a powerful roadster. "We'll take Kan-Tar."

Cassie looked surprised. "Excuse me?"

"I nicknamed all of my cars. I have Clarence, Kan-Tar, and Winston Churchill. I use to have one called Adolf Hitler, but I destroyed it last year."

"You were in a car wreck last year?" Megan asked in a concerned voice.

"No, I said I destroyed it. I saw a news short at the theatre about Hitler's invasion of Hungary and, in a fit of rage, I destroyed the car. With a baseball bat. And a tire iron. And a small stick of dynamite. And then I pushed it off of a cliff."

"Oh." Megan said softly.

"Why were you so surprised that I name my cars?" Pam asked the small blonde woman.

Cassie looked at Pam for a second and then smiled nonchalantly. "Oh. No reason. Let's get going."

The powerful roadster pulled out of the garage and roared away into the night.

Luthor Gibson's limousine silently pulled away from the curb in front of the old armory building, currently being used by the U.S. War Department. The long, sleek machine was delivered to the Montgomery Limousine Service earlier in the day and this was her maiden voyage. Sylvester 'Sly' Montgomery, manager of the M.L.S., piloted the dark automobile through the evening streets of Manhattan with ease, displaying his years of experience behind the wheel. Gibson sat in the back, facing forward. He was a handsome man, well groomed and neatly attired. The dark suit was expensive and tailored to perfection, with a silk handkerchief protruding from the coat pocket. The shoes were polished to a high sheen. The black cane leaning on the seat next to him, however, was more than just another appointment to his attire. Luthor Gibson was completely blind.

Behind the dark glasses, the skin surrounding his eye sockets was horribly burned and scarred. When asked about his injuries, he would merely reply that he had received them during the war and offer a sad, forlorn smile. He was rarely asked to elaborate. The truth of his mysterious injuries would cause most people to doubt the sanity of this millionaire playboy.

The remainder of Gibson's face was quite handsome. He possessed a long, straight nose, high cheekbones, wide forehead and a strong chin. His straight, black hair came to a widow's peak at the forehead and contained a white streak above the left side of his face.

Sitting, with their backs to the driver, were two friends of Doc Titan. Big Tom and Percy had known Gibson for nearly fifteen years and considered him a close friend. They might have reconsidered this, if they ever discovered his secret identity. To the world at large, Luthor Gibson owned one of the most widespread private investigation firms in the United States, with offices in New York, Chicago and Los Angeles; employing several hundred investigators and freelancers. But unknown, except to a select few, Gibson was the crime fighter the criminal underworld knew as … the Darkness.

"Thanks for the lift, Luthor." Percy said with a polite smile. "I still don't understand how you always know exactly where to find us. Even I wasn't informed of our meeting at the War Department until this morning."

"That's my job. To be aware of things." Gibson said, knowingly. He leaned slightly forward in his seat and asked Percy, "I assume you found the Tibetan Egg with the directions I provided?"

"Right on the money. That ancient map gave the exact location. Another mysterious artifact that Adolf Hitler will never get his hands on. Thanks for the information." Percy said confidently.

Gibson turned in Big Tom's direction. "And how did the new aircraft handle? Did Mr. Hazzard create another masterpiece of aerodynamics?"

Big Tom's mouth dropped open. "How do you know about …? Aww, never mind. I know the answer. 'That's your job, to know things.' I'm just glad you're on the right side of this war. We'd be in big trouble, for sure, if you worked for the Nazis. Just remember; loose lips, sink ships. The plane is beautiful. I put her through a full course of tricks and she handled it as smooth as peanut butter."

"I'm certain Doc will be pleased, if you're satisfied. I'm meeting him at the Chromium Club at eight and, if you wish me to, I'll let him know how the flight went." Gibson offered.

"Yeah, sure. Just wait 'til he sees the name Hazzard painted on her. He'll flip." Big Tom chuckled and shook his head. Pointing a thumb over his shoulder, he indicated the driver behind the tinted glass. "Who's driving tonight?"

"Mr. Montgomery, of course. He won't let anyone else drive for me when I come from Chicago for a visit." As Gibson sat back in his seat, he placed an open hand on the package lying next to him, as if confirming its presence. It was twice as large as a cigar box, wrapped in brown paper and tied with string. Lying next to it was a plain manila envelope.

Big Tom thumbed the button that lowered the panel between the driver and passengers. "Hey, Sarge, you old rascal. How are you doing?" Gunner Sargent Sylvester Montgomery had been Big Tom's commanding officer during the war.

"Hi, Big Tom. How are things at 20,000 feet? You ready to retire, yet? I could offer you a job driving one of my limos." The heavy-set black man offered with a broad smile.

"Never, Sly. I'll still be flying when I'm a hundred. Hey, you want to stop by after work? You, me, and my pal Percy, could go out for a couple of beers."

"Sorry, pal. I have to pick up James Chan from the airport at 9:00 and be back at the Chromium Club by midnight to pickup Mr. Gibson."

"Actually, Montgomery, I'm thinking of spending the night at the Club. There is a rather large stack of paperwork I need to work on and I'm certain it will take the rest of the night." Luthor offered. "Why don't you visit with your friend and return to the Club around ten o'clock tomorrow morning. I should have my New York business finished and be ready to fly back to Chicago."

"Very good, sir." Montgomery replied to Gibson and then spoke to Big Tom over his shoulder. "I'll pick up Chan and meet you and Percy back at your building."

"Sounds great. Park in the back and we'll take my new roadster." Big Tom suggested. "Wouldn't want to get this new car dirty." He bluffed an imaginary fingerprint from the chrome door handle and smiled.

"Here's your stop, Big Tom." Sly said as he pulled to the curb. "See you back here about 9:15."

Big Tom stepped out of the large vehicle and waved at Sly in the front seat. Gibson grabbed Percy's arm. "Percy, before you go, I have something I need to give you." He offered the manila envelope. "This contains a map to an artifact called the Golden Serpent. I'm still trying to find more information on it but I have a feeling it's important. You might want to do some research on it as well. It's supposed to be a weapon capable of great destruction. In the wrong hands …." He left the sentence unfinished.

"Thanks, Luthor. I'll look into it right away." They shook hands and the car pulled away. Percy tucked the envelope into his inside coat pocket.

Big Tom and Percy had separate loft apartments on the fourth floor of a turn-of-the-century brick monstrosity. The rent was reasonable, the building was located close to Titan Towers, and the apartments were quite large - each filling half of the fourth floor space. Big Tom's apartment was sparsely decorated with well-worn furniture and very little else. He spent the majority of his time at the airfield or in the hangers. He was a quiet, solemn man who rarely entertained.

Percy's apartment had even less furniture but was filled to overflowing with artifacts, maps, books, and scrolls. He had briefly studied archaeology in college, but found he was far more interested in the treasures and the adventure. Over the years, he had been called a grave robber, a tomb raider, and many other unpleasant names. He was, however, well known for finding things that had remained hidden for centuries. Most museum curators would drool if they were given an opportunity to examine the thousands of relics housed in his simple apartment.

Although John Titan had apartments in the upper floors of the Titan Tower set aside for the two men, they preferred keeping separate quarters. Gibs, Kong and Bart, however, did live in the skyscraper.

Big Tom slapped his old friend on the back and rumbled, "Come on, Bean Pole. It's been a long day and I need a shower before we hit the town with the Sarge. Get your gear unpacked and I'll meet you in the lobby in about an hour.

Tomorrow morning we can head over to Doc's office and see how the other guys are doing."

"I assume you served with Montgomery in the war?" Percy asked.

"Yeah, Gunnery Sergeant Montgomery is what we called him back then. He was the meanest old roughneck you'll ever meet. He's a great guy. I just call him Ol' Sly these days. Or Sarge."

Percy was several inches shorter than Big Tom and weighed nearly half as much. Folks often described him as a living skeleton, an emaciated cluster of bones wrapped in sun-hardened skin, fragile as an October stalk. He gave the appearance of being frail, but this was deceiving. He had never been sick a day in his life. His gaunt body concealed muscles like wire ropes and his physical endurance was incredible. His current wartime contributions included re-enlisting as an American Secret Service Agent, a position he previously held during the Great War.

Big Tom, on the other hand, gave a different appearance. At six and a half feet tall and two hundred and eighty pounds, he looked as solid as a brown bear and twice as ornery. His handsome puritan features were mostly concealed by a thick beard and mustache. His most distinguishing feature were his monstrous fists, each nearly the size of a quart container. They looked like giant, gristled mallets. In a fight, when he punched a man with these monstrosities, his adversary rarely got back up again.

Hailing from Botany Bay, Australia, Big Tom became one of the greatest pilots of the First World War, flying hundreds of successful military missions. Although shot down and captured several times, he always managed to escape and rejoin the battle. While still in his mid-twenties, it was discovered that he suffered from a rare hormonal disorder called acromegaly, an enlarging of the extremities, specifically the hands, feet and jawbone. In 1918, Doc's father, Doctor Clarke Titan, was able to surgically remove a tumorous mass on his pituitary gland to prevent further damage.

Lieutenant Colonel Randolph Garnett 'Big Tom' Thompson and Kenneth Xavier 'Percy' Percival Pierce had been friends for nearly thirty years and had traveled from one end of the world to the other, looking for trouble and generally finding it.

As they walked toward the apartment building entrance, Percy voiced a concern. "Big Tom, have you noticed the unusual trajectory of that black truck?"

Big Tom eyed the vehicle. "Yeah, it's been following us since we stepped out of the limo. Do you have your machine gun pistol?"

Percy confessed. "Negative. I lost most of my personal belongings on my expedition through the mountains."

Big Tom cracked his huge mitts together, a sign of frustration. "Damn. I left mine back at the airfield."

"Ah well, SSDD." Percy exclaimed and then translated the abbreviation, although Big Tom had heard it hundreds of times before. "Same stuff, different day."

As the van pulled up alongside of Doc's aides, several men piled out of the back. Before the first man landed on his feet, Big Tom drove one massive fist into his stomach. All of the air went out of his lungs and the man collapsed on the ground. As he wheezed for a breath of air, a second man joined him, also a victim of Big Tom's lethal pugilistic abilities. Percy's first victim joined the first two on the ground, this one a heavy-set ex-boxer. As the two men wheeled around to continue the battle, a sound came to their ears. A sound both men recognized instantly. The triggers of multiple Thompson machine guns had been cocked.

A tall man with a pencil-thin mustache stood in the doorway of their apartment building. He was well dressed but carried the air of a greasy gangster. One of his upper front teeth was gold-plated and it sparkled in the dim streetlight as he displayed a large, nasty smile. On both sides of this man stood two men with machine guns. All of them were pointed at Big Tom and Percy.

George 'Goldie' MacDonall warned. "I suggest you gentlemen surrender, unless you think you can dodge bullets from these four Tommy guns."

Big Tom raised his arms in surrender. "Dang!"

Percy followed Big Tom's lead. "Aw, SNAFU!!" He often resorted to using military slang abbreviations during times of trouble.

Goldie frowned at Percy. "What did you just say?"

"SNAFU." Percy said with an air of resignation. "Situation Normal, All Fouled Up. It's an old military term."

Goldie guffawed. "Yeah, but it does seems to fit the occasion, huh?"

Big Tom and Percy would have fought and certainly beaten these men, if it weren't for the four machine guns. The three men on the ground had recovered enough to begin binding Percy. The man he had punched now sported a black eye and staggered slightly. He was wondering what Percy had hit him with, because Percy didn't look like he weighed one hundred pounds soaking wet. After a second pair of handcuffs had been placed on Percy's wrists, the ex-boxer kicked him hard in the ribs.

Big Tom was a blaze of motion as he struck the man three times before anyone else had even moved. The ex-boxer dropped to the ground again. This time he didn't get up. Big Tom joined him a second later as a sap struck the back of his head. Four handcuffs were placed on his wrists, with his arms pinned firmly behind his back, while he was still stunned. Obviously, Doc's men had a reputation for escaping handcuffs in the past and these men were taking no chances. Big Tom, like Kong and Doc, had been known to break the links on a single pair of cuffs before. Four new stainless steel handcuffs, however, were more than he could handle.

"Geez, check out the mitts on this fella. They're huge!" One of the men exclaimed in amazement.

Goldie ordered. "Load 'em in the back of the van, boys. We'll attract unwanted attention if we stay here much longer."

Percy and Big Tom were roughly handled and thrown into the back of the van. The ex-boxer was lifted and tossed hard onto the floor of the van. He was still out cold and probably would be for an hour or so. He had messed with the wrong fellows.

Goldie confessed. "Never seen Oxe get knocked down before. Once saw him go fourteen rounds with 'Man-Mountain Monte, the Manhattan Masher.'"

Percy smiled and chuckled, then winced from the pain in his chest, from the kick he had received. "Serves him right. Wish I could have finished the job myself."

Big Tom warned his captors. "He's lucky. I only gave him a few bruises. Percy would have ripped him a new one."

Goldie laughed. "Tough guys, huh? Well, I've taken lots of tough guys for their final ride. When they discover their time is up, however, they all cry like newborn babies."

Big Tom eyed him and prophesized. "We'll see who's crying later."

Goldie MacDonall pounded one fist on the back of the truck cab. "Let's go. We have two more pickups to make, before we head back to the airplane. Egorov is paying us good money to make this snatch and grab."

Percy turned and stared at Big Tom, but kept his tongue. Big Tom understood the look and nodded in acknowledgement. He had heard the name Egorov only one other time and if it was the same man, they were certainly in dire straits.

Chapter Eight
What Lies Beneath (The Chromium Club Gallery)

April 5, 1945 8:15 pm

Luthor Gibson's long, black limousine pulled up in front of the prestigious Chromium Club. The massive brick and stone structure was several stories tall and housed over one hundred common rooms and conference areas. This gentleman's retreat was one of the oldest surviving male-only clubs in New York City and, like the dinosaur, was one of the last of its kind. Originally founded in the early 1800's, the institution dated back over one hundred and forty years.

The original name of the retreat was The Renaissance Fellowship. The original founding members were as unique as the lodge itself. A gathering of men some described as renaissance or new age heroes. Forty-seven years ago, in 1898, when the club developed financial setbacks after a fire destroyed a large portion of the building, a half-dozen influential men stepped forward. A newer, more prestigious building was erected on the sight and the institution was saved. Their names were embossed into a new bronze plaque at the main entrance to the brick and stone building. Names that every man, woman, and child in New York City, and beyond, knew at a mention. These were all great men, who dedicated their lives to performing great deeds. Some were also known as founding members of the Baltimore Gun Club.

The new name over the door was changed to '*The Adventurers Club. Established in 1898.*' A few of the names on the bronze plaque were Professor George Challenger, Allan Quatermain, Phineas Fogg, Colonel Richard Henry Savage, Professor Clarke Titan, and Hareton Ironcastle. All extremely wealthy, influential men.

In 1930, another fire destroyed portions of the building. Again, several wealthy members of the fraternity stepped forward and not only restored the damaged building, but also filled the entire vacant lot next door with an elaborate addition to the structure.

This time the name read '*The Chromium Club. Funded and founded in 1930.*' The list of names on the new dedication plaque was equally impressive. John Titan, Simon Blake, Luthor Gibson, Charles Burton Van Pelt, Preston Stockbridge II, Max Grant, and Lord Kevin Claybourne.

Gibson left the rear of the car, the square package tucked securely beneath his arm. He leaned near the passenger window of the limousine and addressed Sly Montgomery. "Have a nice evening off, Sylvester. I'll see you in the morning."

"Yessir. Thank you, Mr. Gibson." Sly always liked it when Gibson called him by his first name, like they were old, close friends, instead of boss and employee.

As the black limousine pulled away from the curb, Gibson noticed three uniformed law enforcement officers standing near the entrance. Something was wrong but not seriously so or the policemen would have been inside the building. Obviously, someone was trying to be discreet about one of the patrons of the club.

Luthor entered the main doors and removed his hat, gloves, scarf, and coat in the luxurious foyer. From behind his tinted dark glasses, he appeared to ignore the ornate décor in the room, the crystal chandeliers, the deep, rich carpeting, polished hardwood floors, and Art Deco mouldings. Several rare and priceless paintings of the Renaissance Art period graced the oak paneled walls. His highly polished leather shoes glided across the extravagant carpet and up the half-flight of stairs. His eyes played around the quiet rooms, occasionally acknowledging a verbal greeting from another member of the club. He was relieved to note the absence of Commissioner Wheaton. Gibson was on a mission and didn't have time to mimic the role of the disinterested blind playboy millionaire.

Luthor was climbing the stairs to the second floor when he noticed someone waiting for him. Although he knew that man well, he had to continue playing the role of a blind man. He raised his head and sniffed, as if tasting the air, and smiled. "Sebastian. Are you there?"

Sebastian, one of the club's gentleman valets, approached, holding a plain manila envelope out toward Luthor. "Yessir. I am here. I don't know how you could possibly know. I was extremely quiet this time."

"My other senses have made up for my blindness. I could sense someone standing nearby and could smell your aftershave."

"Very good, Mr. Gibson, sir. This package arrived this afternoon, marked to your attention."

"Thank you, Sebastian. Is there a return address?" He asked, although he could plainly see that there was not.

"No, sir. It is simply marked 'Urgent' and is to your attention, in care of the Chromium Club. Do you wish me to open it and tell you of the contents, sir?"

"No, thank you, Sebastian." Gibson held out his hand to the left of where the valet stood, enforcing the perception of being completely blind and accepted the envelope.

"Is there anything else I can get for you tonight, sir?" Sebastian inquired in a servile tone. Gibson liked the polite man. He made a mental note to have Sebastion's wages increased.

"No, thank you, Sebastian. I will be working in my private office tonight. I do not wish to be disturbed."

"Very good, sir." Sebastian responded.

"Oh, Sebastian? My chauffer mentioned that there were uniformed policemen standing outside the entrance of the club. Has there been a disturbance?"

"They would be with me, Mr. Gibson." A polite voice came from around the corner. "We are looking for Preston Stockbridge II. Have you seen him?"

Gibson frowned, as if he were trying to access a distant memory, although he knew exactly to whom the voice belonged. "Police Commissioner Jack Lockhart, if I'm not mistaken."

"Uncanny. We've only met once before and that was nearly two years ago. How could you possibly …?"

Gibson raised his hand to silence the commissioner. "When you're blind, you must develop a memory for voices, smells, and textures. I notice you are still smoking those Havana cigars, Commissioner."

"Well, um, yes. Anyway, have you seen Mr. Stockbridge recently, Mr. Gibson?" Lockhart asked in his usual stern voice. With a wave of his hand, he quietly dismissed Sebastian.

"To answer you original question, I haven't *seen* anyone recently, Lockhart." Gibson teased, with a friendly smile, and then continued. " But, several weeks ago, Preston invited me to a cocktail party at his family mansion. After living in penthouse apartments for the last several years, he thought it would be a nice change of pace to move back to the old homestead. You might find him there, Commissioner." Gibson offered seriously.

"Yes, I was there just last week. That's where we were going next, as a matter of fact."

"Has Preston committed some crime we should be made aware of, Mr. Lockhart? Pilfered the silverware, or some other dastardly offense?" Gibson asked, lightheartedly.

Jack Lockhart looked sternly at Luthor Gibson and cleared his throat. "Nothing so innocent, I assure you. But, for right now, this is strictly confidential police business and I cannot discuss it with you or anyone else. If you see Mr. Gibson, please inform him to call my office immediately."

"Very well, Commissioner. Have a pleasant evening and good hunting. And please give your step-son, Preston, my best regards when you find him."

Lockhart flushed with embarrassment and then frowned as he watched the millionaire walk away. Something wasn't quite right about that man, he would bet his pension on it. He would have to keep an eye on Luthor Gibson. But, for tonight, he had another, more important mission.

Luthor, and the other founding members of the Chromium Club, had private offices and quarters housed in the new addition to the structure. Gibson had two such rooms, one under the name Gibson and the other under Grant. He turned the lock in the door marked *Luthor Gibson* and entered his private room without making a noise. If polled, none of the other members or staff of the Chromium Club would remember seeing anyone ever enter the door with Max Grant's nameplate. Or meeting Mr. Grant, for that matter. Few people knew that these two men were actually the same person. Fewer still, knew that both were simply aliases for the night creature known as the Darkness.

Unlike the rest of the Chromium Club, where flamboyance was the general rule, this room was very simply furnished. A chair, dresser, desk, and bed were the only furniture. Gibson walked past these items and opened the only other door in the small room, into a smaller closet. A full-size mirror was mounted to the inside of the door. Luthor studied his profile and adjusted his expensive silk tie.

Many women thought that the handsome millionaire was one of the best looking men in New York. Of course, his being a millionaire might have colored their perceptions slightly. He removed his glasses and rubbed his sore nose. The thick, black lenses were heavy, however, without them, he was completely blind. He replaced the glasses and his vision returned. In the past, Doc had offered to surgically remove the burned tissue where his ruined eyes had once resided and examine the damage to determine if an optical graft would work. However, if it failed, he would be completely blind once again. Not a condition he wished to suffer from again.

There were only a few articles of clothing hanging inside the closet. He pushed these aside and shoved hard against the rear wall of the closet. There was a barely audible 'click' sound and the wall slid to one side, revealing an equally small room beyond. Luthor stepped in and the wall panel slid back into place. There was a movement and the room in which he stood slowly dropped. It was a cleverly concealed elevator. Seconds later, it came to a halt and he stepped out. A slightly musty smell touched his sensitive nostrils and voices could be heard around the corner. He entered a brightly illuminated, subterranean room of massive proportions.

Glass display cases of various sizes housed miscellaneous relics of many a bygone battle. An enormous menagerie of curious weapons were locked in various repositories and vaults, built of nearly indestructible clear-glass. An archive of newspaper headlines were on exhibit, arranged methodically like souvenirs throughout the decades. This room was like a museum or treasury of important events of the last century and a half. This area was simply known as The Gallery.

Beyond this was a simply decorated, stone room with a large, round table and half a dozen chairs. The voices he had heard were those of three men who had been awaiting his presence. Each man had his own entrance to this hidden sanctuary, deep below the foundations of the Chromium Club addition. Only a dozen men in the world knew of the existence of this place. Even the aides and agents of the men gathered here, were unaware of this lair. It was a very tightly kept secret. When the new addition to the Chromium Club was built in 1930, these rooms were secretly added.

The archives of The Gallery were the personal records of various adventures, and the dangerous weapons and specimens taken during those travels. Memoirs, diaries, and journals were locked away in these vaults, safe from the prying eyes of the common man. These rooms were designed to withstand ... anything. They had been carved directly into the netherworld bedrock of Manhattan Island and the ceilings and walls of the rooms were several feet thick, comprised of reinforced concrete and steel plating.

Luthor Gibson entered the Gathering Room, with the round table, and greeted his friends. Doc Titan stood several inches taller and weighed one hundred pounds more, than Gibson. They shook hands firmly, two old friends confident and true. They had shared several adventures together over the years. Simon Blake offered his gloved hand, but his voice and manner were as cold and lifeless as they had been before the Cry of the Banshee adventure. He was a hard man to read and Gibson was sometimes uncomfortable around the man the underworld of crime called the Guardian. Gibson did not even offer his hand to Preston Stockbridge II, the famed criminologist. They were close enough to be brothers and never passed up an opportunity to taunt one another.

"Leave your violin at home tonight, Guido Salvatore?" Gibson chided.

Stockbridge parried. "I had a *hunch* you didn't like my music."

"Actually, I was distracted. I was looking for the little monkey." Gibson confessed.

Stockbridge frowned and rolled his eyes. "I'm imitating a street musician, not a street organ grinder."

Gibson continued his harassment. "I understand that entire neighborhood raised money ... to send you away."

Stockbridge ignored the jab. "Hey, it's a great disguise."

Gibson smiled. "I especially like the hunchback, the long wig and the smelly clothes. Very inconspicuous."

Stockbridge returned the attack. "Beats being a janitor named Karl at the local police station. You smell like an old shoe in that costume."

Gibson absent-mindedly tossed the envelope on the round table. He had been carrying it since Sebastian had handed the package to him upstairs and had almost forgotten about it. He placed the paper-wrapped box on top of it.

Gibson continued ribbing his friend. "At least my costumes don't involve wearing fangs. Real scorpions don't even have fangs, you know."

Stockbridge reddened with embarrassment. "Hey, I stopped wearing fangs last year. Kept biting my own lip. You keep harassing me like this and I'll have to shoot you. There's only enough room in this town for one caped crusader with a slouch hat and a cape."

Gibson smiled. "Well, at least we don't run around town wearing a stovepipe hat like that Apparition fellow. How silly does that look?"

Stockbridge, imitating Bugs Bunny, agreed. "Yeah, watta maroon. Maybe I'll shoot him instead. Nah, actually I can't do that. When I marry Whitney, he'll be my brother-in-law."

Doc simply smiled during this exchange. They reminded him of Bart and Kong. Simon Blake sat with his arms crossed and watched without emotion.

"Speaking of relatives, your step-father, Police Commissioner Jack Lockhart, is looking for you. And he had three police officers waiting outside the club entrance, probably to arrest you. What did you do this time?"

"Damn. I was involved in a shootout earlier tonight and lost one of my guns. And my hat, too. But I stopped a shipment of machine guns from being unloaded at Pier 52 and Bossman Krieger is now in police custody. They caught him red-handed with the goods. He'll be keeping Al Capone company for the next twenty years. And twelve of his men will be shaking hands with the devil by midnight."

Doc Titan sighed disapprovingly. He tried to never take a human life, even the life of criminal. Admittedly, at times it was a difficult code to follow, but he tried.

Stockbridge, still imitating Bugs Bunny, turned to Titan and asked, "Eh. What's up, Doc?"

Doc shook his head from side to side. "You fellas are a little too bloodthirsty for my taste. Would I be able to convince you to use an alternative to lead bullets?"

Stockbridge responded defensively. "I believe in the Chicago way. Come at me with a knife, I'll come back with a gun. Put me in the hospital, I'll put you in the morgue. I've shot a lot of men in my life, but none I believed to be innocent."

Doc offered a compromise, knowing it was useless. "I could supply you with anesthetic slugs that would put your enemies to sleep. All of my captives are taken to the Titan Rehabilitation Institute and Clinic for professional lifestyle retraining and continued education."

Stockbridge confessed. "I don't believe in rehabilitation."

Darkness' haunting voice came from Gibson's mouth. "Crime is a cancerous plague, and I am the cure."

Stockbridge frowned playfully. "What? You know, half the time I don't even know what he's talking about."

Doc started to explain. "I believe he is referring to ..."

Stockbridge raised an eyebrow at Doc. "I was only kidding, Doc. You're a gullible boy scout, aren't ya? Besides, I don't hear you talking to Simon Blake that way. He shoots folks in the head every day."

"Yes, but I don't kill them. And he doesn't say anything to me because I've been using his 'mercy' bullets for several years." Simon Blake confessed, much to their surprise.

Gibson walked slowly around the large table. "I thought you nicked their scalps with a .22 caliber bullet and knocked them unconscious?"

Blake chuckled, but his face did not reflect humor. "Are you kidding? Nobody is that good of a shot. The injury alone would probably cause interior hemorrhaging and possible death. People started noticing a small amount of blood on the scalp after I shot someone and assumed that I had nicked their skull with a bullet. The tiny cuts were actually from the thin-walled, gas bullets that Doc created. I merely let everyone continue believing whatever they wanted to. As good as I am with a gun, I'm not that good."

He removed a small rectangular box from a sheath on his leg. It measured an inch on both sides and eight inches long. It appeared to be a solid block of aluminum with four holes at one end. Blake aimed it at a nearby wall, pressed a concealed button, and a small pellet struck the brick surface.

"I can hit a target one hundred feet away with a single pellet or all four at once, if I desire. I usually carry at least two of these on me at all times. And a few razor-sharp knifes, if I'm forced to battle hand to hand."

Suddenly, he was holding an eight-inch long stiletto in one hand. As if to illustrate his skills, he balanced the long knife by the point, using his index finger. With a flick of his wrist the knife flashed across the room and stuck deep into the surface of an oak cabinet.

Stockbridge looked unimpressed. "Cute. And do you give your weapons names, such as Mike and Ike?"

"You've read one too many pulp novels, Preston. Nobody gives their gun a name, do they?"

"Sure. I've got Betty, Veronica, and Helen ..." Preston started.

Blake interrupted, "Okay. Doesn't this worry anyone else, that he gives names to his guns? Women's names?"

"Well, personally, I never considered knives very manly. I have always depended on these." Stockbridge pulled out his double .45 caliber handguns.

Gibson drew out his guns as well. "I agree with Preston. With these you can shoot through an engine block."

Stockbridge smiled mischievously. "And you wouldn't believe how many times I've had to do that. The only problem I have, is that I tend to run out of bullets too quickly."

Doc continued with his proposal, offering a presentation. "Well, even if I can't convince you to use mercy bullets, let me show you some other things I've developed. This is a rapid-fire pistol. It's like a hand-held machine gun. With the flip of a switch, you can convert it to single fire action. Mercy bullets, grenades, tracers, and flares are only a fraction of the various ammunitions available. At full speed it will shoot several hundred rounds per minute. Bullets are one-third the size of a .45 caliber, but deliver the same impact. A new addition, twist the barrel of the gun 360 degrees clockwise and you engage the silencer. Magazine clips can contain several hundred bullets, depending on which type of ammunition you are using."

"Holy … it's like a Swiss Army gun ... I'll take a dozen! Do they also have a hidden screwdriver and a toothpick? Maybe a decoder ring?" Stockbridge teased.

Doc was so accustomed to Bart and Kong kidding around, he continued, quite seriously. "No, but they do have a built-in compass in the handle. The handgrip is removable and is made of a braided piano wire. It can cut through stainless steel handcuffs in less than a minute. Additionally, Kong and I recently developed rubber bullets that can be used as well. They are capable of knocking down a full grown man at one hundred feet, but all he'll have is a large bruise in the morning."

Stockbridge laughed loudly. "Oh, that's a deterrent for crime. *'Run away! It's the Scorpion … he'll leave bruises on you!'*"

Doc Titan's tone became more serious. "You are aware that this vigilante killing will not be ignored forever? Sooner or later, the police will be forced to hunt you down and bring you to justice. It won't matter whether or not your victims are crooks. Gibson mentioned that Lockhart is ready to arrest you."

Stockbridge was not in a serious mood tonight. "Well, what can I say, Doc. Lockhart has tried to arrest me for Scorpion-related crimes in the past and failed. And not all of us have a protective, magical red ruby on their hooded blue cape to vanquish evil, bestowed upon us by a grateful, mystical Tibetan monk."

"What the heck does that mean?" Blake, his solemn face a frozen mask, questioned Stockbridge.

Stockbridge continued. "Well, according to his most recent adventures in Knightraven Books' *Doc Titan* comic book series, the writers and publishers claim that he wears a jeweled blue hood when he fights crime. It gives him superpowers!"

Gibson asked incredulously. "Are you kidding?"

Stockbridge presented a bent and folded comic book from the folds of his leather trench coat. "No, it's right here is his comic."

Doc was blushing from embarrassment. "I am so mortified. Kong and Bart showed that to me last week. I ... I honestly don't know what to say."

Gibson snickered. "I can hear the bad guys now. *'Oh, no! It's Doc Titan and he's wearing his blue hood with the mystic jewel! Aiiee! Run away!'*"

Everyone began laughing. This was such a strange thing to witness. These four men lived such serious, stern and stoic existences and here they were, acting like children. This was perhaps the only place on Earth where they felt they could relax, with men who were truly their peers. Finally, the laughter died down.

Stockbridge wiped tears of laughter from his eyes. "I can't believe Luthor Gibson made a joke. Well, you're really going to laugh when you find out this month in *The Darkness* comics, you start wearing a mystical pink tutu and a beanie cap."

Gibson pulled out his gun and aimed it at Stockbridge's forehead. "Take it back or I'll shoot you. Twice. I'm not kidding."

Preston Stockbridge already had his guns drawn and pointed at Luthor Gibson. "You do and I'll shoot you back."

Doc Titan turned to Simon Blake, shook his head and smiled.

Chapter Nine
The Robinsons are Taken for a Ride

April 5, 1945 8:15 pm

Gabriel and Isabelle Robinson strolled slowly down the sidewalk, passing under the hum of the electric streetlight. They had been married most of their adult lives and were still madly, passionately in love. They met at Tuskegee College, where they were both honor students. They were married soon after graduating college. In 1938, while searching for employment in Manhattan, an accounting firm hired them, as domestic help. Like thousands of people in New York, during the last years of the depression era, it was difficult to find steady work. And being of African-American descent made it that much harder. Bartholomew Blackwell understood this and recognizing hard-working, intelligent people, he promoted the married couple to assist with his stock investment organization.

Months later, Doc Titan and Simon Blake met for the first time. Blake mentioned needing someone to oversee his investments and Bart suggested that he hire Gabe and Isabelle, with his highest recommendations. On their first day at Unsolved Mysteries, Incorporated, the couple was kidnapped and soon became embroiled in a wild adventure. And they loved it.

Afterwards, the Guardian had asked them if they would consider staying with the Unsolved Mysteries group. They became invaluable resources, able to invisibly infiltrate an organization as hired domestic help. Criminals of the 30's and 40's in New York City had a blind eye when around black or 'colored' folks, as they referred to them.

The ability to adapt to any given situation made Gabe and Isabelle the perfect undercover agents. Between investigations Isabelle took care of the bookkeeping and accounting for Unsolved Mysteries, Incorporated and the satellite warehouse facility Praetorian Securities. Meanwhile, Gabe managed a small staff of domestic help for the offices and warehouse, including mechanics for the fleet of cars and planes. Isabelle and Gabe also did various investigation footwork, researching background information on current and potential clients. Simon Blake was the leader of the group of investigators but Gabe and Isabelle were certainly the hub that kept everything running smoothly. And they both loved it.

Isabelle was a pretty woman of average height and build. Gabriel Elias was taller, lean but not thin, as strong and fast as a black panther in the jungle, when the situation demanded it.

Gabe spoke quietly. "We need to tell Simon soon. Tell them all."

Isabelle agreed, but had concerns. "I know, Gabe. It's just … I feel like a traitor, like we're abandoning the people we trust the most. And with the financial situation the way it stands …"

Gabe patted his wife's hand reassuringly. "Oh honey, you know they won't feel that way. Besides, I'm not certain Mr. Blake is going to continue in this line of work. Recently, he's even had Andrew Carter stand in for him on a few cases."

Isabelle frowned but agreed. "Simon does seem to be doing quite a bit of soul-searching recently. Cassie has also noticed this. She's concerned about him. That's why I'm hesitating. He needs our support right now."

"Mr. Blake and the others will get along just fine without us." Gabe reassured his lovely wife.

"That's good to hear, 'cause you're going on a little trip, pal." A voice with a New Jersey accent came from behind them. As they both turned to see who was talking, the voice warned, "Eh, slowly. Don't make any sudden moves. We've been instructed to take you alive, if possible."

A man in a nicely tailored suit stood a dozen feet away. But Gabe and Isabelle could recognize a greasy gangster-type from a mile away. George 'Goldie' MacDonall flashed a wide smile, displaying his gold-plated front tooth.

"But the boys have itchy trigger fingers. Especially after those last two palookas we picked up."

The couple immediately noticed the four men with machine guns. Isabelle Robinson squeezed Gabe's arm where she had been holding him, so fiercely he nearly winced in pain.

Isabelle whispered, "Gabriel, don't try anything. There's too many of them."

"Listen to your wife, pal." Goldie sneeringly advised.

They were quickly handcuffed and led to an enclosed truck parked at the curb. As they were roughly shoved into the back, Gabe's jaw dropped in surprise. He immediately recognized both men, also handcuffed, lying on the floor of the van.

"Mr. Thompson, Mr. Pierce. What is going on? What is this all about?"

"Quiet, ya mug. No talking. We have one more stop to make and we're running outta time." Goldie warned, as he signaled the driver.

The truck lurched forward and disappeared into the night.

Chapter Ten
Totenkopf's Deaths-Head Squad.

April 5, 1945   8:30 pm

Preston Stockbridge II reloaded his automatic for the third time and pointed it at the far wall. "So why did you want to meet in these catacombs, beneath the Chromium Club, Doc?"

Gibson rolled his eyes. "These are not catacombs. It's a basement."

"Yeah, but catacombs sound much more mysterious."

"You're a moron."

Stockbridge began working on his other automatic. "Yes, but a mysterious moron," he muttered under his breath.

Gibson turned to face Titan and Blake, ignoring Stockbridge. "You are both public figures, why don't we meet at your offices?"

Doc shook his head. "My office isn't safe." He smiled at his own response. "I suppose that is a strange word for us to use, considering our professions." Doc continued. "I received a communication from a close friend in the military." The other men knew Doc was talking about General Dwight D. Eisenhower, Supreme Commander of the Allied Expeditionary Force, an important man who could easily become the President of the United States someday. "He requested that we meet a liaison of his, in private. That's why we are meeting here. I knew this man's father from World War I. Frank Gunn was a highly decorated combat aviator. I trained with him in Europe."

Stockbridge looked up. "Frank Gunn? I also met him, while training in the United Kingdom's Royal Flying Corps. He reportedly shot down Baron Manfred von Richthofen, the Red Baron, early in his flying career, He was a United States citizen who had enlisted in 1915 and was stationed in France under the Third Republic. A good man."

Doc continued. "Yes, and I believe his son, Richard, is made of the same fiber. He has seen plenty of action already on the European front and has been decorated for bravery many times. I believe he currently holds the rank of Sergeant in the Army and an honorary rank in the Allied Forces. He would have been promoted to a much higher position but the AEF has him performing special reconnaissance operations and in case he is captured behind enemy lines ... you understand."

Gibson volunteered, "Doc asked me to have him escorted here."

As if on cue, a large steel door in the middle of the room swung open. The barrier was several inches thick, with heavy reinforcing straps around the perimeter and criss-crossing the center. The door was set in a solid steel frame with fortified hinges on one side and a heavy bolt on the other. The wall it was housed in was several feet thick and constructed of reinforced concrete and steel. It was built to withstand any attacking force. Three men and a teenager stepped through the opening.

The first man through the door stepped to one side to allow the others to enter. He wore a hat pulled down over his forehead and his face was partially concealed in shadow. He wore a black leather trench coat that covered his entire body except his feet and hands. He wore ankle-high leather boots and leather gloves. The collar of his coat was pulled up and hid the lower part of his face.

Gibson nodded at the quiet man. "Thank you, Valentine."

Valentine tipped his head in acknowledgement, but did not speak. Doc, Blake, and Stockbridge had always wondered what Agent Valentine looked like, and would continue wondering. He was as mysterious as his master, the Darkness. This was the man who relayed messages from the Darkness to his agents, and back again. Besides Gibson, Valentine was the only other man who knew the name and location of every agent in the millionaires employ. He was the hub of Gibson's entire private investigation operation.

The next man was clad in a nicely tailored Army military uniform, neatly pressed and spotlessly clean. His short hair was tussled slightly and a curly lock of stray hair hung down over one eye. Even though he was a young man, certainly still in his early twenties, his chest was covered with dozens of military awards. He was six feet tall and solidly built. This was Sergeant Richard Gunn.

Gunn scratched the short stubble on his face. "I felt my ears burning. Someone must have mentioned my name."

The man who followed was the most impressive of the group. He was nearly as tall and large as Doc. He walked with an air of confidence and power. His red, white, and blue costume mimicked the American flag hanging on a nearby wall. When he noticed the flag he seemed to stand even taller, as though empowered by its presence. A micro-fine, chain-mail fabric covered his head, broad, muscular back and shoulders. His pale blue eyes scanned the room and its inhabitants. Despite the fact that he had surfaced only a few short years ago, every red-blooded American knew his name. The Sentry. The Sentinel of Justice.

The Sentry was actually James Ethan Adams, an American patriot who volunteered to subject himself to a secret process that might allow him to fight in the service of his country. He had been marked as a F4, a military reject, due to the fact he was overly thin, anemic, and a physically weakling. But he possessed the heart of a born warrior. When a colonel approached him and offered him the opportunity to help America, James Adams did not hesitate. He had been injected with a radical biological formula and exposed to a mysterious spectrum of ray beams, in an effort to increase his body's potential. The process was a huge success. Unfortunately, the scientist in charge was killed immediately afterward and James Adams became the first and last test subject. Attempts to replicate the project had met with … bad results.

Since then, the military trained him night and day to become their best soldier. A virtual super-soldier.

The last person to enter was a young man, still in his early teens. The colors of his uniform mimicked those of the man beside him. He wore a simple Domino mask, an oval of material covering only his eyes and nose. This was the Sentry's young sidekick, Kid Sentry. Christopher 'Cody' Sawyer was the Army base mascot where the undercover Sentry was stationed. After discovering Adam's secret, he agreed to keep quiet, but only if he could become the legend's partner. The military leaders approved, agreeing that it would inspire a younger generation of recruits.

Rick Gunn addressed the men. "Gentlemen, we appreciate you meeting with us on such a short notice. We bring important information and require your assistance. I am going to introduce you to a man who has taken on the heavy burden of personally representing the USA in the Allied Forces. This is the Sentry. And the young man with him is his sidekick, Kid Sentry."

Introductions were made and the men gathered around the large table. Only Valentine stayed in his position at the doorway, once again bolted and barred.

"You know we've all volunteered to help with the war effort in any way we can. Just tell us what you need." Blake said.

Sentry stepped forward. "Yes, and the President wants to convey to each of you his appreciation for your assistance. I'm afraid I don't have much time, so I will need to keep this brief. I have to catch a military transport in one hour. America and the Allied Forces face a very real danger. A Nazi agent named Totenkopf, code-named Black Skull, is overseeing a top secret experiment that might alter the balance of the war. Unfortunately, military intelligence is very limited in regards to his location at this time. Recently, however, M. I. has discovered information on a top secret project, code-named Operation Gladiator."

Doc glanced at the Sentry. "Isn't that similar to the name of the project you volunteered for?"

Gunn smiled. "Now you understand our concerns. If Nazi Germany could replicate the Super-Soldier process …" He didn't finish the sentence, allowing each man to make his own conjectures. He added, "I have met and fought this man, Totenkopf. He's a fanatic, willing to sacrifice anything to accomplish his goals."

"Nazis, again? I really hate those guys." Stockbridge became serious and gave Sentry his attention. "What else can you tell us about him? What's his background?"

The Sentry continued. "His origins before 1941 are a complete mystery, as is his true name. But I can tell you this; Black Skull is the true embodiment, the personification, of the Third Reich and the Nationalist Party. Adolf Hitler himself personally indoctrinated him. Disappointed in the training of the SS Stormtroopers by his subordinates, Hitler randomly recruited one of the soldiers to be retrained properly. He ordered his finest military minds and toughest drill instructors to teach the young man everything they knew. Little realizing that the student he had inadvertently selected was a known bully and troublemaker, Hitler had chosen a truly evil man. And he became a sadistic and ruthless soldier.

"As a reward for his unfaltering loyalty and dedication to the beliefs of the Third Reich, Hitler gave him a costume to set him apart from all others. The Sentry was created as an iconic representation of the liberty and justice of the USA and the Allied Forces. As my counterpart, Totenkopf wears a fearful countenance of death incarnate and represents the Fatherland. Dressed in the most magnificent black and leather Nazi SS uniform, topped with a black skull mask, Totenkopf is a horrific sight. Strong, brave men tremble fearfully when he enters the room.

"Black Skull is a force to be respected. Questioning his direct orders leads to death. Failure to perform a mission, regardless of its impossibility, means death. His specially trained Stormtroopers will sacrifice their lives to assault the enemy, simply to avoid the wrath of this man. This was exactly what Hitler wanted. Totenkopf is a fierce, deadly man who will fearlessly follow orders and complete impossible missions under Hitler's command. Totenkopf's only flaw is, while certainly loyal to Hitler and the Third Reich, his ambitions are not limited to the success of their goals alone.

"He feels his role is to be the embodiment of Nazi intimidation and was recently appointed as head of Nazi terrorist activities with an additional large role in external espionage and sabotage. To that end, he has been spectacularly successful, wreaking havoc throughout Europe.

"During one of these espionage campaigns, he discovered a small group of scientists experimenting on cures for deadly viruses and bacteria. After torturing and killing several of the men, he had convinced the survivors to create something horrifyingly awful. It is called The Death's Head. If introduced to a human host, it will destroy the skin and flesh of the face and leave a horrible, bloodied skull. This has become Black Skull's trademark signature. After the scientists created this horrible abomination, his reward for services rendered was to murder them all. Totenkopf took the only known formula and antidote, before destroying all of the records. We're not certain if this Death's Head is a new molecular acid, a type of virus, or something even deadlier."

Stockbridge looked concerned. "Great. One more weapon of mass destruction in the hands of an insane megalomaniac wearing a skull mask over his face. It sounds like he belongs in a circus freak-show or an asylum. Guess I should be accustomed to this by now."

"We need you men to locate Totenkopf's base of operations and stop him from completing his goals." Rick Gunn added.

"I would go myself but I have to leave immediately as there is another project that warrants my attention. England faces a very real danger, a threat of mass destruction. Gentlemen, America needs your help." Sentry explained. He reached into his coat pocket and removed a photograph. "This photograph cost the lives of four military intelligence officers. It is the only known picture of Totenkopf."

Totenkopf's appearance was exactly as Sentry had described him. In the background stood two other men, but they were indistinct and out of focus. The picture was passed from Gibson to Blake to Stockbridge and lastly to Titan. Doc focused on one of the faces in the background. Something was familiar about it but, whatever it was, it eluded him for the moment.

"Who are the men in the background?" Blake voiced Titan's question.

"We're not certain. They don't appear to be soldiers or scientists." James Adams, the Sentry, answered. "Military Intelligence is distributing the photograph to every sector. We'll get an answer sooner or later."

Doc was impressed by this young man. John Titan himself had been secretly asked by the President to help train him in armed and unarmed combat. The man learned very quickly. He was also trained by the best military minds in the Allied Forces. Combat training and strategies, military campaigns, everything he needed to become America's ultimate soldier. He met and exceeded all expectations. The Sentry was truly the next generation of hero.

Sentry looked concerned. "One last thing before we go. If Black Skull discovers you are after him, he will stop at nothing to destroy you. He will go after your headquarters, your friends, your families. If you accept this assignment, protect those closest to you."

Gunn glanced at his watch and placed his hand on Adams' shoulder. "Sentry, we have to go. The transport is waiting."

Sentry and Rick Gunn walked toward the door where Valentine stood waiting. Kid Sentry had quietly watched the entire exchange, without interrupting. Now he finally saw his chance to speak.

Christopher Sawyer, codenamed Kid Sentry, was smiling excitedly. "Wow. I can't believe I'm meeting you guys. I grew up reading your pulp adventures. I just wanted to say what an honor it is to meet you."

Doc placed his hand on Sawyer's shoulder. "Do us a favor and be careful out there, son."

Kid Sentry smiled so broadly his face seemed ready to split in half. "Yessir." He turned and followed his friends through the door. Directly before it closed, they could hear him telling Sentry, "Doc Titan talked to me! And placed his hand right here on my shoulder! Maybe I could shave my head like he …" The door slammed and the sound of heavy bolts being thrown into place echoed in the large room.

The room was silent for several seconds after the door closed.

Stockbridge looked around at the others. "Well, where do we start?"

Blake was looking at the center of the table. The paper-wrapped box that Gibson had brought in lay there. "What is in that package, Gibson?"

"One of my contacts found the legendary Spear of Destiny. The one used to pierce and kill Christ while he was on the cross. Hitler now possesses a forgery of the true spear. I thought the Gallery would be the safest place to keep it. I also have some newspaper clippings to add to the Archive." He lifted the box and placed it on a nearby shelf. He would deal with it later.

"And what's in the envelope?" Preston asked.

Gibson stared at it for a second and replied. "Actually, I don't know. Sebastian gave it to me when I arrived." As he reached for the envelope he noticed a small doodle on the corner that had escaped his earlier quick glance. A small penciled figure of an angel. His heart pounded as he ripped open one end. He extracted several files and stared at them for a moment. "Oh, my God."

Stockbridge leaned forward. He knew for Gibson to voice concern like this, it couldn't be good. "What's the matter, Luthor? Your club fees go up again?"

Gibson tossed the folders on the table. Dozens of photographs and typed pages of agendas, schedules and meetings fanned out on the tabletop. Friends, families, agents, everyone these men came into contact with in their daily lives. The warning Sentry had spoken to them seemed to echo in the large room. *'He will go after your headquarters, your friends, your families.'*

Darkness spoke into a small transmitter, "Valentine, relay this message to all agents. Code Red. Full defense mode. Effective immediately."

Doc Titan and Simon Blake each pushed a button on their watches. They had created these as a warning to their respective headquarters. Anyone at those locations would be alerted by a buzzing sound and red, flashing lights would be activated. Windows and doors would be locked and barred. Local police and fire departments would be alerted.

"If they suspect we've met with Sentry …" Blake started.

Doc finished Blake's sentence. "… they will be moving up whatever timetable they had."

Stockbridge looked from Doc to Blake. "Who are we talking about?"

Gibson pointed at one of the splayed files. "Whoever attacked and killed Captain Lucifer and his crew." Photographs of Lewis Afar and his eight friends were visible.

Preston glanced at the pictures on the table. Whitney Van Pelt, Police Commissioner Jack Lockhart - his stepfather, the Stockbridge Mansion, and others. Stockbridge whispered under his breath. "Oh, My God! Whitney. She was going to the mansion. So was Lockhart." He bolted for an emergency exit that would lead to the alleyway behind the Chromium Club. As the door was slammed shut behind Scorpion, a low rumbling sound came from overhead. Another quickly followed.

Gibson was suddenly the shadowy figure called Darkness. "Someone is attacking the Chromium Club above us."

The reinforced structure overhead muted the sound of explosions, but it was obvious that the building was under attack. The three men quickly armed themselves and ran for separate exits. The Chromium Club was cunningly designed to hide a multitude of secret passages. Doc Titan and his friend Big Tom had overseen construction of the new addition, but even Big Tom was ignorant of the enormous meeting rooms in the sub-basements of the Club.

Darkness was the first to emerge, seemingly springing from the shadows of a bookcase alcove. Smoke and flame blocked his vision for a few seconds. The fire was minor, but a huge, gaping hole allowed Darkness to see the soldier in the next room. The garb of this man was something no Chromium Club member had ever expected to see in their building. He was covered, head to foot, in a costume of black leather. A silver Totenkopf, a deaths-head emblem, adorned each shoulder and a larger one was on the stiff hat he wore. A Nazi Swastika and SS bars also adorned his uniform. Black leather boots, gloves and a full black leather face mask completed the outfit. A crimson-red skull stood out brightly, affixed to his neck. In all of his life, the Darkness had never been witness to anything like this.

The leather-clad man was armed with a large gun in each hand. For every round he fired, an earth-shaking explosion shook the Chromium Club.

Explosive rounds ripped through walls and doors, exposing and destroying water lines and electrical wires. Other explosions could be heard in distant parts of the building, as additional guns roared thunder. This man was obviously not here alone.

Darkness drew both automatics from their concealed holsters and advanced on the invader. He fired two rounds into the thick frame of the man and started forward. He had expected the man to fall. The slugs hit like a ten-ton sledgehammer. Much to his surprise, the soldier staggered but immediately straightened and turned in his direction. Rounds whistled past his head and the wall behind him exploded. Darkness fired again, once at the body and one striking the man in the forehead. Again, the man only staggered momentarily before resuming his attack. Darkness fired one more shot, this time striking the red skull at the neck of the soldier.

A burst of crimson spray encased the man's head and he screamed in horror. Clutching the leather mask, he tore it from his face. While Gibson watched, the facial features dissolved, melting away like flesh and crimson hued candle wax. The skin and muscle was slowly stripped to the bone by some unseen force. The soldier dropped to the floor and didn't move.

The claustrophobic passageways between the rooms were filled with smoke and destruction. Darkness clambered through the rubble and wreckage that once was elaborately decorated sitting rooms. Crystal chandeliers were shattered into a million fragments. Deep, rich carpets burned, emitting thick black smoke. The rare and priceless paintings hanging on the walls were scorched and burned beyond recognition. Panic and confusion ensued amidst the club members. The screams of men and the smell of burning, human flesh reminded Gibson of the trenches of the Great War and the lingering odor of death. The horrible stench of burnt human remains was scorched into the core of his memory, never to be forgotten. Dante's Inferno paled in comparison to the horrors that he had witnessed.

Several rooms away, Doc Titan was battling his own opponent. This Nazi infiltrator was almost the same size as Doc, a giant in black leather. Doc managed to relieve the man of his firearms but after punching the man in the face, he watched in amazement as the soldier stood back up and attacked again. This time Doc felt the man's nose break beneath the leather mask. Without slowing down, the large man hit Doc twice. His speed and strength were incredible. Doc struck again, this time breaking the man's jaw. The emotionless Nazi automaton didn't even attempt to dodge the blow. He was a lumbering juggernaut, an unstoppable force with no sense of self-preservation.

Darkness stepped into the room and shouted. "Get away from him, Doc."

Darkness shot the man in the neck, striking the scarlet skull. This man suffered the same fate as Darkness' opponent. Two more similarly clad men stepped into the hallway, drawn by the sound of gunfire. These Swastika-bearing, Stormtroopers advanced without uttering a sound. Darkness fired twice, unerringly aiming for the crimson targets at their necks. They screamed and ripped off the masks. Both fell to the floor, their faces completely obliterated, leaving leering, gory skulls.

Two men rolled into the hallway, wrestling for control. Despite Blake's greater than normal strength, he was obviously fighting a losing battle. The soldier punched Simon in the face and the imprint of his fist remained on Blake's cheek. Before Doc Titan or Darkness could come to his aid, three more black leather-clad soldiers advanced on them. A small beep sounded and the men stopped. The skulls at their necks started glowing. Half a second later, the small skulls exploded into scarlet clouds. The man pinning Blake to the floor spoke hoarsely. "Heil the Third Reich and Black Skull." His neck ornament also exploded, covering Blake and himself in a cloud of crimson death.

Doc started forward. "Simon!"

Darkness grabbed Doc and tried to hold him back. "He's already dead, John! You can't help him!"

Blake and the soldier screamed in horror as the cloud performed its deadly ritual. Seconds seemed like an eternity as Doc and Darkness were forced to watch their friend suffer. But something different happened this time. The last awful liquescent vestiges of the Nazi's face vanished, leaving a ghastly crimson skull. Blake tossed the ravaged body of the soldier aside and raised himself to one knee. He had his face covered with his gloved hands, but he was still moving. Blake stood on his feet and slowly pulled his hands away. In the blinding smoke and dim light, it appeared as though parts of his face and hands were eaten down to the colorless bone and tendon.

"Simon?"

He walked toward them and wiped his fingers down the front of his face. Long streaks painted his features as the makeup was wiped away. His skin remained whole, but was as white as pure, mountain snow. Blake stared at his messy hands, the leather material of his gloves hanging in tatters, exposing his colorless fingers.

"Damn. Guess the secret is out now."

Doc was still in shock from what he had witnessed. "But, how ... why ...?"

Gibson laughed, happy to see that his friend was still alive. "This is a first. Doc Titan is dumb-struck."

Blake appeared perplexed and disoriented. "Maybe something in the make-up neutralized the acid, or whatever is in those bombs ..." He stopped speaking when he realized his explanation didn't make sense.

Doc stared at Blake doubtfully. "Make-up? And it ate through your gloves, but didn't burn your fingers?"

Blake looked at Doc and Gibson and they could tell that he was ashamed. He removed the coal-black wig, exposing his closely-cropped white hair below. "I was never 'cured' of my white skin and hair." He confessed. "I've been using make-up and hair dye or wigs. I see you managed to destroy another shirt, John."

Doc looked down at the shirt that hung in tatters on his massive frame. In his peripheral vision, Doc noticed two men slink out the rear entrance of the Chromium Club. Titan knew every member of the lodge and these two men were strangers.

"Simon, see if you can help put out the fires and get everyone out." Then Titan was gone.

Simon Blake turned to say something to Gibson and realized he was standing alone amidst the carnage of the Chromium Club. Darkness had already vanished into the shadows. Blake was a little rattled by the near-death experience and leaned against one wall.

Blake shrugged good-naturedly and talked to himself. "Simon, old man, they don't get closer than that. Thought I was a goner for sure."

Grabbing a bar towel, Blake placed his face above a broken water pipe and washed the remaining makeup from his pale, emotionless face. The ghastly apparition known as Guardian had returned.

Within seconds, Blake was organizing a fire brigade and helping the injured. In a few minutes, the police and fire departments arrived, closely followed by Police Commissioner Wheaton and detective Jim Carson, close friends of Luthor Gibson. Blake, Carson, and Wheaton directed the efforts of the emergency services personnel and helped find victims still trapped in the burning building. Per Blake's instructions, the bodies of the Nazi soldiers were carefully removed and taken to a secure morgue until a disease control unit would arrive.

Twenty minutes later, Police Commissioner Wheaton turned to ask Simon Blake a question and noticed that the white-faced man had vanished into the gathering crowd of spectators.

Chapter Eleven
A Kidnapping Gone Wrong at the Stockbridge Mansion

April 5, 1945   9:00 pm

Whitney was driving much too fast. Rav Chandra, the giant bearded warrior, sat mutely on the passenger side of the car. Even if he still had his tongue, he would have never questioned Whitney's actions. And it would have fallen on deaf ears anyway. Whitney Van Pelt was head-strong and had a mind of her own and explaining something, anything, to her was a waste of breath. Not only because she was a Vassar College graduate or a wealthy debutante. And she was not entirely at fault. Anyone who had been through all of the horrible things that she had survived in one short lifetime had to be a little headstrong. She had fought and been taken captive by madmen, aliens, gangsters, and even Cro Magnon Neanderthals. She had also tolerated the obsessions of her soul mate, and Rav Chandra's master and friend, Preston Stockbridge II, for over fourteen years.

Both Rav Chandra and Whitney would give their lives without hesitation to save Preston, but there were times he was simply impossible. He seemed to be willing to sacrifice everything and everyone to win the day. He always did succeed, but usually only after being shot, stabbed, or tortured by some nefarious criminal. And his tortured soul was always in conflict over the decisions he had to make.

After the Great War, a haunted Preston Stockbridge wandered aimlessly throughout Europe and upper Africa. At the border of Afghanistan, he was witness to a silent warrior single-handedly battling seven armed men. Preston intervened as one man prepared to strike Rav Chandra from behind, deftly placing a bullet in the man's skull. When it was discovered that Preston had killed Rav's brother, a power-hungry madman attempting to kill his own siblings, he was imprisoned and, by order of Rav's own father, was sentenced to be executed on the following morning. Rav risked his own life to help Stockbridge escape the prison and incurred the wrath of his father, a powerful Rahdja king.

Christened Ghoshdashtidar Raviprakash Chandramouleeswaran Dakkar, this proud giant stood before his father and confessed to freeing the condemned prisoner. By speaking to his father as an equal, in the defense of the American, Rav committed the greatest possible offense. For this crime,

Rav was severely beaten, had his tongue cut out, and was forever banished from his native homeland.

Upon returning to the United States, Stockbridge revealed to Rav his plan to pursue justice as the masked vigilante, the Scorpion. The faithful mute swore his allegiance to his friend and master.

The sporty, 1939 Stutz Bearcat roadster slid a little sideways, taking the corner on two wheels. The Bearcat was an American-made luxury high-performance sports car and owning one became a famous status symbol for the very wealthy. So, naturally, Preston Stockbridge II owned several. Whitney pressed down on the accelerator with her dainty foot and took the next corner even faster. This auburn-curled beauty with lavender eyes loved danger. Perhaps even more than Preston Stockbridge. More than once, when he had been seriously wounded and could not perform as the Scorpion, Whitney had disguised herself and played the part. She had even confronted Police Commissioner Jack Lockhart and fooled him into believing that Preston was not the Scorpion.

Personally, she was glad he had stopped masquerading in that horrible Guido Salvatore disguise, with the vampire fangs, lanky gray/black wig, battered old hat, and disgusting hunchback. On occasion, he had worn a skirted mask that concealed his entire lower face. She much preferred the Domino eye mask; it made him appear gallant, distinguished, and handsome. Like Zorro, from the pulp magazines. Above all, she preferred the tall, athletic playboy with crisp gray eyes and impeccably tailored suits named Preston Stockbridge II, but she rarely saw him these days.

Preston Stockbridge II was the sole living member of a wealthy family. Several weeks ago Preston, Whitney, Rav Chandra and Allen Coleman had moved from their city penthouse apartments and into the enormous, long-vacant Stockbridge Mansion. Recently, it seemed to Whitney, the Scorpion had become Preston's dominant personality. His life as a wealthy clubsman and concert violinist were only used as tools to gather information and then quickly stored back into the closet again. He was truly a man obsessed with stopping the criminal world. Sometimes Whitney was plagued by a terrifying thought. How long before Scorpion began taking over completely? Would Preston Stockbridge cease to exist at that point? Did he even realize how close to the edge of the abyss he stood?

Rav Chandra solemnly asked, using sign language with his hands. "Mistress Whitney. Is there an emergency, of which I should be aware?"

Whitney laughed sweetly, her eyes bright and intelligent. "No, I merely want to change clothes and get to Pam's beauty shop ASAP. I'm just running a little late. I didn't expect you and Preston to need my assistance at Pier 52 this evening, it was rather last minute. But putting Bossman Krieger behind bars made it worth the trouble. When I go back out again, if you prefer, you can stay at the mansion and play cards with Benson, the butler, and Allen Coleman." Coleman, a soldier of fortune, was an old friend of Preston Stockbridge's from the Great War.

Rav Chandra hand-spoke without smiling. "I think not, mistress. Benson owes me his salary for the next year and Coleman cheats at cards."

Whitney's warm, luxuriant lips curled into a smile and she started to reply, when she saw the flames. She slammed on the brakes and turned the steering wheel on the powerful, little car. It slid sideways and came to an abrupt halt as another explosion blew out several windows on the second floor. Her heart slammed in her chest and tears welled up in her eyes when she saw her home ablaze. Covering her mouth with the back of her hand she stifled a scream. Shifting into reverse, Whitney began backing away from the intense heat. She had to stand on the brake pedal to avoid hitting the van that had silently pulled up behind her sporty car.

Jumping out, the quick thinking Whitney ran to the driver's side of the truck. She pounded on the glass and yelled at the driver. "Please find a telephone and call for the police and the fire department, my house is on fire!"

Goldie's voice came from behind her. "He knows, lady, we started the fire."

Machine guns were pointed at Whitney and Rav Chandra. Too many to fight. Despite this, she lashed out at the man showing one gold tooth with her sharp fingernails. Crimson ran down the man's face from the scratch. She expected to be slapped hard, but the man simply smiled. "Put them with the others." Tears ran down her face as handcuffs were locked onto her petite wrists and those of the faithful manservant. Rav had prepared to pull out his long, razor sharp knife and end the life of the infidel, if Goldie McDonall had slapped Whitney. She gave Rav Chandra a distinct look that told him not to resist, their turn would come. Rav grimly resolved to make these infidels pay, and pay dearly. They joined four other captives in the back of the moving van and the vehicle sped away into the night.

If Whitney Van Pelt and Rav Chandra had arrived ten minutes earlier they would have known the full story. Police Commissioner Jack Lockhart had arrived with three uniformed police officers to arrest Preston Stockbridge. Lockhart was a tall, lean man with quiet, blue eyes and soft, brown hair that was mostly hidden under his gray fedora hat. Lockhart had often suspected, but never directly admitted to himself, or anyone else, that Stockbridge was the

Scorpion. He always lacked the conclusive, ironclad proof. Besides his stepson always seemed to have the perfect alibi. And if he ever proved that Stockbridge was the Scorpion, how could he bring himself to arrest the greatest force of justice ever known?

Jack Lockhart had known Preston for several years and they had been close friends, before Jack met Preston's mother, Marian Stockbridge. The courtship had been short and, unfortunately, so had the marriage. Marian was the mortal victim of a violent crime and Police Commissioner Jack Lockhart had been forced to release the accused killer on a technicality. He steadfastly refused to disclose the identity of the murderer to Preston. Lockhart and Stockbridge allowed this to drive a wedge between them.

Stockbridge was often caught in a nerve-wracking trap between his own role as an amateur criminologist, his identity as the murderous Scorpion, and his strained relationship with his old friend and stepfather, Police Commissioner Lockhart. Earlier tonight, one of his officers had discovered a handgun and a battered hat near a murder scene. It was believed that the fingerprints on the gun would match Stockbridge's.

Allen Coleman, the tall, wide-shouldered chauffer, had been making a multi-layered Dagwood sandwich, a mountainous pile of dissimilar leftovers precariously arranged between two slices of bread, in the kitchen. "Commissioner, can I offer you and your men a bite to eat?"

Lockhart pulled a warrant from the breast pocket of his tailored three-piece suit. "Official police business tonight, Coleman. Have you seen Preston?"

"He said he was heading downtown; had a meeting." Coleman volunteered.

Lockhart removed his felt hat. "We'll just wait for him in the front room."

Coleman had been a military man most of his life and a soldier of fortune for the last several years. Preston Stockbridge was one of his oldest and dearest friends, and it seemed he had fewer every year. The life of a gun for hire is not a long one. The three law enforcement officers relaxed against the plush cushions on the richly upholstered sofa in the spacious front parlor. Police Commissioner Lockhart paced the floor impatiently. Finally, he stopped and stood before an intricately carved wood and glass case mounted to the paneled oak wall. Protected behind the glass was Stockbridge's Stradivarius violin. Only last week, Lockhart had visited Stockbridge and listened as the man passionately stroked the bow across the strings, as gently as a lover's caress.

As they waited for Preston to arrive, there was a knock at the front door.

Harold Benson, the withered, silver-haired butler, had served the Stockbridge family since Preston was a lad. As he approached the front door, the dapper, wax-mustached Police Commissioner and his men followed. They met four men with Thompson machine guns in the doorway. Poor Benson was caught in the crossfire between gangsters and police. He was the first to fall. The police were caught off guard and were no match for the machine gunners. Jack Lockhart hesitated when he saw Goldie and received three slugs to the chest before he dropped.

Allen Coleman was still in the kitchen when the melee had broken out. Never without an arsenal of weapons, Coleman attacked the foyer from the kitchen area. One of the gangsters fell instantly, a bullet buried in his forehead. Unfortunately, one of the other attackers had brought along a rocket launcher. This was fired down the hallway and into the large kitchen, where it struck a ten-burner gas stove. The resulting explosion blew out half of the windows in the large mansion and started a raging fire that was currently burning out of control.

Allen was slightly shell-shocked but still alive. Blood poured from a wound on his head and temporarily blinded him in one eye. He witnessed the van driving away, but was too late to stop it. He dragged the dead and injured from the blazing fire that still threatened to burn the mansion to the ground. A tear formed in the hardened man's eye when he realized Benson, the Stockbridge's faithful family butler, was beyond help. The Police Commissioner was also near death. All three police officers were dead. Allen had a slug in one shoulder and his right arm had been burned in the fire, but he seemed to hardly notice his own injuries.

Chapter Twelve
Beware of the Black Skull.

April 5, 1945   9:00 pm

The man stepped from the elevator cage at the 116th floor of the Titan Tower and strolled to the single, smooth, copper-colored door ahead of him. On a small plaque was embossed the name *John Titan* in plain, unimpressive text. There was nothing bold or outstanding about the entrance to the offices of Doc Titan. The man stood for several seconds before the door, as if uncertain what to do next. Most people who arrived here were nervous or frightened. Often their lives, or the lives of friends or family, were in peril and they had come here for salvation. Sometimes it was representatives of companies or even entire countries that were here to appeal to the considerable talents of the man known as Doc Titan. They all had one thing in common. They all needed his help.

This man was no exception to the rule. However, he was not frightened or nervous. Of average build and appearance, he was as plain as the door before him. His simple gray suit was nice, but not expensive. Light brown hair covered his scalp and his face lacked beard, mustache, scars or any outstanding blemishes. If he had committed a crime, it would be difficult for witnesses to remember anything about him. In the hustle and bustle of New York City, he was only one of the unseen many. A modern day invisible man. Even his facial expression left no memorable impressions. And to match this plain and simple man, was a plain and simple name, Harold Bekker. He took a shallow breath and pushed the door open.

The reception room he entered was rather large and spacious, simply furnished with a few comfortable chairs and a large, wooden inlaid table. As the door closed behind him, Harold noticed the rather odd pair of gentlemen. The first was seated at the table. Impeccably dressed and exuding an air of confidence, the dapper man nodded his head in Harold's direction. "Good evening, sir. My name is Bart Blackwell. How may we assist you?" His soothing voice and polite mannerism matched his appearance. This fellow was a true gentleman.

The man, using the term loosely, standing next to the well-dressed Bart Blackwell, was his opposite in every detail. He wore a loudly colored sweatshirt that appeared to have been slept in. His hair was uncombed and a day's growth of rust-colored hair covered his face. And what a face. *Homely* was the only term that Harold could think of to describe the man. Scars and marks made it look as though a chicken had paraded across his face, several times. The loose sweatshirt could not hide the fact that the man was built like a large gorilla. He was barrel-chested, with short legs, and long arms. And the part of his arms that stuck out of the sleeves was covered with thick, coarse hair that looked like rusty nails. "Well, c'mon fella. Give. It's late, whatcha want?" If the man's appearance was in contrast to Bart Blackwell, his speech and mannerisms were even more so.

"Ignore Kong Larson's gruffness; you awoke him from his slumbers, and he needs all of the beauty sleep that he can get." Bart spoke politely.

Henry Marmaduke *'Kong'* Larson was slightly over five feet tall and yet he weighed over 300 pounds. His simian exterior, most notably his thick, caveman brow and abnormally long arms, often made him the object of ridicule. Nicknames such as 'chimp,' 'apeman,' and 'monk' followed him as a youth in Oklahoma.

"Hello, my name is Harold Bekker. I have come a long distance to see Doc … err … John Titan." Like his appearance, Harold's voice was plain and unimpressive. "I was told to give him an important message."

Bart nodded. "I'm sorry, but Doc is out of the offices right now. I could give him your message, if you would care to leave one."

Harold looked disappointed. "This can only be given directly to Mr. Titan. I shall wait for him here until he returns." Harold approached Bart and his forward momentum was abruptly halted by an unseen force. He took one step backward and stretched out a hand. It met with a thick panel of nearly invisible glass, barring his way.

Bart apologized. "Sorry about that. We have learned to take precautions with unknown visitors. That barrier is a bulletproof glass that drops down from the ceiling. Would you mind emptying your pockets, so we can confirm that you are not carrying a dangerous object?" Bart's voice was calm and reassuring. Bartholomew *'Bart'* J. Blackwell was one of America's leading mathematicians and cryptologists. Bart assisted the Allies in deciphering the supposedly unbreakable secret codes of the Axis Forces and in creating the 'Windtalkers' code with the assistance of the American Navajo Indians. With a keen mind for numbers, he was also Doc's investment broker and oversaw the financial aspects of Titan Enterprises. Bart studied the man carefully. "Excuse me, Mr. Bekker. Have we ever met before? You look distinctly familiar."

Kong nodded in agreement. "I was thinkin' the same thing. I never forget a face … or a pair of legs." Kong smiled broadly. He had once solved a case by remembering a woman's shapely legs. He, and Bart as well, had a weakness for the 'weaker' sex. They were renowned skirt-chasers. Much to Bart's chagrin, Kong was very popular with the girls, despite his Neanderthal-like appearance.

Before Harold Bekker could respond to the question, an alarm sounded. A red light flashed above a small bank of phones. Attached to one of the phones was a loudspeaker, and Doc Titan's voice sounded from this box. Even though there was no hint of panic in his well-modulated voice, Doc's tone carried the warning of immediate danger. "Red alert, brothers! Prepare for possible attack."

Large automatic pistols appeared in the hands of Kong and Bart. They were odd-looking guns, fitted with oversized magazine clips. Bart pressed several buttons with his left foot, on the floor, below the wood inlaid table. Metal shutters slid down to cover the exterior windows. The quiet, plain room had become a virtual fortress in less than ten seconds.

However, before restraining bolts could slide into place in the entrance door and pin it closed, it was opened abruptly. Four men rushed into the room and pulled machine guns from within the folds of their oversized trench coats. Before Bart or Kong could respond, Harold Bekker met his end in a hale of lead bullets. When the gangsters realized a bulletproof shield separated them from Kong and Bart, they ceased firing. As Harold slowly slid to the tile floor, Bart heard him voice a warning. "Beware of the Black Skull." These were the last words Harold Bekker would ever speak.

One of the attackers had rushed forward and smashed a small, fist-sized ball of mud against the glass. Bart was staring at this with a puzzled expression when Kong hit him full force and carried him into the doorway of the next room. "What the hell ...? Get off of me, you great ape!" Bart began, indignantly.

Suddenly, the world became all sound and movement. An explosion rocked the entire skyscraper, down to its foundations. The ball of mud had been a powerful explosive, shaped so that the majority of the devastation and destructive was directed toward Bart and Kong. Their ears rang from the loud explosion. Bart was searching for his dropped gun when he saw the four men step toward them. Anyone who had been around Bart and Kong for long would have been surprised by Bart's next move. He turned, so his body would become a shield for Kong, if only for a few seconds. They argued and sounded like they would kill one another but Bart and Kong were truly the best of friends.

The four men smiled evilly and began to raise their guns. Then something odd occurred. There was a 'pop' sound and the first man fell to the ground and didn't move. Several more pops could be heard in rapid succession and all four men were down. Kong realized a second later that his sense of hearing was still ringing from the explosion and the pop sound was actually the firing of a pistol. He stared at the men lying in the rubble and knew from experience; they wouldn't be getting back up. He had been witness to many a dead man in his line of work. Bart and Kong turned to look behind them, to see the man who had saved their lives.

The man's full name was Gilbert 'Gibs' Elliot Maddox. He was holding one of the rapid-fire machine gun pistols. So quietly that Kong barely heard him with the ringing in his ears, Gibs said, "I wish they hadn't put me in that position. I didn't want to kill them." He then turned and looked at his two friends. "How are you guys doing? Are you okay?"

Gibs was teased as a child, that his name was bigger than he was. He had suffered from a hormonal deficiency known as dwarfism. Technically, he was a midget, not a dwarf. A midget was a medical term referring to an extremely short but normally proportioned person, and was used in contrast to dwarf, which denoted disproportionate shortness, especially noticeable in the hands and fingers.

Barely four feet tall, this tiny man possessed a giant intellect, especially in his field of expertise - electricity. As a young man, he studied under the tutelage of Nikola Tesla, Thomas Edison, and George Westinghouse. Besides his lust for adventure, his second greatest obsession was the creation of an electrical bug killer. Gibs fervently hated insects of any kind. He held hundreds of electrical patents and because of them he had become the wealthiest of all of Doc's aides. He was a wizard with electricity, or as Bart called it 'The Juice.' Whenever he wasn't following Doc Titan around the world, he could be found at his desk, designing some new electrical gadget.

Gibs apologized as he helped his friends stand up. "I would have been here sooner, but I was playing with my bug-zapper. I ran down here as soon as I heard the first gunshot." From the moment Harold Bekker entered the room, until Gibs had saved Kong and Bart, barely two minutes had passed. In this lifestyle, things moved quickly. One misstep, or stopping to make a split-second decision, could mean the difference between life and death.

Bart brushed dust from his black, pin-striped suit. "What the heck was that chunk of mud they put on the wall? Kong, you seemed to know what it was."

Kong shrugged his broad shoulders. "It was just a guess, but it made sense ta me. The British have recently been using something called Nobel 808, or C-4. It's a mixture containing RDX, mineral oil, and lecithin. They call it a plastic explosive. It's safer than dynamite and more powerful than nitroglycerine. As with many plastic explosives, the explosive material in C-4 is RDX also known as cyclonite or cyclotrimethylene trinitramine. C-4 is made by combining RDX slurry with a binder dissolved in a solvent. The solvent is then evaporated away and the mixture is dried and filtered. The final material is an off-white solid

with a feel similar to modeling clay. It sure did a number on our bullet-proof glass shield."

Bart was wiping dust from his black cane with his handkerchief. He still carried the cane as a reminder of a wound he received during the Great War, although the injury had left no permanent damage. "Yes, and the entire reception room as well. It's a good thing Doc had the walls, floors, and ceilings on this floor reinforced." Gibs could tell Bart and Kong were shell-shocked. They weren't arguing or ribbing each other and Kong wasn't even pretending to be a moron. Kong's small bullet-shaped skull didn't look like it could contain a thimble full of brains, but he was actually the one of Doc's most valuable aides. Possessing a nearly photographic memory, he could commit to memory any professional journal, design specification, or technical research and recall every minute detail. He could memorize the layout of any city at a glance or learn any written language in less than an hour. But when Kong was relaxing around Bart or his friends, he talked and acted like an uneducated holligan.

Gibs was looking at the faces of the dead men to see if he recognized any of them. He also searched each man for identification. When he got to Harold Bekker, Gibs noticed the clothing was different, a more casual attire. This was no gangster.

Gibs turned to Kong and Bart. "Hey, who shot this guy? I only shot four men, not five."

Bart brushed off his pants cuffs with the no-longer-clean handkerchief. "He arrived only seconds before these other mokes barged in and started firing. He came to see Doc about helping him with something. A quiet little guy. Damn, this suit is absolutely ruined."

Gibs tsk-tsked with his tongue. "Wow. He picked a bad night to come by the offices. Wrong place at the wrong time."

Bart frowned, knelt down and exclaimed Bekker's neck. "Kong, Gibs, check out the back of this guys neck. Look at this." He indicated an inch-long white scar at the base of the skull, behind the right ear.

Kong and Gibs stared at the scar for a moment and then each other. Finally, Bart broke the silence.

"Doc's going to want to know about this right away."

Kong snapped his fingers. "Geez, I forgot … Doc called in right before the ruckus and warned us to go on full alert. We need to send out a signal to Percy and Big Tom."

"I got it." Gibs flipped a switch on the wall and a red light came on. He and Doc had created a special insert in each members watch. When the switch was turned on at the office, the back of the watch would heat up and vibrate. This was a signal to report to the main office as soon as possible.

"Kong, did you hear the last thing Harold Bekker muttered after being shot?" Bart asked.

"Yeah, something about 'Beware of the Black Skull.'"

Gibs bit his lip. "You think he was referring to that place in Black Skull canyon in Arizona?"

Bart smiled. "Wasn't that the time Snaps Malone kidnapped Kong?"

Gibs smiled, too. "And Kong's secretary, Leanne Laster, saved his hash?"

Kong's face took on a foolish, dopey look. "Yeah, that Leanne was some pip. And she had legs that went all the up to ... "

Gibs, who wasn't a ladies man like Kong and Bart, interrupted. "That was ten years ago. Maybe he was referring to that Nazi psychopath who wears a Black Skull mask. I've read about him in the Department of Justice memos." Gibs Maddox was the government liaison between Doc Titan, the FBI, and the Department of Justice.

Kong scratched his bullet-shaped head. "I bet Doc can tell us when he gets here. And he can tell us why this man has that scar on the back of his neck."

"I believe I'd like to know the answer to that myself." Bart said with a worried look in his eyes.

Chapter Thirteen
The Doc Titan Trap

April 5, 1945   9:00 pm

Doc Titan emerged from the Chromium Club, at the rear of the building. He heard the engine of a car as it sped away from the alley. Two men were in the front seat. Their names were Teppleman and Gross. Reaching into his utility vest, Doc plucked out a small object that resembled a shirt button. He tossed the object at the speeding car and it hit the right shoulder of the car's passenger, Teppleman, where it adhered itself. From another pocket, Doc removed another item, about the size of a cigar. At one end was a blinking light. The blinking became faster as Doc pointed it at the speeding car. Satisfied with the results, he began running after the automobile, staying to the shadows whenever possible.

Twenty-five blocks later, the sedan pulled up in front of an abandoned hotel. In fact, most of the buildings in the block were no longer used, except by derelicts and winos. Teppleman and Gross entered the structure and for several moments there was no evidence they had ever been there. Then, on the ninth floor of the ancient hotel building, lights came on. Doc Titan emerged from the doorway of the building across the street. Amazingly enough, he had been able to easily match the speed of the fast car and arrived only seconds after they had stopped. Doc wasn't even breathing hard. He studied the dark monolith from his position, waiting for further signs of activity. There were none.

Darting across the open street, Doc ducked into the alleyway next to the old hotel. Grasping the ledge of a window sill, he effortlessly pulled himself up with one powerful arm. Like a human fly he clung to the side of the building, finding finger holds and toeholds in the brick joints and the minor projections on the outside face of the building. He quickly traversed this way until he reached the ninth floor. Hanging outside of a window he listened, searching for signs of movement or the sound of voices. Pushing upward, he managed to open the window, as it emitted only a slight groan of protest. The corroded window latch shattered and tumbled onto the filthy floor.

He swung inside and landed on the tiled floor with the grace of a stealthy feline. Watching each step to avoid weak spots in the creaking floor, he made his way across the room to the partially open door. He peered into the next room, which was dimly lit by a dirty, old light bulb. Doc strained his senses to their utmost, seeking any signs of life in the adjoining room. So keen was his sense of hearing, he should have detected the sounds of the men breathing, but the room was completely silent. Cautiously, he entered, glancing about for signs of a trap. Except for a filthy old sink and a claw-footed, cast-iron tub, the only other inhabitant of the room was a wooden chair with a missing leg. Teppleman and Gross had completely vanished!

Only Doc's training and experience saved his life. First, he noticed the board resting on the sill of a window was moving slightly, slowly being pulled from the room. Obviously, the two men had used this makeshift bridge to cross over into a window of the adjoining building. He took one step forward, into the dim light, just as the board slid off of the window sill and plunged into the alleyway below. Suddenly, spotlights on either side of the building were switched on, catching him in the bright illumination.

The rooftops on either side of the hotel were one story taller than the floor Doc was on and allowed the men, armed with Thompson machine guns, a perfect view of the bronzed man. He had only one second to react to the threat and he used the time wisely. Grasping the rim of the iron tub, he gave a mighty heave and tore the fastenings that held it to the dilapidated floor. It had taken four strong men to bring this tub, weighing several hundred pounds, into the building when it was installed. As though it weighed nothing, Doc flipped the heavy bath upside-down on top of his prone form, as he fell flat on his back.

Hundreds of bullets struck the sides of the ancient iron tub and it rang like a large bell. Doc covered his ears to drown out the sound, until he was able to fit them with earplugs. Despite its size and thickness, Doc knew it would only take a few seconds for the guns to crack the forged metal, leaving him exposed to the violent, steel hornets searching for him. In the confined space under the tub, he could only pull his fist back six inches, but when he struck the floor, it cracked. A small hole appeared. Using his powerful fingers, the opening widened, until he was able to squeeze his large frame through and drop down onto the floor below. At the same instant his feet touched down noiselessly onto the floor, the rusty iron tub broke in several places. Bullets bounced off of the inner surface of the bathtub and rained down around Doc. He moved quickly to the far side of the room to avoid the deadly ricochets.

While he was formulating a plan of escape, Doc heard a noise over the steady stream of machine gun fire. Thoom. Thoom. Thoom. It was the undeniable sound of a large bore automatic, .45 caliber in size, judging by the sound. Doc heard the sound of a man running across the roof of the old hotel building, as maniacal laughter echoed into the valleys and canyons of the old, abandoned buildings. Doc could hear the yells and panic of the gunmen in the neighboring structures. For each bullet fired by the automatic handguns, there was one less machine gun firing its lethal projectiles. And one less gangster, as well.

After several seconds of gunfire, the city block became silent again. The only sound was the receding laughter of the scourge of the underworld of crime, the Darkness. Even though he must certainly have known Doc was in the decrepit hotel building, Darkness had not even slowed his progress through the barrage of gunfire. And now he was gone. Stopping only long enough to battle the killers, Darkness was obviously on another, more urgent, mission.

Doc looked out of the windows facing north and was witness to a dozen slain men at the roofs edge. The southern windows provided the same type of view. To his surprise, from the rooftop fire escape, a man stepped forward, holding a tube several inches in diameter and about four feet long. Doc recognized the man as one of the occupants of the car he had followed. It was Teppleman. Doc recognized the face but he still didn't know the man's name. And the tube was ... a rocket launcher!

Without hesitation, Doc ran for the stairwell located in the center of the building. He grasped the rail with one hand as he leapt over. The old stairwell was a winding rectangle, with a large unobstructed area in the center, open all the way down to the ground floor. The musty air whistled in Doc's ears as he plunged downward through layers of dusty cobwebs. He struck the floor at the bottom and continued moving without hesitation. Even though he had plummeted nearly one hundred feet straight down, he made it appear as easy as jumping from a step stool. His powerful leg muscles had absorbed the impact without any injury.

The rocket exploded in the center of the old building and a plume of scorching fire and heat extended out and downward. The blast weakened the few supporting members that had kept the structure upright and seconds later the entire tower of brick and wood collapsed. Smoke and dust billowed out and covered the surrounding area for a long minute. Nothing could have survived such total destruction. The lifeless body of Doc Titan was buried under tons of debris. Teppleman, still holding the rocket launcher in the crook of his arm, stared down at the smoldering pile of rubble, searching for any signs of movement or life. Finally, after several minutes, he was satisfied that Doc must be dead.

Teppleman turned to walk back to the rooftop door. His lower jaw dropped and his eyes bulged. Doc was standing five feet away. With a growl, the man recovered from his surprise and reached into his jacket for his gun. Before the revolver could be removed from it's holster, Doc had clasped the wrist in a steely grip and squeezed hard. A sharp snap sounded and the man's forearm twisted at a weird angle, the bones broken. Surprisingly, the man simply glared at Doc and snarled. He managed to grasp Doc's collar with his good hand and pull himself close, before Doc could even react. The broken arm struck a button on Teppleman's shoulder and a light blinked on. The red skull epoxied to the man's throat glowed slightly. From recent experience, Doc knew he only had a fraction of a second to respond to this threat.

Dropping straight backwards, he landed cleanly on his back and kicked the man over his head. There was a thud as the man struck the parapet wall at the edge of the roof, then a 'phoom' noise as the red skull exploded. A crimson mist encircled Teppleman's head and he died horribly only seconds later, arms and legs thrashing wildly. The scarlet mist dissipated, leaving a bloody, gore-covered skull and upper skeleton. The grisly sight was enough to make even Doc Titan nauseous.

During his adventures, Doc been witness to many strange phenomena. Men stripped to the bone by something that made a sound like sizzling bacon. Humans consumed by black smoke or turned to dust. Men screamed and died as their eyes bulged out. He had even witnessed the horrors of war in the trenches of France. Working triage during the battles, where medical or emergency personnel had to ration limited medical resources as the number of wounded and dying exceeded the resources available. Hopelessly watching as men died, while waiting for medical assistance. It humbled him, both as a man and as a surgeon, knowing he could not save everyone. But in all of his travels, all of his battles with madmen and scientists wielding monstrous weapons of destruction, Doc had never witnessed anything remotely like this … virus. Originally, he had thought it might be acid-based, but now he was certain it had to be a deadly form of virus. This was the weapon that Sentry had warned them about.

The other man from the car, Gross, had escaped many minutes ago, probably while Doc was being shot at by the gangsters. Doc had narrowly escaped death during the hotels collapse, by bursting through the exit doors and into the rear alley. He used the enveloping blanket of dust to approach the next building. He quickly climbed up the side of the brick structure from the outside and approached the man with the rocket launcher from behind. He had hoped to take the man alive, to question him and discover why Doc and his friends had been under attack.

Doc tried his wrist radio again but received no response from his headquarters. Praying Kong, Bart, and Gibs were okay, Doc began running toward his downtown offices. Suddenly, he turned right. First, he would stop by and make sure Big Tom and Percy were safe. He could also get to Titan Towers faster by borrowing Big Tom's new roadster.

Chapter Fourteen
Death of Police Commissioner Jack Lockhart

April 5, 1945   9:15 pm

Preston Stockbridge slammed on the brakes in front of his mansion, nearly crashing his car into Whitney's sport coupe. The cargo truck had left only five minutes earlier with Whitney, Rav Chandra, and the other four prisoners. Stockbridge bounded up the granite steps three at a time. His heart pounded in his chest, fearful of what he might see. When he reached the top step he hesitated, staring for a full second at the bodies that lay scattered around the front lawn. Patches of blood had painted the dark grass almost black.

Allen Coleman was holding the still form of Police Commissioner Jack Lockhart. Preston's eyes searched the other bodies, recognizing the bullet-ridden form of Benson. His heart ached at the sight and tears welled up in his eyes. Three other still forms were policemen, but two figures were not here amongst the dead. He had half expected, and greatly feared, seeing Whitney and Rav Chandra lying in the cold night grass. However, they were nowhere to be seen.

Lockhart's eyes opened and he lifted one hand toward Stockbridge. Preston knelt down beside his stepfather and clasped his hands over the Commissioner's.

Jack's quiet blue eyes stared into Stockbridge's steely gray pupils. "I'm sorry, son. They caught me ... off guard. Benson was in the doorway ... I couldn't fire back ... then it was too late." The dying man spoke with great difficulty. Blood slowly oozed from his fatal chest wounds.

Stockbridge held back tears with great effort. "Its okay, Jack ... Father. You'll be okay." Preston couldn't remember the last time he had called Jack 'father.'

Jack spoke weakly. "No ... I'm dying. Nothing can ... save me ... Preston. I want you ... to do something ... for me."

Stockbridge glanced up and searched Allen's eyes for a positive diagnosis, but the mercenary simply looked away. These two soldiers of fortune had witnessed enough men near death to know the signs. The policeman had fought to hang on this long but he was reaching the end of his personal reserves of strength.

Stockbridge found it hard to speak. "Anything, old friend."
Lockhart's eyes blazed. "Avenge ... me. That son-of-a-bitch ... with one gold ... tooth. I want ..." Jack coughed and the sentence remained unfinished, but Preston clearly understood.

"But ... I'm ... I can't ..." Stockbridge stammered.

Lockhart's hand tightened on Stockbridge's. "Damn it ... stop ... I know you're ... the Scorpion. I'm no ... fool, son. I've always ... known. I have to ... tell you something. Something I ... couldn't tell you before. Goldie McDonall ... is the man ... who killed your ... mother. I can't prove it, but I know ... it's true."

The Police Commissioner coughed jaggedly and blood trickled from the corner of his mouth. His lungs were filling with blood from his fatal wounds. He finally regained enough energy to continue but only with great effort.

"I want ... to see him. I need ... the Scorpion." One bloodshot eye flittered and began to close. "Please, son."

Stockbridge seemed to barely move but suddenly in his place was the Scorpion. The deadliest man alive.

Jack smiled weakly. "Damn. Ain't ... that something ..." His breath trailed off as he exhaled slowly. He never inhaled. Police Commissioner Jack Lockhart was dead.

Scorpion closed his stepfather's staring eyes. "You *will* be avenged, old friend." The night wind caused his black cape to billow and flap.

Allen placed his hand on Stockbridge's shoulder. "There were half a dozen men with machine guns, Major. They fired a bazooka into the house to get at me ... they left ten minutes ago, heading north down Pennsylvania Avenue. I tried to stop them. They got Whitney and Rav Chandra. I'm sorry, Preston."

Scorpion was silent for several seconds. "I'm sure you did everything you could, my friend. I need to go after these men. Will you be okay?"

"Well, I've been shot and burned, but I've lived through much worse. Hell, I even came back from the dead once, remember?"

"Yeah, I remember."

Allen heard sirens in the distance. "Police and Fire Departments will be here soon. It would be better if you weren't here. Those guys kidnapped Whitney and Rav Chandra. Preston, you have to go save them. Jack mentioned a man with one gold tooth; he seemed to be the leader. He didn't kill our friends, yet. But it doesn't mean he won't."

"This is all my fault. They were after me." Scorpion was worried about Whitney and Rav Chandra. The idea that his beloved, ever-loyal Whitney, was in the hands of ruthless gangsters made his heart broil.

Allen disagreed. "That's what was odd ... I don't think they were. If the police hadn't been here, I believe they would have taken Benson as well. 'Course, I still would have ..."

Scorpion smiled without humor, acknowledging Allen Coleman's soldier-of-fortune ways. "I understand."

"Go. Get out of here, Major. I hear the sirens heading this way." Allen warned again.

Scorpion clasped hands with his oldest friend. "I'll be back ... with Whitney and Rav Chandra. You take care of yourself, Coleman."

Before Allen could respond, Scorpion was halfway to his roadster. Gravel was catapulted into the night air as the tires spun, then the powerful vehicle roared away. Scorpion's eyes were mere slits as he sped down the winding road. Criminals had taken from him again, just as they had so many years ago. Before tonight was over, he would make certain these murdering lunatics had paid for their crimes. And the only currency the Scorpion traded in was blood and bullets.

Chapter Fifteen
Killers at Work

April 5, 1945   9:15 pm

Jimmy Chan slowly sipped his coffee from the thermos cup. The warm liquid felt good going down his throat. Although a faithful servant of the mysterious, cloaked man known as the Darkness, he always felt uncomfortable when waiting for something to happen. And something *was* about to happen. He could feel it in his bones, as though they were a barometer for measuring trouble. He loved adventure and danger, ever since he was a small lad. Not that he was that old, only in his mid-thirties. He had worked with the Darkness for over ten years now. Ever since that foggy night when the Darkness had sprung from the shadows and prevented him from making the biggest mistake of his life.

In November of 1931, Chan had a total sum of one dollar and thirteen cents to his name. He was not close to his family and had no friends, no job, nothing to live for. He chose a self-destruction path. Looking back, he could never quite figure out why. It simply wasn't like him. The mysterious character known only as Darkness saved his life and gave him an assignment, to assist in solving a crime and become an agent of Darkness. He also demanded obedience, absolute obedience. Jimmy had been given a second chance, to live his life with adventure, danger, and excitement. A chance to risk life and limb for a noble cause. He had been reborn and the Darkness was the reason. Jimmy Chan owed him everything.

From that day forward, danger lurked around every corner and Jimmy loved it. He left his old life behind and never looked back. Born of a Chinese father and a white American mother, Jimmy was fluent in both languages and, with the aid of makeup, could pass for either race. This made him invaluable during undercover assignments, especially in New York's Chinatown district.

Over the years, many other similar souls had joined Darkness' organization, but Jimmy was one of the first. He soon met Sylvester 'Sly' Montgomery, Charles Manning, and Nick Drago, and became acquainted with a mysterious man named Valentine. Chan still didn't know if Valentine was his first or last name. Megan Meriwether was the final member to join the group, about three years ago. Together, these agents were the daytime eyes and ears of the Darkness. And the eyes of the Darkness were everywhere.

Two years back, Jimmy, Sly and Megan had discovered one of the Darkness' deepest secrets. The shadowy figure was actually employed by the blind millionaire, Luthor Gibson. The playboy owned the largest private investigation firm in the Unites States and employed hundreds of detectives, including the Darkness. Gibson made Jimmy and the others swear to keep this a secret between the four of them. To not even let Darkness know what they had found out. They had solemnly agreed.

Jimmy yawned and stretched. "How many years have you worked with the Darkness now, Sly?"

Sly poured another cup of coffee. "Ah, kid, I joined up with him only a few months after you did, remember?"

Jimmy Chan nodded, remembering when he and the Darkness had saved Sly from street thugs. "Drago is a good man, I've worked with him several times. And Megan, well she's a brick. I suppose I'll always think about what happened to Charles Manning. He introduced me to the world of the Darkness, and instructed me on how and where and when to report, things like that." The memories made him smile. He glanced over at Sly and thought to himself that the black man appeared larger than ever. He probably topped the scaled at three-fifty and was nearly as big around as he was tall.

Sly agreed. "I'm told he was a polite, amiable fellow. I didn't get a chance to work with him much."

Jimmy's face grew solemn. "Yeah, and it's the only time I've ever known the Darkness to fail one of his agents. Manning was gunned down by gangsters while visiting a friend in Chicago."

"Chicago was a dangerous place back then, Jimmy. Besides, Manning was on vacation when it happened, not working on a case for the boss. By the way, be careful with that coffee or the boss will kill me. This is a brand new limousine; he wouldn't appreciate stains or spills on the leather. Hey, you want a donut? Got a couple of bear claws in the bakery box on the seat."

"Heck no, Sly, those things'll kill ya." Jimmy almost mentioned about watching his weight, but politely changed the subject. "Hey, Sly, I have a question for you. Have you ever met Valentine?"

"Nah, he's just a voice at the other end of the phone."

"Ever wonder who he is? Why he works for the Darkness?"

Sly removed his chauffeurs cap, wiped his forehead and nodded his bulbous head. "Kid, in this business, it doesn't pay to ask too many questions. I follow directions and report everything I know. The Darkness takes care of the rest. He's saved my hash more times than I can count." Sly leaned closer to Jimmy and whispered. "Personally, I think Valentine worked with the boss back in the First World War, back before they gave them numbers. I saw him only once, in the dark, but I noticed he had some nasty scars. O' course it could have been a disguise. Hell, it could have been the Darkness in disguise. Maybe Valentine is the … awww, this is why you shouldn't ask questions. It'll only make your head hurt."

Jimmy chuckled. "I know what you mean. I've seen the boss in so many disguises that I gave up trying to figure out who he really is a long time ago." Jimmy took another sip of his coffee. There was a long minute of silence. "By the way, what are we waiting for? Valentine said to meet you at the airport. We've been sitting in this alleyway for twenty minutes. Are we on a stakeout?"

Sly shrugged his shoulders. "Naw, I forgot to tell you. We're gonna pick up an old war buddy of mine. Big Tom was the best damn pilot in my outfit, and a crack shot with a pistol, too. He could probably land on a tabletop and shoot a fly at a hundred yards. I dropped off him and his buddy Percy about an hour ago and they said to meet them behind their apartment building. Hope that's okay with you."

"Sure, I'm off-duty for the rest of the night, big guy."

Sly glanced at his watch and frowned. "Thought they'd be out here by now."

While they were talking, Jimmy and Sly watched two men walking down the alley, still several blocks away. The men didn't seem in a great hurry. They walked slowly, but surely, in the direction of the stationery, black limousine. The limousines that Sly drove were like his second home. As an ex-cab driver in New York City, Sly knew every street, short cut and back alley.

He managed the Montgomery Limousine Service, but the town-cars and the company were actually owned by Luthor Gibson. Sly was content because he was allowed to run his company without interference. His only obligation to the millionaire was to personally and discreetly provide transportation for Luthor Gibson and his various agents and investigators upon request and without question. Always on call, he had rescued the mysterious Darkness many times. Or followed a suspect. Or transported agents on assignment. That was his main job. Sly believed that Gibson was simply an eccentric millionaire and amateur criminologist with some rather strange associates, one being the man known as the Darkness. On a personal note, Sly truly enjoyed Mr. Gibson's company.

Similar to when he drove a taxicab for a living, Sly Montgomery didn't even carry a firearm, just an old baseball bat. He could shoot fairly well, but claimed he had little use for guns. He left the shooting to the Darkness or one of Gibson's agents. The bulky automobile had been rigged with a powerful engine and could outrace any car on the road. And the large, heavy-set black man could handle it like a racecar professional.

Two more men had joined the first two as they came closer. Both Jimmy and Sly noticed this immediately. When your very life depends on observing every detail in your vicinity, you developed a third eye that was constantly watching for hidden death. You lived longer if you were always expecting the unexpected.

Jimmy squinted his eyes. "That's odd."

Sly agreed and sat up straight. "You mean those fellas? I've been watching them, too." He brushed donut crumbs from his cubby ebony cheeks.

Jimmy felt the hair rise at the base of his neck. "Maybe we should drive around the block once and see if they move on."

Before Sly could reply, the four men stepped directly in front of the limousine, blocking the way. The long trench coats they wore were pulled to the side and machine guns came into view. During the prohibition in Chicago and New York, the *'Tommy'* gun was a favorite weapon of law enforcement officers and underworld criminals alike. In Chicago, it had been nicknamed the *'Chicago typewriter.'*

Sly shouted. "Oh, BOHICA!"

"Holy Jehoziphat! Start the engine. Let's get out of here!" Jimmy barked instructions and reached for the pistol beneath his left armpit.

Before Sly could reach for the key, the Thompson machine guns started emitting a staccato of noise. Bullets, like angry metal hornets, hammered the black car and shook the entire frame. Glass and metal were pelted repeatedly, and the noise was deafening. This abuse continued for fifteen or twenty seconds. The air was filled with gunpowder smoke and visibility became limited. Then it was quiet, deathly quiet. Certainly no one could have survived the deadly assault on the limousine. The four men waited in the alley for the smoke to clear, to confirm the fate of the two men in the automobile. Jimmy and Sly were looking at each other in surprise. Each had expected to feel the bullets riddle their body, feel the flesh and bone torn and rendered. Sly's round face turned from surprise to anger upon discovering he had sustained no injuries.

Sly pounded the steering wheel. "Dammit! I wish Luthor Gibson would let me know when he modifies my limo. Bulletproofed the windows and armor-plated the body. I thought it handled differently tonight." He looked out the front window and saw the surprised faces of his attackers. "Okay, boys. My turn!" He said with a smile.

The powerful engine revved under the armored hood of the car. Before the startled men could move, Sly shifted into drive and the car shot forward, as if propelled by a rocket engine. Two of the men fell under the wheels of the heavy car and would never move again. The third man was thrown into the air and struck the ground hard. The fourth man, however, dodged the hurtling projectile and avoided serious injury.

Sly said quietly, almost to himself. "They didn't know who they were messing with!"

Jimmy leapt out of the car with a revolver in his hand, ready to confront the last man standing. Unfortunately, the fourth man of the group had already recovered from the attack. One shot rang out and Jimmy felt a sharp sting on his shoulder. The bullet barely grazed the skin, but the shock caused him to jump. His gun clattered onto the pavement and slid under the car. The Thompson had jammed after that single shot, but the gangster thumped the cartridge release with his palm and cleared the obstruction. The machine gun leveled and aimed in his direction and Jimmy knew he was going to die. His last adventure. Gunned down in the streets, just like Charles Manning had been. For a brief instant, the two adversaries faced one another.

Then came the mocking laughter. It was low, but carried on the night wind. It seemed to come from everywhere at once. The man with the machine gun spun in a circle, looking for the origin of the sound. A shadow appeared on the blank, brick wall of one of the large empty buildings. Even though it was obvious that the shadow belonged to a man, wearing a coat and slouch hat, there was no one visible in the alley. It was the shadow of the Darkness. Jimmy's attacker lifted his machine gun and prepared to spray the entire alley with lead, hoping to catch the shadow's wielder. Two shots rang out and the man fell hard. One shot to the heart and one in the forehead. Jimmy had dropped to one knee and retrieved his gun but neither shot had come from his firearm.

The laughter sounded again, the laughter of the Darkness. "The weeds of crime bear bitter fruit," was the strange phrase directed at the dead man, in a hollow mocking voice.

A piece of the alley shadows separated and a blurry silhouette strolled forward. The figure became more distinct and spoke to Jimmy and Sly, who had just stepped from the cab. The tall, dark-clad man with blazing red eyes looked from Jimmy to Sly. As he re-sheathed his pistols somewhere beneath the black cape, Jimmy caught sight of the blazing red, fire opal on the Darkness' hand. It blazed with an internal glow. Someday, Jimmy would have to ask the Darkness about that unique gem.

Darkness spoke in a hoarse whisper. "Are you both uninjured?"

Sly chortled. "Yeah, we're fine. Thanks to that new armored tank Luthor Gibson has me driving."

Jimmy placed his fingertip in the tear at the shoulder of his coat. The bullet had missed him by a fraction of an inch. Lady Luck had been looking over his shoulder tonight.

Darkness issued orders to Chan. "Jimmy, contact Valentine and assist him in relaying a message to all agents. We are operating on red alert status. Cancel all surveillance projects. I will be leaving the country for a while."

Jimmy never felt comfortable standing next to the Darkness. He always felt like he was talking to someone not quite … human. All that could be seen of the Darkness' features was a small portion of his face and his glaring red eyes. His collar was pulled up to cover his lower face and the broad-brimmed, felt slouch hat angled down, covering everything above the brow line. His voice was well-modulated and, if he didn't speak in such a harsh whispering tone, would have been rather pleasing to hear. But when he laughed, that inhuman, horrible sound, it was not pleasant at all. The Darkness' laugh was something you never forgot.

The third man, who had been hit by the cab and fallen to the ground, got up slowly. From inside his long coat he extracted a long cylindrical object, perhaps four feet long and three inches in diameter. Slowly, quietly, he raised the weapon onto his shoulder and pointed it toward Jimmy, Sly, and the Darkness. His finger sought the trigger. One shot rang out and the man fell to the ground, a small circle on his forehead leaked blood. The long, metal cylinder clattered harmlessly to the hard pavement. The Darkness spun and prepared to defend himself, both guns drawn and ready to throw lead. A figure lowered himself from the shadows of a fire escape, a cloaked man sporting a pair of .45 caliber automatics. He was the Scorpion. The most dangerous man alive.

Scorpion's feet touched the ground. "You have to be more careful. This guy was preparing to blow you to kingdom come. Can you believe it? A rocket launcher? And machine guns? Whatever happened to the good old days, when crooks carried simple handguns?"

Jimmy stared at the intruder. "Who the heck are you?"

Darkness spoke reassuringly. "This is the Scorpion. He's one of the good guys."

Scorpion removed a silver cigarette lighter from one pocket and moved toward the dead man. He pressed the lighter to the man's forehead and when it was removed a red burn remained, in the shape of an eight-legged Scorpion with a long, barbed tail. The Scorpion's calling card.

Sly looked disgusted. "Okay, that's really gross."

Darkness took control. "Scorpion, we need to get to the Global Navigator Consortium warehouse on the riverfront. But first we have to make a stop. Sly, Jimmy, make sure everyone gets to their safe houses and then … " Darkness hesitated for a second. "Then find someplace safe to hide. Use one of the aliases I've set up for you. I'll contact you when I return."

"No problem, chief." The heavy-set Sly headed for his limousine, following orders without hesitation. He slapped his forehead. "Dang, I completely forgot. I'm supposed to pick up the boss in the morning at the Chromium Club."

"I've already seen to Luthor Gibson's safety. He is being escorted out of the city, even as we speak."

Jimmy addressed the Darkness. "You sound like you're not coming back, chief."

Darkness answered without emotion. "This case is dangerous. I'm not sure everyone will return." Turning toward Scorpion, Darkness continued. "Scorpion, let's go."

Scorpion walked over to the other dead man, the one who had been shot by the Darkness. He also placed his crimson Scorpion seal, with its multiple legs, deadly pincers and barbed tail, on this man's blood-splashed forehead.

"Hey, you didn't kill that fellow, the Darkness shot him." Jimmy exclaimed defensively.

Scorpion turned and gave Jimmy an evil smile. "Whatever you say, kid. He got him once, but so did I. Besides, anything that helps spread the myth and legend of the Scorpion."

As the limo left the alleyway, Jimmy Chan whistled to himself. "Wow. If the Darkness thinks things are too dangerous, that's not good."

Sly Montgomery nodded in agreement. "Amen, ta that, brother."

Chapter Sixteen
Death in the Air

April 5, 1945   9:30 pm

They could see the flames licking the night sky from nearly two miles away. The mansion was barely visible, except as a charred, monstrous skeleton amongst the orange and red holocaust. Megan found that she was holding her breath and forced herself to inhale a small gasp of air. Firemen were battling the conflagration with every hose and hydrant available, but it was certain that the destruction would be total. The Stockbridge family mansion would be completely gone by daylight.

Cassie Greyson saw a man with his shoulder and arm swathed in bandages. Two ambulance attendants were trying to convince him to go with them to the hospital. His attention was focused on the burning building. And something else. Something that Cassie couldn't see until she got closer. When she finally did, a gasp of surprise stuck in her throat. There were five bodies covered with white sheets lying on the small lawn and a sixth by itself, nearly thirty feet away. Blood had saturated the cotton fabrics in several places; making it obvious that these victims had not died peacefully. When she was finally able to look away, Cassie turned her attention back to the injured man. Recognition showed in her eyes, as she confidently strolled forward. Megan Meriwether and Pam Titan were still watching the fire, and trying to ignore the covered bodies. It didn't have to be spoken out loud. They were all hoping that their friends weren't under those sheets. Or still in the building.

Cassie smiled and asked, "Allen? Allen Coleman?"

The injured man had a confused look on his face. "I'm sorry, do I know … Cassie Clayb ...?"

Cassie seemed to cut him off abruptly. Pam could swear he was about to call her by a different last name. "That's right. It's been a long time since I last saw you."

Allen smiled weakly at the small blonde. "Yeah, at least ten years. You're still a cute little thing. How's your father? Still playing at being the lord of the jungle?"

Cassie gave her friends a look that made it obvious they shouldn't ask her questions about this comment. "Oh, you know, some things never change." As delicately as she could, Cassie changed the subject. "What's happened here, Allen?"

Allen tried to act nonchalant. "Oh, it's nothing, honey. Only a fire and a little cops and robbers stuff."

Cassie scolded the wounded man. "Allen, I'm not twelve years old anymore. My friend, Whitney Van Pelt, is engaged to the man who lives in this mansion. Please tell me ..." She stopped talking, but nodded her head in the direction of the covered bodies.

Allen apologized. "Oh. I didn't know you knew Whitney ... she's not there, Cassie." He assured her, indicating the bodies. "Three of them are policemen, one is Police Commissioner Lockhart, and the fifth is Benson, the family butler."

Cassie breathed a sigh of relief. "And the last one? Over there."

Allen snarled, looking at the covered body. "That's one of the gangsters. I shot him myself."

Cassie continued her questions. "Why were there gangsters here?"

"They kidnapped Whitney and Rav Chandra. Cassie, the police will handle this. You should go on home. There's nothing you can do here."

Cassie's face tightened. "You're wrong, Allen. I'm a member of Unsolved Mysteries, Incorporated. This is what I do these days."

"Damn, it's a small world. I know Simon Blake. I didn't know you were associated with him. How well do you know Whitney and Preston?"

"Well enough to know that they had a problem with an insect in their lives. An arachnid. A scorpion." Cassie whispered the last part.

Allen grabbed her arm and led her away from the ambulance. "Hmm. Yes. Who are your friends, Cassie?"

Cassie made quick introductions. "The bronzed goddess is Pamela Titan, Doc Titan's cousin. The brunette is Megan Meriwether."

Allen nodded knowingly. "I understand she has a problem, that she's afraid of the ... dark."

Cassie understood the inference instantly. Allen was a sharp cookie. "Exactly."

Allen continued, keeping his voice low. "I didn't tell the police, but Preston was already here. A few minutes after the gangsters left. I told him that the van was heading north and he took off before the police and fire trucks arrived."

Cassie held up one tiny finger. "Wait right here." She walked confidently over to the sixth body, the dead gangster. She lifted the sheet and studied the face. Allen was impressed by her moxie. The gangster had been shot in the head and the sight must have been grisly, but Cassie didn't even flinch. She returned to her position next to him.

Cassie continued. "I recognize him. I study every file we have at Unsolved Mysteries, Inc. and he's one of 'Goldie' MacDonall's men. Goldie is 'Man Mountain' Marko's chief lieutenant, one of his enforcers."

Megan appeared impressed. "You never cease to amaze me, Cassie. Do you know where he would take Whitney?"

Cassie thought for a minute. "No, but Blake would. We need to swing by the office and talk to Simon Blake. Marko is a very dangerous man, we might need some help."

Allen raised himself erect. "Let me grab a gun …"

Cassie placed an arm on his shoulder. "Oh, no. You've done your part. You need to get to the hospital and take care of your injuries."

Allen had been through a stressful event and appeared to have aged ten years in the past several hours. Despite this, he tried to appear tough. "You know, you're a tough little minx, but I could still bend you over my knee and spank …"

"I'm sorry, Allen."

"Sorry? About what?" The large man asked, confused.

"This." Almost faster than a blink of the eye Cassie struck the side of his neck, below the skull-line, with her little thumb. Allen's eyes glazed over and then shut completely. Unconscious, he dropped like a sack of potatoes. Pam caught him in one arm and waved to the nearby ambulance paramedics.

Pam volunteered. "He just keeled over. His injuries must be more serious than he let on. You'd better get him to the hospital immediately."

Cassie watched them strap Allen Coleman to a gurney and sighed. "Take care of yourself, you big hunk."

"What the heck did you do to him?" Megan whispered.

Cassie face tightened. "Just a little JuJitsu move I learned. He'll wake up in about six hours, none the worse for wear. Let's get to Barren Street and then find our friends."

Chapter Seventeen
Death Deals Double

April 5, 1945 9:30 pm

Scorpion and Darkness had watched the black limousine disappear around the corner. As if sharing one mind, they raced for the Scorpion's motorcar and sped through the evening streets. Traffic was light and there were few pedestrians on the sidewalks. The speedometer climbed upward, until the needle couldn't move any further.

One minute after they had left, Doc Titan arrived on foot. He noticed the bodies and surmised that Darkness had already been here. And from the marks on the dead men's foreheads, Scorpion as well. Seconds later, he raced away in Big Tom's car.

Scorpion reloaded his automatics and checked his backups. "I don't mind you driving my car, but where are we going?"

Darkness drove quickly through the quiet, Manhattan streets. "I recognized that last mobster back there. He worked for 'Man-Mountain' Marko. Marko is a gun-runner from the Bronx, buying and selling deadly weapons. He's been on my list of gangsters to take down."

Scorpion smirked. "Bet you wish now that you had already taken care of him."

"Let's just say, he made it to the top of my list tonight. I've had one of my operatives watching him, for just the right moment."

"Operatives? How do you have time to maintain a staff of agents?" Scorpion asked, but received no response.

The powerful roadster sped through the dark downtown streets. Preston Stockbridge had installed exhaust mufflers and the engine sounds were almost non-existent, except for the low guttural roar of massive horsepower. It took corners at breakneck speeds and the tires hugged the asphalt greedily. Scorpion sat silently in the passenger seat as the Darkness drove the car with all the skills of a racing champ.

Scorpion asked, his tone becoming serious. "Do you know of a man, a criminal, with one gold tooth?"

Darkness responded without hesitating. "Yes. He is one of Marko's main enforcers. Ruthless, but he follows Marko's orders without question."

"If we find him, he's mine."

Darkness read the look of vengeance in Scorpion's eyes and didn't need to respond. They were both vigilantes that dispensed frontier-style justice, as judge, jury, and executioner. Scorpion shifted restlessly in his seat.

"The weeds of crime bear bitter fruit? Did I really hear you say that back there? What the heck does that mean, anyway?" He finally said.

Darkness shrugged his shoulders. "Heck, I'm not really certain. I heard Orson Welles say it on a radio show the other night and figured I'd try it out. I get tired of using the same old phrases. I thought I'd use it a few times and see if it made sense to anyone else."

"Keep looking. You sounded like a moron, if that helps. Maybe he meant the *seeds* of crime bear bitter fruit, that makes more sense. I'll let you borrow my thesaurus later." Scorpion taunted.

"The seeds? Oh yes, that's so much better than the weeds."

"Whatever."

There was a long moment of silence between the two crimefighters.

"Maybe Orson was only messing with you. Remember that War of the Worlds radio show? Scared a million people half to death. And he made everyone sit through a two-hour movie, merely to find out what Rosebud meant. A man's last thought in the world is about some sled he had as a kid? Mind my words, that fat man is trouble. You should fire him from your show." Scorpion said venomously.

"What are you talking about? He's not fat."

"Ha. Maybe not yet. But Whitney and I were at a charity function last week and watched as he devoured five cream filled bearclaws at one sitting."

Darkness shook his head knowingly. "I know what this anger is all about. You're just upset because your pulp publication was cancelled."

Scorpion gritted his teeth. "It NOT cancelled, it's on hiatus. Just like Blake's was. Wartime paper shortage and all of that stuff."

"Blake always hated the publicity from the pulps anyway. I'm sure he's glad to be left alone."

Gibson could tell Preston was concerned about Whitney and Rav Chandra and hoped he wouldn't do something stupid. Entering into a conflict in the wrong state of mind could get you seriously hurt or worse. Preston was close to allowing his personal angst to cloud his judgment, just like he always had in the past. And Simon Blake wasn't much better. He appeared to be on the verge of a nervous breakdown at times.

Miles disappeared behind them and in a short time Gibson pulled up outside a luxurious mansion. The main building was several hundred feet from the road. If someone had been staring directly at the parked car, they would have barely noticed a movement of shadows in the darkness. However, seconds after the car had stopped, its occupants were nowhere to be seen. Twin silhouettes vaulted over the ten-foot high wall that surrounded the property and then disappeared into the shadows of the trees and bushes.

The Scorpion briefly became visible near the garages at one end of the mansion. The monstrous house spread out over the ground like a giant octopus. A growling noise came from under a nearby tree and two Doberman Pinschers emerged. Stockbridge abhorred the use of violence on animals, but he knew this was a rare occasion and he was left with no choice. Pfft. Pfft. The silencers whispered their announcement of death. Another thing that Scorpion rarely used, silencers on his automatics. But this was a battlefield and sometimes war called for extreme measures. He glanced into the garages and confirmed that there were no trucks matching Allen Coleman's description of the kidnap vehicle.

Darkness had managed to enter the residence without setting off an alarm. Like Scorpion, he had outfitted his automatics with silencers. Nine men had been 'dispensed with' on his path to the house. Six of them would wake up the next day with a nasty headache and a large lump on their head. The other three would never wake up again. Darkness was not usually this bloodthirsty, but tonight comrades of these men had nearly murdered his agents. They were all criminals and as he had so often stated, "A life of crime does not pay." Four more guards were eliminated from his path as he made his way to the third floor, to the offices of the man called James 'Man Mountain' Marko.

Three men sat in the office quietly talking to one another. Without making a sound, a dark silhouette detached itself from the dimly lit area in one corner of the room. Two of the men were seated in comfortable, leather-clad chairs, facing a large, oak-paneled desk. The third man, a monolithic giant in size, was leaning on the massive desk with both elbows. Obviously, the nickname Man-Mountain was not a play on words. One of the two men noticed the shadow moving and plunged a hand into his overcoat. A revolver appeared in his hand. Before he could use it, Darkness shot him twice in the chest. Pfft. Pfft. And the room was silent again.

The man in the second chair merely raised his hands into the air, showing no signs of resistance. Marko had managed to slide one of his hamlike hands toward a wooden box that sat on his desktop. An icy, metallic cylinder pressed against the flesh at the back of his thick neck. He had been in the business long enough to know what that sensation meant.

Scorpion warned. "If I were you, I would place both hands flat on the desktop. I haven't come here to kill you tonight, so don't force my hand in this matter."

Marko did as requested. "Okay. Fine. So why have the Darkness and the Scorpion both come to my …?"

Darkness growled deeply. "We are not here to play games, Marko. You know exactly why we're here."

Marko seemed unconcerned, even with a gun barrel pressed against his thick neck. "I have thirty men on the grounds of this property, you'll have trouble leaving here alive. Donny? Jimmy? Charley?" He waited for a response, but none came.

Darkness laughed and the sound was deafening in the private office. "They won't respond. Your men are in no position to help you." Darkness didn't mention that they weren't all dead. He let Marko fill in the blanks with his own imagination.

"What have you done to them? I have nothing to say …" Marko began perspiring heavily.

"The seeds of crime bear bitter fruit." Scorpion whispered huskily.

Darkness glared daggers at Scorpion.

"The seeds of … what does that mean?" Marko asked.

The large man grunted loudly as the Scorpion bounced the handle of the automatic off of the top of his cranium. A trickle of blood poured from the cut and reddened the collar of his white shirt. Although this must have hurt quite a bit, Marko simply grimaced and then smiled.

"Oh, right, the kidnappings. It was just a snatch and grab operation. Nobody was supposed to get hurt. I heard about the shootout with the police at the Stockbridge mansion. That was just bad luck." Marko waved his hands dismissively.

Scorpion controlled his anger. "I assumed as much or you would already be dead. Who paid you to do this job?"

"Hey, I'm no snitch. Get stuffed!" Marko spat.

Marko sensed Scorpion raising his gun for another blow and spoke quickly, before he was subjected to more punishment.

"Okay, okay. The man's name was Egorov, Konstantin Egorov. Big Russian. He offered to pay me one hundred thousand dollars for each person we kidnapped on the list. For a few hours of work, I could make a cool million dollars. My family is from Russia; my parents still live there, so I agreed to help him."

Darkness' eyes burned red in the shadows. "You're a fool, Marko. Egorov is working with the Nazis. You've helped the same people that the Russians have been fighting for several years."

Marko began to get angry, his large features flushing scarlet. "What do you know about my people? About the Russian people?"

Darkness shoved the blood-red girasol jeweled ring under the large man's nose. "Do you know what this ring signifies?"

"Oh, my God. You're him. The Dark Eagle. Colonel Grantov." The Man Mountain's eyes grew larger than it seemed possible and then they narrowed to mere slits. "Egorov lied to me. I will tell you everything. I sent my chief lieutenant out to kidnap a group of people, from a list. The list was provided by Egorov. We had orders not to kill anyone, only kidnap them and take them to an airport."

Scorpion leaned forward and whispered. "Which airport?"

"The small, private one called Roanoke Point Airport on Neptune Island."

Darkness glared. "If you were given orders not to kill anyone, why did someone attack my agents tonight with machine guns?"

Marko responded defensively. "It wasn't us. That was Mike 'Iron Jaw' Johnson. He stole a shipment of Tommy guns and broke off from my gang two weeks ago. I've heard stories from the streets that two Germans hired him to kill everyone on that same list. I've also heard rumors that he sent his men to attack Doc Titan's headquarters, too."

"Who's the man with one gold tooth?" Scorpion asked.

"That's George 'Goldie' MacDonall. He's my chief lieutenant."

Darkness straightened. "Since you came from Russia, I will give you this one opportunity to leave the country. When I get back, don't still be here, in New York."

"But, I ..." Marko started to question.

Darkness' eyes blazed red. "This is not open for debate."

Darkness and Scorpion prepared to leave the room. Man Mountain Marko flipped open the wooden box on his desk and reached for the pistol hidden within. Scorpion began to reach for his weapon. Before he had a chance to pull it from the leather holster, a shot rang out, followed by three more. All four shots hit Marko point blank, dead center in the middle of his chest. He sighed once and fell forward on his desk. The second man who had been sitting quietly with his hands raised in surrender, now held a smoking gun in one hand. Scorpion's view of the man had blocked by Darkness during the entire questioning. Scorpion leveled his automatics at the man, just as Darkness stepped between them.

"Scorpion, this is my agent, Nick Drago."

The man stood up and shook hands with Scorpion.

"It's a pleasure to meet you, sir."

Nick Drago was a big, tough guy, with chiseled features. He had a firm, strong handshake. Drago roamed the underworld with the reputation of a killer and lone wolf. Only he and the Darkness knew this to be false. Nick was living constantly undercover in the criminal underworld and badlands, and was totally dedicated to the Darkness' cause of justice. Only the Darkness knew of the man's illustrious past.

Drago traveled about criminal hangouts, trying to pick up information on impending crimes. Because of his reputation, he could usually join any gang that the Darkness wanted him to infiltrate. Nick was good with his fists and a gun, and useful in battles. Because his features were rugged but not hard, he could occasionally team with Jimmy Chan for honest work. Jimmy had once overheard Nick make references to the war episodes, but those references were vague at best. So, like the legendary Darkness and the enigmatic Valentine, Nick had his own mysterious past.

Nick nodded at the dead Russian, 'Man Mountain' Marko. "Sorry about that, chief. I didn't know if you saw him reaching for that gat."

Darkness nodded. "He was given a chance and he took it. A life of crime does not pay."

Scorpion smirked. "Actually, I understand it pays better than crimefighting. Doc must spend a fortune on new shirts alone. And do you know how much I spent on ammunition last year?"

Darkness ignored the Scorpion. "Drago, assist Jimmy Chan and Sly Montgomery. All agents are to drop out of sight. Use the aliases we set up for emergencies. There might be secret files on all of the known associates of every crimefighter. I will be out of the country for an indefinite period of time. Contact will be made when I return."

"Understood, chief. Anything else I can do to help?" Drago asked.

Darkness warned his agent, "Protect yourself and the others, Nick. These are dangerous times."

"You too, chief."

Scorpion was already heading for the door. "Come on, Darkness. We need to catch that plane."

Nick Drago started to ask another question and realized he was standing alone in the room. The two masters of shadows had vanished. On the forehead of Marko was a wetly embossed scarlet arachnid seal, a scorpion with a deadly barbed tail.

Scorpion removed the silencers from his automatics. "How long will it take to reach Roanoke Point Airport on Neptune Island?"

Darkness' cape blew in the night wind as the car accelerated. "We're not going there."

Scorpion frowned. "But Marko said that the people they kidnapped are being taken there."

"He lied. There is no airport on Neptune Island, private or otherwise."

Scorpion's jaw muscles flexed. "Can we turn around and go back to the house?"

Darkness looked at Stockbridge questioningly. "Why ...?"

Scorpion stated earnestly, "Because I want to shoot Marko again."

"It's okay. I know where they are going. We'll be there in twenty minutes. There are two places near downtown New York where a plane can takeoff or land without special permits. Doc Titan owns a warehouse in the old historical wharf district called the Global Navigator Consortium. His building has high-level government security and is under constant surveillance. The other one, Praetorian Securities, belongs to Simon Blake. He abandoned the warehouse last year, but it still has high-level security access. No questions would be asked if someone landed a plane or lifted off from there."

"I'm sure Titan and Blake would be concerned to find out you know all of this information about them."

"They don't seem to understand *how* to keep a secret. All of this is public information, hidden under a subtle cover of false companies. Besides, it's my job, to know the secrets that men wish to remain hidden."

Scorpion pounded his fist on the dashboard. "Damn it. Trespassing in our very back yard."

Darkness cleared his throat. "Speaking of trespassing, stop stealing my cryptic catch phrases! Get your own!"

Scorpion smiled mischievously. "Just trying it out for you, Lew. Besides, it still doesn't make sense. Maybe you ought to try 'The *deeds* of crime bear bitter fruit.'"

"Just so we're clear on this, Preston. If you call me Lew again, I'll shoot you. Twice."

Chapter Eighteen
A Farewell to Unsolved Mysteries

April 5, 1945   10:00 pm

Pam sped up when she saw the man standing in the street, holding a rocket launcher. He had started to turn and fire at the car. In one swift movement, she slammed on the brakes, turned the car sideways and whipped out her massive revolver. One shot rang out and the man dropped, a large smoking hole in the center of his frame. The rocket launcher clattered harmlessly on the concrete street. Smoke danced thickly through the night air, making visibility difficult.

A second man was two hundred feet away, also armed with a rocket launcher. Pam doubted she could hit a human-sized target from this distance. She warned Megan and Cassie to abandon the vehicle. With a roar of power, a roadster approached from the opposite direction. The man turned away from the women to face this new threat.

Cassie could see the dark silhouette of Guardian leaning out of the drivers' window, a small rectangular 'pistol' clutched in his hand. Two shots rang out in rapid succession and the man holding the rocket launcher felt the impact strike his weapon, but he was unharmed. Smiling evilly, he aimed the launcher at Guardian's car and pulled the trigger. The explosion of the backfire was deafening. When the smoke cleared, the man had completely vanished. Blake exited his car and met the three ladies in the center of the street.

Cassie coughed at the thick smoke. "What happened?"

Guardian reloaded the pellet-shooter and returned the small 'gun' to its holster. "I shot both bullets into the barrel of his launcher, locking the rocket into place. He had a choice and he made the wrong one."

Cassie ran forward and wrapped her arms around Simon Blake.

Tears of relief filled Cassie's eyes. "Oh, chief. It's so good to see you. I was worried …"

Her voice broke off as she sensed something was wrong. In the darkness of the night and with the poor visibility, she hadn't noticed.

"Simon, your hair, your face. What happened?"

Very calmly, without any sign of emotion, he looked into Cassie's eyes. "I'm sorry. I lied to you, to everyone. My … condition was not reversed during the Cry of the Banshee incident."

"But I saw ..." Cassie started.

Simon shook his head. "You saw what I wanted you to see."

Cassie's petite face didn't hide the pain of his betrayal. It was one thing to lie to the world, but it was another to lie to her.

"Cassie, we need to talk about this ... later. Right now, let's find our friends."

Cassie sized up the situation and bravely agreed. "Yes," was all she could say. Megan found herself openly staring at Blake's solemn, pale face but managed to glance away as he turned in her direction.

Cassie Greyson felt her heart rise into her throat. The entire block of buildings were burning rubble. This certainly made her feel a new appreciation for the English, who had suffered and survived the continuous bombings from the German forces. These buildings had become her home, her one area of security in a dangerous world. No matter how bad things would get during their battle against crime, she knew she could come back to this place and safely kick off her shoes. She would never feel safe here again.

Pam and Megan stood on either side of Cassie and placed their arms around her for moral support. Tears formed in her eyes but she fought them back. She would not cry, not now. Her friends might be trapped in the rubble. They might need her help. This area of town was deserted at night. There were few spectators and the heat from the fires forced them to keep their distance.

Pam reassured the petite blonde, "I'm sure they're okay, Cassie. We'll find your friends."

"I can't believe this. In one night, there were three separate attacks?" Megan questioned.

Pam frowned, considering the query. "Doesn't seem like a coincidence to me, either."

At the far end of the street a roadster slowed to a stop. A large man, nearly seven feet tall, walked toward them. Pam couldn't see him clearly through the smoke and debris, but she was taking no chances. One hand reached into her jacket and pulled out the turn-of-the-century, custom made, six-shooter from her shoulder holster. As the figure got closer, she recognized the gait of the large figure as belonging to her cousin, Doc Titan.

"It appears we are under a full scale attack. It might not be safe for you ladies to be here. Pam, could you ..."

Pam held up her hand. "Whoa, stop right there, Doc. We were also under attack, at my beauty salon. Men with machine guns."

"Nazis?"

Pam gave Doc a puzzled look. "What? No, not Nazis. Gangsters."

Guardian analyzed this. "It appears that there is more than one group at work here. Or perhaps these gangsters are working for the Nazis who attacked the Chromium Club."

Cassie added, "I don't know about that, but it might be at least three different groups. You guys say you were attacked by Nazis. We were attacked by a group of men who were obviously ready to kill us without hesitation. Whitney Van Pelt and Rav Chandra were kidnapped and taken away by another group of men. The attack on **Unsolved Mysteries, Inc.** doesn't look like they were trying to kidnap anyone. I feel like we're in the middle of a war."

"How do you think we feel?" Wall asked, as he approached.

"Wall!! You're okay?!" Cassie had to step on tiptoe but she managed to give the giant Norwegian a friendly embrace. His thick beard tickled her cheek. She really liked Wall. They were the best of friends. And, at times, she had her suspicions that he would like to expand on that relationship.

"I don't know about okay, but I'll live." Wall said quietly and smiled.

"Auch, dinna I get a wee hug?" Mick asked dourly.

Cassie smiled. "Of course. I'm so glad you guys are ... okay." She stopped herself from using the word 'alive'. She was still looking around for Gabe, Isabelle, and Andrew.

"Have you seen the others, Mick? Gabe, Isabelle, or Andrew?" Guardian asked.

The Scot replied. "Last time we saw Andrew, he was on the roof of that garage." He indicated by pointing a thumb over his shoulder.

The group began sorting through the rubble and finally discovered Andrew Carter. His face was battered and bruised, thickly covered in dust and small debris.

Wall placed a hand on his shoulder. "Geez, Andrew. You okay, pal?" Andrew groaned in pain as they lifted various building debris off of him. "You're one tough bird, little fella." A steel beam, weighing several hundred pounds, had pinned Andrew's leg. Wall hefted it as if it were made of Styrofoam.

Guardian examined his friend. "Feels like he has a few broken ribs and his leg is broken for sure. We shouldn't move him until the ambulance arrives. I've called an old friend, he'll take Andrew somewhere safe until we return."

Wall smiled. "The little Robin Hood should be proud of himself. He saved the day and our lives."

Doc Titan scanned the wreckage of the buildings. The destruction was total. "What happened here?"

Wall started relating their story. "I was working in the rear of the laboratory on one of my electronic doodads, when Isabelle's remote beeper flashed on and her voice came over the loudspeaker. She had me build a miniature radio into her bracelet and she must have activated it. It sounded like someone was kidnapping her and Gabe. They were ordered to get into the back of a truck. We heard Gabe mention two names, Mr. Thompson and Mr. Pierce." Wall nodded at Doc. "I assume he was referring to your friends. I started for the front door when I noticed a man standing in the street. It took a second to realize he was holding something that looked like a pipe on his shoulder. It was a rocket launcher!"

Mick took over the narrative at this point. "The big galoot here grabbed me by the collar and lifted me off of my giant feet. We had barely entered the next reinforced building when the explosion shook the world. There must have been several men because another explosion happened less than two seconds later. The building on the other side of us collapsed and we were trapped in between them."

Wall resumed. "That's when I saw Andrew Carter across the street on the roof of the building. He was shooting at the men in the street. But one of them fired a rocket at the building and it collapsed. Andrew was buried in the debris."

Mick added, "Wall was about to charge into the street when I saw another rocket shatter the front window. It bounced off the wall and landed in the rear of the building. I tackled Wall as he was passing the basement stairs and we plunged down into the cellar. Ach! The entire structure dropped down on us. Fortunately, the chief reinforced all of the floors, too. It took us a few minutes to dig our way out but we were unharmed."

Megan was holding Andrew's hand to comfort him and, even though he smiled, it was obvious to everyone he was in pain. Doc knelt down next to him and pressed on several nerves on Andrew's neck and shoulders. His pained expression brightened a little.

"Thanks. That's much better."

Doc warned Andrew, "There will be less pain but Simon was correct. You have several broken ribs; so don't try to move around. There is still the danger of puncturing a lung."

Andrew suddenly exclaimed. "Hey, chief, your hair …"

"I will explain later." Blake said quietly.

Wall confessed, "Mick and I already know, chief. You were never cured."

Guardian looked surprised. "How did you …?"

Mick placed his large hands on Blake's shoulder. "It's hard to fool an old fool. All of the signs were there, if you knew what to look for, Simon."

"I'm sorry about lying …" Guardian started.

Wall cut him off. "You did what you felt you needed to do. You know we won't judge you for that."

Cassie whispered to Megan. "Now I feel guilty. Everyone else is so understanding about this."

"Yes, but they're not in love with him."

Cassie started to reply, but didn't have the words. Megan found herself staring at Blake's cold eyes and pale features again and forced herself to look away.

Guardian straightened and stood facing Doc. "This supports Cassie's theory about there being more than one gang. Gabe and Isabelle were kidnapped and it sounds like two of your aides, Big Tom and Percy, were also captured. Whitney Van Pelt and Rav Chandra makes six. There may be more. Meanwhile, Pam's beauty salon was attacked by killers, as was Unsolved Mysteries, Incorporated. On the way over here, Kong contacted me and said they were also attacked by men hell-bent on murder. The Chromium Club was destroyed by men in Nazi uniforms. Cassie was right, we are in a war."

"Right now the safest place is in my offices. We can plan our strategy from there. They were designed to withstand a full scale attack." Doc offered.

Guardian stated the obvious. "So was this block of buildings."

Nobody wanted to voice what everyone was thinking. They were facing the battle of their lives.

Chapter Nineteen
Kong Gets a Bite

April 5, 1945   10:30 pm

Doc Titan led the small group from the bank of elevators. In tow were Simon Blake, Wall, Mick, Pam, Cassie, and Megan. Much to everyones surprise, except Pam's - she had witnessed this magic before, the main door to Doc's offices opened as he approached. He had a small piece of radioactive isotope in one shoe that set off a sensor in the door. They stepped through the doorway and entered the world of carnage beyond.

The windows had been blown out of the reception area on the 116th floor, along with a small section of exterior wall. The hole had been sealed with a quick-expanding foam, one of Doc's inventions. Pieces of reinforced glass were scattered about the floor and even embedded in the walls and furniture. One leg of the large inlaid wooden table was bent at an odd angle. Bart and Gibs were sweeping up debris at one end of the room. Kong had already moved the bodies of the four dead gangsters and placed covers over each one. He was crouched over the prone form of the man they had briefly known as Harold Bekker. In one hairy palm, he held a large metallic medallion. With the other hand, he was tapping at something protruding from one of Harold's inner coat pockets. In a split second, Doc recognized the item, a small grisly-looking red skull. As Kong tapped it again with his hard knuckles a small light flashed on and blinked rapidly.

Doc Titan had never moved so fast in his entire life. His movement was instantaneous and without any hesitation. With three large strides he reached Kong. He firmly grasped the man's massive bicep and pulled hard, still moving forward. Even though Kong weighed over three hundred pounds, he was lifted off of his feet as though he weighed no more than a feather. As Doc's movements, and Kong's bulk, capsized the men, Doc hit the floor several yards away and Kong struck the granite floor next to him with bone-jarring force. Even while they were moving away from the deceased body of Mr. Bekker, the red skull exploded into a scarlet mist. One knuckle of Kong's tough hands passed by the life-threatening fog and a nearly microscopic particle splashed onto his callused skin.

Everyone in the room watched breathlessly as the body of Harold Bekker was quickly consumed by the crimson cloud. Megan became physically sick on a pile of rubble. Gibs sat down hard and looked more pale than usual. Kong was staring unbelieving at the horrifying fate he had so narrowly escaped. Thirty seconds after it started, the body had been partially consumed and left behind a grisly, gory upper torso. The cause of the destruction had stopped and nobody moved or even breathed for a long moment. Suddenly, Kong jumped several feet into the air and let out a terrific bellow. Nearly everyone else in the room jumped at the noise. They watched wordlessly as Kong bounded about the room, clutching his hand.

"Yow, yow, yow! It's got me! I'm being eaten alive!" Kong cried aloud and showed them the bloody mark on his hand. A quarter inch circular hole had been eaten into his knuckle, exposing flesh, gristle and bone. "I'm gonna die!"

Doc grasped Kong firmly by the shoulders and stared into his homely face. "Kong, the virus can only survive exposure to the air for about thirty seconds. You'll be okay."

If anyone else had spoken to Kong at this moment, he would have ignored them. So great was his respect for Doc and the knowledge that he possessed, Kong calmed down quickly. He studied the raw wound with fascination.

"Geez, Doc, thanks for saving me. What a horrible way to go." Kong stared at the sickening remains of Harold and shuddered. "Okay, that's just gross." He rubbed his sore bicep. Bruising, in the shape of Doc's strong fingers, was already darkening on the surface of his thick skin.

Bart studied the remains of Bekker. "Almost like that sizzling death stuff we discovered on Fear Key. Except, that completely stripped a man to the bone."

Guardian turned to Doc. "I originally thought it might be an acid-based fluid but I think your assessment of it being a virus is correct. We ought to run a few tests to see what we're up against."

Megan shielded her eyes from the dead body and bent down to pick up the round medallion. It was the metal disc that had fallen from Kong's grasp and bounced across the floor. "What's this? Some type of coin?"

The large, brass-colored disc was several inches in diameter, larger than any modern coin. It was covered with strange markings, a unique pattern of hieroglyphics, embossed into the face of the metal. Rare-looking emeralds and other sparkling jewels were embedded in its worn surface and reflected a rainbow of colors.

Kong volunteered. "I found that in his pocket, right before you folks arrived."

Doc quietly extended one hand and Megan passed the object to him without a word. He studied it intently for several seconds, flipped it over in the palm of his hand, and estimated its weight. His eyelid twitched slightly.

Megan noticed the small movement and asked. "Discover something, Doc?"

Titan did not respond to Megan's question. Instead, he turned away and walked up the stairs leading toward his laboratories. "This demands further examination," he stated, almost to himself. Bart placed a cover over the remains of Harold Bekker.

There was a quick period of greetings between the gathered group. The giant Wall had once saved Bart from certain death. This was only hours before Wall met Simon Blake for the first time. Cassie had shared a private car on a train with Kong and Bart for six hours. Three months later, after her father was murdered and she was framed, she became the fourth member of Unsolved Mysteries, Incorporated. Fate, it seemed, had conspired to link this unique conclave of people together.

Doc climbed the stairs, past the next floor - the 117th, where Kong, Bart, Gibs and Doc kept modest apartments. The entire 118th floor of the building contained a massive library with hundreds of thousands of volumes on every field of science and study. Doc had read every one and even written several of them. His fields of expertise were extensive. The enormous library was noteworthy for the completeness of its reference works and educational volumes. There were no works of fiction housed in this library.

The following floor, the 119th, was an expansive laboratory, filled to capacity with an enormous collection of experimental and industrial equipment. One entire corner was reserved for Gibs' electrical experiments.

Doc pulled a small, sealed specimen vial from his vest pocket. He addressed the solemn Scotsman, Mick.

"At the Chromium Club, Darkness, Blake, and I were attacked by six men. This is a blood sample from one of the dead Nazis. Despite the fact they were severely injured or even shot, they continued fighting. I suspect a drug was responsible for their ability to withstand the pain. Please analyze this blood sample to see what you can find out."

Mick looked questioningly at Doc and then Kong. "I thought Kong was …"

Kong interrupted. "Despite what the pulps say, I only dabble in the field of chemistry. Strictly for personal research, however, I do read nearly every journal published on the subject, and specializing toward gases, minerals, and fluids. But I don't have your background in biochemistry and I'm certainly not qualified to study this problem. I understand you're something of a pharmaceutical wizard, even declined a nomination for the Nobel Prize."

"Ach. I didn't need a prize to be happy at my work. Actually, I do know something about pharmaceutical biological medicines."

Doc nodded, "Bart can assist you if you need anything."

"Sure, Doc, no problem." Bart agreed and confided quietly to Mick. "Kong is just being modest. He's been experimenting for years, trying to create a special formula. A new type of Cola. The last mixture he concocted was overly saturated with sugar and caffeine and was a bright yellow color. He drank one sample and couldn't sleep for two days."

"Hey, that one will sell someday, you mark my words. I just need the right advertising limerick." Kong said confidently.

"Watch out where the huskies go, and don't you drink that mountain snow." Bart offered, snickering.

Kong looked skyward, as if seeking inspiration. "Mountain Fizz … Mountain Mist … dang it, I just need the right name for it. Maybe I'll add some citrus flavoring, too."

"I also have a degree in biological research." Blake volunteered.

Doc turned to him. "I know. I was hoping you would use that background to find out everything you can about this Death's Head virus. I believe you are uniquely suited to this research."

Simon Blake didn't need it spelled out for him; he alone had survived a full exposure to this deadly agent.

"I'll get right on it."

Doc held up his hand and apologized. "Sorry, Simon. I'm accustomed to taking charge. I didn't mean to sound …"

Blake's face remained immobile, but his eyes smiled, as he interrupted Doc. "No problem, Doc. You're a natural born leader. No reason to practice restraint on my account. I'll start testing these samples now."

Doc turned to his ape-like aide. "Kong, I might need your assistance with this medallion."

Kong stepped up, "Sure thing, Doc."

Chapter Twenty
Coffin Nails

April 5, 1945   11:15 pm

Conall 'Mick' McGrath began mixing several combinations of chemicals, powders, and liquids. Even though he was in a strange laboratory, his movements were quick and sure. Bart assisted as needed. Several minutes later Mick smiled. "Ah-ha! Got it."

Bart studied the vials and beakers. "So what caused these men to continue fighting, even after they should have dropped, Mick?"

"It's actually a mixture of several drugs. In the pharmaceutical industry it's commonly known as Phencyclidine." Technically, that's a contraction of the chemical name phenylcyclohexylpiperidine, abbreviated PCP.

Kong walked over to listen in and added, "I recently read about that stuff. It's a dissociative drug formerly used as an anesthetic agent, exhibiting hallucinogenic and neurotoxic effects. Pretty powerful stuff. And nasty to boot."

Mick continued, "Aye. It is commonly known as The Dust of Angels. Most medical facilities have banned the use of the drug. Addicts dipped their cigarettes into the solution and would smoke it. They nicknamed it 'embalming fluid.'"

Bart, sitting on a stool on the opposite side of the lab table, asked Kong, "How come you are such a dunderhead under normal conditions, but you speak like a college professor when it comes to technical research?"

Kong frowned. "Heck, shyster, I don't joke around when it comes to my chosen vocation."

Bart chuckled, "Maybe not, apeman, but we're not talking about you chasing skirts right now."

Kong smiled broadly. "Heck, that's not a profession, it's a pleasurable preoccupation."

Gibs looked up from his work. "You guys are both dunderheads. How many times have you clowns gotten into trouble chasing members of the opposite sex?"

"One hundred and thirty-nine times, if you must know," Bart confessed.

"That would be one hundred and sixty-two for me," Kong admitted.

Bart frowned at Kong. "You're not counting that little blonde from your seminar in Houston last month?"

"Better than you, taking a dip in the company's secretarial pool with that perky brunette last week," Kong countered.

Gibs rolled his eyes. "Women are nothing but trouble. I'm better off without them in my life."

"I'm very glad to hear you say that, Gibs." Kong stated earnestly.

Gibs looked surprised at Kong's comment. "You are?"

"Sure. It means there are more women for me," Kong chuckled.

Bartholomew 'Bart' J. Blackwell neatly folded his handkerchief and tucked it in his suit coat. He had taken a few minutes to change into a clean three-piece, dark pin-striped suit. "What kind of desperate woman would want a throwback Neanderthal like you?"

BJ, a coal-black rodent, scurried to one of Bart's neatly tailored trouser legs and looked up. BJ was Kong's pet ferret. He had named it BJ after Bart's initials. It had short legs, a flexible, round body, and an extremely long, bushy tail. His mouth opened and in a squeaky little voice he clearly said, "Your personal secretary, Carol, seemed to like him just fine the other night. She called him her hulking ape-man and even stuck her tongue in the bullet hole in his earlobe."

Bart looked down sternly at the small creature with color markings around the eyes that resembled a white domino mask and smartly said, "Mind your own business, Roadkill, or I'll carve you into beef strips and feed you to Duke. And stop brushing against my new pants. You're shedding hair everywhere."

Mick, who couldn't see the other side of the table, queried in his Scottish brogue. "Who are ye talking ta, Bart?"

Bart poked his black cane at the floor. "This little rat, BJ, of course."

Mick, looking around the corner of the table, stared at the cute furry creature. "But squirrels dinna talk."

BJ stared wide-eyed at the Scot and said, "You ever hear the one about the two kilt-wearing Scots who walked into a bar?"

Mick's eyes grew large. "Oh, my Lord! Yer wee rat speaks! Tis possessed by a demon! Cassie, didja hear?"

"I've seen Kong's ventriloquist tricks before. I'm not impressed. He likes using his skills to pickup up girls." Cassie confessed. "I once spent several hours in a train car with Bart and Kong."

Mick scoffed and gave Kong a nasty look. "e's a bit of a skurlie dodger, eh?" Having voiced his opinion, he walked away to see how 'Muster Blake' was doing with his experiments.

Bart leaned near Kong and whispered, "I'm not really certain that that was a compliment."

"And I'm absolutely certain that it wasn't." Megan confided.

Gibs snorted. "You're correct on that account. But Kong's ventriloquistic skills have saved us more than a few times. And he has trained his little mousy friend to untie knots and fetch things. You'd be surprised how often the ladies fall in love with the pair of them."

Kong was tossing small treats across the room and BJ was managing to catch each one before it hit the floor. The small ferret was very quick.

Mick returned to the table and shook his head. "Ye're a strange lot o' characters, ta be sure. Do these fellas argue all the time?" He jabbed a finger in the direction of Kong and Bart.

Gibs confided, "Arguing for these fellows is like wrestling with a pig in the mud."

"How's that?" Wall inquired.

"Sooner or later, you realize the pig's enjoying himself!"

The five men and three women began laughing, but after receiving stern looks from Doc and Blake, they settled down and got back to work.

So, who is Duke?" Asked Cassie as she casually tossed treats to BJ. "You mentioned feeding BJ to Duke."

"Duke!" Bart exclaimed loudly. The air was filled with the sound of hard nails dancing up the stairwell and across the floor. Cassie envisioned the hellhound of the Baskervilles, bounded across the moors. A huge beast lumbered into the room. Duke was a two hundred and fifty pound English Mastiff. His short thick brown coat, however, resembled that of his American cousins, the Bull Mastiff. Duke was nicknamed after Bart's friend, Henry Marmaduke 'Kong' Larson.

The dog spotted the ferret and prepared to chase him around the laboratory. Considering the dangerous experiment Blake was conducting, Bart wisely stepped in Duke's way and gave him a simple, stern order. "Down!" Duke immediately followed Bart's direction and sat on his hind haunches. Cassie approached him cautiously and held out the back of one hand for him to sniff. He quickly gave her a friendly lick and she rubbed the top of his large head. Seated, he was nearly as tall as the petite woman.

"Oh, he's a good boy, yes he is." Cassie said as she stroked his ears. He growled happily and leaned against her, nearly bowling her over.

"Holy Cow!" Wall exclaimed. "He's huge!"

"Yeah, Monstro, was a gift from the queen of a small country we saved." Kong offered. "Eats more food than I do and he'll gnaw on anything you leave laying around. He and BJ get along just fine, they are best of buddies."

Bart looked around searchingly. "Speaking of Roadkill, where'd he go?" He quickly jabbed several fingers into his watch pocket and searched frantically. "Dang it, he stole another one!"

"Another what?" Cassie asked.

Bart face flushed with frustration. "My watch. That little thieving rodent steals my watches, right out of my pocket. And my cuff links, tie pins, spare change."

Kong chuckled. "Somewhere, BJ has a stash of sparkly treasures."

One floor down, in the huge library, BJ climbed into the recess at the top of a tall bookcase. He carefully added another watch to his treasury of shiny metal objects. In addition to Bart's jewelry, there were hundreds of items belonging to Doc and all of his aides. BJ curled into a ball, feeling safe amongst his various treasures and quickly fell fast asleep.

Gibs excused himself and returned to his electronics workbench. This bench was custom-built to his four-foot tall scale. He had been on the verge of completing another electronic gizmo when Harold Bekker and the four gangsters had interrupted. Wall found himself drawn toward the area, like a moth to an electric light. His eyes scanned a multitude of mysterious gadgets, deciphering and understanding each, before moving on to the next. His gaze finally rested and focused on one item in particular.

"Please forgive my intrusion, Gibs, but I'm curious about this device. It appears to be a variation of the Tesla coil resonant transformer. I notice this high voltage capacitor is designed to expel electrical discharges using high-frequency alternating current." Wall pointed at the contraption in question.

Gibs beamed brightly. Rarely did he meet a person capable of understanding his complicated devices, especially with only a rudimentary glance. Only Doc was his equal when it came to 'The Juice.'

After Nikola Tesla died on January 7, 1943 the FBI took possession of his property and papers. J. Edgar Hoover and the war department had declared it all top secret. The only problem was, they didn't know what most of it did. They soon contacted the only living man who might know, Gilbert 'Gibs' Elliot Maddox. For the last two years, Gibs had been studying and deciphering Tesla's notes, with the help of his friend and one of America's leading mathematicians and cryptologists, Bart Blackwell.

"Yes. It is one of my longest running experiments and greatest headaches. I designed this as an insect killer, to help farmers destroy certain pests … and because I hate bugs."

Wall studied the design and offered, "I believe it could be adapted for wireless power to create an electronically charged transmission. A miniature winding generator and storage battery, coupled with an electrical discharge focalizer ..."

Gibs' eyes widened. "Yes! I see where you're going with this. It would have limited range and power, but utilizing miniaturized transistors as semiconductor devices ..." He seemed on the verge of finishing and suddenly lacked something.

Wall continued Gibs' thoughts. "... and by modulating the signal and voltage frequencies ..."

"... and regulating the primary and secondary circuits to amplify the conduction output at the same frequency ..." Gibs added.

"... you could greatly amplify the total output of the high-voltage discharge." Wall finished with a large smile.

Bart had been listening to the two men discuss their electronic theories. They might as well have been speaking Russian. Bart was completely clueless about what they had just agreed on. They turned and looked at him, smiling like two children celebrating Christmas morning.

Bart nodded and said, "That's exactly what I would do. But I didn't want to suggest it, until Gibs asked."

As a government liaison, Bart had learned several secrets over the years. One was to know when to stop talking. He quietly clasped his black cane and walked away. Wall and Gibs began tinkering.

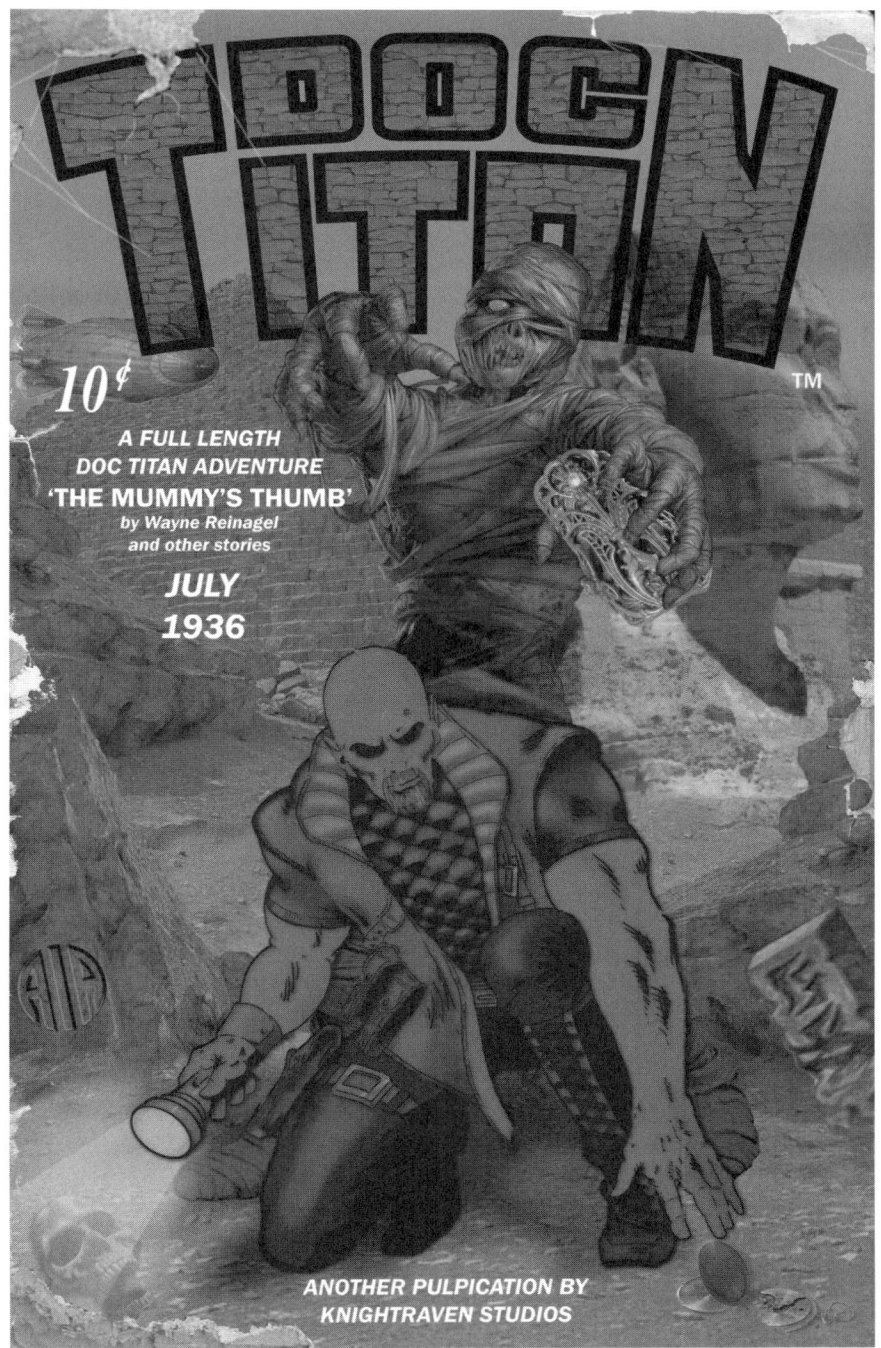

Chapter Twenty-One
Detective Work

April 6, 1945   12:15 am

One hour later, Simon Blake called the others into the laboratory. On a blank wall was the view of a slide under the lenses of a powerful microscope, projected and enlarged several times.

"Have you figured out the reactive agent in Totenkopf's deaths-head, Blake?" Doc asked.

"You won't believe this stuff, Doc. It's unlike anything I've ever seen before. What you are seeing on the microscope is obligate intracellular parasites. These are parasitic micro-organisms that cannot reproduce outside of their host cell, forcing the host to assist in the parasite's reproduction. Once the host cell runs out of genetic material to feed the parasites; skin, fat, and muscle tissue; they simply break down and die away. Additionally, less than a minute of exposure to normal air causes it to dissipate with no harmful effects."

Doc nodded. "They are playing with a genetically-modified biological pathogen that could destroy mankind. Black Skull is using an infectious biological multi-cellular weapon as his personal plaything, but nature refuses to be bound within set parameters."

Blake continued, "The Black Death of 1347 to 1352 killed twenty-five million in Europe in a little over five years. The introduction of smallpox, measles, and typhus to the areas of Central and South America by European explorers during the fifteenth and sixteenth centuries caused pandemics among the native inhabitants. Between 1518 and 1568 disease pandemics are said to have caused the population of Mexico to fall from twenty million to three million. But for all of these plagues there were people who were immune to the viruses. However, if this deaths-head virus mutated to the point where exposure to air would no longer stop its transmission to other hosts …"

Bart followed Blake's train of thought. "So you are talking the Black Plague, Smallpox, and Malaria, all rolled into one."

Blake nodded in agreement. "It would cause widespread devastating epidemics that could destroy all life on Earth. Most animals would also die from exposure to the virus."

"Gotcha. Important note to self, stay away from the red stuff." Kong said under his breath.

Bart placed a hand on Kong's shoulder. "That was a close call, brother."
"Yeah, and what a nasty way to go."

Bart snorted, "Better living through chemistry, indeed."

Doc considered this and asked, "What's the chance that someone could be directly exposed to this and not suffer the fate of these dead men?"

Mick volunteered. "None. This virus would kill anyone or anything it comes into contact with, bar none. Unless … you somehow already possess an immunity to the virus, perhaps by pre-indigesting a powerful pathogenic antibiotic. A biological antidote of sorts. It might be as dangerous to the host as the virus itself. Personally, I'm not sure I would recommend anything but staying the hell away from it. Why do you ask?"

Doc looked at Blake, who had actually survived direct exposure to the deadly virus, and simply replied, "No reason. Good work, Simon."

Wall and Gibs approached Bart, Kong, and Mick. They were smiling broadly, very pleased with themselves.

Kong warned, "I recognize that look on Gibs' face."

Mick nodded in agreement. "Aye. He and Wall appear to have tinkered together some new kind of gizmo."

Wall opened a box, roughly the size of a suitcase. Housed within were a dozen pistols that Doc's men called rapid-firers, with slight modifications. A rubber sheath encased the handle and a small textured button protruded from the top of the main body. Gibs pulled out one of the guns and pointed it at a slab of granite leaning against the wall. He aimed and pulled the trigger. A small lightning bolt jumped from the end of the gun and splashed against the stone, dancing across the smooth surface. Duke lay down on the floor and covered his head with his large paws.

Kong watched the display and calmly stated, "Impressive guys, but doesn't have much bang, does it?"

Wall grabbed a second gun from the case. He wound the button on the top, similar to winding a pocket watch fob, and pointed at the same granite slab. A burst of power shot forth and the stone exploded in a shower of dust.

Kong nearly fell off of his stool. "Cheese and crackers!"

Gibs began to explain. "It's a simple generator built into the base and the increased power is amplified in a cascade …"

Kong waved his hands excitedly. "I'll take one, if you'll stop explaining how you did it."

"Me, too." Bart pulled one of the guns from the case with a mischievous smile painted on his features. "Is the lower charge lethal?"

"No, the human body easily can withstand a charge of that magnitude ..." Wall began explaining.

The tip of Bart's gun touched the metal leg of the stool Kong was sitting on and sparks shot from the muzzle. Kong's rusty-red hair stood straight up and he leapt several inches off of the stool. He landed on his butt and growled at Bart.

Kong shook his fist. "You did that on purpose! I'm gonna wring your scrawny neck, you clothes-horse!"

Bart smiled. "Not much of a bang, eh?"

Kong approached Bart with his hands clinched into fists. A low, deep growl emanated from his right shoulder. Duke had approached with incredible stealth, considering his size, and was standing next to Kong. His massive jowls were pulled back and his large teeth were exposed, as he prepared to protect Bart against the apelike Kong. Bart snapped his fingers and Duke quickly laid back down. But the Mastiff kept one eye on Kong.

"Wow, he's something else, isn't he?" Kong's face had gone from angry to impressed. "He would have fought me to protect you." Kong reached down and scratched Duke behind one ear. "Good boy." The Mastiff rolled on its side and allowed Kong to stroke the thick fur on his stomach.

Bart held out his hand to Kong. "Sorry about the shock, big guy. I was just goofing off. It didn't hurt you, did it?"

Kong chuckled. "Kinda tickled actually. I'm gonna go help Doc, now. Hey, when we get back from this adventure, let's find out where BJ has been stashing all of your watches and other stuff."

"Sounds like a plan, brother."

Chapter Twenty-Two
Harold Bekker and The Mysterious Medallion

April 6, 1945   12:30 pm

Doc held out the medallion to Pam and asked. "You've seen a lot of expensive jewelry in your line of work. What is your first impression of this amulet, Pam?"

Kong chimed in, "Gotta be worth a fortune, with all of them jewels."

Pam smiled mischievously. "Gaudy. It wouldn't match any of my outfits." She took the circular disk from his hand and stared at it for a second. "Well, for one thing, all of the jewels are fake."

Kong gawked. "What? How can you tell that merely by looking at it?"

Megan studied her painted fingernails. "A woman knows these things, Kong. I could tell from five feet away. They're only cut glass."

Pam hefted the medallion as if trying to judge its weight. "That's odd. It feels heavier than it appears. As if … "

Doc volunteered. "As if something else is hidden inside? I believe the real message Harold Bekker brought us is actually beneath the surface layer."

Pam smiled in agreement. "Exactly what I was thinking."

"Thanks, Pam. If you ladies aren't busy, I could use your help."

"Sure, Doc. What's up? How can we help?" Pam offered.

Doc handed her four file folders. "These were given to us tonight by … a friend. They contain information on all of us. I haven't had time to look at all of the information inside each folder." He smiled a little. "I've been kind of busy. Could you three look through these files and see if you find anything unusual? They appear to be the work of a professional detective, possibly someone from the Manhattan area. Maybe you can discover who he is and find out more information. Perhaps he can give us an important lead on his client, or clients. Lastly, search for any information on the four dead men in the reception room. According to Kong and Bart, the lone gentleman claimed his name was Harold Bekker. The others are obviously mobsters. Knowing who their leader is might provide clues about what has been going on tonight."

"We'll get right on it." Pam was very pleased. Doc had always treated her as a burden. Now he was giving her assignments, just like he did his merry band of men.

Thirty minutes later, Cassie approached Doc, as he continued his experiments on the metal disk.

"Doc, I found something on the man who introduced himself as Harold Bekker. He arrived yesterday afternoon on a steamer ship, the Newcastle II, bound from Greenland. Stayed overnight at a small hotel called the Kensington Arms. Nobody really seemed to notice him. Even the hotel clerk only remembered the name after re-reading the registry book. He didn't speak to anyone or do anything memorable while on the steamship. No records of him exist in Greenland. He simply showed up out of nowhere and boarded the ship."

Doc pondered the information. "Hmm. Anything else?"

Cassie continued. "Well, the name Harold Bekker was probably false. The only Harold Bekker on record was a ruthless gangster who used to work for the Belcher mob in Queens. But he vanished from the face of the earth seven years ago. Rumor has it that he crossed the wrong mob boss and is buried out in the New York woods somewhere."

Bart snapped his fingers. "He crossed the wrong guy all right. That's where I've heard that name before. After that incident at the bank in '38, we sent him up to the Titan Rehabilitation Institute and Clinic with some of his more illustrious friends. That explains finding the mark on the back of his neck. Doc, you must have operated on him."

Doc continued working on the medallion and did not look up. Bart knew Doc was keeping his own council on this subject. When he was ready he would let them know what he was thinking but not before. Not until he was absolutely certain of his facts. As soon as the words left his mouth, Bart regretted even mentioning the Titan Rehabilitation Institute and Clinic. Not everyone knew about it and some secrets should remain secret.

Megan had several newspaper clippings in her hands and she spread them out on the surface of the workbench.

Megan spoke confidently, "Those files you received from your, uh, friend, appear to be the research of a down and out detective in lower Manhattan named Darius Angel. He runs a business called the Daring Angel Detective Agency. Mostly works finding petty larcenists, criminals, and dead-beat husbands. Occasionally, he does cloak and dagger surveillance jobs."

"Did he mention who he was working for?" Doc asked.

Megan tsked with her tongue and nodded her head. "Sorry, I should have said he *ran* a detective agency. Right now he occupies a slab at the county morgue. Somebody shot him six times and he fell out his office window, from three or four floors up."

Doc breathed out slowly, his eyes closed. "Another dead end." Megan Meriwether smiled at the unintentional pun.

"One last thing, Doc. At one time he called himself 'The Avenging Angel Detective.'"

Doc nodded. "I remember him. He was avenging his father's murder. Another masked detective, like Scorpion or the Apparition Detective. His real name was Gabriel Wilder."

Pam added, "I glanced through those files, Doc. He did a pretty thorough job of tracking everyone who works with you and the boys. Even managed to find out Scorpion was actually Preston Stockbridge. There is no mention of the Darkness' alter ego, but he did manage to discover several of his agents."

Megan flipped through her notes. "Allen Coleman mentioned that a man with one gold tooth was leading one of the gangs. The ones who kidnapped our friends. Did a quick search through the files you have on New York gangsters. The name George 'Goldie' MacDonall came up. He's an enforcer for 'Man Mountain' Marko."

Kong cracked his knuckles. "Doc, you want Bart and me to pay Mr. Marko a visit? Find out what we can about Big Tom and Percy?" He punched his knuckles together forcefully. Kong enjoyed his position as the team's tough guy.

Megan interrupted, "About five minutes ago they announced on the radio that Marko and his thugs were all found dead."

Bart chimed in, "Anyone want to bet that it was the work of the Darkness? Or the Scorpion?"

Doc stated flatly. "Or both."

"No bet here. Sounds like their handiwork," Megan agreed.

Everyone was quiet for a moment. Doc quietly announced a discovery. He had been laboring at a long workbench. The surface was pitted and burned by various experiments and covered with beakers, vials, Bunsen burners, rubber and glass tubing, and hundreds of other scientific equipment. Dozens of carefully labeled bottles, organized alphabetically, were filled with chemicals and powders. These filled a 'spice rack' of enormous size, mounted to the wall behind the laboratory bench.

The adjoining table was equally as large and covered with microscopes of varying sizes. Books were spread open and randomly scattered throughout and in between the equipment. More piles of books towered atop stools and every empty work surface. Precariously balanced mountains of tomes also littered the floor space under the benches. This area was Kong's inner sanctum. Sometimes it would be days or weeks before he would finish a complicated experiment and would allow the area to be re-organized and cleaned. He did his best work in a chaotic, haphazard environment.

Doc held up the metal disk. "I think I have discovered the secret of this medallion. I've been trying to figure out the puzzle of how to open it without destroying the outside. I believe that is actually part of the deception. The outside is merely a decoy, a red herring, in case it fell into the wrong hands. They would waste their time attempting to unlock the mysteries of the jewels and the gibberish printed on the outside. The true message is concealed within. Doc scraped the surface of the golden metal, exposing a dull gray substance beneath. "Kong, what does this material look like to you?"

Kong used a magnifying glass and studied the scratch for a second.

"At first glance, I would say it looks like magnesium. But you wouldn't want a coin or medallion made of magnesium."

Bart frowned. "Okay, I'll bite. Why not?"

Kong explained, "Unlike most metals, magnesium is extremely unstable under certain conditions. Magnesium is a highly flammable metal, but while it is easy to ignite when powdered or shaved into thin strips, it is difficult to ignite in mass or bulk. However, once ignited, it is difficult to extinguish, being able to burn in both nitrogen (forming magnesium nitride) and carbon dioxide (forming magnesium oxide and carbon). Magnesium, when it burns in air, produces a brilliant, white light. When glowing white, Magnesium has many chemical properties that it does not possess at lower temperatures. It also becomes more toxic. Magnesium powder is still used in the manufacturing of fireworks and marine flares where a bright white light is required."

"There you go again. If I didn't know better, I'd think you had more than half a brain." Bart taunted.

"Don't you have an ambulance to chase?" Kong retorted. Bart had studied law before the Great War and failed the final examination. Kong had never let him live it down.

Doc grabbed the medallion with a pair of metal tongs and placed it directly in the exposed flames of the Bunsen burner on the workbench. Little sparks spat forth and then effervescent flames climbed across the surface of the metal. Doc dropped the burning token into a beaker filled with water. The medallion continued to burn briskly for nearly a minute, throwing off bright illumination.

Using the metal tongs, Doc reached back into the beaker and removed a substantially smaller metal disk. The amulet was now approximately three inches in diameter. For its size, it was still quite heavy. On one side was an indistinguishable image, perhaps a face, with what appeared to be a star directly overhead. Numerical figures near the star read 90 00 00 00. On the flip side was more of the gibberish they had noticed on the medallion earlier. Bart quietly studied the disk from Doc's shoulder.

"Dang, if that don't clear things up." Kong scratched his head and placed his pinky in the hole in one earlobe, where a criminal had shot through it several years ago. "We went from a silly-looking medallion covered in gibberish writin' to a smaller medallion with gibberish writin' on it. And a face that's been messed up so bad we can't make it out at all. And what does that ninety million mean?"

Doc quietly placed the amulet in his pocket and walked over to Pam. He knew exactly what hidden secret the mysterious coin was and the meaning of the 'gibberish' written on its surface.

Chapter Twenty-Three
The Dangerous Life

April 6, 1945   1:00 am

Doc placed his hand on Pam's elbow and gently guided her away. "Pam, can I talk to you three ladies for a moment? In the next room?" His face was fixed and quite serious.

"Sure, Doc. Want do you need?"

Doc looked at her sternly. "Pam, this is a very dangerous case. I think that you, Cassie, and Megan should leave the city and find a safe haven. I will find and contact you, when I return."

"Ha! And I think you should have your head examined, Doc. I'm not going anywhere, except with you and the boys. I care just as much about the safety of Percy and Big Tom as you do and I want to help rescue them." Pam retorted.

Kong, who had followed them as far as the doorway, rolled his eyes and started to speak, then decided he was better off staying quiet.

Doc's icy calm was beginning to show some aggravation. His cousin was obviously not going to back down without a battle.

"Why must we always get into these debates?" Doc asked quietly.

Pam's face reddened with anger. "Because you are a bull-headed, male chauvinist who believes that a woman can't take care of herself when faced with danger. Percy and Big Tom were kidnapped by street gangsters. Kong, Bart, and Gibs allowed your offices to be demolished. But Cassie, Megan, and I fought off three gangsters armed with guns and walked away without a scratch. I had to shoot one man in the street tonight. He was carrying a bazooka, for heaven's sake."

"Hey, we didn't *allow* ..." Kong started defensively.

Pam and Doc turned on him at the same time. "Shut up!"

Kong slowly sidled from the doorway and joined Bart and Gibs in the next room. Cassie and Megan stood on either side of Pam in support of her position.

She stood toe to toe with Doc, "You might as well give in because there is no way you're leaving us behind."

Doc did not reply. He appeared to be searching for a response to Pam's bold position. Slowly turning his head, he looked from Pam to Cassie to

Megan. He opened his mouth, hesitated for a second, and closed it again. Pam smiled broadly, pleased with herself for standing up to her cousin like this. She remembered several years ago, when he had given her a package and told her to leave the state and guard the item with her life. After three days, she got curious and opened the box, only to find it empty. She swore he would never send her on another snipe hunt like that again. Too many times in the past he had left her behind. Not this time.

"Cat got your tongue? I expected more of an argument from you, Doc." Pam's broad smile suddenly vanished. "Are you holding your breath? You bastar ..."

In mid-sentence, Pam's eyes rolled back into her head and she dropped to the floor. Megan and Cassie followed a half-second later. Doc Titan raised his foot and looked down at the glass capsule he had broken beneath his heel. He calmly walked over to a nearby window and opened it, allowing a breeze to blow into the office. After thirty seconds had passed he took a deep breath. The gas had dissipated by then. Pam was snoring delicately on the floor. She and her companions would wake up again in six hours. By then Doc and the others would be long gone. One at a time, he carried the women into a nearby room.

One might think it was a small guest room, simply furnished with a single chair and a small bed. Actually, it was closer to a prison cell with reinforced walls, floors, and ceiling. The door was solid steel and weighed several hundred pounds. It was supplied with a timed lock that could be set for a specific schedule, much like a bank vault. The only weak spot was a tiny grate welded into the door, to allow fresh air into the otherwise air-tight room. The grate would not allow even a small dog to pass through, much less a human. He closed the heavily reinforced door and set the timer for twenty-four hours. By then, Pam would cool off and go home. Doc rejoined the others in the laboratory.

Kong asked Doc, "Where's Pam? Did she settle down? She was really getting hot for a moment there."

Doc replied calmly, with absolutely no sign of agitation, "She and the other ladies are resting comfortably in the other room."

Kong frowned and scratched his bullet-shaped head, "They're just sitting in there?"

"Actually, they're asleep." Doc volunteered calmly, stroking an open palm over his bald scalp.

Kong looked confused. "But Pam was just ... Doc, you didn't!?"

"Didn't what?" Bart questioned.

Doc calmly shrugged his shoulders, "I gassed them. They'll be asleep for several hours. I locked them in the 'guest room' and set the timer. The door will open in twenty-four hours."

Doc glanced over at Simon Blake, Mick, and Wall, expecting an argument. Without consulting with them, he had locked up Cassie, a member of the Unsolved Mysteries, Inc. group.

Guardian simply shrugged his shoulders, "Maybe it's just as well. This way we'll know Cassie is out of harms way."

Wall agreed. "We already have one in the hospital. I'd hate to see anything happen to our little Cassie."

"Well, since you all agree, we need to gather our gear and get going right away." Kong moved quickly.

Bart toyed with his black cane, "What's the rush, nature boy?"

Kong warned, "'Cause when Pam wakes up she's gonna kill someone and I want to be far away from here when the shooting starts. Doc, I suggest you wear a bullet-proof vest for the next couple of weeks."

"She'll calm down and see that I was right to leave her behind." Doc stated, still calm.

Kong waved his hands excitedly in front of Doc. "Excuse me? Do you even know your cousin? She's already shot one man in cold blood tonight."

Mick quietly confessed, "Doc, I suppose we should warn you. If Pam doesn't kill you, Cassie probably will."

Gibs, who was never a big fan of women, chimed in. "For the record, I think Doc did the right thing. This adventure will be no place for women. It's far too dangerous."

Kong smiled broadly, his mouth stretching from ear to ear. "I'll be sure to let the ladies know that. Maybe after Pam shoots you and Doc, she'll calm down enough that she'll forget about Bart and me."

Gibs wrinkled his nose at Kong. "Snitch!"

Kong stowed the last of the gear in the small cockpit of the vehicle. He had nicknamed the strange, sleek sled the 'Hell-Rocket.' The others simply referred to it as the 'Slipstream.' It was, simply stated, a three-mile long, pneumatic-tube system linking the 124 story Titan Tower skyscraper to the Global Navigator Consortium, a massive warehouse/hanger on the waterfront, where Doc kept a multitude of specialized vehicles.

Wall glanced around the cockpit, "That's a weird-looking elevator. Where does it go?"

Kong smiled again, "Straight down and out. It's one heck of a ride. The other end is at our warehouse."

Bart warned Wall, "The first time we rode in it, everyone else nearly lost their lunch. But Kong just about wore it out that first week, riding it back and forth. He's crazy like that."

Mick buckled himself into one of the seats and asked, "What's at this warehouse?"

"I call shotgun!" Kong jumped into a front seat. "The Global Navigator Consortium? Man, you gotta see it to believe it." Kong leaned over near Bart and whispered, "Bet one of them loses their lunch on the Hell-Rocket."

Bart whispered back, "I'll be lucky if I don't lose mine."

Fortunately for the giant Wall, one of the seats was designed to fit the large engineer, Big Tom. Once everyone was buckled in, Gibs turned around and inquired, "Is everyone strapped in and ready to go? Then hang on."

Doc pulled a lever that released the safety clamps and the bullet-shaped car dropped abruptly. Gravity propelled the small craft toward the street level and below. At one hundred feet below the streets of Manhattan, the vehicle sharply angled and then leveled out horizontally. The nearly frictionless ride was incredibly fast and surprisingly smooth. After less than a minute of travel, the car came to a braking halt. Bart, Gibs, and Mick exited the vehicle quickly and seemed pleased to be standing on solid ground again. Kong and Wall had huge smiles and appeared to be unaffected by the speed of the Slip Stream. Doc and Blake exited last, neither showing any visible signs of discomfort or pleasure. Doc pushed a button near the exit door and heavy clamps locked the craft down. This would stop anyone, specifically Pam, from calling the car back to the skyscraper.

Wall and Mick walked into the main section of the Global Navigator Consortium building and stared in awe. Housed in the sprawling complex were dozens of automobiles, motorized land and water vehicles, and even armored tanks. Resting on a gigantic steel frame was a submarine called the Seablade. Overhead a dirigible, named the Windjammer, hovered weightlessly. Planes of every size and description filled the rest of the space.

Doc commanded the men. "We'll be loading the Windjammer today, brothers. Pack the cold weather gear, we're heading toward the South Pole."

Chapter Twenty-Four
The Battle at the Praetorian Securities Warehouse

April 6, 1945 1:15 am

Scorpion trod the accelerator of the powerful roadster, as it roared around the street corner. He immediately recognized the danger they were facing. Two men stood in the street, each with a rocket launcher. Before a full second had passed, the deadly projectiles were airborne. They flew toward the automobile, resembling fiery comets. Darkness and Scorpion leapt from the car an instant before it exploded; shooting flames high into the night air. The thunder echoed in the man-made concrete canyons of the city. Both men were quickly back on their feet, their hands filled with death-dealing automatics. The firearms spit lead at the two gangsters and they dropped in the street.

At the far end of the block, massive doors opened at the Praetorian Securties warehouse. The mighty roar of powerful engines came from the opening. A large plane rolled out and taxied to a loading dock at the water's edge. Immediately after the pontoons struck the water the pilot throttled the engines and the craft leapt forward.

From every direction, men emerged from doorways and alleys, armed with various weapons ranging from revolvers to machine guns. The barrage of exploding firearms was nearly deafening. Scorpion and Darkness ran for cover behind vehicles parked along the streets, while firing their weapons with deadly skill. Each bullet seemed to find its mark as men crumpled and dropped, each wound a killing blow. The gangsters, try as they might, failed to target their elusive quarry. The twenty against two odds were quickly changing. One man loaded a second rocket launcher and fired at Darkness, or where Darkness had been a split-second earlier. Instead, the explosive device struck a car, the resulting explosion killing three men who had also been shooting at Darkness.

The airplane had plowed through the dark waters and taken flight. The trajectory carried it over the abandoned Praetorian Securities warehouse and then it quickly gained altitude. The pilot displayed great skill as he throttled the plane hard, without stalling the engine.

One man fired from the fourth floor of a fire escape, narrowly missing Scorpion's head. Scorpion spun around and fired without aiming. The man plunged off of the fire escape, as the bullet drilled a hole through the center of his forehead. Even though Scorpion was unaware of the gangster's identity,

Mike 'Iron Jaw' Johnson's last vision on Earth was Scorpion standing over his body, preparing to place a scorpion emblem on his forehead. The crimson seal with the deadly pinchers and poisonous barbed tail. The mark of the Scorpion. The gangster's shallow breathing stopped.

One last man was still standing, and he decided that fleeing was the smartest option. Darkness had other plans. He glided forward and returned shots with the man attempting to hide behind the driver's door of the sedan. The large bore automatics perforated the thin metal of the car door and the gangster dropped to the ground. As he passed the open door, Darkness noticed a rocket launcher lying on the floor board of the car. He grasped the metal cylinder and moved quickly to a position where he could see the escaping airplane. The craft was lined up in the crosshairs and his finger pulled back on the trigger. An iron-hard fist hit the side of his head, knocking him to the concrete sidewalk. Simon Blake, the Guardian, stood over his prone form. He had followed the explosions and gunfire, and realized his abandoned warehouse was where the battle raged.

"Some of my people are on that plane!" Guardian stated through clinched teeth.

Before another word could be said, Darkness moved. He seemed impossibly fast as he flowed toward the white-faced man. Guardian's back slammed hard against the brick wall and his arms were pinned by an inhuman force hidden within the depths of the dark cloak. Darkness' face, a terrible, grimacing mask, was inches away from Blake's, and his eyes seemed to glow with crimson fire. Blake could feel the cold, hard barrel of a .45 caliber automatic pressed against the soft skin of his exposed neck.

Darkness spit angry words at him through tightly clinched teeth. "We're fighting a war here. In war, there are casualties."

"Those people in that plane aren't casualties, they are my friends!" Blake's emotionless face showed no signs of concern for his own safety. He continued. "Is this what it will come to?! Friend against friend?! Killing each other?! Damn it, we're on the same side! Doc's right, Gibson, you're out of control!"

Darkness slowly released his grip and Blake dropped to the ground. Darkness' face was completely hidden in the dim illumination of the alleyway. Only his blazing red eyes burned through the shadows. There was a moment of silence between the two old friends.

Darkness finally spoke. "You and I fight crime in very different ways, Blake. I do not believe in allowing dangerous criminals to escape. I will continue this battle on my own terms. Do not interfere again." Darkness backed away and the shadows seemed to embrace his form.

Blake started to reply and realized he was standing alone in the filthy alleyway. Darkness had vanished from sight. There was no laughter or prophetic announcement about crime. The airplane had also vanished into the dark stillness of the night skies. The bodies of two dozen men lay scattered in the streets or consumed in the fiery blaze of the burning vehicles. If any man had escaped death at the hands of Scorpion and Darkness, they had quickly left the battle zone. Perhaps Darkness was correct about this being a war.

Scorpion was casually strolling through the carnage, placing his scorpion emblem on the foreheads of every dead gangster he could find, whether he had shot them or not. Finally, he calmly walked up to Simon Blake.

Scorpion smiled. "God, I love this job." Realizing Blake was disturbed about his recent confrontation with Darkness, he continued. "Don't be concerned, we're probably better off without him."

"Perhaps, but I have a feeling before this is all over, we'll wish he was with us." Blake stated ominously.

"I don't mean to be rude, but what the hell happened to your hair and face?"

Blake turned to Stockbridge and quickly recapped the events of the last few hours. "I was never cured. I've been wearing a wig and make-up. After you left the Chromium Club, we were attacked by Nazis Stormtroopers. They wore small crimson skulls at their necks and when the skulls exploded a virus was released that consumed all of the skin and flesh from their faces. I was directly exposed to the virus and somehow survived. Then the Unsolved Mysteries, Inc. offices were completely destroyed by men with rocket launchers. Even Pam's salon and Doc's offices were attacked by gangsters."

"You're putting me on, right?" Stockbridge chuckled. "You've been wearing make-up?"

As Blake opened his mouth to speak, they were both thrown to the ground by an earth-shattering blast. The Praetorian Securities warehouse exploded, throwing debris several stories into the sky. As Blake regained his footing, he stared at the ruins of the warehouse. Being constructed mostly of brick, concrete and steel there was very little left to feed a fire. But the blast had been sufficient to destroy the building completely.

Blake was in shock. "They've annihilated everything," he said quietly.

Stockbridge slapped him on the back. "Welcome to the club, Simon. They burned down my family mansion, too. Good thing we're millionaires and can afford to rebuild everything. After all, it's only stuff."

Simon nodded and silently agreed, "Yes, it's a good thing we're millionaires."

Scorpion could hear the sound of an airplane engine revving up and preparing for takeoff. He dashed for Doc Titan's Global Navigator Consortium building, with Blake close on his heels.

"They're leaving us behind," Scorpion stopped and pointed.

Passing the opening between the large buildings, he witnessed a large airplane exiting the massive hanger doors. It roared upward and turned in an arc that would carry it back over the Global Navigator Consortium warehouse. The pilot was certainly an expert, maneuvering the large craft easily. A whistling noise filled the sky, even over the sounds of the airplane engine. The two men were witnesses as another rocket was launched directly at the plane. Half a second later, the craft exploded into a million pieces of debris that dropped, hissing, into the river. No one could have survived the explosion.

Scorpion whipped out his automatic and took aim. He saw the silhouette of a man on the neighboring roof. Two shots filled the morning air and the dark shape fell from the roof parapet of the building. The body hit the ground with a disgusting crunch of bones. Stockbridge and Blake walked over and stared down at the dying man. The man with one gold tooth. George 'Goldie' MacDonall, James 'Man Mountain' Marko's chief lieutenant, lay dying on the hard concrete. His body was twisted at an odd angle and one leg appeared to have several joints, instead of one. Blake could tell at a glance that the man's back was broken.

Scorpion sheathed his gun when it was obvious that the man no longer posed a threat. Goldie's eyes were fixed on a position behind them. Scorpion quickly pulled the gun from its sheath and spun around, prepared for an attack. His hand was caught in an iron grip as Doc pointed the dangerous end of the automatic in another direction.

"Geez, Doc, that's a good way to get shot, sneaking up on a fellow." Scorpion hesitated for a second, and then asked. "Hey, weren't you on board that plane that exploded?"

"No. It was remote controlled." Doc explained calmly. "This man appears to be the last of the attackers."

Guardian knelt down next to the broken man. "You're dying and there's nothing we can do for you. Will you explain why you attacked us?"

Goldie coughed and expelled a shower of blood. He smiled weakly. "Guess it don't matter now, does it? Besides, Marko will just send more men after I'm dead."

"I guess you haven't heard yet, Marko is already dead." Scorpion volunteered and then added, "And so are all of the men who were at his estate."

Goldie laughed and coughed again. "Figures. I have to admit, you guys are tough birds."

"Why were you kidnapping our friends?" Guardian asked the dying man.

Goldie stared for a minute, and then decided it didn't matter. "Man named Konstantin Egorov was paying us fifty thousand per head to snatch everyone we could on a list of names."

"Marko told me he was getting one hundred thousand." Scorpion told Goldie.

Goldie snarled. "Cheating bastard. I'm glad you killed him." He chuckled and spit up more blood.

"So why were some men trying to kill …" Doc started to ask.

Goldie interrupted him. "That jerk, 'Iron Jaw' Johnson, was working for two Germans. Their names are Teppleman and Gross. They wanted everyone on the list killed. He wanted to be the man to wipe out you heroes in New York. Figured he would become a 'made' man in the Mafia. He wanted Marko's territories."

Scorpion asked angrily. "Where can I find this 'Iron Jaw' Johnson?"

"You've already met him." Goldie saw the questioning look in Scorpion's eyes. "You shot him off the fire escape, back there in that gunfight."

"Why did you shoot down Doc's plane?" Guardian asked.

"Johnson wasn't wrong. You heroes are a pain. B'sides, I already clipped the wings of an angel …" Goldie laughed at his own joke and coughed up more blood.

Doc frowned. "So you're the man who killed Darius Angel, the private detective?"

"Yeah. Guess I'm paying the devil now, huh?"

"Where are the prisoners being taken?" Scorpion wanted this man to suffer for Lockhart's death. And for the death of Stockbridge's mother.

Goldie shook his head and grimaced in pain. "Don't know. I was to deliver 'em to the airplane. Egorov was supposed to have a courier deliver the money straight to Marko. He double-crossed us. After we reached the plane and helped load the prisoners, his men opened fire on us. I was the only one to escape alive."

"Another dead end. Describe this Konstantin Egorov," Doc asked quietly.

"Big man. Bearded. A Russian." Goldie coughed and a large volume of blood poured from his mouth. His eyes rolled back into his head and his breathing stopped. Scorpion reached forward to close the man's eyelids. When he pulled his hand away, the mark of a scorpion was embossed on Goldie's forehead.

"Rest in peace, Jack Lockhart. You've been avenged." As had Stockbridge's mother and Benson, the family butler.

The three men re-entered the Global Navigator Consortium warehouse. Kong and Bart were arguing over a bet they had placed with one another.

"I bet you the plane would get blown up." Kong was arguing.

"Yes, but I said it would get shot down." Bart returned.

"But they did blow it up."

"Only *after* it was shot down."

Doc Titan ignored the constantly bickering men and asked. "Is the Windjammer all loaded and ready to go?"

The bearded giant Wall stepped forward. "Yep. All of the winter gear is loaded and we strapped down the equipment you requested. You think it's safe to go out? We won't be shot at again?"

Guardian stated calmly, "It appears that the coast is clear." He decided to tell his friends about the destruction of the Praetorian Securities warehouse at a later date. They had all been through enough for one day.

Doc took charge. "Stockbridge, Blake and I will fly in the Windjammer. You five take the large, all terrain airplane. We might need the backup craft in case we encounter problems."

Kong acknowledged the instructions, "Right, Doc. Maintenance log says it was checked out earlier this week and should be ready to go."

"See you fellas in the air." As Doc walked toward the Windjammer, he whispered to himself, "Take care, brothers."

Five minutes later, the massive airship called Windjammer lifted into the dark skies through the gigantic doors at one end of the warehouse. Kong watched as it headed directly south and walked back to the plane he nicknamed 'The Spruce Goose.' Rumors were that the Howard Hughes Aircraft Company was working on something similar they called the Hughes H-4 Hercules. Supposedly, Hughes' ship was ten times larger than this craft.

Bart was behind the pilot's yoke and prepping the plane for takeoff. They were running through the checklist when Wall enquired, "So, where is our destination?"

Kong looked knowingly at Bart and then Gibs, who both frowned back at him. He had assumed they knew the answer.

"Didn't Doc tell anyone where we were going?" Kong asked.

"Other than *south*?" Bart retorted.

Gibs offered, "Must have slipped his mind." Kong looked at him doubtfully.

Bart had flipped the ignition switch and nothing happened. He tried again, with the same results. Kong turned on the radio and called to Doc, informing him there was a problem. For a long moment there was silence. Then Doc's voice answered loud and clear.

"Brothers, this is one adventure that might be too dangerous. I'm sorry, but I sabotaged the plane. Take care, my friends."

"But, Doc, we can …" Bart began, but the only reply coming back was static. Doc had switched off the radio.

Kong began cursing up a storm. When he was riled, as he clearly was now, Kong could curse for several minutes straight, without repeating himself. Finally, he calmed down enough that the men could talk amongst themselves.

"So there's no way to track him?" Wall asked.

Kong's face lit up. "Of course, we recently added those new long-range trackers in all of the ships." Bart flipped on a switch and a radar screen lit up. To the South a blip showed up, tracking the zeppelin's position. Suddenly, the blip disappeared. Doc Titan had turned off or disabled the tracking device. Not to be daunted, Gibs pulled a device from one of his equipment cases, approximately the size of a cigar box.

Gibs pushed a button. "Maybe he can turn off that one, but I added a backup transmitter that would function on a battery backup, after the power was turned off." On a small screen, similar to the dashboard model, a tiny blip occurred every few seconds, heading directly south. The men all smiled at Gibs' ingenious invention, and then promptly lost those smiles as the screen went blank.

"Guess Doc found that one too," Kong said sullenly.

Five minutes later, they had checked all of the other vehicles in the warehouse. They were all victims of a similar sabotage. Doc had been quite thorough.

Gibs tossed a wrench across the hanger. "I suppose this only leaves us with one choice."

Kong looked depressed, with his homely face resting in one cupped hand. "Yeah, guess we go back to the office and wait for them to return."

Gibs looked at Kong in surprise. "No, we fix the airplane and follow Doc anyway."

Kong frowned. "How do we fix it? Doc … "

Wall interrupted. "Are you kidding? With all due modesty aside, you are standing in a room with two of the greatest electrical engineers of the century. And you've probably memorized every engineering and technical specification written on these airplanes, right? If we can't fix that plane, we could probably build a new one from scratch, using only paperclips and duct tape."

Kong's face broke into a quick, broad smile. "Yeah, you're right. Let's get to it. We'll get this bucket of bolts up in the air and catch up to Doc. He'll need our help before this is all over. He always does."

The five men began tinkering with the airplane and soon discovered Doc's handiwork. Fast-spreading foam had been dropped into one of the engine ports, preventing air intake. They could mix a solvent, but this would take several hours to discover the correct formula. Doc had used this chemical once before, during an adventure in Egypt, to prevent the bad guys from stealing his airplane. It would dissolve on its own in 48 hours, but they couldn't wait that long.

Instead, Wall and Kong removed and replaced the massive engine components. They carried these engine parts, weighing several hundred pounds each, into another work area and opened crates that contained replacement parts. They held these overhead as Mick and Gibs bolted them into place. Gibs and Wall rewired the new components. An airplane shop would have spent more than a day to complete this work but they accomplished it in mere hours.

Chapter Twenty-Five
Bart Solves a Mystery

April 6, 1945 4:30 am

While Kong, Wall, Gibs, and Mick worked on rebuilding or replacing the sabotaged parts of the plane engine, Bart studied charts, graphs and maps of the world. He had lived most of his adult life as a thinker, studying people, memorizing facts, and piecing together information. He was known as one of the most brilliant minds in mathematics and cryptology but with his keen mind he could have been successful at any career he chose. He had watched Doc carefully while he examined the amulet. Even though he had said nothing, Doc obviously found some meaning to the scribbles and gibberish on the medallion. But what had Doc discovered?

Even Doc would be impressed as Bart rewrote the strange symbols, relying solely on his memory to reproduce the unusual images and figures. He then replicated a rough drawing of the deformed face from the amulet's flip side. He leafed through several volumes of old books in a small storage closet. Some were written by a virtual genius in the world of archeology, Kenneth Xavier Percival Pierce, his friend 'Percy.' Bart was specifically looking for northern dialects. Some of the figures had looked familiar to him, even though he had no knowledge of the spoken languages. He suddenly found a correlation between the figures in the book and some of his own images.

He strolled over to a large map of the world, hanging against one wall, and stood staring at it for several minutes. Occasionally, he tilted his head to the left or right, seemingly looking for some vital missing clue. Suddenly, his face brightened. Bart had solved the puzzle! He waved at the four men across the massive building, indicating for them to approach.

"Whatcha got, math whiz." Kong asked.

Bart was so thrilled with his discovery, he ignored the jibe. "I know where Doc is heading."

Kong looked doubtfully at Bart. "Yeah, he already told us. South. Some place cold, because he packed winter gear. Maybe Antarctica."

Bart snapped. "Quiet, dimwit."

"What did you find, Bart?" Gibs joined the conversation.

Bart began explaining. "Remember the distorted face on one side of the medallion Doc showed us?"

Wall wiped grease from his large hands, "Yeah, did you figure out who it belonged to?"

"It's not a who, it's an it." Bart pointed at the piece of paper he held.

Kong frowned, "Huh? Speak English."

Bart held up a rough outline that resembled the face on the disk. "Does this look similar to the one on the coin?" Everyone agreed that it did. "It threw me at first because I had glimpsed it upside down. But if I rotate it around this way and compare it to the map; look at the Northern hemisphere."

"Ach, it's the outline of that island on the map!" Mick exclaimed in his thick Scottish brogue.

"That's right, it's Greenland," Bart explained.

Wall remembered something and snapped his fingers. "That's where Cassie said Harold Bekker came from."

Bart continued, "That's right. And if I remember correctly, there was a star above the outline. Maybe it signifies a land mass North of Greenland."

Kong nodded his head side to side. "Huh uh. I might have slept through some of Percy's lectures, but I do remember there is no island above Greenland. There's only the North Pole. And it's just a huge chunk of ice, floating in the Pacific Ocean."

"The Arctic Ocean, dunderhead," Bart slammed him.

Kong snorted. "Whatever. No land."

Bart agreed, "Yes. That is correct. And there are no dinosaurs on islands that time forgot, or witches living on the edge of a swamp ..."

Gibs joined in, "... or lost races of people, or blue people living in an upside-down city with arms like a spiders ..."

Bart continued, "... or ghosts of pirates, hinting at buried treasure, or ..."

"Okay, I get your point," Kong surrendered.

Wall shook his head in amazement. "You fellas sure lead interesting lives."

Gibs added, "Yeah, sometimes too interesting."

Bart tapped his cane on the floor. "That's not all. This theory would also jibe with those numbers."

"You mean the ninety million written near the star?" Kong asked.

Gibs slammed his fist into an open palm, "Of course. 90 00 00 00 would mean ninety degrees zero minutes latitude, zero degrees zero minutes longitude. Right at the very peak of the world, along the Prime Meridian. This would be exactly at the North Pole."

Kong asked doubtfully, "So we're gonna go visit Santa's Secret Village at the North Pole? What about the gibberish nonsense written on the other side of the amulet?"

Bart confessed, "I'm still working on that."

"Well, let's do it from the air. The plane is ready to go and so am I." Kong smiled to himself and shook his head.

Bart noticed and had to ask. "What? You almost look like you had a thought and it tickled something."

"Doc nearly sent us on a wild snipe hunt to the South Pole, at the other end of the globe. I'm sure glad you figured out this mysterious clue."

Bart said sternly, "Me, too. Doc might really need our help, before this is all over."

Twenty minutes later the large airplane was ready for takeoff. Bart flipped the ignition switch and nothing happened. He flipped it several more times with the same result.

"Damn." Bart looked disgusted.

Kong raised his hands in resignation. "Ah, for the love of Pete! What now?"

Gibs thought for a second and then asked, "Before you guys removed the alternator coil, did you ground it first?"

Mick shook his head, his freckled face more dour than usual. "Nae, we dinna. So now the battery is discharged?"

Gibs had a sudden flash of genius. "Hey, no problem. Check this out." He removed one of the electrical guns that he had designed with Wall's assistance. He opened a panel below his seat and exposed one of the large batteries. Twisting the knob on the handle of the gun, he then placed it against the battery post and pulled the trigger. An electrical discharge could be felt in the air.

Kong giggled, "I can feel that all the way down to my nether regions."

"That's something I could have lived a lifetime without knowing." Bart wrinkled his nose.

Gibs finished. "Okay, Bart, now give it a shot."

The ignition switch was flipped and the engines roared into life. Gibs was jotting down a notation in his pocket notebook.

"Whatcha writing in yer idea book, Gibs?" Kong asked.

"Another invention to patent. Emergency battery charger."

"How many patents do you have now?" Bart queried.

Gibs closed his idea book, "Four hundred and fourteen."

Wall nodded. "Not bad, but Thomas Edison had one thousand and ninety-three patented inventions when he died on October 18, 1931."

Gibs flipped open his little notebook, to a page in the rear. "Perhaps so, but this figure corresponds with my current bank account balance." Wall saw a numerical figure followed by a lot of zeros. His eyes became very large and he let out a low, long whistle. Gibs simply smiled.

Chapter Twenty-Six
Out of the Frying Pan

April 6, 1945   4:30 am

Megan heard a loud pounding noise inside her head, as consciousness slowly reasserted itself. *Boom. Boom. Boom.* Her brain throbbed with each reverberating impact. With great effort, she opened one eye, allowing blinding light to pour into her aching skull. She grimaced, blinked, and tried again. This time it wasn't quite as bad. *Boom.* Pam was across the room from her with a wooden post that used to be a bed leg, pounding on the steel door. *Boom.*

Megan groaned. "Pam, please stop doing that. I think my head is going to explode."

Cassie stirred nearby and slowly sat up, wobbling unsteadily. She smiled groggily, slurring her words together. "Wat hoppn'd? Wher 're we? Were we drinkin'? Why dos my hed hurt?"

Pam turned savagely to Cassie and Megan. Her face was flushed and the look in her eyes was molten lava. She was furious.

Pam spat venomously, "My cousin drugged us and locked us in a holding cell in the back of his offices."

Megan frowned at Pam. "So what exactly are you doing?"

"I'm trying to break down the door!"

Megan smiled knowingly, "And how's that working for you?"

Pam tossed down the heavy wooden post. "It's hopeless. The walls, floors, ceiling, and even the door are all reinforced steel. I should have guessed, Doc never does anything halfway."

Cassie moaned and covered her eyes, "I feel like I've been on a three-day drinking binge."

Megan held her throbbing head in her shaking hands. "Wait until you feel the hangover that follows. It's a doozy."

Pam held out two glasses of tap water, "Drink some water and it'll help dissipate the nausea caused by the anesthetic drugs."

Moments later all three women were nearly recovered.

Cassie glanced around the small cell. "So, how do we get out of here?"

Pam explained. "The door is on a timer, it will open automatically. Knowing Doc he would have set it for about 24 hours. I estimate we've been out for about three hours … maybe four."

"There's no other way out?" Megan asked.

"Well, if you were the size of a mouse, you could crawl out through the grate in the door," Pam retorted.

She was referring to a small opening that would allow food to be passed through the door without opening it. The hole was approximately eight- by ten-inches with a reinforced welded wire mesh covering the opening.

Cassie studied the grill and turned to Pam, "Can you tear out that wire mesh?"

"I think so, but what good would that do? The opening is too small to climb through and my arm isn't long enough to reach the timer panel."

"If you can remove the mesh, I can climb out through the hole." Cassie replied, removing her jacket and kicking off her shoes.

Megan eyed the small hole. "You're kidding, right? I couldn't fit my head through there."

Cassie smiled confidently. "One summer, when I was seventeen or eighteen, I worked as an assistant to circus magician. One of my tricks was to squeeze my entire body through the head of a tennis racket."

Pam raised one eyebrow. "This I have to see with my own eyes. One wire mesh, coming up."

Tearing strips from the bed sheet, Pam wrapped her fingers and hands for protection. She sat down in front of the door, placed both feet against its smooth, hard surface and reached forward, between her feet, grasping the wire mesh firmly. Muscles bunched on her arms and shoulders, tendons exposing themselves through the delicate female flesh, resembling bundles of piano wire. Her cousin Doc was certainly stronger but Pam Titan was no weakling. A grimace formed on her beautiful face as she pulled even harder. A metal against metal grinding noise became audible and the grill gave slightly. Seconds later it weakened further, and with a loud snap, it ripped completely loose from its housing.

Pam took great gasps of air and wiped her sweaty brow. "Tah dah. How's that for magic?" She tossed the metal grill into a far corner and stepped aside for Cassie.

Megan stared in amazement. "Sometimes you scare me, Pam. What did they feed you Titan children when you were younger?"

Cassie was equally curious. "Were you and Doc stronger than average when you were children?"

Pam shrugged. "I was raised as a tomboy in a lumberjack community. Women were just naturally tougher. I don't know about Doc. I didn't meet him until after my father died. I was about nineteen, he was about thirty. That's probably why he always treats me like a kid sister. Always concerned about my safety."

Cassie placed her jacket over the metal in the lower part of the opening to protect her delicate skin from the cold, rough edges of metal.

"Well, you've done your part. Guess it's my turn now. See you ladies on the other side." She flipped onto her back, so she was facing up, and pushed one arm and then the other through the tiny hole. With a smile, her face disappeared through the opening, followed by her narrow shoulders.

Megan stared in astonishment. "I never would have believed it, without seeing it for myself. This has certainly been worth the price of admission."

The upper part of Cassie's chest disappeared through the opening that was not much larger than a lunchbox. For a moment there was no further movement.

Megan tapped the door and placed her forehead against it. "Cassie, dear, are you okay? You seem to have stopped."

"Actually, I *do* have a small problem." Cassie confessed.

"What's that, dear?" Megan asked in mock sweetness.

"One of you ladies will need to help me get through this opening by pushing down on the girls," Cassie responded.

Pam laughed loudly. "Excuse me? 'The girls?' I thought you could fit through the head of a tennis racket." She covered her mouth to stifle further laughter.

Cassie replied in her own defense. "Well, I could, before I fully matured into a woman. Certain parts have … grown larger."

"You call this being fully mature? I was your size when I was only 12 years old," Pam chided the petite woman.

"Oh hush, Pam. Not every woman can be a six foot tall, bronzed Amazon Goddess and a two time winner of the Golden Globes award."

"Excuse me?" Pam said with mock indignity.

"I think she's referring to your …." Megan indicated Pam's healthy bosom.

Pam glared at Megan. "I *know* what she's referring to."

"If you're stuck now, what happens when you get to your hips?" Megan asked Cassie, in mocking sympathy.

"What!? What are you trying to say about my hips?"

Megan knelt down to assist Cassie. "Just teasing, darling. Bet the boys wish they were here to help you with this part of the escape. Speaking of the boys, did you ladies notice Doc's tight little …?"

Pam's face reddened and she quickly interrupted. "Hello!? I *am* his cousin … I *don't* want to hear things like that."

"Is that why you dropped your purse three times, Megan?" Cassie's voice asked from the other side of the door as her hips vanished through the hole.

Megan smiled mischievously. "He's such a big Boy Scout, he didn't even catch on. Remind me to bring my purse when we get out of here."

Pam rolled her golden-brown eyes. "That is so immature."

"Like I care," Megan taunted.

Pam tapped at the door. "Speaking of 'before you matured,' Cassie, what was it that Allen Coleman was saying about your father? Not to be callous, but I thought your father died or was murdered, and that was why you joined Unsolved Mysteries, Incorporated."

"I joined because I was bored, and I wanted to see more of Simon." Cassie confessed.

Megan shivered. "Yick. Doesn't the dead white face kinda creep you out a little? It's just plain eerie. Like a corpse. I keep finding myself staring at him when he's around."

Pam turned to Megan. "This coming from a girl dating a blind guy with burn marks on his face and body who becomes some kind of night creature. And those red eyes. Brrrr. Like a vampire. Besides, you already asked her this question before. Of course, you *were* drinking heavily earlier tonight."

"Gibson and I are not dating. It's strictly a professional relationship. And I was not drinking heavily." Megan replied defensively. "By the way, does this room have a mini bar?"

Pam ignored Megan. "Anyway, Cassie. Back to the question."

Cassie's feet disappeared through the opening. "I'm through! I told you I could fit through that hole, Pam."

"Good job. But I still want an answer to my question. Entertain us while you're picking the lock."

Cassie began working on the door lock. "When the crew of Unsolved Mysteries, Inc. first met me, they just naturally assumed that great-uncle Archer S. Portman was my father. He was a retired Professor of Archaeology from Columbia University. I always loved archaeology, so he agreed to become my legal guardian. They assumed his last name was Greyson, because that's the name I was using at the time. Have you ever noticed that every doddering old fart scientist or geologist or archeologist has a stunningly beautiful daughter? I always wondered if one of these boy scouts ever came across a case where some old fart died mysteriously, and the daughter was a hideous, homely frump, would they still take the case?"

Megan snorted with laughter. "I've noticed that, too."

Pam shook her head in agreement. "So the man portraying your father was actually your great uncle? So who's your father? Kan-Tar?"

"How did you guess?" Cassie asked in a surprised tone.

"Hah! Very funny." Pam mocked. "You're saying your father dresses up like Kan-Tar the Ape Man? Wears a loin cloth and swings on vines?"

The door slowly swung open and Cassie stood in the opening, smiling broadly, and very pleased with her rescue.

"No, he doesn't dress up like Kan-Tar. My father *is* Kan-Tar. The Ape Man. The Lord of the Jungle. Kevin Claybourne, the 8th Duke of Greyson. Lord Greyson. Mom is Lady Jane Portman-Claybourne. Lady Greyson. Her father, my grand-dad, was Professor Archimedes Portman. My real name is Cassandra Allison Claybourne. Everyone always calls me Cassie, short for Cassandra."

"You're pulling my leg, right?" Pam stated incredulously. "Your father is Kan-Tar? For real?"

Megan looked puzzled. "I don't get it. Who's Kan-Tar?"

Pam frowned at Megan. "Now you're pulling the other leg. Don't you ever go out to the movies? She says her father is that jungle man from the movies."

"Johnny Weissmuller?"

"I give up." Turning to Cassie, Pam spoke softly. "Personally, I wouldn't give Blake too much grief about lying to you about his true condition and hiding behind some make-up. Maybe he merely wanted to feel … accepted. Especially, not when you're lying to him about your father."

Cassie tried to defend her position. "It's not like I meant to lie about it. But how do I fix this? It's not like I can just say, 'Oh, by the way, the man you thought was my father was actually my great-uncle; and my true dad runs around the savage jungle wearing nothing but a loin cloth and a knife. Swinging on vines and beating his chest. Oh, and he's the Lord of the Apes.'"

"They'd probably have you committed!" Megan chuckled.

Pam stepped through the doorway and looked around. "Let's grab our stuff and go after Doc and the boys."

"Wow, look what they left behind. I saw Gibs playing with one of these."

Megan was referring to the electric guns. Gibs had assembled a bakers dozen, but left a few behind to experiment with later. Megan jerry-rigged a double shoulder harness for the rapid-fire pistols and armed herself with two of the electric guns.

Megan smiled. "Now I'm ready. I never did like real guns. The final results are too messy."

"I'll stick with my grand-dads custom-made six shooter." Pam found her purse with the large gun still inside.

Dainty Cassie looked at the huge revolver. "Geez! I couldn't even hold that dinosaur up to shoot it. I'd take off my own foot."

"Try these out for size." Pam handed Cassie one of the rapid-fire machine gun pistols. "Light weight, easy to use, never jams, and no kick to them. They even come with mercy bullets or rubber bullets, if you don't want to shoot to kill."

Cassie hefted the lighter gun. "Perfect. I'll take two."

"Okay ladies. Let's roll. Damn it!" Pam exclaimed.

Megan turned. "What's wrong, Pam?"

"Doc locked the Hell-Rocket so it won't return to the skyscraper."

Megan raised an eyebrow. "What the heck is a Hell-Rocket?"

"It's a shortcut to the Global Navigator warehouse. We'll just have to take the express chute and drive over there." Pam started toward the pneumatic elevator.

Cassie stepped into the compact elevator. "How come there are handles and straps on the walls?"

Pam smiled, her copper-hued eyes twinkling. "Trust me, you'll want to hang on for dear life."

Megan asked, a worried look on her face. "Why is that?"

Pam smiled and pressed the down button. The elevator hovered for an instant and then it plummeted like a stone. "Climb down to the floor, if you can. It stops rather abruptly. The shaft is airtight and the compression of air is the only thing that slows this elevator down."

The elevator felt like it had collided with the ground floor, it slowed so abruptly. All three women were driven to the floor of the car by the increased gravity. The only person known to be able to stand up straight when the brakes were applied was Doc Titan. Even Kong, with his short powerful legs, was driven to his knees.

Megan coughed and lifted her head slowly. "Would we be able to take this elevator back up to the fiftieth floor?"

Pam wobbled slightly as she stood erect. "Sure. Why?"

Megan groaned. "I think that's where I lost my stomach."

Cassie laughed. "I thought looking green was only an expression, Megan."

"Ha. ha. I'm just glad I was wearing my best support bra." Megan confessed, making adjustments to her attire. "Now I know how old ladies feel when their 'girls' sag down to their knees."

Pam's roadster flew out of Doc Titan's private parking garage, located in the basement of the skyscraper. All four wheels left the ground for a second. She gunned the engine as gravity brought the car down and the powerful vehicle bolted forward. Megan and Cassie hung on as Pam took the first corner on two wheels. The three occupants of the plain, black sedan watched from the curb side, in front of the Titan Tower building. As Pam's car sped past, the sedan quickly followed.

Megan was still recovering from the elevator ride. "Pam, honey, you might want to slow down a little."

Pam focused her attention on the road and replied. "Megan, I will not let those men leave me behind again. I've missed way too many adventures in the past. Not this time."

Megan objected. "The police will …"

Pam smiled confidently as she passed a police officer, who waved her through the intersection. "They've all been instructed to let Doc's cars through as a priority. Doc has so many honorary police merits, they've lost count. He even has letters of accommodations from the President of the United States and the Director of the FBI."

"Bet that's handy." Megan said, flashing a quicksilver smile.

Pam glanced into her rear view mirror. "Especially, when you're being tailed. You girls might want to strap yourselves in. There's a black sedan following us and they don't look friendly."

The words had barely been uttered when machine gun fire echoed through the man-made canyons of the New York City streets. Slugs ricocheted off of the bulletproof trunk of Pam's car, like angry steel hornets. She whipped the wheel of the car and turned down an alleyway.

"Megan, be a dear and open the glove compartment and flip the little red switch inside." Pam instructed.

Megan did as Pam requested and glanced back just in time to see a large sheet of lightweight steel armor rise up from behind the rear passenger seat. More slugs stitched themselves along the rear of the car and bounced off of the metal shield.

Cassie tapped the bulletproof barrier. "That's pretty convenient. I take it that you get shot at fairly often?"

Pam turned another corner. "Often enough. A girl's got to protect herself these days."

The sedan attempted to pass Pam's car on the driver's side but she cut them off quickly. The ladies were allowed a brief glance at the men in the other car.

Megan waved and smiled. "Oh, look. It's our friends from Pam's beauty salon. Guess they escaped. This must be why Gibson shoots gangsters. Otherwise, they just keep coming back."

Bullets attacked and embedded themselves in the rubber of the rear tires. This would have caused a blowout in a normal car. However, Pam's auto, like all of her cousin's cars, had solid rubber, bulletproof tires that resisted punctures. She handled the car like a racing professional, expertly and effortlessly dodging and weaving around various obstacles while blocking the shadowing vehicle. She turned another corner and found exactly what she had been searching for.

"You ladies might want to keep your heads down. I'm about to let them come up on the passenger side." Pam warned.

"Why on earth would you …" Megan glanced ahead and understood what Pam had planned. "Oh, no. Tell me you're not going to …"

"Hang on, here we go." Pam pushed a small button on the dashboard and a plume of smoke issued forth from the front passenger wheel-well. It spread so quickly that the sedan behind them had limited visibility. She pulled the wheel to the left and, as if on cue, the driver of the sedan saw the opening and decided to approach the unguarded passenger side of Pam's car. Graves was hanging out of the passenger side window, attempting to aim his machine gun over the hood of his car. From the corner of her eye she saw the driver, the semi-bald Kirby; pull his revolver from its shoulder holster. He wanted the killing shot to be his own. Pam must have really ticked him off with her waxing torture.

He was busy watching Pam's heavy car and avoiding crashing into her as she weaved and dodged. He glanced forward and his eyes nearly popped out of his skull. He had just enough time to look at the other car and see Pam smiling and waving goodbye. He instinctively covered his face with both hands. Then his heavy sedan struck the solid concrete loading platform that extended into the alleyway. The automobile exploded in a fiery blaze, killing the driver and both passengers instantly.

Pam said dryly, "I don't think they'll bother us again, Megan."

Pam slowed the car to a stop and lowered the rear shield so she could look for survivors. She felt a twinge of guilt over killing anyone, even hardened criminals like these men. But they made their choice and would have killed all three women, if given half a chance. Shifting into gear, she continued driving toward the Global Navigator Consortium warehouse.

Five minutes later, she stopped in front of the large, brick building that purposely appeared derelict and abandoned. She opened the small side door and Cassie and Megan followed her into the warehouse. At the far end of the building, a large airplane was exiting the hanger and preparing for takeoff. She thumbed the call button on a nearby radio set and called to the occupants of the plane, requesting that they turn around.

Chapter Twenty-Seven
Kiss Kiss, Bang Bang

April 6, 1945 5:00 am

Kong's voice came over the speaker system. "Pam, this mission is too dangerous for you. Stay in Manhattan and we'll keep you updated."

Under her breath, Pam muttered, "Like Hell you will. We'll just grab another plane from the hanger and trail you."

"Sorry Pam. Doc sabotaged all of the other planes so we couldn't follow him. It took us six hours to get this one running."

Slowly walking out onto the pier, followed by Cassie and Megan, Pam pulled out her father's massive six-shooter. She swung open the breach and unloaded all six chambers into her hand. "Hold these, please." She said confidently, dropping the large caliber bullets into Megan's small hands. Pam reloaded her gun with some rather odd-looking bullets, longer than standard issue ammunition for her revolver. They watched as the triple-engine plane made its turn in the air and headed back toward them to head north. Powerful engines thrummed and the large plane gained altitude. Pam leveled her gun with both hands and pointed directly at the aircraft.

"Pam, what are you doing?" Cassie asked, wide-eyed.

Pam replied, her face breaking into a quick, broad smile, her golden-brown eyes sparkling brightly, "I'm getting their attention." There was a roar of thunder as the revolver exploded in her hands.

"Holy Cow! Pam's firing on us!" Kong said, jumping at the loud boom.

Bart slapped Kong's arm. "That'll teach you to treat her like a delicate flower. You've ticked her off and now she's gonna try to blast us out of the sky."

Gibs looked only slightly concerned. "She *does* know this plane is bulletproof, right? It'd take more than her cannon to punch a hole through the undercarriage."

"Not a whole lot more. Besides, right now I don't think she cares." The gun boomed again and Kong reflexively ducked as a bullet careened off the window in front of him. "Damned if she's not a crack shot with that old blunderbuss."

Wall shook his head in amazement. "You fellas are insane. One of your own friends shoots up your plane and you merely joke about it."

"Aww, Pam is just a fireball." Kong said with a smile.

Another bullet struck the bottom of the aircraft. "Ach, the lass is bleeding bonkers!" Mick barked in his Scottish brogue.

Bart agreed. "Heck, she probably thinks Doc is in the plane. Bet she's still ticked at him."

Gibs added gloomily. "Personally, I'd rather take my chances with the Nazis and gangsters shooting at us."

As the plane zoomed overhead Pam took careful aim and fired her last shot. This bullet struck the undercarriage and Mick jumped, as if struck by a thunderbolt. "Ach, she's a temperamental lass, ta be shore."

Cassie was yelling at Pam on the ground. "Are you insane? You could have shot down the aircraft."

Pam smiled widely. "Nah. That plane is heavily armored. It could withstand worse than my six-shooter. Besides, I wasn't firing real bullets." She held up a single bullet, similar to the ones she had fired. Cassie and Megan could make out that the strange bullet was actually glass, not metal. Contained within the glass bullet were wires and coils. "Doc and Gibs created these a few years back. They contain a miniature tracking device and transmit a repeating signal. We can track them with this." She held up a palm-sized black box. On its surface were eight arrows, evenly spaced. As Pam moved her arm, the arrows pointing in the direction of the plane flashed red.

Cassie smiled admiringly. "You're just full of surprises, Pam. I'm astonished Doc gave you all of this equipment."

Pam confided. "Oh, he didn't. But I have my ways of getting the things I want."

"This allows you to track the plane, but how do we follow them, without transportation of our own?" Megan asked.

"Leave that to me." Pam Titan sighed happily. "Time for me to call in an old favor." As they ran back to the roadster, Pam pondered the fact that Doc had left his friends behind. How dangerous was this mystery? What secret was Doc hiding?

"Look." Cassie had stopped running and pointed at the warehouse several blocks away. The Praetorian Securities warehouse was still burning. They had not noticed the fire when they first entered Doc's warehouse/hanger and ran for the pier. "They've destroyed everything. The offices and the warehouse are gone." Her features became fixed and eyes burned with a new fire. "And they've taken my friends, maybe even hurt or killed them." Her hard glaze turned toward Pam. "If you have access to transportation, let's get to it."

Chapter Twenty-Eight
Victor Kaine's Secret Plan

April 6, 1945   6:00 am

Black Skull paced back and forth across the length of his private offices. His arms were locked behind his back and he appeared deep in thought. His two giant guards, Ernst and Orban, stood silently watching as he paced. The large mutes never left his side. Clad entirely in black leather uniforms with matching boots, gloves, and even face masks, they were his most loyal officers. Professor Schmidt was sitting behind a small desk in one corner, making notations in a small journal. Totenkopf liked having Schmidt nearby, where he knew the elder man was safe. He felt a kindred soul in Schmidt; they had common goals and aspirations. He remembered the first time he and the professor had come to this island. When standing where Totenkopf currently stood, the distant mountain resembled a large skull. He had insisted on having this large window installed, so he could look at that part of the mountain from his private headquarters.

There was a knocking sound and a guard at the door admitted a soldier, still dressed in civilian apparel. This was the man Doc Titan had followed from the Chromium Club and had escaped from the rooftop. He saluted Totenkopf and clicked his heels together. Totenkopf glared at the man for several seconds, before acknowledging the salute. He believed in keeping his subordinates off-guard.

Black Skull turned to the messenger. "Report, Agent Gross. Was your mission a success?"

The man began sweating and wiped his brow. Black Skull did not like to hear bad news or reports of failure. The messenger usually did not survive. Unfortunately for Agent Gross, Totenkopf had rigged the Death's Head crimson icon at his neck with a timer device. If Black Skull did not unlock it, the bomb would automatically detonate in forty-eight hours. Gross had no choice but to return to the island so Black Skull could remove the device. The epoxy was firmly attached to the skin and any tampering with the small skull bomb could cause it to explode. And Gross had witnessed, first hand, the effects of the virus that would be released.

Agent Gross explained nervously, "Herr Totenkopf, we attacked the American obermensch in the place called The Chromium Club. Your suicide squad was defeated. Karl Teppleman and I barely escaped ..."

Black Skull interrupted. "And where is Herr Teppleman?"

Agent Gross licked his lips. "Der bronzemann, Doc Titan, killed Karl on a rooftop. I returned to the plane and flew straight here to report to you."

Victor Kaine and his Russian friend, Konstanin Egorov, had entered the room as Gross told of the events in New York. Black Skull noticed the tall man watching him, studying him carefully. This man, Kaine, was a very dangerous man. Totenkopf decided to let Kaine and Egorov see what happened to men who failed their commanding officer on this island. He turned his gaze back to the soldier. He was glad the mask hid the angry flush on his face, but his fiery eyes still made Agent Gross cringe.

Black Skull glared. "So, instead of returning with a report of successfully killing the four American heroes, you return to admit failure of your assignment."

Agent Gross was sweating. "But, sir, I thought you should know that the Death's Head bombs on your soldiers were pre … "

If Gross had been permitted to finish his sentence, Black Skull might have had many more questions. The soldier was about to explain that an outside agent had somehow prematurely activated the bombs. Instead, Totenkopf decided he had heard enough from this soldier who had failed his assignment. He pointed an object that resembled a fountain pen at the soldier and clicked a small red button on one end. The bomb epoxied to the man's neck began to flash red.

Black Skull stated calmly, "You failed your mission. You are well aware what penalty failure brings."

"But I have always been loyal, I have never asked for anything ..."

Black Skull leered. "And you receive it, in abundance!"

Agent Gross screamed as he clutched the skull-shaped, crimson object glued to his neck and tried to pull it free. A second later the virus bomb exploded, releasing a cloud of scarlet dust. Gross screamed louder, in absolute horror, but only for a second. The sound of frying bacon filled the air. The flesh quickly dissolved from his face and upper torso and by the time his body struck the floor, the horrible deed was complete. Black Skull smiled insanely at this display, then turned and looked at Kaine, voicing a warning.

"This is how I reward failure."

Victor Kaine looked directly into Totenkopf's eyes without flinching and spoke confidently. He knew this was a moment to show his own strength and ingenuity. He motioned to Egorov and the large Russian left the room.

"Then you will be glad to know that I succeeded where your men failed." Victor offered.

Totenkopf studied the tall, pale man. "How so?"

Kaine continued. "As a backup plan, I sent my man Egorov to New York City. While your soldiers tried to kill Doc Titan and the others, we kidnapped six of their friends."

As if on cue, Egorov and several soldiers led six hooded figures into the room. The prisoners were forcefully knocked to the floor. Egorov removed the hoods of two of the captives. Big Tom and Percy blinked in the bright light and looked around the room. Big Tom noticed Egorov and did a double take.

"I thought you were dead." Big Tom stated bluntly.

"Oh BOHICA!" Percy exclaimed, using his favorite acronym.

Egorov bared his broad smile. He was a huge ox of a man with a massive amount of dark hair covering his head and face. He reminded Big Tom of a large bear. "As your American Mark Twain said, rumors of my demise were greatly exaggerated."

Let me out of these handcuffs and I'll remedy that error." Big Tom glared at the Russian.

Percy looked over his shoulder and his mouth fell open. He nudged Big Tom and cocked his head. They both stared at the tall man who stood behind them.

"Victor Kaine. I thought you were chopped to bits by that angry Mongolian horde in Tibet." Percy said bluntly.

Kaine smiled. "I am harder to kill than other men. Three times Doc Titan has made the mistake of assuming I was so easily defeated. However, I did not escape completely unmarked." He indicated the long scar that started on his forehead, through the eyebrow, and several inches down the cheek. The knife that caused the scar must have missed the eyeball by a fraction of an inch."

"And now you're working with this Razi scum?" Percy sneered.

Egorov struck Percy so hard he saw stars. "Silence, little dog," he ordered.

Kaine calmly added. "We are collaborating on a project of great importance. Toward a common goal." Kaine turned to Black Skull. "If I might I would like to introduce Kenneth Xavier 'Percy' Percival Pierce, treasure hunter and tomb raider. Recently, he snatched the Tibetan Egg from Hitler's grasp. Our paths very nearly crossed in that very country in 1938."

"So that was you?"

"Yes, Mr. Pierce. His friend is Randolph Garnett 'Big Tom' Thompson, aviation expert and has test-piloted nearly every craft the Allies are currently flying. These men might have secrets your government will be interested in acquiring."

"And these others?" Black Skull indicated the other four prisoners.

"Merely friends and family of the heroes who call themselves Guardian and Scorpion. Not as important as these two men."

Totenkopf confronted Kaine. "Why have you brought these prisoners to this island? Everyone knows these crusaders of justice will fly to the ends of the earth to rescue their friends."

Egorov spoke to the Nazi leader. "Exactly so. When you hunt the wolverine or badger in the deep snow, you do not crawl on your belly into his lair with your axe and hope to take him by surprise. You leave a trail of blood for him to follow and when he comes to investigate ... you chop off his head."

"Are you going to follow the advice of this Russian moron?" Big Tom taunted.

Totenkopf looked around the room from face to face and pondered for several moments. He replied to Big Tom. "You had best hope I do, otherwise you have no value to me. Kaine, you have proven yourself as an asset. However, in the future, you will keep me apprised of any missions. You and your associates are not to leave this island without my approval."

Victor Kaine nearly lost his composure but realized he was playing dangerous games with a deadly mastermind. He simply nodded in agreement. Totenkopf instructed his men to take the prisoners to the old dungeons and lock them in cells. Guards were to be assigned to watch them at all times.

Black Skull waved them away. "You are all dismissed. I wish to be left alone."

Once more, Victor fought to remain calm. He was not a man to be dismissed like some underling. He reminded himself that the proper time would come and he would take command of this island. But now was not that time. He made a mental note to himself that these insults would cost Black Skull dearly. The prisoners were taken down a separate hallway, followed by a dozen armed guards.

Kaine watched them and then turned to Egorov. "Did everything go as planned in New York?" He whispered the question to his old Russian friend.

Egorov nodded. "Dah, Viktor. The remote bomb detonator Schmidt gave us worked as he said it would. Titan and his three friends survived the attack."

Schmidt approached, having heard what was said.

"When the time comes, I hope you will remember this moment." Professor Schmidt whispered.

Victor reminded Schmidt. "If Doc Titan is to die, it will be by my hand alone and no one shall stand in the way of my revenge."

Schmidt nodded. "Do not forget our agreement."

Kaine grabbed the collar of the elderly scientist and pushed him back against the wall. "I held my tongue with that insane madman, but I will not be talked to in that manner by you, old man."

Schmidt looked directly into Kaine's eyes without glancing away or flinching. Kaine was not accustomed to men standing up to him and found this rather unnerving. But he was certain he could break any man's will eventually. Victor shook his head in bewilderment, released the professor and watched him walk away. These Germans were all crazy.

Egorov growled angrily. "Black Skull is a very dangerous man, but there is something about that old man. Something in his eyes."

Kaine waved his hand, as if shooing a pesky fly. "Bah, he's merely a crazy old scientist. He only wants to get away from Black Skull. I can't blame him. I don't like dealing with that masked lunatic, either. When the moment comes we will make our move and neither Doc Titan nor the Third Reich will be able to stop us."

Black Skull was astounded as he witnessed one of the modern miracles of science. The phenomenal advances in microbiology and biochemistry that Professor Schmidt and his brain trust had accomplished were incredible. The bright glow of the super-heated, glass cylinder slowly dimmed. Totenkopf could finally see the small figure floating weightlessly in the steel and glass womb. The difference was unbelievable.

"That was amazing. Simply amazing." Black Skull acknowledged.

"Phase One of Project Gladiator took a fertilized egg and accelerated it to an embryonic state. Phase Two enhanced the bone, tissue and muscular structure to withstand the next phase. Today's process amplified the growth factor from embryo to newborn. And all of this has only taken two months." Schmidt reviewed the progress.

"And the fourth phase?" Kaine questioned, peering into the thick glass cylinder. He understood basic science, but this technology was years ahead of anything he had ever witnessed. He placed a long-fingered, gloved hand against the warm glass womb, sensing the power contained within it.

"In one week we proceed with Phase Four. The subject will be injected with the completed Danner Formula and subjected to a Beta Ray bombardment. If the final phase of Project Gladiator is successful, we will witness development from newborn to full grown adult in mere minutes." Professor Walters added. Walters' intellect was second only to Professor Schmidt's.

Black Skull was extremely pleased with the successes of Professors Schmidt and Walters. They were truly modern-day wizards. Adolf Hitler and the Third Reich would soon hear of the progress, and ultimate success, of Project Gladiator. And Black Skull's reward would be anything he desired. Anything.

Chapter Twenty-Nine
Born Better

April 6, 1945   6:00 am

Doctor Karl Drakoft, the 12th Count Drakoft, fumed as he paced back and forth in his private quarters. He carefully stepped over a dark puddle on the floor and then continued pacing. The great stone rooms were simply furnished with antiquities that had been in his family for several centuries. He was a thick-set man, five feet nine and one hundred and eighty pounds. His heavy leather boots stomped on the granite floors and echoed into the vast rooms. He was furious. Once more, he read the message tightly clasped in one hand. Not that he needed to re-read it, his memory was perfect. He was perfect. He was the embodiment of Arian supremacy. He had been born ... better.

His eyes burned as the words twisted the dagger deeper into his heart. It was from that upstart Black Skull. The mongrel dog that Hitler had taken under his wing. A simple peasant. Count Drakoft's inferior. And yet, here was a message from this member of the lower caste. No. Not simply a message. An order. Black Skull presumed too much.

Allied Forces have successfully completed experimental drone aircraft. Proceed to Northern England immediately. Capture ship and return to Berlin. If captured, destroy prototype aircraft.

Drakoft did not need to read between the lines. This was a mission designed to fail. Infiltrate an enemy base, certainly heavily guarded, and steal a prototype drone airplane. Destroy the prototype, if captured? In the twisted mind of Black Skull this could mean only one thing, failure meant death. Black Skull was plotting to rid himself of Drakoft, the man who should be his superior. Damn Black Skull! And damn Adolf Hitler! Drakoft had met disgrace at the hands of The Sentry one time and Hitler had turned his back on him.

All because of the damned mask!

He reached up to his face and for the thousandth time, he tore at the covering adhered to his skin. The thick, dark-umber leather remained tightly affixed. Drakoft cursed and cried aloud in frustration. How could his have happened to him? Why was he doomed to be forever entombed in this horrible mask, like Alexandre Dumas' *The Vicomte de Bragelonne, The Man in the Iron Mask?* This was not supposed to be his fate! He had been destined for greater things.

Count Drakoft was a brilliant, scientific genius, one of the top scientists in the Nazi Party. He had made great advances in the field of laser technology, genetic manipulation, and the creation of androids. Drakoft's first and most notorious invention was his 'death-ray' gun that could literally disintegrate its targets. The death-ray was actually a laser beam. The term laser was an acronym for Light Amplification by Stimulated Emission of Radiation. He was decades ahead of his peers and enemies in his advanced research. Sergeant Rick Gunn and his special squad of commandos had invaded Drakoft's castle in order to destroy the only existing death-ray gun prototype. Drakoft blew up the castle, with the ray-gun inside, rather than allow the commandos to capture it.

American and British newspapers had portrayed Drakoft himself as a satanic figure. The embodiment of Hitler's superior race. As a result, Count Drakoft became the most wanted man within Nazi Germany by the Allied agents. Assassination or capture, either would be considered a success. Hitler offered Drakoft a new secret laboratory, hidden deep in the rebuilt foundations of Castle Drakoft. And a mask to conceal his true identity. His code name became, the Black Mask.

It had only been a short time later when the Allied hero, The Sentry, invaded his castle. Drakoft had been working on an experimental genetic compound called Weapon X. During a brief struggle, a vial of this substance was shattered by the Sentry's bullet and splashed the leather mask Drakoft was wearing. The chemical caused the leather to bond with his very skin on a molecular level. Drakoft could still see through the eyeholes and hear, speak and breathe through the mask's thick fabric but he could no longer use his mouth to eat and had to be fed intravenously. The Weapon X compound made the fabric preternaturally resilient, and Drakoft simply chose not to risk damaging his face further by surgically removing the mask. Further tests only confirmed his original theory, the grafting of human skin and leather was permanent. For a short time, Drakoft was driven violently insane by this disfigurement. During those months of isolation, Totenkopf - codenamed the Black Skull, had risen in the Nazi organization.

With Hitler's approval, the notorious Count Drakoft began leading combat and espionage missions against the Allies and was rivaled in these only by Totenkopf. Naturally, the two men quickly became fierce rivals. And now Black Skull had the arrogance to consider himself Drakoft's commanding officer. His superior. But Drakoft was more than a mere soldier, a pawn to be manipulated by lesser men. He had been born better.

Suddenly, Drakoft smiled broadly. This could be a great opportunity. Black Skull expected him to fail; he might even sabotage the mission to rid himself of the Count. But what if Drakoft turned this mission to his own advantage? Totenkopf was no match for a man of Drakoft's superior intellect. Perhaps it was time to eliminate the Black Skull and perhaps Hitler as well. They were both mad dogs, and Count Drakoft knew exactly how to treat mad dogs. As he plotted, he paced quickly about the enormous room, cautiously avoiding the dark puddle on the cold, stone floor. When he stopped, he was facing one of his newest inventions. A giant, android robot. It towered over Drakoft, standing nearly ten feet tall. He gazed up into its lifeless, dark eye sockets. Drakoft's icy-blue eyes sparkled. He stroked a gloved hand over the cold, smooth, metallic surface.

He called for Simms, his devoted man-servant. Then he remembered. Simms lay dead across the room, six bullet holes in his chest. A large, dark pool of blood had spread out on the stone floor. Drakoft had been carefully avoiding the puddle as he paced about the large room. Simms had the misfortune of bringing Drakoft the message from Black Skull. In a fitful rage of anger, Drakoft had, as they say, killed the messenger. He called for his other servant, Schuster. He quickly jotted a reply to Black Skull's missive, translating it into the cipher code that the German High Command had created, using only his sharp intellect.

Instructions understood. Will proceed to destination immediately.
Will send message of success after returning to Berlin.

When his mission was completed, he would take his place as leader of the National Socialist (Nazi) Party and the Third Reich. He would embrace his rightful destiny. Even if he had to do so over the cold, dead bodies of Black Skull, Adolf Hitler, The Sentry, and the entire Allied Forces. He would rule and at the end of his days, his children would inherit his legacy. His sons would follow in their father's footsteps. Because the Drakoft's were born better.

Little did Count Drakoft realize how accurate was his vision of the future.

Chapter Thirty
Calling in a Favor

April 6, 1945   6:00 am

Pamela Titan was driving very fast. With the top of the convertible down, it felt even faster. Pam, Megan, and Cassie were leaving the New York City limits and there was no traffic. She loved this car. It was a 1928 Mercedes-Benz 680 S Saoutchik Torpedo Roadster. It was equipped with an oversized six-cylinder engine, fitted with a supercharger that engaged when the throttle was floored. Off the production floor, it was capable of achieving 180 horsepower and 112 miles per hour. But Pam had a mechanic friend make several modifications and now it was capable of greatly exceeding those numbers.

Her hair was whipping like a flag in a hurricane and the telephone poles in her peripheral vision were going by like a picket fence. Her mouth was stretched nearly ear to ear in a huge smile. Pam loved danger.

Megan shouted over the roar of the road, from the small back seat. "Pam, dear, if you drive any faster, we'll be flying."

"Yes, isn't it great."

"That's not what I meant." However, Megan was not shouting this time, so Pam did not hear her.

As originally designed, the chassis and suspension worked well, but the roadster was not agile enough. To compensate for this, Pam had the wheelbase lowered and the engine block moved back on the chassis, centering the weight better. Now she could follow the curving highway without needing to slow down. And the appearance of the car was rather spellbinding and dramatic, with its long hood, wheel wells, running boards, and custom gold-plated appointments. It had been painted coal-black with crimson undertones. Only 124 of this model had ever been built and Pam owned several, in case one should break down. Like everything she owned, it was sleek, powerful, and most importantly, quite fast.

Cassie Greyson was riding 'shotgun' in the front and was having the time of her life. "Woowhoo! This is a blast. I have got to hang out with you more often, Pat. Everyone in Unsolved Mysteries, Inc. drives like old ladies compared to this."

Even though Pam was only five years older than Cassie, the petite woman looked up to Pam and Pam felt like she had adopted a kid sister. They were like long-lost siblings. The roadster approached a car from behind and Pam changed lanes and then back again without even slowing. She pushed a button on the dashboard and a red light glowed in the early morning dawn. The dashboard resembled something from an airplane cockpit. The voice of Rex Hazzard came over a speaker mounted near the glove compartment.

"Pam, is that you?"

"Hi, darling. How's my handsome hunk?" Pam said, smiling broadly.

"Doing good. Are you driving?" Hazzard asked. "There's some background static."

"I'm just taking the Torpedo out for a spin, Rex darling. I need a favor. I have a small emergency and I am in urgent need of one of your speediest toys."

"For you, my dear, anything you want. I have the perfect craft all warmed up and ready to go. In fact, I just finished it yesterday. Big Tom took it out for its maiden voyage this morning and put it through every maneuver he could think of. It passed with flying colors."

"Hang onto your hats, girls." Pam whipped around another slower-moving vehicle and re-entered her own lane, narrowly avoiding a large, cargo truck in the oncoming lane. Megan Meriwether's eyes were as large as platters and her heart was pounding hard.

"Are you nearby?" Hazzard queried.

"We'll be there in thirty minutes … maybe twenty-five, Rex."

"How fast are you driving, darling?"

"Don't know. Speedometer doesn't register above one-twenty."

"Hot damn! I'll see ya soon, Pam."

Pam switched off the radio and speaker. "Someday, I'm going to marry that man. He's a keeper."

"I hope we live that long." Megan muttered and then shouting to be heard again, she asked, "Are you sure you don't want me to drive for a while, Pam?"

Pam smiled and looked in the rear view mirror. "Hang on, Megan, I'm going to shift it into high gear."

Megan turned pale as Cassie and Pam laughed like two little schoolgirls.

Chapter Thirty-One
The Strange Prisoner

April 6, 1945   6:15 am

The weary prisoners were forced into a dank, medieval room that housed four old cells. The steel bars at the front of each cell were massive and, even after several hundred years of rust, they were still quite solid. The other three sides of each cell were carved into the stone mountainside. Their thick hoods were removed and the six men and women glanced around the main room, blinking to adjust to the light. The stench of mildew and mold was strong in the air. The sound of dripping water could be heard. One of the guards prodded Big Tom forward with the business end of his rifle. The large engineer had tested his bindings several times during the flight to the island, but four stainless-steel handcuffs were more than even the powerful Big Tom could break.

Whitney had worked on escaping her handcuffs by using a small piece of her bracelet. She had succeeded in unlocking one wrist and had secretly gotten Percy and Gabe free as well. They had been waiting for the best moment to spring their surprise. Once they were confined in the cells, their element of surprise would be lost. One of the Nazi guards prepared to unlock Whitney's handcuffs. She grabbed his arm and twisted sharply, snapping the elbow joint. The soldier cried out in pain and dropped to his knees. Rav Chandra kicked the man under the chin and knocked him out. Chaos ensued.

Big Tom, still handcuffed, ducked his head and rammed another guard in the stomach. Gabe punched one Nazi in the face and shoved another off balance. In a fight, he displayed the speed and strength of a black panther. Percy turned to the guard Big Tom had head-butted, and finished him with a blow to the head. They were making quick work of the guards. Unfortunately, Victor Kaine, Egorov, and the giant sisters, Hermia and Xena, chose this minute to enter the room. Egorov grabbed the big-fisted engineer and slammed him into a stone wall. Gabe punched the Russian several times, but the huge bear of a man merely staggered backward and attacked again.

Percy was lifted above Hermia's head and tossed across the room, as a child would toss a rag doll. Gabe and Xena squared off but his blows had very little effect on her, while she swung haymakers that would remove his head if they connected. Whitney struck Egorov in several nerve points and the large man collapsed to one knee. She was a hell-fury in a tussle. Hermia punched Big Tom, who was unable to defend himself with his hands still bound. He saw stars, before she knocked him unconscious with a haymaker. Hermia and Xena Reeves might have been vaudeville stage names, but the Amazon women were unbelievably strong.

"Enough!" Kaine lifted Whitney and Isabelle off the floor, with his long fingers around their necks. They were struggling but he held them as though they were weightless. Isabelle was already feeling faint from the lack of blood to her brain. "I will break their necks unless you surrender ... NOW!"

The fighting ceased and the defeated prisoners were soon securely locked in their cells. Victor preferred live prisoners to dead ones. He enjoyed proving his superiority by domination. Gabe and Isabelle were in the first cell, Whitney and Rav Chandra in the next, and Big Tom and Percy in the last. Well, actually it was the second to last. The last cell already had a prisoner. The filthy man sat in the middle of his small prison, not even moving during the roughhousing. He appeared to be the victim of several sessions of physical torture. Egorov swore long strings of very bad Russian words at the prisoners, especially Whitney Van Pelt. She had made him look bad in front of Victor Kaine. None of the prisoners understood Russian, but they could tell that Egorov was using words that were unlikely to be found in most Russian dictionaries.

Black Skull entered the room. "Is there a problem, Herr Kaine?"

"No. No problem. Merely locking up the prisoners. Who is that fellow in the last cell?"

Totenkopf waved his open hand dismissively. "He is not your concern. Professor Schmidt is prepared for the delivery of your final Danner Journal; Phase Four is ready to proceed. Kindly fetch the journal now."

Kaine's eye twitched, accenting his Marquis De Sade scar. "And my diamonds?"

"Will arrive tomorrow." Totenkopf stated, without hesitation.

Victor really did not like this man. He managed to say things that irritated Kaine, such as 'fetch' the journal. But Kaine had to be patient. His moment was coming soon. As Victor left the room, followed by his lieutenant, Egorov, and the two giantesses, he noticed Black Skull glaring daggers at the stranger sitting in the fourth cell. Who was that man? Why was Totenkopf keeping him prisoner? There were too many mysteries for Kaine to feel comfortable. Egorov was still cursing under his breath.

Victor studied his old Russian friend. "Are you okay, Egorov?"

Egorov's pride was injured, nothing more. "Da, soodar. I was the strongest man of my providence in Russia, Viktor. And that little girl knocked me to my knees."

Kaine smiled at the simple Russian.

Lieutenant Colonel Randolph Garnett 'Big Tom' Thompson and Kenneth Xavier 'Percy' Percival Pierce were not present the first time Victor Kaine confronted Doc Titan. Big Tom was in France, serving as a consultant in the construction of a number of new flying fields designed for high-speed modern transport planes. Percy was in Egypt, opening up another pharaoh's tomb that had recently been discovered. They were there for the second encounter, but barely saw him before he was chased down and supposedly killed by an angry mob. Both were surprised to hear that John Titan and Victor Kaine had met a third time. Doc had never mentioned this encounter to his friends. Percy had to admit, Kaine seemed to be a formidable foe. But Black Skull seemed to be a true megalomaniac. Percy wondered how his other friends, and Doc Titan, were doing. Big Tom was still unconscious from the beating Hermia gave him but didn't appear permanently damaged.

The mute Rav Chandra knelt before Whitney and talked to her, using sign language. "I am sorry we failed to escape, Miss Whitney. It was my fault ..." Whitney blinked her deep, lavender eyes at the loyal man-servant. "Nonsense, Rav Chandra. We will not give up. Preston will come for us, he always does, if we don't succeed in escaping on our own." Whitney placed her auburn curls near the prison bars and whispered to Percy. "Hey, who the heck is this Kaine guy?"

"His name is Victor Kaine. Doc Titan once described him as the most dangerous man alive." Percy whispered back.

"Looks like some kind of pansy to me." Whitney exclaimed toughly, her pastel eyes burning with liquid fire.

Percy admired Whitney's moxie. He whispered, almost to himself, "We might be in some deep trouble here. I'm wondering what the heck a Danner Journal is?"

Black Skull returned to the cell block half an hour later. His silent bodyguards followed close behind. Their emotionless faces, as always, were completely covered in the black leather masks and goggles. Whitney found herself envisioning what their faces looked like beneath those dark coverings. Probably horribly scarred. The vision her mind provided caused her to shiver. Ernst and Orban entered the last cell and removed the silent resident. The other prisoners watched as he was dragged past their own cells. He put up a mild resistance, apparently too weak to resist the overpowering strength of the twin giants. For an instant, his face glanced in the direction of Big Tom and

Percy. Black Skull led the way to a dark room at the end of the hallway. The heavy, steel door slammed shut.

Big Tom turned to Percy with a frown on his solemn face. "Did his face look familiar to you, Percy?"

Percy considered his response and then replied. "Yes, but it can't be. The person I'm thinking of, he's been dead for several years."

Big Tom grabbed the thick iron bars of his prison and flexed his powerful arm and back muscles. The bars remained rigidly fixed in place. "That's exactly what I was thinking. That man looked a lot like Doc's father." He said, stroking his beard.

Whitney whispered from the next cell, "Did you say you recognize the prisoner they just dragged away?"

Percy placed his head against the iron bars, but couldn't see the auburn-haired beauty. "Yes. But it can't be him. He resembles a man we used to know but he's dead. Been dead for fifteen years."

Whitney smiled broadly but Percy couldn't see it from his cell. "Been there before. We've fought mummies, zombies, even dancing dead men. Faked my own death several times. Did you actually see him die?"

Percy met Big Tom's gaze. They were sharing the same thought.

Chapter Thirty-Two
(How Many) Bullet Holes

April 6, 1945 6:30 am

Scorpion was standing at the front of the Windjammer's cabin. He was concerned about Whitney and Rav Chandra. This profession, dealing with madmen and criminals, would worry him at times. How long would their luck hold out? He had just lost a close, dear friend, Lockhart. And his loyal butler, Benson. How would he survive if anything happened to Whitney or Rav Chandra? All too often they treated these adventures like a game. But it was a game of chance and, unfortunately, the odds were stacked against anyone winning every time. And the Grim Reaper held the final, winning hand.

Simon Blake noticed a crimson drip fall from Stockbridge's sleeve. It struck the floor and splashed, beginning a red puddle.

"Excuse me, Stockbridge? Are you bleeding?" Blake asked.

"Yes, I sure am. Hey, you're a doc, right?" Stockbridge seemed completely oblivious to his wounds.

"Yes, I have several medical degrees. Why do you ask?"

"Well, I got shot a couple of times back there during the street fight and I was wondering if you could stitch up the holes." Stockbridge asked off-handedly.

"What! You were shot?" Blake asked, incredulously.

"Must you get shot every time you're in a gun fight?" Gibson stated from his lounge chair in the main cabin.

"Hey, it's no big deal." Scorpion did a double-take. "Holy … how did you get on board this airship?"

"Only the Darkness knows." Gibson said, his face breaking into a quick, broad smile. He adjusted the dark spectacles that hid his eyes.

Scorpion frowned. He was beginning to dislike that phrase. "But didn't we leave you in New York?"

"I thought you might have need of my special abilities." Turning to Blake, Gibson continued. "Blake … Simon, I apologize for my … outburst back there. I suppose sometimes I get carried away."

Blake waved away the past offense. "No problem, Gibson. Glad to have you with us, Luthor."

"I'll pilot the ship, while you stitch up our friend." Gibson volunteered.

"I was shot before and it hurt like blazes!" Blake said. "I've been shot four more times but, fortunately, I was wearing a bulletproof jacket each of those times. Still hurts like hell. Like being kicked by a Missouri mule. Take off your cape and coat and let me see, Preston."

Gibson countered. "I've been shot nine times. You never quite get use to it."

Doc had been quiet, until this point. "I've only been wounded by bullets half a dozen times, and I've been stabbed twice as many times. Fortunately, I was trained to ignore the pain."

Gibson raised an eyebrow. "And that really works? You can ignore the pain?"

Doc flashed a quicksilver smile. "Not really. Hurts like hell." Turning to Scorpion he asked, "Where did you get shot?"

"I told you, during the shootout in the street."

Doc frowned. "No, I mean ..."

Scorpion laughed. "Just teasing you, John. Once through the arm and once in the upper chest."

Doc's mouth dropped open. "What? Why didn't you say anything until now?"

Scorpion smiled. "I suppose I was too busy ignoring the pain."

"He does tend to get shot quite often." Gibson confessed.

"Usually I have Rav Chandra or Allen Coleman patch me up." Scorpion removed his coat and everyone stared in amazement at his abused body. "Oh, and by the way, here's my score. I've been shot sixty-four times, stabbed forty-two times - three times through the lungs, and even had a guy hit me with an axe. Don't even ask how many bones I've broken, you don't want to know."

Doc blinked and quietly said, "I don't know what to say. I don't even know how you are still alive."

Scorpion turned to Doc. "While Blake is patching me up, why don't you tell us who this Konstantin Egorov character is?"

"It's not Egorov that worries me. It's the man he works for. Victor Kaine." Doc said the name with almost a reverence in his voice. He removed a photograph from his shirt pocket. It was the one that Sentry left with them. Doc was now certain he knew exactly whom the men in the background were, standing behind Black Skull. Konstantin Egorov and Victor Kaine.

Gibson frowned. "Victor Kaine? I wonder why that name sounds familiar."

Doc continued. "In 1938, Kaine discovered my Hidden Acropolis buried in the Northern snows. Breaking in, he found several fully-functional weapons of death and began selling them to countries at war."

Preston interrupted. "You have a Hidden Acropolis? I always wanted a Secret Sanctuary or a Citadel of Solace. Right now, I use a hidden room behind Whitney's shoe closet." Realizing the mood was serious, he indicated for Doc to proceed.

"I followed the trail of death and destruction and after a brief battle, Victor escaped into a blizzard of snow. I trailed him for two days and discovered polar bear tracks and a bloodied battlefield. Assuming Victor Kaine had met his doom, I left the area. If I had stayed a little while longer, I might have found evidence that Kaine had survived. He more than survived. It appears he had actually killed the bear, not vise versa. Several of the deadliest weapons were never found. I moved most of my experimental equipment to a new location, in case he would ever re-emerge. I'm afraid I never completed the clean-up of the old facility. Because of extradition rights, Konstantin Egorov was remanded to the custody of the Russian government.

"Months later, Kaine found his way to the mountains of upper Mongolia. Preying on the superstitions and naiveté of the warriors in the foothills of Tibet, he established himself as the reincarnation of Genghis Khan. Unfortunately for him, fate and I interfered once more. I convinced the horde of followers that he was a fake and a charlatan. Several dozen bloodthirsty warriors ran him to the ground and it appeared that they chopped him to pieces. But if Egorov is back, I assume they managed to grab the wrong person in all the mêlée. Kaine must have escaped again and freed his friend from prison." Doc did not mention the third time he and Victor Kaine had faced one another. And the things that Kaine had hinted at.

Blake finished stitching up the first wound. "How dangerous is he, Doc?"

Doc stared out of the window of the Windjammer a long time before answering. "On a scale of one to ten, he's an eleven." To himself, Doc thought, "Maybe more, if Kaine is who I think he is. If the rumors of his origins are true."

For several minutes the room was silent. An old memory replayed itself in the back of Doc Titan's mind. During the First World War, he had met a lovely woman. With his limited experience and knowledge of the opposite sex, having been raised on a remote island, she might have been the first woman he had true feelings for. Countess Matryvonav, Iriana Noviskovaah. She was an exile from her mother country, Russia, and an influential Austrian named Count Drakoft had offered her sanctuary within his country's borders.

John Titan was a young man, barely 16 at the time, but mature for his age. He was already a highly decorated combat aviator, attained the rank of Captain in the United Kingdom's Royal Flying Corps. During one dangerous flight, after his airplane was shot down, he was captured and detained as a prisoner of war. He soon met Count Drakoft's ward, the Countess Matryvonav, at the prison camp where he was confined. He was enthralled with her beauty and mesmerized by her charms. One of her most interesting features were her long, thin fingers, each being the length of a normal persons hand.

They began meeting secretly and shared several passionate embraces. But the war was not over and John felt he must escape and rejoin the battle. During the escape, Iriana appeared to be shot and killed. Titan had regained his freedom, but at a terrible cost. Months later, and much to his amazement, he received a letter from the Countess. She had not died during the escape, as he had believed.

The war ended several months after he received the letter and John spent weeks searching for Iriana. It seemed that she had completely vanished until; at last, John finally found a clue, leading to a simple tombstone. The grave marker read, Countess Matryvonav, Iriana Noviskovaah, Sister, Friend and Mother.

Mother? No further mention was made and all records of the birth were destroyed during the bombing that had taken Iriana's life. Eventually, as all men must, John Titan moved on and continued his life. But he never forgot his first love.

It wasn't until the second time he faced Kaine that he noticed the resemblance between Iriana and Victor. Despite Doc's exhaustive research, further evidence was never found. Too many records were lost during the war. The third time 'they met, Doc Titan was completely convinced that Victor Kaine was Iriana Noviskovaah's son and might be his …

"Doc, are you okay?" Blake interrupted his mental flashback.

"Uh, yes. I'm fine. Sorry, just lost in my thoughts. How long have I been …?"

"You've been staring out of the window for an hour. I finished stitching up Preston's wounds and he is resting in one of the cabins."

"Thanks, Simon." Doc patted Blake's shoulder. He walked to the co-pilots seat and relaxed. He removed a small plastic container from the dashboard and handed it to Gibson, who was sitting quietly in the pilot's seat next to him. Gibson had removed his glasses and was rubbing the bridge of his nose. "I nearly forgot, Luthor. I designed a new pair of glasses for you. You were complaining about the weight of the old glass ones. These are made from a new type of lightweight plastic I recently discovered."

Gibson opened the case and tried on the new dark glasses. "Big difference. These are much lighter. Thanks, Doc." He glanced around the cabin of the Windjammer. "Oh, by the way. I placed a radio call to Valentine and had him do some research on Konstantin Egorov. With the war going on in Europe, some records are difficult to find but, apparently, Egorov was released into the custody of a high-ranking military official, about six months ago. No name could be found, but the warden of the prison described the man as tall, thin, long white hair and all dressed in black. Apparently, the fellow left quite an impression."

"That certainly matches the description of Victor Kaine." Doc acknowledged.

Blake summarized the situation. "So Victor Kaine and Black Skull are working together. And according to Military Intelligence, Totenkopf is overseeing a top secret experimental project code-named Operation Gladiator. But why would Black Skull need Kaine? What is the common link that we are missing? And why attack, kill or kidnap our friends?"

"I believe I know. But if I am correct, the world is in mortal danger. The entire balance of the war could be shifted in Hitler's favor. I think all of this might be tied to something called The Danner Journals."

Chapter Thirty-Three
Captain Hazzard and The Pamela

April 6, 1945   6:30 am

Megan Meriwether asked Pam Titan, "Who is this man we're going to see?"

"I've known Captain Rex Hazzard for several years. He has designed and flown nearly every type of aircraft known to man. Rex and his closest friends were addicted to danger. He reminded me of my cousin John in many ways. He and his team operated out of Hazzard Laboratories, a Long Island complex of massive buildings that housed scientific and mechanical labs, as well as aircraft hangers. His adventures, research, and inventions earned him amazing wealth and the honorary rank of Captain in the Army and Navy Air Corps.

Unfortunately, early in his career as a crimefighter, a gangster planted a bomb in one of his experimental airplanes. Three of his closest friends died in the explosion. Rex took it very hard. He became reclusive for several years. Got lost in a bottle of gin. His business was nearly bankrupt. Somehow, Doc found out about Hazzard, like he always does. He helped Cap get back on his feet, spiritually and financially. Now, Hazzard designs and builds most of Doc's aircraft. Doc tends to have a lot of them burn, crash, and explode. Even more are shot down or stolen. His personal air-fleet costs a small fortune. Big Tom tests every new prototype that comes from the shop."

"Hazzard sounds like a great guy. Is his name really Rex?" Cassie asked.

Pam smiled. "Actually, it's Kevin Douglas or something. Rex is just my nickname for him. But, yeah, he's a great guy. Makes my toes curl when he's around. Someday I'll let him make an honest woman out of me."

Pam slowed and brought the roadster to a halt in front of a complex of massive, derelict-looking buildings. A tall, lanky man, dressed in a cowboy hat and weathered denim overalls, waved a greeting salute. His right hand was missing one finger. From his exaggerated gait, Cassie could tell he had a fake leg. Pam whispered, before exiting the car, "That's Jake Cole. He was in the plane that exploded. Lost one leg, a couple of fingers and has a metal plate in his head. He's a quiet, taciturn, but not terribly bright, cowboy." Pam walked over to the scarecrow with arms raised and gave him a breathtaking hug. "Jake, you old sod, how are you doing?"

"Ah, not bad, Pam." Jake said with a slow Texas drawl, his smile stretching from ear to ear. "Rex said ya'll called and were heading out here.

He's over in the big hanger, prepping your plane. Big Tom flew it this morning, said it was a real hoot." Pam made quick introductions and the group strolled over to the structure. Inside the huge metal hanger were a dozen crafts, ranging from a B-52 bomber to a small, streamlined single-passenger vehicle that looked like something from the pages of a science fiction pulp. "Governments had Cap working on some new designs for their aircrafts. Buck Rogers type of stuff. Been keeping him real busy. He's even helped the Brits design a new prototype of unmanned drone plane."

From the engine compartment of an airplane the lower half of a man could be seen, dressed in simple, greasy overalls. Cassie noticed the muscular torso of the man was a fine display of male anatomy. She smiled, raised one eyebrow and nodded her head at Megan, making it completely obvious what she was admiring.

Pam noticed this display and mutely mouthed the words to Cassie. "He's mine." Cassie shrugged her shoulders with an, *'Oh well, worth a look,'* sigh.

"Captain Rex Hazzard, come out of there and give your girl a hug," Pam exclaimed loudly.

The man who turned to the group was a surprisingly young man. From the description Pam had given them, Megan had expected a man in his late forties or early fifties, with graying temples, a large potbelly, and a weathered, unshaven face. But 'Rex' Hazzard turned out to be a younger man, perhaps in his middle-to-late thirties. He was ruggedly good-looking, with a Clark Gable handsomeness about him. Rex had large, muscular arms and a thick chest. He sported a thin moustache, beautiful blue eyes, and a thick crop of hair, with a goofy little quiff of hair at his forehead. Rex resembled a cover model for one of the pulp hero magazines, only lacking the gun in one hand, a damsel in distress clinging to one arm, and a crouching villain preparing to attack in the background.

"Pam, darling. It's so good to see you again. Got my fastest, sleekest, sportiest aircraft all ready for you. Handles like a champ. Top speed of over five hundred miles per hour. You'll be able to out-race, out-maneuver, and out-distance anything else in the air. Once your cousin, Doc, flies this baby, he'll order a dozen of them. Of course, knowing him, he'll donate them to the U.S. Air Force."

Megan leaned to whisper into Cassie's ear. "She doesn't fly as fast as she drives, does she?" Cassie simply smiled, her eyes brightening.

Pam gave Rex a huge bear-hug. "You are such a sweetheart, Rex." She tilted her head sideways, indicating her companions. "Rex Hazzard, I would like to introduce you to my friends, Cassie Greyson and Megan Meriwether."

"Enchanted to make your acquaintance, ladies. Any friend of Pam's, is a friend of mine. Hope you girls are here to keep her out of trouble." Rex smiled and his face looked even younger. He had a good smile. Looking back to Pam, he continued, "Doc financed the building of this craft, he'll be mighty upset if you damage or destroy it."

Pam smiled evilly, raising one eyebrow. "He'll just have to get over it. By now, he ought to know better than trying to leave me on the sidelines." They approached the airplane and everyone was in awe. Technologically, this aircraft was years ahead of its time. Incredibly streamlined, the powerful turbine engines were housed in sleek metal cylinders, replacing the standard propeller blades. "Wow, she's a beaut!"

Rex Hazzard stroked one hand along the wing, proud of his work. "Automatic sensors allow takeoff and landing on any surface … land, snow, or water. Sensors engage wheels or skis or pontoons depending on the need. Rivets and seams have been eliminated, greatly reducing wind resistance. The copper color paint is a hardened liquid polymer and fiberglass mixture that creates a bulletproof skin covering and also reflects most radar. In-line twin turbines in each housing allows for shorter takeoffs and landings and increased air speed. The cabin is completely soundproofed and has all of the modern bells and whistles you could possibly want. Short and long-wave radio, radar equipped, autopilot, and an air-conditioned cockpit. Flip a switch and machine gun turrets on the wings pop out. Another switch loads and fires heat-sensor tracking, short-range rockets. Doc gave me the designs from that little Balkan country that tried to hoodwink him into becoming their king. In fact, Doc and Big Tom provided several new engineering innovations for this airplane. Doc helped me create an amalgamation of lighter metals and enhanced fuel mixture ratio. There's no other airplane on Earth like this one."

"Why don't you come along with us and test her out?" Pam said, and regretted it immediately.

Rex's face saddened and he looked down. Pam felt like kicking herself. He was still haunted by the death of his close friends. "Thanks, Pam, but my adventuring days are in my past. You kids have fun, but be careful. And try to bring my plane back in one piece. Oh, I have one more detail I wanted to show you." He smiled as he pointed at the name of the plane, painted in bold, black lettering on the side of the body. It simply read, '*The Pamela.*'

Pam actually blushed a little and said quietly, "I don't know what to say."

Hazzard stood next to Pam. "I call her the Pamela, because she's fast and sleek and every time I see her, she takes my breath away." He wrapped his muscular arms around Pam's waist, pulled her close and their lips met.

Cassie whispered to Megan, "Wow, he's even romantic. And loaded. And smart. Do you think he has a twin brother at home, looking for a nice girl like me?"

"Right. Like you're ever going to settle down, Cassie. Besides, I thought you had a thing for Simon Blake?"

"I'm not sure if anything will ever come of that. He's still haunted by the loss of his wife and son. There are times he can be so cold and distant. I hoped that would change after he regained his black hair and his face was no longer paralyzed. Or was *supposedly* cured. I mean, I like Simon, but I don't think I love him. Besides, Wall is the man who really has the hots for me. And I *really* like him, too." Cassie confessed. "He's my big Viking hero."

"And you're in *love* with him, too, aren't you? Why don't you tell him?"

Cassie fidgeted uncomfortably. "I guess I'm merely waiting for the right time, Megan."

"In my opinion, there is no such thing as the right time. Especially, in this profession."

"You're probably right." Cassie admitted.

Pam gave Rex another kiss. "I have one last favor, Rex. Did you receive those leather, racing outfits that I ordered from France last month?"

"Yep, they arrived yesterday. They're in the office over there."

Pam jumped with excitement. "Okay, girls. I have a surprise for you. Time to get dressed for action."

"What's wrong with what I'm wearing?" Megan asked Cassie.

"Oh, Megan darling, don't get me started. Besides, Pam has a garment fetish, with a fixation on leather, but she also has excellent taste."

Pam flashed a quicksilver smile, her eyes twinkling. "Besides, Megan, those electric pistols we stole from Doc's office clash with your outfit."

"You think so? Okay. Maybe you're right."

Jake and Rex watched as the three beautiful women walked to the office to change clothes.

Jake Cole spit tobacco. "Rex, ya ol' sod. Ya'll oughta make an honest woman of that lil' filly some day soon. If ya'll don't, Ah will."

Minutes later the ladies returned, wearing skin-tight leather breeches, aviation jackets trimmed with gold fur and black leather, knee-high boots. Both men gawked openly at the trio.

Megan was fidgeting in her outfit. "Could these pants be any tighter? If I had a dime in my pocket, you could tell if it was heads or tails!"

Cassie looked pleased. "I feel like a dominatrix in this outfit, with all of the leather."

Pam smiled, feeling naughty. "You say that like it was a bad thing, Cassie."

"Actually, I was wondering if it came with a cat-o-nine tails whip. Meow!"

Megan closed her eyes and shook her head in surrender. "You two are such bad girls."

Act II: To the North Pole

Chapter Thirty-Four
The Invitation

April 6, 1945   6:30 am

Bart finished deciphering the last of the hieroglyphics on the paper he held. He reread the contents of the message and let out a long, low whistle.

"Fellas, I do believe I figured out the message on the flip side of the amulet."

"And you still think that the North Pole is still our final destination?" Wall asked.

Bart nodded. "Correct. And that gibberish on the other side? It's an ancient dialect of the Norwegian Vikings. Remember when those Vikings from Kwui came to New York? Percy stayed with them for a short time and wrote a rather lengthy thesis on the subject."

"Yeah, after those gangsters tried to turn him into a popsicle. He nearly died. Percy wrote a book about the people of the Kwui? I don't remember that." Kong scratched his skull.

Bart retorted. "Because while you were picking your nose and napping, I actually listened to what he told us about the culture."

Kong looked hurt. "I can't help it if Percy studies boring things, like thousand year old dead people and dusty ruins. However, I do remember that cute little chick during that Viking adventure. Ingrid. Not tall and thin, actually rather husky, but with curves very pleasing to the eye."

Gibs, who thought women were a distraction, at best, interrupted Kong. "Anyway, what does the writing say?"

Bart continued. "As close as I can make out, it's an invitation from *'The People of the Light.'*

"Well that sure solves the mystery. We just have to look for the light people." Kong added sarcastically.

Bart ignored Kong and explained further. "Actually, there *is* a group known as The People of the Light. Some cultures call them the Illuminati. Others refer to them as The Unknown Nine. Some believe the Freemasons were an offshoot of the Illuminati or vise versa. Freemasonry is a fraternal organization with millions of members. It exists in various forms worldwide, with shared moral and metaphysical ideals and in most of its branches requires a constitutional declaration of belief in a Supreme Being. All of these 'secret societies' appear to be linked somewhere in the long-lost, distant past.

George Washington, John Hancock, and Ben Franklin were supposedly Freemasons. One of their symbols, the All-Seeing Eye of Ra, is on the backside of the US one dollar bill. Franklin, also a Rosicrucian Grand Master, was at the heart of the Illuminati operations to take over America and replace the visible control of the British Empire with the invisible control of the secret brotherhood. This was the most effective and ongoing form of mastering the underclass. It is said the Illuminati, via the Freemasons, controlled and manipulated both sides in the American War of Independence and were also deeply connected with the French Revolution in 1789."

Kong wrinkled his button nose. "And they've invited us to visit them at the North Pole? Can we pass? They don't sound like folks I wanna meet."

Gibs reassured Kong. "You have to remember, history is written by the survivors of conflicts and by those who enjoy embellishing the truth. People love the intrigue of secret societies and hidden government agendas, but most of it is simply the creation of someone's overly active imagination."

Kong laughed and shook his head. "Yeah, you're right. Next thing you know, they'll be writing that someday Ronald Reagan will be President and J. Edgar Hoover wears dresses. Whatta lotta garbage."

Chapter Thirty-Five
Flashback to 1916 - Grant and Rasputin

April 6, 1945   6:30 am

Thunder and lightning was playing around the large airship. Doc had piloted the zeppelin named Windjammer upward until they were above the raging storm. The motors and framework were insulated to withstand bolts of lightning, but sometimes it was easier to play it safe. Luthor Gibson was relaxed in one of the comfortable lounge chairs in the main room. It was spacious enough that if the muffled noise of the powerful motors could be ignored, a person might think they were in the pleasant lobby of a small hotel or a luxury ocean liner. The gusting winds slowly rocked Gibson into a state of relaxation, nearly asleep. Old memories played in his head. Memories of Russia.

Beginning of Flashback to December 16ᵗʰ, 1916.   The Day Rasputin Died.

Grigori Yefimovich Rasputin stroked his long, gnarled fingers through the delicate hair of the little blonde girl. Anastasia pulled away slightly in fear of the reputed madman. She didn't like his wild appearance or the way he smelled of garlic and pepper. He was, in her young mind, a horrible, evil man. Even though Rasputin had counseled the royal Russian family for many years, she had never liked him. And, apparently, others shared her feelings. Tonight, several men had already tried to poison him. He had ingested enough poison in his food to kill ten men but the legendary Rasputin was not affected. When two of the conspirators, Prince Felix Yusupov and the Grand Duke Dmitri Pavlovichv, realized their plot to poison him had failed, the Prince shot Rasputin in the back. When that failed to kill him, they had attacked with knives. One still protruded from out of his back, below the left shoulder blade, but he didn't even seem to notice it. His foul breath assailed her nostrils and she wished he would simply leave her alone.

Rasputin had been born a peasant in the small village of Pokrovskoye, along the Tura River in the Tobolsk guberniya in Siberia. In 1905 he helped Tsarevich Alexei, Queen Victoria of England's great-grandson. Alexei was diagnosed with hemophilia, a blood disorder, and had recently suffered internal injuries. Doctors said he would soon die. Rasputin healed the boy and became close friends of the Russian Tsar and the Royal family. Russia's economy was declining at a rapid rate and many blamed the Royal family and, more specifically, Rasputin. Two years ago a woman, Guseva by name, stabbed him, thrusting a knife deeply into Rasputin's abdomen. Again, he had survived.

Rasputin whispered to the young girl. "My pretty, Anastasia. You must come with me now. I must flee this country tonight, little one. The hounds of Russia are on my heels and I am not prepared to battle them all." Even though she was Anastasia Nikolayevna Romanova, Her Imperial Highness Grand Duchess Anastasia of Russia, and the youngest of four daughters of Emperor Nicholas II of Russia, the last sovereign of Imperial Russia, Rasputin had always felt this child was his own. Either the Russian gypsy did not know of her disdain for him or, more likely, he simply didn't care.

The door at the end of the large Fellowship Hall crashed open. Silhouetted in the doorway was Max Grant. As lightning crashed behind his form, all that could be seen was a dark figure, a shadow of a man. Anastasia called his name but could not be heard above the loud cascade of thunder. A monstrous storm was raging outside, matching the inevitable clash of titans inside the Russian palace.

Rasputin scowled at the newcomer. "Comrade Grant. Or do you prefer the name Dark Eagle? I was hoping to have the pleasure of your company one last time before we left. We have unsettled history, you and I."

"You aren't going anywhere, you Russian madman." Grant spit venomously.

Rasputin smiled, his wild eyes painted with madness. "We shall see. Anna and I were just preparing to leave, and only you stand in my way."

Grant roared in anger as he charged forward. "Let's finish this!"

Rasputin's crooked smile widened and he charged toward the renowned aviator of the Great War. He pulled a massive revolver from his waist and it exploded round after round at Grant. Max had both .38 caliber Army revolvers in his hands and they blazed with long tongues of orange and red flame. As they ran toward the middle of the room, they continued firing. Grant was struck in the right shoulder. Rasputin felt two ribs break as twin bullets struck his chest. Max felt one round pass within an inch of his left eye. His thick leather aviation vest deflected the full, impact of several of the bullets.

Grigori felt the sickening bore of another in his right thigh muscle, barely missing the large thigh bone. He continued forward without any hesitation and smashed hard into the American. Grant dropped to the floor on his back, raising his guns as he dropped. Click. Click. Both guns were empty! Rasputin seemed to tower above him. The crazed Russian slowly pointed his large bore revolver at Max's skull. Click. Rasputin had also run out of ammunition.

Voices could be heard from downstairs as Prince Yusupov and the Grand Duke Pavlovichv led a score of men to the second floor. Rasputin growled and cursed, before turning away. He smiled at Anastasia and said, "My imperial schwibzik, my little imp. I must leave you tonight, but I shall return for you soon."

Grant rushed forward and both men crashed through the etched glass window. They hung in the air for a second, before dropping to the rain-soaked ground. Water poured around them as the storm continued. Lightning and thunder filled the dark skies. Max was stunned for a moment. Gigori took advantage of this and struck him hard across the skull with one of his large fists. Max didn't think anything had ever hit him quite so hard. One large hand wrapped its long fingers around his throat and his body was lifted from the ground. Despite being poisoned, stabbed and even shot, Rasputin showed no signs of being near death. Max began to doubt this insane lunatic could even be killed. He had been witness to many unusual sights since joining the battle of The Great War. He had traveled the width and breadth of Europe, seeking his fate and his future. Max decided his travels would not end at the hands of this Russian madman. The palm of his left hand shot up and struck Grigori's nose. Grant felt the cartilage break and Rasputin's broken nose burst with a fountain of blood. The death-grip was loosened and Max fell to the ground, gasping for air. A cascade of water continued to pour past them and joined the overflowing river below.

Both men quickly rose to their feet. Rasputin's eyes seemed to glow red as he growled and charged without hesitation. Grant dropped below one of the clutching hands and as Grigori passed, he pulled the blade from the Russian's back. Max was amazed that any man could survive having a seven-inch long blade plunged into their body. Not only had this man survived, he had nearly killed Max several times tonight. As Rasputin lunged forward, Max saw his opening. The long blade whistled upward and struck Rasputin under the chin. The blade sank up to the hilt. Rasputin straightened, took one halting step and then another. He clutched at the blade, as if to remove it and fell backwards. His body slid on the slick, rain-soaked stones beneath his feet and he plunged into the small river. Max saw the body for a brief second; floating in the steady current and then it disappeared beneath the hard ice of the frozen waters.

Grant sank slowly to his knees, his strength finally giving out. He heard shouts behind him from the palace. Men were running out to where he had fallen. To where Grigori Yefimovich Rasputin had met his end. Prince Yusupov and Anastasia were the first to reach Max. As they helped him to his feet, he noticed a young boy on the opposite river bank. The boy glared hatred toward Max.

"Who is that boy?" Max asked, matching the lad's steady gaze.

"That is Joachim, the illegitimate child of Rasputin." Prince Yusupov leveled his rifle at the boy and prepared to pull the trigger. "The spawn of that devil Rasputin should be destroyed."

Max placed his hand on the barrel of the rifle and gently pulled it down. "There has been enough killing this day." Max said weakly.

The Prince sighed deeply and closed his eyes. "Perhaps you are correct, Comrade Grant. I shall respect your council. I will have all of Rasputin's family exiled from Russia. We will never see that boy again. I pray in the years to come, we do not regret this moment of mercy."

They all watched as the boy turned and walked downriver. His eyes never left them until he was out of sight. Grant swore he would never forget those eyes. Max wanted to say more, but he lost consciousness.

He awoke several days later, his wounds bandaged and he felt well rested. The past few weeks and months had been ... difficult. His first guests were Prince Yusupov and Anastasia.

Anastasia held his hand. "We owe you ... our entire country owes you a debt of gratitude. How can we reward you for what you have done?"

"I simply served justice, nothing more. Your well-being is reward enough." Grant replied modestly.

Anastasia removed a ring from her finger. "Please accept this royal ring. It has been in the family for centuries. It was rumored to be a gift from one of the great emperors of China. If you should ever need anything, the Royal family of Russia will do whatever is asked of the bearer of this ring." The blood-red, girasol jewel embedded in the center of the ring was a translucent opal with flaming orange, yellow, and red colors. It was truly a unique gemstone, unlike anything Grant had ever seen. He forced himself to look away from the depths of the jewel.

Grant smiled at the Grand Duchess. "It shall never leave my person, Imperial Highness."

"Please ... call me Anastasia."

Grant smiled. Perhaps he could spend some time here in Russia. There was certainly no hurry to return home. He had made one decision today. In the future, he wanted larger caliber pistols and more bullets. Maybe the new .45 caliber colt automatics.

End of Flashback to December 16th, 1916. The Day Rasputin Died.

Chapter Thirty-Six
Flashback to 1916 - The Secret

April 6, 1945   7:00 am

Doc Titan had retired to his private cabin on the Windjammer. Even though he required very little sleep and could go for days without tiring, Doc realized the necessity of allowing the body and mind to rest. He lay down and within one minute he was sleeping soundly. His internal clock was so finely tuned, he could 'instruct' his mind and body when he wanted to awaken. Exactly two hours later, to the second, he re-opened his eyes.

He began his daily two-hour exercise routine. Performing calisthenics, simple movements performed without weights, and various cardio-vascular activities, his bronzed skin was soon coated with a fine sheen of perspiration. While his physical body ran through a gauntlet of regimented exercises, Doc occupied his keen mind with complicated mathematical logarithms.

Next, he opened a variety of small containers and studied the contents. He would use every sense to determine the origin and contents of each sample. These were gathered from around the world and sent to a cataloging service that randomly sorted, labeled, and supplied them to Doc. During one examination he might find samples of evergreen pine needles from Canada, clay mud from a lake in Nevada, scales from an African crocodile, and pottery from a remote South American village. He would sometimes attempt this blindfolded, relying only on his olfactory senses or using only his sense of taste. Occasionally, he had to resort to using a jeweler's magnifying glass on more unique items. After years of daily trials, he could study all hundred samples in an amazingly short period of time. Often when captured, he could tell exactly where he was, by the smell of nearby trees or the texture of the dirt on his boot heels.

This was an exercise he had learned from a man known as the world's greatest detective, Sherlock Holmes. Doc had studied only briefly under the tutelage of Holmes but had learned the lessons of a lifetime.

Sherlock Holmes had once studied every available brand of tobacco available in England. He could identify each by smell, texture of the leaves and by the ash left behind after burning. If a killer left ashes at a crime scene, Sherlock could immediately tell whether it was a domestic brand or imported. More than one case was solved by his compulsive in-depth study of such ordinary, everyday items.

The last sample was a blue-gray sample of tobacco. Doc lifted the container and smelled the thick, course leaves. The sense of smell can often jump-start memories in the mind, sometimes decades old. A person might find a scent that reminds them of their first car, a girlfriend's perfume, or flowers at a lake in the springtime. Doc would sometimes be reminded of an adventure in the Florida everglades, a South African cattle ranch, or a particular building in Northeast Asia.

The human eye can recognize sixteen point four million different shades of color. The human sense of smell can be equally sensitive, if properly honed.

Doc felt an old memory stir near the surface but couldn't quite place it. He closed his eyes and smelled the tobacco leaves again. He could almost place it, but it evaded his abilities of recognition. Finally, he surrendered and glanced at the label on the bottom. Except, this container had no label. He glanced into the box where the samples had been stored. There was no label there, either. Odd.

Doc finished his exercise routine by performing one hundred one-armed pushups in a hand-stand position. Despite the slight movement of the Windjammer's deck as winds gusted outside, he remained perfectly balanced. He had completed ninety-five pushups when a flash of recognition came to him. He stopped moving, still balanced on one hand, upside down. He attempted to extract the memory from the depths of his past.

Ned.

The name came to him and suddenly brought with it a torrent of memories.

Beginning of Flashback to December 16th, 1916.

John Titan liked Ned. The old groundskeeper smelled of the sea, fish, freshly cut grass, and his own unique brand of blue-gray tobacco. He was a solidly-framed man, about the same height as John. He had a thick, hairy chest, arm muscles hardened by years of working on the open seas, and sandy-colored hair and beard. A dozen men exactly like him could be found in most large ports, but here on Wilder Island he was unique. All of the men his father had brought to the island were cut from a different cloth than Ned. They fell into two classes, the educated professors and the professional trainers. But Professor Titan insisted that they were all well-groomed and well-mannered around his son. They were his mentors and were expected to show John respect at all times.

Ned was different.

One day John was walking down one of the paths that bisected the island, reading his chemistry homework. He noticed Ned pulling weeds from the area surrounding the gravesite of John's mother. He placed a small bouquet of flowers at the base of the tombstone, removed his cap, and bowed his head respectfully. When the elder man looked up, John was standing nearby.

"Are you the new groundskeeper? I heard my father say he was thinking about hiring one." John asked politely.

Ned squinted an eye in John's direction. "Me? Why … eh, yes. Yes, I am. And you must be young John Titan."

John looked surprised. "You know me?"

"Of course. You are the only young man on the island, unless I've been misinformed."

"No, that is true." John replied quietly.

"My name is Ned …" He seemed to hesitate for a second. "But all of my friends just call me … Ned. Just Ned."

John smiled broadly after he realized Ned's jest, and held out his hand. Ned extended his weathered appendage and shook John's hand.

"Good to meet you, 'Just' Ned." Ned smiled at John's own sense of humor.

This was the start of a new type of relationship for young John Titan. Ned was not an instructor, a professor, or his father. He was simply a friend. And in the last sixteen years of his life, John had never had a friend. Every few days they would meet, usually near his mother's gravesite. Sometimes they would rest against the old pylons of the abandoned wharf and dip their bare feet in the cool waters of the lagoon.

They would talk about the great ocean voyages and traveling the wide-open seas. Or about the shapes of clouds overhead. Or creatures that Ned had witnessed in his global adventures. Bar room fights and buried treasures. And about women. John was sixteen years old and had never met a woman. He understood every part of the physical biology of the female, of course. He knew about courting, and kissing, and even reproduction. But he had never actually seen, smelled, or touched a real live woman.

For several weeks, the two men grew closer. The old man of the sea and the young castaway on a remote island. There were tales of ancient mariners and modern day pirates. Doubloons. Keel-hauling. Beasties from the ocean depths. Tales of Davy Jones' locker. Even one story about an honest-to-God submarine voyage. In all of Doc's studies, he had never been allowed to read a tale of fiction or adventure. He greedily drank in all of Ned's wild stories. One evening they sat on a hilltop, watching the sun dropping into the horizon. The skies were ablaze with scarlet and crimson colors.

Ned puffed on his old pipe. "Red sky in the morning, sailors take warning. Red sky at night, sailor's delight." He stated almost without realizing it.

John loved the quotes and phrases that Ned would recite from his years on the open seas.

John leaned back onto the thick grass and stared into the skies. "Ned, were you ever married?"

Ned puffed deeply on his pipe and had a faraway look in his eyes. "There was one woman who stole my heart, child. There is nothing like being in love. Your stomach cramps like you ate some bad oyster stew and your heart races like when you've sprinted across the island. All you can think of is her face."

John wrinkled his nose. "Sounds horrible."

Ned smiled, looking at the ocean and at nothing at all. "Nah, it's the best feeling in the world. Women are the most wonderful and terrible things you'll ever meet. You'll never discover anything that can be as soft, and as beautiful, that can fill your empty heart to overflowing. Of course, they can also rip out your heart and step all over it."

John was quiet for a minute. "What happened to her? Where is she now?"

Ned dragged on his pipe again and his eyes teared slightly. "We had a daughter, the most beautiful creature on God's green Earth. I thought about retiring from the sea, maybe taking up farming. Two months after our little girl was born, my wife died of consumption. I was distraught. I left my daughter behind, to be raised by my brother. I signed onto the first outgoing freighter and didn't return for over thirty years. I received word that my grand-daughter was to be wed. Her mother, my daughter, had died six months prior. I missed her entire life. I swore I would not abandon my grand-daughter the same way. I was there the day she was married. I was so proud."

Ned puffed quietly for a long minute. John waited, thinking he would continue. Ned seemed to be contemplating some idea. Finally, he spoke again.

"John, there is something I want to tell you. Your moth …"

Professor Titan barked loudly. "Johnny! Your instructors have been looking for you. You have a chemistry exam."

Ned leapt to his feet and raised his hands waist high toward John's father, palms forward, fingers up, in a calming gesture. "Professor Titan. Your son and I were only …"

John noticed his father was glaring lividly at the elder seaman. John stood up and hesitated, looking from Ned to his father and back again.

Professor Titan's gaze turned coldly to his son. "Johnathan, now!"

John could always tell when his father was serious. He called him Johnathan. He used the word as a domination feature, similar to Ivan Pavlov's phenomenon known as classical conditioning reflex. And like Pavlov's dog, which would drool when a bell was rung, when his father would call John

'Johnathan,' he would always respond immediately. John turned and walked down the hill. Behind his back, he could hear Ned and his father speaking loudly, arguing about something.

He heard his name. Johnny. Everyone called him John, except his father, who insisted on calling him Johnny. Nobody on the island would have called his father by his first name. They all called him Mr. Titan or Professor Titan. The young man crept closer but stayed to the darkest shadows of the hallway. This was an old part of the building, with stone foundations and alcoves placed randomly in the corridor. He had been trained since a very small boy to stalk silently through the island jungles. He could creep up on a skittish fawn and touch her, before she could hear, smell, or see him. The voices were louder now. John backed into the deep shadows of the alcove, across the hallway from the open door. As he moved a few more feet to the right, his father and the man he knew only as Ned came into view.

Professor Titan was shouting at Ned, "You risked everything today, old man. I forbid you to interfere ..."

"You forbid me?! You forbid?!" Ned cut off the elder Titan in mid-sentence.

Professor Titan reinforced his previous sentence. "Yes, I *forbid* you to interfere with how I raise my son. He has a mission ..."

Ned pointed a weathered finger at Professor Titan. "No, *you* have a mission. You are simply imposing it on your child. Young John needs ..."

Professor Titan slammed his fist down on the hard wooden table. "Do not presume to tell me what my own son needs or doesn't need."

Ned lowered his voice, in hopes of calming the other man. "Your son is more like a prisoner on this island. He needs kids his own age. Your agenda and mission for his life of fighting crime is more than any child should bear. You are pushing him too hard. He will crack if you don't let up. He's not a machine."

Professor Titan answered without hesitation, "No, Ned. He's the perfect man. He's only sixteen and since the age of fourteen months he has been trained in every discipline known to man. He has learned from the masters in a dozen different fields and has started surpassing their knowledge. He knows three dozen languages. He has been trained in every type of combat. What will he be like by the time he's twenty years old? Twenty-five? There has never been a man alive like young Johnny. He is the perfection of mankind. He will lead mankind into the world of the future." Professor Titan calmed himself a little, as if realizing he was starting to rant.

"But what can he offer the world, if he doesn't even know himself?" Ned replied calmly.

Professor Titan frowned at the elder seaman. "What do you mean?"

"Children need more than lessons, they need love. A father and a mother. A family. There has never been a woman on this island since John's arrival. What happens the first time some woman meets John and she breaks his heart? The boy you have trained to become the ultimate man will someday meet his match. All of that pent-up animal aggression has to go somewhere. You intend to send him out into the world to right wrongs and battle evil. What happens the first time he discovers that evil men do not fight fair? That they will kill his best friend, his wife, his son, just to destroy him? To avoid that pain, he will have to keep everyone at arms length, in fear for their safety. He will be alone for the rest of his life. Or worse, what if he decides the only way to battle evil men is to destroy them, to kill them? Where does that stop? When he has killed a hundred men? A thousand? When does a good man, defending truth and justice, finally cross that line and become a vigilante killer?"

There was a moment of silence. Young John suddenly became aware of the presence of a third person in the room. In the far corner, hidden almost completely in the shadows, stood a dark figure. The hood was pulled up around his head and nearly hid his face completely. For a second, John couldn't figure out why he hadn't noticed the man until now. Then it dawned on him. The man was immense, gargantuan. He dwarfed the other men, and they were large men themselves. The hulking behemoth must have stood nearly eight feet tall. John had been so focused on the two men arguing, he had not noticed this massive creature in the background. A shiver ran down his back as his eyes searched the shadows that enshrouded the hidden face.

He could see a long scar that ran along the huge neck and disappeared into the recesses of the cloak. A mis-aligned bottom lip showed several yellow, broken teeth. Black hair cascaded from the bottom of the hood's opening but failed to cover the horrible scab on the collar bone. It looked like someone had attempted to patch a bullet hole, but it had never completely healed. As John looked up, he nearly screamed out loud. The dark figure's eyes were staring directly at him! One iris was blue and the other was green, as though they had come from two different skulls. The pupils were a sickly yellow color. The eyes were sunken far back into the skull. And they were staring at him, through him. Was it possible this … man could see him hidden here in the complete darkness of the alcove in the hallway? Impossible … but the eyes never left him.

Professor Titan continued, "That wouldn't happen. Johnny is stronger than that."

"And what if you're wrong?" Ned asked quietly. "Is that why you keep the Other, hidden here on the island? Your last failed experiment, that poor white-faced creature. If John fails, will you simply imprison him, too?"

"No, I could never … " Professor Titan started, appearing shocked that Ned would even suggest such a course of action.

"Enough." It took a second for John to even recognize this rumble as a voice. The coarse sound was so deep that it sounded like a bear in a cave. The monstrous, scarred figure slowly stepped forward, as if maintaining its balance with some difficulty. Apparently, one leg was slightly longer than the other. A massive, grotesquely scarred limb extended forward and clutched the top edge of the thick, wooden door. John saw more horrible scars on the hand and extending far into the sleeve of the hooded coat. The fingernails were dark, broken and dirty.

John realized he was backed up against the wall and still wanting to retreat further. His sensitive nostrils detected the scent of decay and he experienced a second of nausea. In all of his young life, he had never seen anything like this … hulking abomination. As the door slammed shut, he looked once more into the creature's eyes. More than before, he was absolutely certain that this misshapen man was staring directly into his eyes. What John saw there was … sadness. Resignation. As if he had seen the fear reflected in John's eyes, the same fear he saw in every set of eyes he had ever looked into. For a second, John wanted to knock on the door. Talk to the … man. That's what he was, just a man. John felt truly ashamed of his reactions and he fought back his tears.

John stood outside the door for several seconds. Then the words that Ned had said, repeated in his mind. *'The Other, hidden on the island. Your failed experiment.'* What other? It sounded like there was someone before him. Someone else his father had trained, developed … created? What had his father done to make John the young man he was? He knew from a very early age that he was faster, stronger, smarter, better than nearly everyone he met. The things he didn't know, he learned easily and quickly. He had also come to know that this was not normal. Not … natural. Men who had studied a science all of their lives, soon found out their pupil had become their superior, in just a few short years. His father had dismissed this by explaining to John that these older men lacked the focus and dedication that he exhibited. And, perhaps, to a certain extent this was true. All John had was his studies. Every hour of every day he spent mastering the arts, sciences, and even perfecting his body. Even though he was only sixteen years old, he was already over six feet tall and weighed two hundred and twenty pounds. What had his father said? Wait until John was twenty years old. Or twenty-five. What were his limits? Or did he have any?

'*The Other.*' John had to know what this meant. As he quietly walked away from the soundproof door, his mind was working feverishly. Where on the island would they be able to hide this '*Other?*' Ned had mentioned a prison. In the sixteen years he had lived on this island, where had he never been? Where wasn't he allowed to go? Of course. The Catacombs, located beneath the castle ruins on the hill. The crumbling old fortress was at the other end of the island, nearly six miles distance from where he stood. He began running slowly in that direction. He knew the wooded areas of the island like the back of his hand. Despite the darkness of the night he never misplaced a footstep or stumbled over an obstacle. The moon was shining and to John's fantastic eyesight, it was like moving in broad daylight.

Half-way there he realized he was running full out, perhaps as fast as he had ever run. His breathing was barely labored, so he pushed a little harder. A minute later he pulled up short when he realized he was already at the foot of the massive stone castle ruins. He had covered six miles in a little over twenty minutes and was still breathing regularly. Before leaving the main building he had grabbed a small flashlight. He quickly made his way down the dark tunnels, occasionally using the light to confirm his path. Much sooner than he expected, he detected a dim illumination ahead. He tucked the flashlight into his pocket and quietly eased forward.

What he saw that day would stay with him for the rest of his life.

Ned was gone the next day. Professor Titan refused to explain where he had gone or why he had left. John's world returned to studies and training. But, whenever he could escape the vigilant eyes of his instructors, John would climb to the top of the hill and watch the sun disappear behind the horizon. Two weeks later, he escaped the island and never returned.

End of Flashback to December 16th, 1916.

The entire time this memory had flashed through his head, Doc had been supporting himself with one arm. He slowly lowered himself to the deck of the Windjammer and sat on the floor. He closed his eyes as he remembered his young life on Wilder Island. Looking back, he knew that a weaker man would have certainly broken under the pressure. Damn his father for not seeing that. Damn him.

Chapter Thirty-Seven
Flashback to 1919 - Too Many Degrees?

April 6, 1945 7:00 am

Wall, the giant Norwegian, yawned and stretched his huge arms. "This is going to be a long trip. Since we'll be here for a while, I have a question for you fellas. I've heard rumors that Doc Titan has degrees in about two dozen professions. How can one man be such an expert in so many things?"

Gibs closed his notebook and placed it in his shirt pocket. "He was trained for this unique vocation since he was barely a year old. His father hired the finest men and minds in every vocation to train his son."

Bart added, "And he did not neglect the physical acumen. His father hired experts at boxing, wresting, savate, karate, and nearly every art of unarmed fighting. And tumblers, acrobats, jugglers, and circus performers. Then, men who used weapons, from guns, knives, swords, and many other, lesser known, weapons. By the time he was twelve, Doc Titan was one of the most dangerous men alive. And one of the greatest intellects."

Kong took a bite of sandwich and spoke between bouts of chewing. "By the time he was sixteen, he knew more than most of his masters and instructors. Sixteen grueling hours a day, seven days a week, fifty-two weeks a year, Doc trained, practiced and studied. It was the only life he knew."

"Doesn't sound like much of a childhood," Mick shook his head sadly.

Bart nodded in agreement. "Perhaps not. However, by the time he was eighteen years old and ready to attend college, he had already surpassed all of his instructors."

Kong set his sandwich aside. "In 1919, after returning home from the war, Percy and I returned to college to finish our educations and Doc joined us. He had been raised and trained on a remote island since he was one year old, so this was his first time in a traditional school."

Beginning of Flashback to January 28th, 1919.

University of New York State - Dean's Office

"Dean Baumhofer? Professor Holland and Professor Bama are requesting a meeting with you, sir."

The small man glanced up and squinted at his secretary from over the top of his bifocals. Frowning, he never smiled, the sixty-two year old man coughed to clear his throat. "What do they want, Miss Artho?" He tugged at his right earlobe and ran his hand over his balding scalp, a sign that he had been concentrating on something and didn't appreciate the interruption. Miss Artho had been his secretary for more years than she cared to admit and knew all of his different nervous signals. He was not an easy man to work for and had gone through many secretaries before she had come along.

"They said it was a private matter and want to discuss it only with you." Of course, she would find out about it later, when the paperwork had to be done. She knew every problem, every decision, and every dirty secret of this entire campus. All she had to do was wait and it would cross her desk sooner or later.

"Very well," He said impatiently. "Let them in."

A moment later, two men shuffled in through the doorway and stood in front of his mahogany desk. He liked his desk. With the chair that was four inches taller than the other chairs in the room and this massive desk between him and anyone before him, he felt like an important man. He compared himself to a great king, whose subjects begged an audience and were given his judgments from on high. Inwardly, he always smiled at this mental picture, while his face displayed an air of indifference.

The first man stepped forward and addressed him from the far side of the desk. "My apologies for this intrusion, Dean Baumhofer. I know you are a busy man, but we have need of your advice on a rather ... delicate matter." Walter Baumhofer always liked it when men assumed he was a busy man, an important man. Actually, he had just finished reading the morning paper and had been contemplating what he would like for lunch. In truth, he was rarely a busy man. The man standing at the edge of his desk was Professor Holland, a very well-respected chemist. He had nearly won a Nobel Prize for new and amazing concepts in his field of expertise. He had written several thesis' on molecular and quantum ... something or other. Walter Baumhofer had flunked chemistry in high school. He was never really a man of the sciences. He did, however, notice the old professor's hands were trembling slightly and there was a deeply concerned look on his face. Something was on his mind. Holland continued, "Professor Bama and I were hoping to talk to you about something ... about something that occurred yesterday."

"Please, gentlemen, take a seat." Baumhofer waved a hand at the chairs in front of his desk. These men of importance, men far more intelligent than he was, had come into his office, apologized for wasting his time, and requested an audience. These were the times he lived for, days where he would make a decision, like royal kings of old, and his final word was law. He even gave them a small polite, friendly smile to put the gentlemen at ease.

After sitting, the two Professors hesitated, as if uncertain where to start. Finally, Professor Bama spoke up. "Sir, we've come to you today to discuss one of our new students. His name is Johnathon Titan. He enrolled in this college last month and signed up for my classes on Advanced Molecular Biology and Professor Holland's classes on Chemistry. These are considered two of the most difficult classes at this college. Many students fail these classes. And nobody has ever taken them both in the same year. Until now."

Dean Baumhofer, naturally, recognized the name immediately. Clarke Titan, the boy's father, had donated a rather large sum of money to help build the new south wing of the college. The name Titan had become recognized with many New York institutions in the last few years. Massive donations were made to hospitals and schools. He already was beginning to visualize the problem, even before it was presented. Many sons of rich men thought they could ride their father's coat-tails to receive their degrees. Spoiled, little rich boys who would one day be the rich fathers of more spoiled, little rich boys. Walter Baumhofer had dealt with many such men in his lifetime and always refused to back down from their pompous preening. He knew someday this would probably cost him his job. Some rich bastard would hire a lawyer and threaten to sue the University, and the board of trusties would be forced to replace him as Dean. He refrained from interrupting and allowed Bama to continue.

"In the first couple of weeks, John seemed genuinely interested in the classes. He has been a model student. However, in the last week we have decided he is quickly becoming bored with the speed of the class. He has had perfect scores on the first few tests in my classroom. I consulted with Professor Holland about offering John the option of testing out of the beginning course and advancing to something more difficult. He had already decided to do the same. As per the University rules, we did not approach Mister Titan directly, but instead; we selected the top four students in each class and offered to administer this test to each of them. The Molecular Biology test takes approximately eight hours. All four students began the test promptly at eight in the morning. Professor Holland and I, and two teacher's aides were in attendance. At nine-fifteen John approached my desk at the front of the room. I assumed that he had a question regarding the test. He quietly announced that he had finished the test."

"I see, he simply guessed at each answer? He didn't even make the effort to try to pass the exam?"

"That was my first thought as well. However, I soon discovered he had actually finished the entire test."

"And his score?" Baumhofer thought he knew the answer even before he asked.

"Out of 1000 questions he answered correctly to 998 of them, per the answer sheet I used to grade the test." Bama nervously licked his lips and appeared a little uncomfortable.

"He only missed 2 out of 1000? Obviously, the boy cheated. Didn't he? Or is he some kind of genius? A savant?"

"That's just it, sir. I created the test and the answer sheet myself. After I checked the test and noticed the two errors, I asked John to accompany me into the adjoining room. I asked him about the two mistakes. After five minutes of discussion with this young man, I found out that the errors in calculations were mine, not his. He had a perfect score. Like you, I was doubtful. How could any eighteen year old man know what I spent my entire life studying? There were still over six hours left, so I asked Mr. Titan if he would be interested in testing his knowledge and take the senior exam. This test usually takes two days, and only 10 out of every 100 students pass. And most of the time, only barely. I have even had colleagues from MIT and several of the world's foremost biologists take this exam and they were not able to complete it. In fact, no one has ever completely answered all of the questions. I pride myself on the difficulty and complexity of this exam. The boy quietly accepted the test and went back to his desk."

"I assume this time our young man had some difficulty and was put in his proper place?" Professor Bama glanced at Professor Holland and looked down. He seemed to be searching for the words. "Well, don't keep me in suspense, how did young Titan do?"

"I watched him answer question after question, without any delay or hesitation. At noon I gave the students the option of breaking for a short snack and to stretch their legs. John Titan continued working. At one o'clock he approached my desk and handed me the exam book, announcing he was finished. By his quiet demeanor I assumed he couldn't go any further on the test. After he left the room I opened the book and discovered he had completed the entire test. Every question."

"Impossible!" Walter could feel his blood pressure rising. He was leaning forward on his desk, captivated by what the professor was telling him.

"Exactly my thoughts. But once more, the boy had answered every question. Correctly. Effortlessly. Calmly."

"And it's not even remotely possible that he might have cheated?" Asked the Dean, still rather dubious.

"Impossible. These weren't true or false questions. To be able to cheat at most of these questions, you would have to be a certifiable genius. This boy's level of intelligence is completely off the charts. When I asked him how he knew the answers he simply replied that he read … a lot. He gave me a list of some of the books he has studied. He claimed his father had one of the worlds' largest libraries. I can believe it. Some of the books he cited haven't even been translated into English! Titan claims to know several languages and read these books in their native language."

"I see why you came to me. What do you do with a student who comes to your school to learn … and it turns out he knows more than the teachers?" Professor Bama frowned at this inference but didn't interrupt. Long ago Walter Baumhofer had developed a habit of asking men what *they* thought should be done and, if it sounded correct and worthwhile, he would then suggest they pursue that course of action. Often he heard these men of greater learning tell his friends that he was a genius who knew the answer to every question. "So what do you recommend we do with our young Mister Titan, Professor Bama?"

"In light of his intelligence, and who his father is, I think we should let him graduate."

"After only one month? How do we explain this to the board of directors?"

"Advertise to new applicants and to the newspapers that one of the greatest minds in Advanced Molecular Biology recently graduated from our fine institution?" Bama asked with a sly grin on his face.

Dean Baumhofer considered this for a second. And smiled. Actually smiled. And the more he considered this proposal, the happier he felt. This was definitely a win/win solution. The board would like it. As he mulled this around in his balding head, he suddenly realized that the entire time he and Professor Bama had been talking, Professor Holland had been sitting quietly.

"Well, Professor Holland, I believe you also came in here to discuss something."

"Yes, sir, I did. I wished to talk to you about young John Titan and the tests he took in my Chemistry course."

Before the Dean could say a word, there was a rap on the door and Miss Artho poked her head in between the door and jamb. She was taken aback for a second when she noticed Dean Baumhofer smiling. She couldn't remember ever seeing him smile. Then she whispered, "Sorry to interrupt you, sir, but Professor Rozen is waiting out here for you. He wants to talk to you about a student named Johnathon Titan. It's about a test he gave him yesterday in Electronic Technologies."

In the following week, a New York newspaper article read, *February 1st, 1919 John Titan graduates from University of New York State with top honors in Chemistry, Advanced Molecular Biology, and Electronic Technologies.*

End of Flashback to January 28th, 1919.

"Very interesting." Wall whistled and shook his bearded head. "I never attended college myself, but I understand Electronic Technologies is an extremely tough class. So how many degrees does Doc Titan currently hold?"

Gibs' eyes looked skywards, as if the answer was written on the ceiling. "Last time I counted … twenty-two."

Bart corrected his friend. "Actually, he now has twenty-four. Let me see if I can remember them all. Naturally, Doc has a Medical Degree. Then there's Law, Psychology, Physical Chemistry, Engineering, Business Administration, Public Health, Musicology, Education/Linguistics, Geology/Paleontology, Doctorate of Humane Letters, Osteopathic Medicine, Chiropractic Medicine, Dentistry, Neurology and Neurosurgery, Theology, Philosophy, International Law, English Literature, World History, … what am I forgetting?"

Gibs nodded and added, "Physics, Meso-American Archaeology, Biochemistry, Comparative Biology, and Culinary Arts."

Mick's jaw dropped in amazement. "My goodness! Quite an impressive resume he has there."

Wall agreed. "Especially considering how much time he spends traveling the globe, righting wrongs."

"And you should see how many books and thesis' Doc's written." Kong added.

"When does he find time to rest?" Wall asked, still amazed.

Bart volunteered, "Occasionally, he retires to his Hidden Acropolis, up north somewhere. Of course, he still works when he's up there, too. Now that you mention it, I don't think he's ever taken a true vacation."

Gibs turned to Wall and Mick. "Okay, quid pro quo. How did Simon Blake learn so much? It seems he's as knowledgeable as Doc on a variety of subjects. He says he's been traveling all his life, all around the world. When did he have time to learn all of those things?"

Mick looked at Wall for an answer and received a blank look from the man-mountain. Wall shrugged his broad shoulders. "I dunno. I guess we've never questioned him about that." Wall's brow furrowed. "Now that you mention it, over the years, he's claimed to have degrees from a dozen different universities."

Bart offered a defense. "I'm sure there must be a simple explanation. Why would he lie to you?"

Mick looked perplexed. "Yes, why would he?"

Chapter Thirty-Eight
The Man of a 1000 Faces

April 6, 1945   7:30 am

Doc placed a hand on Blake's shoulder. "Simon, why don't you get some rest? I'll pilot the ship for a while. Looks like clear skies for the next hour or two."

Simon Blake stretched and yawned. "Perhaps, you're right. Thanks, Doc."

Blake walked to the small cabin, simply outfitted with two single beds, a dresser, and closet. An empty washbowl and pitcher filled with cool water sat on the dresser. A small mirror hung on the back of the closet door. Stockbridge snored lightly on the far bed. Blake removed his gray-blue jacket and eyed himself in the mirror. He wore a white under-shirt. His well-developed arms and shoulders were exposed in the dim light. His skin was nearly as colorless as the white under-clothing he wore. He stood for nearly a minute, studying his pale reflection in the mirror.

Reaching up with both hands, Blake pushed and pulled the lifeless, white skin covering his skull. When he touched the skin, it stayed where his fingers had molded it, similar to a sculptor manipulating soft clay. Seconds later, an albino Doc Titan stood where Blake had been. He moved his face from side to side, admiring the chiseled features. It didn't look quite right without the shaved scalp and goatee.

Once more his fingers began their manipulations and seconds later the face staring back at him belonged to Luthor Gibson. Despite the pale features, the man in the mirror was actually quite handsome. Blake raised one arm in mock semblance of the Darkness and squinted his eyes into slits. His pantomime of the Darkness was dead-on, lacking only flesh-toned pigmentation to complete the astonishing transformation.

"Do you always play dress-up when you have a sleep-over with the other kids?" Stockbridge asked from the far bed.

Simon Blake poured a cascade of chilled water into the basin and splashed his face with the cold liquid. When he finished drying his face with the towel, Blake once more resembled himself.

Stockbridge raised one eyebrow. "I always wondered how you returned your features to their original form."

Blake replied, his face completely impassive. "Cold water seems to tighten the skin. Listen, do me a favor. Don't tell John or Luthor …"

Stockbridge waved one hand in dismissal. "No problem. Why don't you get some sleep?"

"I can't." Blake boldly confessed.

Stockbridge's eyes narrowed and he asked quietly, "Are your dreams haunted by the ghosts of the men you've killed?"

"No. Do you have that problem?"

Stockbridge smiled mischievously. "Me? Heck no, I sleep like a baby. I know that I've never killed a man who didn't deserve it. The only time I have trouble sleeping is when I'm trying to solve a mystery. Got something on your mind?"

Blake nodded slowly. "No. It's not that. I don't sleep."

"Ever?"

"Not since the day I woke up in the hospital, after the plane crash, after my wife and son disappeared. I haven't slept a single night since then." Blake lowered his head and shut his eyes. He appeared exhausted.

Stockbridge was quiet for a moment and then stated, "Wow. That's just not healthy."

Blake's eyes reflected his humor but his face remained emotionless. "Coming from the guy who's been shot sixty-four times."

Stockbridge chuckled. "Touché. Guess we're all a little screwed up, to even want to be in this crimefighter business." He shifted uneasily on the bed and bit his lip. "Mind if I ask you a question?"

Blake shrugged his shoulders. "No, go ahead."

Stockbridge leaned forward slightly. "I've read the account of how you woke up in the hospital with snow-white hair and the pale, lifeless skin on your face. Supposedly, it was caused by the stress of the plane crash and the loss of your wife and son."

Blake nodded. "Yes. That's correct."

Stockbridge held out one hand, as if holding an invisible ball. "But thousands of people have lost family, faced great personal stress, and I've never heard of anyone else having the same results. What made your situation so unique?"

Simon rubbed his chin with one pale hand. "I've asked myself that same question a thousand times." He finally replied.

Stockbridge leaned closer, curious for the answer. "And?"

Blake sighed and responded with resignation. "When I have an answer, I'll let you know. I've been called the man with a thousand faces. Sometimes I would give everything I own to have only one face … my own."

"So is that why you've been coloring your hair and wearing make-up? To blend in? To be like … to *look* like everyone else?"

Blake nodded. "I suppose so. Sometimes it's just nice to be able to walk down the street and not have people stare. Or scare little children."

"Wow, I never thought of it that way. It's almost like you've been cursed or something. Good thing you have all of that Incan gold to finance your adventurous lifestyle. And it'll make rebuilding Unsolved Mysteries a lot easier."

Blake sighed. "That's just a way for the publisher to sell more pulps. There is no Incan treasure hoard. And Doc doesn't have some mythical, lost tribe of Mayans in South America sending him an unlimited supply of gold. The fact is, I'm flat broke. Only Gabe and Isabelle Robinson know of this, because they do the financial bookkeeping. I've done so many cases for charity and so much Pro Bono work, that I haven't replaced any of the money being spent. Every week someone is blowing up one of my planes or destroying one of my cars. And lately, the only employment being requested of Unsolved Mysteries, Inc. has been surveillance on cheating husbands, finding runaway pets, and standard police work."

"So that's why the Praetorian Securities warehouse was completely empty?"

"I've sold most of the planes and other equipment to keep the bills paid."

"Does Doc know about this? He could help you rebuild …"

Blake held up a hand to interrupt. "No. And to be honest, I'd rather he not find out. I'm not looking for charity, Preston. I simply need to decide what I want to do with my life from here. When I saw the Praetorian Securities warehouse destroyed, it was like a great weight had been lifted from my shoulders."

"How so?"

"This all started with the plane accident. On that day, I dedicated my life to finding out what happened to my wife and son. But over the last few years, I have lost my way. Fighting mummies, madmen with doomsday devices, strange creatures, and so on, has certainly been exciting. Recently, however, I discovered that I had completely forgotten about my family. It was never mentioned in detail in the pulp adaptation of my life, but I spent a short time in a mental ward after the accident. I had a nervous breakdown. If Mick hadn't helped me, I might still be there today. He has always been my moral compass; I don't know what I would have done without him. He was there from the first day I lost my wife and son."

"I understand, Simon. That's exactly what Whitney is to me. Without her in my life, I dread to think of what might happen. I'd probably go crazy."

"Crazy. Funny that you should use that term. Sometimes, I fear I might be going mad again, losing my mind. My memory has been failing me. I can't seem to remember the faces of my wife and son. My son, who would be seven years old now. I have bits and pieces of memories that conflict with other memories. I remember being at two distinct places at the same time in my life. Excavating for emeralds in Australia and drilling for oil in Asia."

"Well, you did travel a lot during your youth. Sometimes, the years start to blend together. We've all been down rather long and winding paths."

Blake nodded in agreement. "Perhaps that's all it is. To be honest, I think it's time for me to move forward with my life. Recently, I've been letting Andrew Carter take over the role of Guardian, mostly because I've lost interest."

"I understand, Simon. Sometimes I think it might be time to marry Whitney and settle down. Let men like Sentry take over the fight. Pass the heroic baton, as it were. We're not getting any younger, you know."

Blake's eyes showed gratitude. "Thanks for talking about this. You're an okay guy, Preston."

"If you don't sleep, what are you going to do now?" Stockbridge asked.

"I've taught myself to meditate. To help clear my mind." Blake sat in the middle of the second bed and leaned his back against the wall. He closed his eyes and relaxed. "Thanks, again."

Stockbridge lay back on his bed and closed his eyes. "No problem. But if you start snoring, I *will* be forced to shoot you."

Both men chuckled and the room grew quiet. Minutes later, Stockbridge was lightly snoring again. One lonely tear gathered in the corner of Blake's eye and trickled down his white, lifeless cheek.

Chapter Thirty-Nine
The Titan Rehabilitation Institute and Clinic

April 6, 1945 7:30 am

The four greatest crime-fighters in the world were assembled in the large cabin of the Windjammer. John 'Doc' Titan. Simon Blake, the Guardian. Luthor Gibson, the Darkness. And Preston Stockbridge II, the Scorpion. Daring adventurers, men bred for action and excitement, millionaires, philanthropists, supermen. All four were anxious to arrive at their final destination. They had approached the southern-most edge of the ice mass called the Geographic North Pole.

Blake stared out of the windows at the huge expanse of whiteness. "Doc, I have a question for you. It's about your operations on criminals. Are they truly successful? Did you truly discover a 'crime' gland? Something that can be surgically removed and alter a man's propensity for committing evil deeds?"

Gibson leaned forward. "I'm interested to hear this myself. I've often heard whispered rumors of the Titan Rehabilitation Institute and Clinic."

Doc considered his response and then nodded. "I can answer this, but you must swear to never tell Bart, Kong, and the others the whole truth."

"This sounds interesting." Stockbridge chimed in.

"I don't truly operate on criminals, like you might think." Doc confessed. "The scar on the back of the neck is where a stainless steel, numbered implant is slipped under the skin."

Stockbridge frowned. "So what does that do?"

Doc spread his hands. "Absolutely nothing. It's simply an identity marker."

Blake's eyes narrowed. "And the cure for criminal tendencies?"

"Do you understand the concept of 'The Seven Deadly Sins,' also known as the 'Capital Vices' or 'Cardinal Sins,' a fallen man's tendency to sin?" Doc asked them.

Blake nodded. "Certainly."

Doc began his explanation. "Simply put, I hired a staff of prominent psychologists and psychiatrists and posed them with a series of questions. If the seven deadly sins are greed, lust, envy, gluttony, jealousy, sloth, and wrath, and these sins are the root cause to every 'fallen' man's tendency to sin, how do we cure such men?

"For example, the majority of greedy men tend to have been born poor and have had to fight and scrounge for everything they own and earn in life. Through encounter groups and re-education, most men can overcome this compulsion to hoard and steal. Years ago, it was established that environment often made the man, not vise versa. If a man was born poor and wanted to quickly better his position in the world, he could lie, cheat, or steal. We simply place these men in new environments where they no longer feel the need or desire to depend on these vices to advance. Usually, a well paying job and the respect of their family and peers are all that is required.

"Because of the Depression, there were many men, 'lost men,' as they became known, who simply had no other way to make a living. They found themselves lying and stealing just to get through another day. Trapped in this world, it simply takes another push to resort to robbery. Another push to commit murder. These men were the easiest ones to convert to better lives. Most were thrilled to be given another chance to start over. To be trained in a field that interested them. To provide for their family.

"Every man has some private desire that motivates him to get out of bed each morning and face the world. Essentially, we simply asked each man one basic question. *What do you want from your life?* And then tried to fulfill that desire."

Stockbridge looked doubtful. "And this cured every criminal you've ever met?"

Doc sadly shook his head. "Unfortunately, we have only a ninety-eight percent cure rate. Ninety-three percent are rehabilitated with the methods I just described. Sometimes voluntary treatment, using medications in conjunction with various forms of psychotherapy, may be undertaken. This has proven most effective. Fortunately, chemical imbalances in the brain or other physical ailments only account for about five percent of our cures.

"I'm afraid there will always be those who are essentially criminally or mentally insane. This is the remaining two percent. They are usually transported to asylums and prisons throughout the United States and abroad. Someday I hope to be able find cures for these unfortunates."

"Ninety-eight percent sounds like pretty good odds to me. Why don't you want Bart and Kong to know about this?" Blake asked.

Doc took a deep breath and sighed. "Some people have not embraced the idea of rehabilitation. Prisons remove criminals from the general population but usually does very little to help the prisoners become truly rehabilitated. To once more become a useful member of society. More often than not, it simply breeds better-educated criminals. I'm afraid some of my friends are 'old school.' Eye-for-an-eye retribution is closer to their style."

Blake nodded. "Blood for blood. Like Scorpion and Darkness practice."

Stockbridge sneered. "I don't need to practice, I'm very good at my profession, Simon."

Doc ignored Stockbridge's response. "We have used graduates to maintain warehouses, assist at hospitals, even work in respected banking establishments. These men have tried hard to change their lives for the better. They don't need someone constantly looking over their shoulder and counting the silverware. Trust and respect are essential ingredients to total rehabilitation."

Gibson had listened intently, his hands knitted together, index fingers creating a steeple. "I confess, I have often wondered if there might not be an alternative to fighting crime the way I do. Mind you, if a man comes at me with murderous intent, I believe he deserves the justice I dispense. However, I have sent many men to prison that might have profited more from your charity. If you were so inclined, I would be willing to donate toward your Rehabilitation Institute. Both in patients and in funds."

"And I as well." Blake added.

The three men turned their gazes toward Stockbridge. "I suppose I wouldn't be considered much of a philanthropist if I ignored this opportunity. Okay, count me in, Doc."

Chapter Forty
The World of Man

April 6, 1945   9:00 am

Sherlock Holmes climbed over the ice-slick stone and sat down for a minute. His breathing was harder than normal, but he was not exhausted. This was fairly impressive for a man his age, over ninety years old. The elderly detective was born January 6, 1854 at a farmstead in the North Riding of Yorkshire, England. He was over six feet tall, still straight, thin, and strong in posture. He had long ago abandoned the deerstalker cap and London fog coat. His black thick hair, with graying temples, blew in the cool morning breeze. He had sharp and piercing, gray-blue eyes that seemed to absorb everything around him at a glance.

His breathing slowed and he watched as the beautiful woman in white followed his trail. She was stunning, an angel on Earth. Her hood, with a fur lining inside, covered most of her head with the exception of the gold-plated face mask that hid her true features. If the unseen face matched the beautiful, delicate white hands, it could have been carved from alabaster marble by a sculptor with masterful skills. Her golden-blonde hair cascaded from the opening at the front of her hood. She saw him and smiled beneath the mask, her eyes glowing with a heavenly radiance, and he felt a smile form on his own features.

The Council of Elders simply referred to this woman as the Lady in White. By her request, she had no other name. And they all respected her request.

"Sherlock, if you are too tired to continue, I could finish the journey alone."

Holmes chuckled lightly. "Milady, I am simply admiring the most splendid view on Earth."

The Lady in White ignored his obvious flirtatious remark and gazed at the panoramic view of the surrounding snow-capped mountains. "You are correct; the view is truly breathtaking. I understand why he prefers living up here."

Sherlock Holmes frowned slightly and replied. "He lives up here to be away from 'the world of man', as he so eloquently states it. It is not right for him to sequester himself like this. It's not … healthy."

From behind her golden mask, the Lady in White responded. "Perhaps, you are correct. But he seems to enjoy this … solitary life. And he is not like other men, so why should he live like other men?"

Sherlock closed his eyes and absorbed the warmth of the morning sunlight. "I wish John Watson was still alive to see this splendor. He loved the Highlands and the European Alps. You know, he would be ninety-two this year. He's been gone over five years now."

The Lady in White nodded. "He lived a good and full life."

Sherlock smiled. "You're always a ray of sunshine. The silver lining on a cloudy day. But compared to other members of our fellowship, John and I are merely spring chickens. Phileas is one hundred and thirteen. Quatermain is one hundred and twenty-eight years old. Challenger is the youngest and he's eighty-two this year. Old Adam is one hundred and fifty-five." He found himself wondering how old the woman behind the mask might be. But she volunteered no information in this regard to Holmes.

"You're only as old as you feel." She offered.

Sherlock responded quietly. "It's not the years, milady, it's the mileage. Seen too many things. Things that can't be unseen. I've done too many things that can't be undone."

A deep voice came from around the corner. So deep it sounded like a bear, growling deep in its cave. The voice belonged to the man named Adam. Just Adam. It was a name he chose for himself, many years ago.

"I certainly hope you haven't come all of this way to cheer me up, old friend. Because you really aren't doing a very good job."

The Lady in White looked at the trail ahead. "Adam. It's so very good to hear your voice once more."

Sherlock and the Lady in White cautiously climbed up the remaining incline for several more yards. The path up the mountain stopped here but opened into a cavern, carved deep into the mountainside. The view was breathtakingly spectacular on three sides, open to the mountains and clouds below. By looking out, and allowing the cave opening to disappear from peripheral sight, a person felt like they were perched on top of the world. As Sherlock and the mysterious, beautiful woman approached, the man known as Adam covered part of his face and retreated deeper into his cavern and the shadows. By hiding the scars on his face, he simply exposed the deep ones on his hand and forearm. The flesh was a mottled, grayish color. Sherlock had always hoped that someday this poor wretched man would feel acceptance, but old wounds run deep.

Sherlock offered his open hand. "How are you doing, my old friend?"

Adam graciously accepted the greeting, shaking hands with his old companion. "Perhaps I would feel better if you had brought a birthday cake with one hundred and fifty-five candles. Old Adam? Is that what you call me these days?"

The Lady in White laughed, her voice clear and bright. "You always make me smile." She reached out and caressed his face, her fingertips like butterflies on his cheek. Sherlock had never witnessed Adam allow anyone else to touch him in such a personal manner. She was truly a heavenly angel on Earth. Even though he was slouched over, she had to stand on tiptoes to reach his face. Adam was a giant of a man, standing nearly eight feet tall and far more massive than any man Sherlock had ever met. And yet he could be as gentle in manner as a warm spring breeze. However, his cadaverous flesh gave off the fetid stench of the grave. One of the unfortunate curses he suffered for being only half-alive.

"And you always brighten my life with your visits. It has been too long since we last met." Adam said solemnly.

"You could always move down into the valley …." She began, leadingly.

Adam nodded his head, his coal-black hair danced across his broad shoulders. "I have … other obligations. Besides, my place is here, away from …"

Holmes finished the phrase he had heard so often, "… the world of men."

Adam smiled at Sherlock's tease. "I suppose I've said that once or twice before." In contrast to the rest of him, Adam's teeth were almost brilliantly white and straight.

Sherlock nodded. "Yes. Once or twice. She wasn't asking you to return to the world of men, merely to the valley below. Do you know why we have come?"

Adam's long, coal-black hair blew over one eye and he left it there. His eyes were the hardest feature to ignore, once you came close. Sherlock had known many a man with a grotesque scar here or a deformity there. But Adam possessed one blue iris and one green iris, mismatched in both size and alignment. The whites were a yellowish sickly color, sometimes seen in patients with jaundice. Sherlock could tell a lot about a man by studying the eyes, the windows to the soul. So he developed a habit of looking directly into a man's eyes. Regretfully, he found it hard to look into Adam's eyes. Regretfully, because it was not Adam's fault.

He had been 'born' into this world a poor, wretched soul, malformed, mismatched, a patchwork man; sewn together from random pieces and parts. He had been rejected by men as a wretch, a daemon, a horror, even a monster. Even after one hundred and fifty years had passed, the pain of that rejection was still painted in his deep-set eyes. And his haunted eyes reflected his tortured soul. Was it any wonder he sought the solitary refuge of these peaceful mountains? And similar to the grim gargoyles that adorned church cathedral buttresses and rooftops, this grotesque creature enjoyed his private mountain aerie, where he could silently observe the world.

Sherlock noticed the ring on Adam's little finger. It was a simple band but Adam never removed it. He was forced to wear the wedding band on the last finger on his left hand, since he lost the third digit in a battle to the death with a monstrous, monarch ape. Even though Lady Megan was murdered fifty years before Sherlock was even born, Adam still remembered her fondly. The blind woman was his wife only a short time, but every year he privately honored her memory.

Adam responded to Sherlock's question. "Yes, the Chosen Ones are approaching. They will arrive soon."

"The Chosen Ones? Is that how we are referring to them now? Men do love their titles, don't they? Illuminati. People of the Light. Council of Elders." The Lady laughed lightly. "But, yes. It is time for them to learn the truth ... the whole truth. To put an end to secrets. Veritatem dies aperit itaque Vincit omnia veritas."

Adam acknowledged the Latin phrase. "Yes, 'Time reveals the truth and the truth conquers all things.' I have waited nearly sixty years for this time."

Sherlock sighed heavily and nodded his head. "Yes. And I as well, Adam. Remember, we were both there from the very beginning. Will you come down and spend a day with us? Meet with our guests?"

Adam nodded. "Yes. I was planning on leaving my home today anyway. I've been reading the depressing works of Nietzsche, *'He who fights with monsters might take care, lest he thereby become a monster ...'*"

Sherlock looked deeply concerned as he finished the phrase, "*... and if you gaze for too long into the abyss, the abyss gazes also back into you.'* Is everything okay, Adam? You seem troubled."

Adam was quiet for a long moment. Something had been preying on his mind. "Yes ... and no. My ... father has need of our help. I was going to appeal to the others in the council to assist him, in his hour of need. If they agree, he has desperate and urgent need of the special skills possessed by our order of monks, the Brotherhood of Silence."

It was the Lady in White's turn to look concerned now. "You have heard the voice of your father, Adam?"

"Yes, it came to me in the night."

"In a dream ... a vision?"

Adam smiled broadly and then laughed. If one could look beyond the obvious scars, his face was handsome. "No ... on my long wave radio transmitter/receiver." He pointed a bent thumb, with a black, broken nail, over one shoulder and indicated a large black box with a speaker mounted on top.

Lady in White laughed behind her golden mask. "Adam, you devil, you always make me smile."

Adam turned away and whispered, repeating himself. "And you always brighten my life with your visits."

Sherlock warily glanced around the large cave entrance with keen eyes. He had once met Adam's friend and did not wish to repeat that particular experience. His companion did not care for visitors. The great detective shuddered as his memories flashed back to another monstrous creature, the horrible hell-hound of the Baskervilles.

Chapter Forty-One
Allied Intelligence

April 6, 1945   9:00 am

The Sentry listened intently as these men, the leaders of the Allied Intelligence, discussed various strategies. He had studied under some of these very men, learning everything they knew about modern combat and strategies of ancient wars. They were the best of the best and he was trained to be the best of them all. He had learned quickly, as he seemed to do with everything he studied. A lesser man might have broken under the constant pressure of his training but James Adams was as mentally strong as he was physically. He was often referred to as a Super-Soldier, a term with which he was not entirely comfortable. He was, however, an experienced combatant with superhuman endurance and physical abilities at the absolute peak of human strength and endurance.

He was taught by gifted tacticians and leaders of men, and soon became one himself. His training included the use of every known weapon, including his own body. It was very possible he was the greatest hand-to-hand combatant on Earth, both defensively and offensively. Born in 1918, on the fourth of July, James Ethan Adams felt he was born as a passionate patriot to his country. When James Cagney's Yankee Doodle Dandee came to the theatres in 1942, Adams had watched it several times and was inspired by the main character's patriotism. In fact, he offered to be code-named The Patriot. Unfortunately, there was already another costumed adventurer using the name. With one gloved hand, he toyed with the white, five-pointed star pinned on his chest. He was anxious to get back to combat. Every second he sat in this room, men were dying on the battlefields.

He glanced over his shoulder at the young man beside him. Christopher 'Cody' Sawyer was his young sidekick and an extraordinary lad. Under his tutelage, Adams had placed the youngster into an intensive training program. He met and exceeded every challenge placed in his path. Originally, the Allied Forces were reluctant to allow a minor into combat situations. However, the lad proved to be an inspiration to many young men volunteering for military service. He became Sentry's teenage partner, known only as Kid Sentry. Together they faced dangers, led covert operations, and daunted masterminds and villains, like Count Drakoft and the Black Skull.

Sergeant Richard Gunn was silently chewing on his unlit cigar as he listened to his superior officers. He didn't always agree with the orders he was given, but he was a loyal and unquestioning soldier. Usually someone of his rank would not attend such a high-level meeting, but Gunn also had history with both Black Skull and Count Drakoft. Besides, several times he had been given a choice between being promoted or performing dangerous special reconnaissance operations and he always chose the latter.

King George VI, English Prime Minister Winston Churchill, Australian Prime Minister John Curtain, General Douglas MacArthur, General Dwight Eisenhower, Field Marshall Bernard Montgomery, and Field Marshall Sir Thomas Blarney were all in attendance. Gunn liked Churchill, with his well-known quotations and his no-nonsense manners. 'Without victory there is no survival' was one of Gunn's favorites.

At the end of the long table sat Air Commandant and Director of the WRAF, Jean Lena Conan Doyle. A lady of great merit, she had risen to the highest achievable rank in the Women's Royal Air Force and was Aide de Camp to the Queen of England. She was one of the first women to be admitted into the Allied Command and had often proven herself worthy of the honor. Noticing James Adams glancing in her direction, she flashed him a quick, polite smile. He smiled in return. His thoughts wandered back in time, remembering the late nights he had stayed awake, trying to finish reading one of her father's stories. While he enjoyed the Sherlock Holmes stories immensely, his favorite Arthur Conan Doyle story was the Lost World with Professor Challenger. After all, what young man didn't enjoy dinosaurs and high adventure?

Unfortunately, President Franklin Roosevelt had fallen ill and could not attend the conference. Everyone knew his health was quickly deteriorating. Little did they know that in six days, April 12, 1945, while at Warm Springs, Georgia, he would die of a cerebral hemorrhage.

The communications between Black Skull and Count Drakoft had been intercepted by military intelligence. The Germans were unaware that their secret codes had been deciphered by one of America's leading mathematicians and cryptologists, Bartholomew 'Bart' J. Blackwell, and that the contents of their coded messages were now known to the Allied Forces. It was agreed to allow Drakoft to enter the top secret military base and attempt his sabotage. They would capture the megalomaniac and Nazi Germany would have one less madman working for them. Sentry and his young partner would lead the assault and capture of Drakoft. Sergeant Gunn was assigned to a separate top secret mission and would be briefed the following day, at the Parliamentary offices.

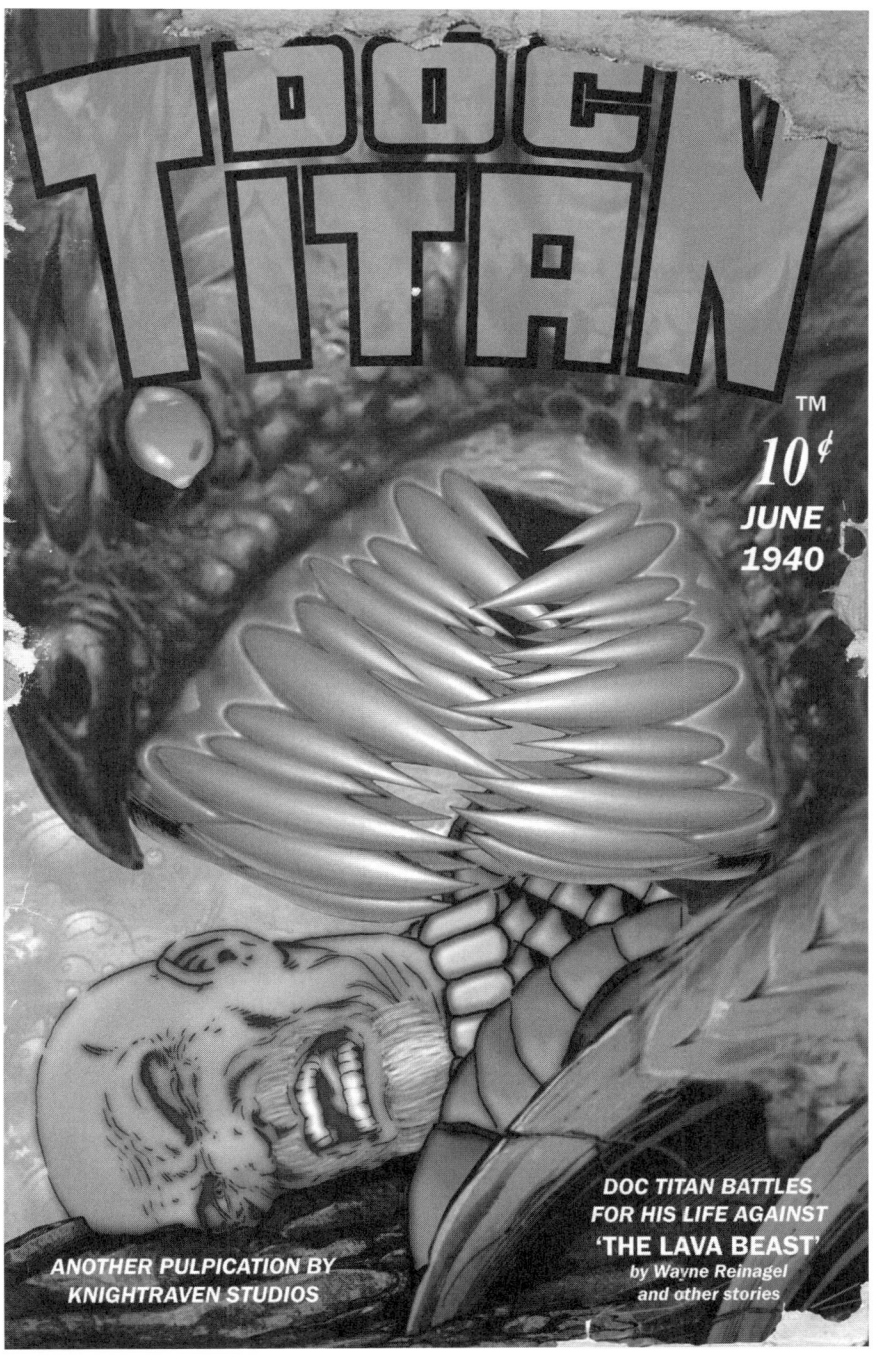

Chapter Forty-Two
The Mystery at the North Pole

April 6, 1945 1:00 pm

The passengers of the Windjammer were struggling to maintain balance. The large airship was being roughly buffeted by horrendous winds that threatened to tear it from the sky. The engines whined as Doc Titan fought the controls and attempted to turn the gigantic zeppelin into the current. Resembling a monstrous whale breeching through the turbulent surface of a sea storm, the Windjammer performed great leaps and dives. Finally the ship turned and Doc adjusted the flight path to avoid re-entering the maelstrom.

Stockbridge hung onto a leather strap mounted to the wall. "What the heck was that?"

Blake studied the dials on the console. "Some sort of natural hemispherical disturbance. Appears to be the merging of several low-pressure mixtures, of varying temperatures, colliding and confluencing into a massive storm system. A natural, self-sustaining, perpetual phenomenon."

Stockbridge looked at Blake, frowned, and repeated his question. "What the heck is that?"

Doc translated. "We entered a strong blast of cold air clashing with warm air and causing near tornado conditions."

Stockbridge looked at Doc and then Blake. "See, was that so hard to say?"

"That is the location we seek but we can't subject this ship to that kind of stress. It will rip the craft apart." Doc warned the passengers. "The wind gauge is reading air velocity gusts at over two hundred and fifty miles per hour. I'll polarize the windshield so you can see the effect for yourselves."

He flipped a switch on the console and the reflective quality of the glass altered. The sky was a shifting spectrum of colors and the swirling storm outside was clearly visible. The view was quite breathtaking, Mother Nature in her naked glory, painting a canvas of beauty from a terrible force almost beyond description. The cold air was a vivid blue and the warm air a crimson pallor, and where they mixed was a kaleidoscope of movement and color. The natural electro-static phenomenon covered an area twenty-five miles in diameter. The collision of electrically charged particles in the magnetosphere with atoms in the Earth's upper atmosphere created a unique form of Aurora Borealis, or Northern Lights. A rainbow pallet of colors danced in the electrified skies. From the ground, visibility would be non-existent for a dozen miles in every direction. Mount Kilimanjaro could have sat in the midst of the swirling maelstrom and gone unseen.

Blake assisted Doc with piloting the behemoth craft. "What could cause this? A volcanic turbulence under the area, throwing off unnatural amounts of warmth, perhaps?"

Doc nodded. "That's a reasonable assumption. We'll have to find a place to land outside the storm and ..."

Stockbridge interrupted them and pointed to the horizon. "How about over there?"

Gibson focused at the distant phenomenon. "What is that?"

In the distance was a sight no man would have ever expected to see at the North Pole. On the hard-packed ice was a series of bright lights, indicating what appeared to be a landing zone. They had been nearly invisible until Doc had polarized the windshield. Now the small flames glowed like a parallel pattern of glittering stars. Doc steered the large craft in that direction.

Doc used a powerful pair of binoculars. "There are several scores of men down there on the ice."

Blake accepted the glasses, as Doc passed them along. "Are we going to land down there? Could be a trap."

"If they were going to set a trap, there were easier places than the North Pole to spring it."

Stockbridge checked his automatics. "All I know is, if I don't shoot something soon, I'm going to go stir crazy."

"Has anyone mentioned to you that you are a little bloodthirsty, Preston?" Blake queried.

Stockbridge shrugged. "Yeah. Doc did, just yesterday. For me, shooting something is a misdemeanor; the more I miss it, the meaner I get."

"There is almost always a peaceful alternative ..." Doc started.

"Blah, blah, blah." Stockbridge mocked. "Listen, I agreed your Rehabilitation Institute and Clinic is a great idea. And it is. But I grew up on the same block as one of the Untouchables, the men who took down Al Capone. Old Jimmy Malone would say, *'You wanna know how you do it? Here's how: they pull a knife, you pull a gun. He sends one of yours to the hospital; you send one of his to the morgue! That's the Chicago way!'* That's how I deal with gang lords. When I started my career as a crime fighter, I sought justice. Since then I have broken every law I swore to defend, but I am content with the knowledge that I have always attempted to do the right thing."

The Windjammer dropped toward the ground and Blake lowered the toll ropes. The men on the ground tied the airship down like trained professionals. Despite the blustering air turbulence around the mountain, this area was relatively quiet. The zeppelin had been designed with reinforcements so it could rest its full weight on the cabins below. This way egress from the ship could be made at ground level.

Doc Titan emerged from the ship first, clad in a knee-length parka and snow goggles to cut the intense glare reflected from the white snow. He wore a thick fur hat to protect his bald head. Simon Blake, Preston Stockbridge, and Luthor Gibson followed, similarly clothed. Each of the heavily-clad men who had watched them disembark, sported a carbine rifle, slung over their shoulder. Many were certainly wearing revolvers and automatics, tucked into holsters under the thick fur coats. However, there were no threatening movements made toward the four heroes.

One large man walked through the throng of men and stood before Doc Titan. He removed his thick glove and extended a bear-claw of a hand. He was tightly bundled against the intense freezing conditions, but his leathered skin gave every indication that he had faced cold climates before. His features were covered in thick dark hair, a full mustache and beard covering the lower half of his face. Icicle stalactites dangled from the hair around his mouth. He removed the tinted snow glasses and smiled broadly at the four men.

"It's a pleasure to meet you, sirs. We have been awaiting your arrival." He turned to face Doc Titan. "Imagine my surprise when I found out R. J. MacReady was actually Doc Titan. Do you remember me, sir?"

"Certainly, you were my assistant meteorologist fifteen years ago, in Antarctica. The name is J. W. Campbell, if I remember correctly."

Campbell nodded. "That's right. I'm impressed that you remember me. However, it's really been closer to twenty years ago."

Stockbridge glanced around at the gathering of men. "You've been expecting our arrival? How did you know?"

"Of course." Campbell flashed a smile, as if he knew a private joke. "The Council of Elders knows everything. They told us you would arrive today. They are also known as The Leaders of the People of the Light."

"Geez, they sound like Darkness, they 'know' everything." Preston teased.

"And you're a member of this Council?" Doc asked guardedly.

"Heavens no, sir." Campbell responded. "They are very great men. I simply … serve a need, when it is requested of me."

The winds were dying down and the men could talk normally again. Blake indicated Campbell and the other men. "And what need are you and these men serving here today?"

"I am to escort you to Sanctuary." Campbell stated pointedly.

"Sanctuary? What is …?" Blake began.

Campbell held out his hand to stop Blake's question and then tucked it back into the warm glove. "Believe me; you'll have to see it for yourself. I lack the words to do it justice." He noticed the machine pistols Blake and Titan had armed themselves with, strapped to their thighs. "However, weapons are strictly forbidden at Sanctuary. You'll have to leave them behind. Trust me, they will not be needed."

Gibson studied Campbell. "Forbidden by this Council?"

"Actually, it is a sign of respect for the Brotherhood, a society of monks who dwell at Sanctuary. No weapons or modern equipment of any kind. They live a very simple life."

Stockbridge took one step back. "Well, you'll have to wrestle my guns from my cold, dead fingers before …"

Campbell held up his open hands in a gesture of peace. "Actually, Preston Stockbridge, you are not going to Sanctuary."

Stockbridge sputtered. "How do you know my name …?"

"What are …?" Doc began.

Campbell held up one hand to calm everyone. "My apologies, that came out wrong. I was asked to request a favor of Mr. Stockbridge and Mr. Gibson. We have urgent need of their unique … skills. A mission of grave importance. If, of course, they are willing to accept the danger."

Stockbridge's face brightened. "Danger? Why didn't you say so? I'm your man. How about you, Lew? You want to take a deadly mission or go sit with some moldy old monks?"

Gibson's eye twitched. "On one condition. Don't call me 'Lew.' Ever again."

Campbell continued. "Your assignment is to safeguard a treasure until it reaches its destination. Joseph will take you to a plane, fueled up and ready for takeoff. I am informed you are capable aviators and will not require a pilot."

The man named Joseph guided Gibson and Stockbridge to a nearby hanger, painted white and completely invisible from the air. Campbell turned back to Doc Titan and Simon Blake.

"Now, we only need to wait for the rest of your group." Campbell explained.

Guardian nodded. "We are the only ones on board the Windjammer."

Campbell smiled knowingly. "I was instructed to wait for the other eight to arrive."

Guardian eyed him with wonder as Doc spoke.

"I assume you are referring to Kong, Bart, Gibs, Wall, and Mick. I had doubts we would be able to successfully leave them behind. And the other three …"

Guardian nodded, understanding where Doc was leading. "… are Cassie, Pam, and Megan."

Doc turned to Campbell. "How do you know …?"

"I told you, the Council of Elders knows everything."

Doc Titan stood silent for a long minute, his eyes studying the faces of the men around them. He turned back to Campbell. "Tell your men to turn their backs to us and lower their hoods." Campbell responded to the request and the other men silently complied. He turned back to Campbell again, without explaining his strange request. "I would like to speak to Simon, alone."

Campbell smiled. "No problem." He and the others walked a short distance away, certainly out of earshot.

Doc whispered to Blake. "These men are all graduates of my Rehabilitation Institute, with the exception being Campbell. This could be a trap, as Gibson suggested. What is your opinion, Simon?"

Blake thought for a long moment. "I haven't been in this business as long as you, but I can usually read men. They all seem to be decent and I believe Campbell is a good man. Plus, your Rehabilitation Institute does have a ninety-eight percent success rate, right?"

Doc agreed with Blake's assessment. "Yes. I believe you are right about them, and Campbell. So we go with them?"

Blake shrugged. "I'm certainly not going back to New York without knowing what's going on. And why we were summoned or invited here by the People of the Light. Whoever they might be." They motioned for Campbell to return.

Doc met Campbell's gaze. "I have one more question I need you to answer. Why do you serve this Council of Elders?"

Campbell sighed deeply. "Fifteen years ago, several members of the Council saved me from a horrible fate, a fate worse than death." He turned to look at Doc. "Worse than that *'thing from another world'* we thawed out of the frozen ice, at the Antarctica science station. I owe them my very life. And I swear on that life, that you and your friends will be safe when we reach Sanctuary."

Doc studied the large man's face as he spoke. "I believe you, Campbell."

"Your eight friends should arrive here in approximately twelve hours. We can all leave for Sanctuary then."

"How is it you are so well informed?" Blake asked.

J. W. Campbell flashed a quicksilver smile. "The Leaders of the People of the Light ..."

Doc and Blake finished his sentence. "... know everything."

Doc leaned close to Campbell. "I do not want to wait that long. They can follow behind us later."

Campbell nodded negatively. "The round trip will take several hours and the dogs would be too exhausted."

"Do you have a second in command, Campbell?"

Campbell nodded. "Of course. Joseph, please come here."

Doc addressed Campbell. "You can take us now and Joseph can bring the others later. I will leave them a written message, so they know everything is okay."

Joseph stepped up, with almost military precision. "I can assure you, sir, your friends will be in safe hands. I pledge my life on it."

Campbell frowned. "But the dogs ..."

Doc smiled this time. "I have something far better than sled dogs."

Five minutes later, the cargo bay door to the small garage, located behind the private cabins in the Windjammer, opened and three sleek-looking vehicles exited. Single passenger snowmobiles with silenced mufflers and powerful engines. Within minutes, although neither had ever used one before, Blake and J. W. Campbell became accustomed to handling and operating them. The three men soon set out in the direction of the mysterious destination known as Sanctuary.

Chapter Forty-Three
The Island at the Top of the World

April 6, 1945   5:00 pm

Kong's head was tilted back and his eyes were nearly closed. In spite of the thousands of hours he and his friends had spent traveling over the years, he never could adjust to the boredom. He could check the sensors and the course only so many times. There were moments he prayed for someone to dive down and attack their aircraft, merely to relieve the boredom. He had been sitting at the console for nearly two hours and was fit to bust. He had eaten another sandwich, in an effort to remain active and awake. Now the warm, rocking cabin and full belly were putting him to sleep. He considered starting a fight with Bart but a nap sounded better.

Gibs flew over the passenger seat and bounced with zeal. He was so ecstatic about his electronic guns working and what it would mean for his larger bug-killer, he had been bouncing off the walls since they left New York. He had already filled half of a legal tablet with doodles and figures as he designed and re-designed some new electrical doodad. Gibs was the richest of all of Doc's men, holding patents on several hundred electrical inventions.

The plane rocked as he landed, but only slightly because he was such a small man. He was only one hundred and forty pounds soaking wet and stood barely four feet tall, certainly the smallest of Doc's crew of adventurers.

Kong eyed Gibs grumpily, with one sleepy eye. "Geez, Gibs, you're as giddy as a school girl. You didn't drink any of my soda pop concoction, did you?"

Bart stood behind Kong and added, "He's probably thinking how much money he can make off his newest invention and how many more doo-hickies he can buy with the pile of cash."

They looked outside at the bright reflection of the snow, through the polarized glass. Hundreds of miles of ice and snow, as far as the eye could see in every direction. They couldn't ask for a more boring landscape.

Bart nudged Kong on the shoulder. "Hey, sleeping beauty, how long have you had the radar volume turned down?"

Kong yawned widely; his gaping mouth was abnormally large. "Only about half an hour. The spinning wheel and the constant ping, ping, ping noise was giving me a dang headache."

Bart tapped the console with his black cane. "So you don't know how long that plane has been following us?"

Kong bolted upright in his chair and stared at the black and green screen. "Holy … not merely following, they are coming right at us! Better buckle up folks, we have company." He announced loudly, waking Mick.

Doc and Big Tom were the two best pilots in the group, but Kong was like chaos personified behind the wheel. He performed the most unexpected moves at the most unexpected times. He pulled back hard on the wheel and Bart was tossed to the rear of the plane, as it suddenly gained altitude. Later, Bart accused him of doing this on purpose, just to wrinkle Bart's new suit. The throttle was goosed and Kong turned the wheel sharply to come up behind the other plane. Much to his surprise, the pilot of the other craft simply mimicked his eclectic moves and stayed on his tail. He reached into his aerial bag of tricks and tried several other maneuvers, ones that would have raised the hair of the bravest of barnstormers. But to no avail. The other aircraft followed him, almost effortlessly. He was about to attempt something truly dangerous when a familiar voice came over the radio receiver.

"Is something chasing us, or are we just having fun?" Pam's excited tones came through the speakers. She was obviously enjoying the aerial acrobatics.

Kong frowned at the speaker box. "Pam? What are you doing out here?"

Pam laughed. "I thought that was obvious, darling. I'm following you."

Gibs grabbed the transmitter. "He means where did you get that plane and how did you find us?"

Pam tsk-tsked. "Ah, boys, a girl has got to keep her secrets. By the way, where are we heading?"

Gibs, who always believed in the rule that women should stay home and out of harms way, replied. "We're following Doc and you're going home."

"Sorry, boys, that's not happening this time. Me and the girls are in this for the long haul, whether you like it or not." Pam responded firmly.

Bart walked to the front of the plane, rubbing a growing knot on the back of his skull, where it had slammed into the rear cargo compartment during Kong's deadly flying. "Might as well give in, she's not leaving. Besides, if she's still upset, she might try to shoot us out of the sky."

Kong surrendered. "Okay, Pam, we're following Doc to the North Pole."

"O'boy, is it Christmas time already?" There was a moment of silence, and then Pam's voice came back, mixed with an expression of awe and amazement. "Wow! What the heck is that?"

'That' was the electro-static phenomenon that Doc and the others had witnessed earlier. Everyone was silent as they stared in awe at Mother Nature's incredible creation.

Ten minutes later, they followed the path that Doc Titan had taken and landed within one hundred feet of the Windjammer. All eight passengers disembarked from the two planes and soon found themselves surrounded by the man named Joseph and several dozen others. Kong whispered to Bart and Gibs.

"Hey, guys, I recognize some of these mugs. They were all sent to Upstate New York, to Doc's Rehabilitation Institute. What do you think they are doing here?"

Gibs shrugged, almost lost in the thick folds of the parka coat. "I'm not sure, but this is the direction Doc took."

Joseph greeted them. "Welcome, one and all. Your friend Doc Titan left this message for you and asked you to follow his trail. We will be your guides."

Bart opened the letter and Kong, Gibs, and Pam all read it quietly. Wall, Mick, and Megan thought it looked like silly children's writing. Cassie, whose uncle had been an archeologist, could almost understand a few of the figures. It was a lost language that Doc and all of his associates could read and speak. It came in handy when they wanted to say or write something that nobody else could decipher.

Cassie wrinkled her button nose at the paper. "I can make out one or two letters, but not the rest. What does it say?"

Kong translated. "Doc says we can trust these men and he wants us to follow them. And to leave all of our weapons behind."

Wall warily eyed the two dozen men surrounding them. "And you don't think they could have faked that message?"

Megan whispered. "Or somehow forced him to write it?"

Kong, Bart, Gibs, and Pam all burst out laughing at this suggestion.

Pam finally said, "Someone *force* Doc to do something? Against his will? That'll never happen."

Joseph waited patiently while they made their own decisions. He met with minor reluctance when he asked them to surrender their weapons, but Doc had made it clear they would not be needed. Lastly, Joseph suggested they dress warmly for the trip. The winds had picked up to twenty-five miles per hour already and the temperature had dropped to zero. And it was getting colder by the minute. Doc had left them a full wardrobe of protective clothing in the Windjammer. Twenty minutes later the five men were still standing in the snow, waiting.

Gibs checked his watch for the fourth time in as many minutes. "Where are the ladies?"

Kong stomped his feet in the drifting snow. His feet were already cold. "How long does it take to put on a coat?"

Bart sighed. "Pam said something about how hideous the fur suits were."

"Hey, if they're good enough for you, clothes-horse ..." Kong stopped talking as the three women strolled from the Windjammer cabins. They were stunningly outfitted and Kong was struck speechless.

Pam flashed a quicksilver smile. "Okay, boys. Let's find out what kind of trouble Doc has gotten us into this time."

Chapter Forty-Four
Sanctuary Discovered

April 6, 1945   8:00 pm

After a ten-mile trek across the frozen Arctic landscape, the group of eight adventurers found themselves standing outside an enormous cave entrance, invisible from the air because of the overhanging projection of ice. The sled dogs panted hard and columns of misty breath circled their heads. There was no movement in the surrounding wasteland, except for the dancing, drifting snow. Megan and Cassie were shivering from the intense cold.

"This is incredible." Pam studied the enormous cave entrance and turned toward Joseph, their guide, and asked, "Is this a steam vent from a volcano, Joseph?"

"That's possible, I really don't know. From here we will leave the dogs and proceed on foot."

Bart looked into the depths of the dark passage. "How far do we travel through this tunnel?"

Joseph shrugged, uncertain. "This path leads completely beneath the storm outside. There is no other entrance into Sanctuary. It's impossible to climb the outside of the cliffs, through the wildstorm."

Kong was glancing around, nervously. "I sure hope we don't run into that abombdi ... abommina ..."

Gibs laughed. "Abominable snowman? Nah, according to Percy, he lives in the Himalayan Mountains, in Tibet."

The sled dogs were led to a small bunker built into the cliff face, only a mile from the raging, swirling maelstrom they had witnessed from the sky. The air was filled with sparks of electricity and the northern lights, the Aurora Borealis. A rainbow pallet of colors danced in the electrified skies. The structure housed a dozen men and the garage next door contained three snowmobiles, covered with a large tarp.

Gibs and Kong looked at one another. Gibs spoke what they both were thinking. "Excuse me, Joseph. I notice there are only three snowmobiles, but there were four men who came before us."

Joseph nodded. "I forgot to mention it earlier. Two of your number, a Mr. Stockbridge and a Mr. Gibson, agreed to volunteer for an important errand?"

Megan looked concerned. "What kind of errand?"

Joseph shrugged again. "I really can't say, ma'am. I was not given the details." Pointing a thumb at the snowmobiles, he explained further. "The third vehicle was used by the man guiding your friends. His name is J. W. Campbell."

Bart whispered to Kong, indicating the dozen men in the small shed. "Do you recognize any of those men, Kong?"

"Yep. They're all men we sent to the Titan Rehabilitation Institute." Kong nodded in agreement.

"Joseph, will these men be accompanying us on our trip?" Gibs asked the guide.

"No, sir. They never leave this post. Just as the men at the last outpost never leave that location."

Gibs frowned. "You mean you've been ordered to never leave?"

Joseph smiled kindly. "Ordered? No, sir. You don't understand. We have all volunteered for this duty. We have pledged our lives to insuring the safety and privacy of Sanctuary."

Cassie glanced around quickly. "This is the second time you've said that word ... Sanctuary. What is it?"

Joseph raised his hands in a peaceful gesture. "Please, let us continue this discussion as we travel. We have several miles to walk before you arrive at your destination." He waved a gloved hand toward the large mouth of the cave entrance. The wind had become more forceful this close to the storm. As the group entered the frozen opening, they immediately noticed how quiet it suddenly became.

Pam turned to Kong and whispered, "Once more we go down into the rabbit hole, in pursuit of the white rabbit." Kong frowned at the reference. Pam explained. "From Alice in Wonderland. She begins her adventures by chasing a white rabbit in a waistcoat carrying a pocket watch."

Bart added, "Guess that makes me Tweedledee and Kong must be Tweedledum." Kong growled at Bart and walked ahead.

There was a loud, low whistling sound as the blowing winds passed in front of the entrance, a noise similar to that of a child blowing into a soda bottle. But several minutes later, this noise grew quieter as they continued walking deeper into the tunnel. The temperature felt slightly warmer, even though it was still well below freezing. The sides of the cave seemed to have a natural fluorescence, illuminating the way without the need of lantern or flashlight. The tunnel was wide enough that several people could walk side by side without crowding. Cassie and Megan huddled against the man-mountain Wall for warmth.

Joseph finally spoke again. "You asked about Sanctuary. It would be better explained by your next guide, since I have never actually seen it myself."

Kong's mouth dropped open in disbelief. "You guard the entrance to a place you've never been to?"

"Yes. Perhaps this sounds odd to newcomers, but we all feel we serve a greater purpose, a greater glory, than simply ourselves. The men you met outside, and I, myself, have done … questionable things in our past. We seek atonement or penance for various indiscretions of our previous lives. We refer to ourselves as The Guardians of the Brotherhood."

"And you prevent others from finding this place?" Gibs asked.

"Yes. But very few have ever traveled this far north. We also perform any errands that the Council of Elders might request of us. We are their main contact with the outside world."

"So the Elders never leave this place, Joseph?" Wall asked in astonishment.

"Almost never. However, since my arrival, I have known two such men who traveled the path from Sanctuary to the outside world and back again."

Kong shook his head. "Wow. Talk about dedicated to your job. Why is it you have never entered this Sanctuary? Aren't you curious?"

Joseph shrugged, almost indifferently. "Yes, I suppose, but I have never deemed myself worthy. I am quite content with my position in life."

Bart reached out and thumped the side wall of the cave. "This isn't my area of expertise, but I've been around Percy enough to know that this is solid rock."

Kong sneered at Bart. "Gee, Bart, I would have thought that was obvious."

Cassie stepped forward and tapped the wall. "You're correct, Bart." She turned her head and addressed Kong. "Don't you understand? This is stone, not ice. But there is no known land mass at the North Pole. This entire place is like an island in the middle of an ocean of ice."

"Oh," was Kong's only reply.

As they continued walking, the tunnel ceiling dropped lower, until Wall could have easily reached up and touched it. They also noticed a high-pitched whistle that grew in intensity. They entered a strange area where outside light poured in, from above. They were standing beneath holes bored through several feet of rock and the air from within the tunnel was being sucked up and out through the holes. Pam's hair was lifted from her head as she lowered her hood. Glancing up into one of the holes, she saw an ever-changing pallet of flowing materials, looking like a golden stream. Electro-magnetic current was generated with the movement and sparks danced happily in the flow. "It's beautiful." When she started to reach up into one of the holes, Joseph placed a hand on her arm.

"I would not recommend such an action, ma'am. We are currently beneath the deadly maelstrom." To illustrate his point, Joseph picked up a fist-sized stone and simply tossed it upward, near the mouth of one of the holes. The rock was sucked out instantly and swept away violently, disappearing in the vortex. "There is enough suction to pull an average-sized man off the ground and carry him away. What looks like flowing sand are thousands of small rocks and various debris being carried along in the wake of the winds. Those hurricane force winds outside would strip a man to the bone in mere seconds."

Pam gulped hard and said sheepishly, "Thanks, Joseph."

The path led at an upward angle and seemed to continue on for several hours. The view rarely changed from the plain gray stone surroundings. Bart gauged they had climbed several hundred feet above sea level. There was no plant or animal life evident. They continued asking Joseph a multitude of questions, and he always seemed happy to answer their inquiries. The temperature continued to become warmer and several of the men had opened their parkas. Half an hour later, they had all removed their coats. They had entered an immense, domed cavern, several hundred feet high at the center. A large pool of crystal clear, blue water filled the entire floor of the natural dome. A glow emanated from below the glassy surface. They were pondering how to cross over, when Joseph led them to the shoreline of the pool. Invisible from a distance, was a ledge of stone that rose up in the middle, dividing the lake down the center. The water was only half an inch deep on this ledge.

Joseph pointed at a light at the far end on the cavern. "If you walk straight toward the light, you will stay on this ridge of stone. This is as far as I go. I have enjoyed being your guide and I hope you enjoy your stay in Sanctuary."

"You're not coming with us, Joseph?" Pam inquired. She liked the quiet man.

"Someday, perhaps, I will enter Sanctuary. But not today." He gave them a friendly smile and returned back along the path they had just taken.

Mick was the first to step onto the ledge and his eyes opened wide. "Ach, this water is warm. There must be some underground thermal activity beneath this lake."

The rest followed Mick's lead and they slowly walked toward the distant light. Warm air gently blew in their faces and even Megan began to thaw out.

"That feels wonderful. Hey. I think I smell ... is that honeysuckle?" Megan sniffed loudly.

Bart sampled the air. "Yes, I smell it, too. I thought I was hallucinating."

They finally reached the end of the cavern and simply stood in bewilderment. The sight that greeted them was like nothing they had ever seen before. And members of this group had been witness to many amazing sights, such as living dinosaurs, lost civilizations, mummies in the streets of New York, and more.

Kong whispered to himself, as if afraid to speak out loud. "Oh my stars and garters. Are you guys seeing what I'm seeing?"

Bart's face showed amazement. "I'm not sure. Are you seeing heaven?"

"I think so. It's only missing the angels with harps floating on billowy, white clouds." Kong responded.

Cassie finally voiced her opinion. "Wow."

"Cursiouser and cursiouser," whispered Pam.

As far as the eye could see were waterfalls, lakes, birds flying in the air, the scents of a thousand different exotic flower blossoms, beautiful blue skies, and ice-caked mountain tops.

Pam spoke so quietly, it was almost a whisper. "Is this Shangri-La?"

"Actually, Shangri La is in Tibet. I've been there once. Quite lovely. But it really doesn't hold a candle to this place. Besides, the Abominable Snowman living in Tibet doesn't really like intruders." Gibs gave Kong a knowing smile at this comment, before realizing it was not voiced by someone in his group. "I'm so glad you finally arrived. I sincerely hope that that you had a pleasant journey."

The man who was talking to them was of average height and build, with grayish curly hair and prominent sideburns. He spoke with a slight English accent. He wore a splendid robe of yellows and oranges. Simple sandals adorned his feet. Bart estimated his age around sixty years old. He bowed at the gathering of gentlemen and kissed the hands of the three ladies.

"Who are you?" Kong asked gruffly.

"Phileas Fogg, at your service, Mr. Larson." The fellow politely bowed again.

Bart frowned. "That name sounds familiar. Have we ever met?"

Fogg laughed pleasantly. "I sincerely doubt it, Mr. Blackwell. I have been living here in Sanctuary since before you were born."

"I might be older than you think." Bart stated boldly. "And how do you know our names?"

Phileas Fogg had a twinkle in his eye and flashed Bart a quicksilver smile. "And I might be older than *you* think. I was born in 1832. And I know a great deal about you. About all of you."

Bart quickly did the math. "Impossible. That would make you 113 years old!"

"Yes, quite correct. But you've met men claiming to be older than me, Mr. Blackwell. Old Ben Thunder from Fear Key was one such man."

Gibs eyed the man doubtfully. "You know of our adventure on Fear Key?"

Fogg nodded. "The Council of Elders know everything, if the rumors are to be believed. However, I prefer not to be called an 'Elder,' it seems rather unflattering."

"So you really are 113 years old?" Cassie asked in disbelief, studying the gentleman calling himself Fogg.

"That's correct. Perhaps it's the environment here. The aging process seems to slow down. All members of the Illuminati are … long lived."

Pam had been studying Phileas Fogg and finally spoke. "Le tour du monde en quatre-vingts jours?"

Fogg's eyes lit brightly. "Ah, en chante mademoiselle." They spoke French for several seconds. Bart smiled and listened. Kong simply scratched his bullet shaped head. The only French he knew were the words Bart had taught him and they weren't to be used in polite conversation. Back in the Great War, Bart had convinced him that the words were complimentary and he should use them when he next met their commanding officer. He spent several days in the brig for that prank.

Phileas Fogg's attention turned to his other guests. "My apologies. It is so rare I get to hear French spoken anymore. It is a beautiful language. Pamela Titan was merely asking if I was the same man who traveled around the world in eighty days."

"Excuse me? Like in that story by Jules Verne?" Kong scowled.

"Well, yes. However, Monsieur Verne did use a certain amount of poetic license here and there when he wrote about my adventures." Fogg answered.

"But, I thought that was only fiction." Kong eyed Fogg, disbelievingly.

"Many great stories have their foundations buried in truth. You will find many such great men here at Sanctuary." Phileas Fogg indicated the valley with his cane.

Wall watched as a massive butterfly landed on Cassie's head. It perched there, slowly beating its wings. "Hey, Joseph said we should ask someone who lived here. Why do you call this place Sanctuary?"

"Good question, Mr. Walker. Several hundred years ago, a silent order of Franciscan monks were driven from their monastery. They traveled, seeking a place where they could worship in peace. They heard rumors of a place, heaven on Earth, far to the north. Many years later, like knights seeking the Holy Grail, they discovered the entrance. They followed the same path you did and discovered … this." Saying these words, Fogg waved his hand, indicating their surroundings. "Paradise on Earth. They have been the caretakers of this place ever since."

Pam glanced around. "They still live here? Are all of the original monks still alive, Phileas?"

"Honestly, I'm not certain. We call them The Order of the Brotherhood of Silence. They never speak. Sometimes, men like Joseph, will enter Sanctuary and join the Order." He noticed that the group was still admiring the view. "Takes your breath away, doesn't it? I remember how I felt when I first came here and saw all of this. By the way, you can leave your coats here, you won't be needing them. It's quite warm here all of the time."

As they walked, several monks in simple brown robes, with the hoods pulled up, strolled past silently. They wore sandals; similar to the ones Phileas Fogg wore. The presence of the group of strangers was completely ignored by them.

Wall watched with fascination as Cassie's multicolored hat, the huge monarch butterfly, flapped away. "Are you taking us to our friends?"

"Actually, they have gone on ahead. You will want to rest and in the morning we will finish your journey. Rooms have been made up and baths have been prepared. Besides, you will want to visit the Museum before you continue your journey. A great many things, many mysteries will be explained there. A meeting of the Council of Elders convenes in the morning and your presence has been requested. If you have further questions, they can be answered there."

Kong grunted and whispered to Gibs. "Museum, huh? They'll probably want us to stop by the Sanctuary gift shop too." Gibs smiled at Kong's jest.

Phileas Fogg offered his arm to Pam and he walked next to her. "I understand your friends arrived in a modern-day flying balloon, called a zeppelin. You simply must tell me all about it."

Chapter Forty-Five
The Museum - Secrets Revealed

April 6, 1945   8:00 pm

Pam Titan was drying off after her long bath. The scented oils and perfumes in the water made her skin silky smooth and her nostrils tingle. While Pam owned a spa and health club, she was one of those rare women who didn't feel a need to spend hours in front of a mirror. Not that she needed it; she had natural beauty that most women would sell their souls to attain. There was a soft knock on her door. Despite the fact that she was not dressed, she was not anxious or embarrassed.

"The door's unlocked. Come in."

Kong and Bart opened the door and stared mutely as Pam walked past them, to stand behind a folding screen to finish dressing. She had left her towel behind and the two men saw her in all of her glorious splendor. She had been raised as a tomboy and had gone skinny-dipping with young boys in the wilds of Canada. Pam had never been a shy girl and had no reason to be modest. She had the body of a goddess. These two men had been with their share of beautiful women in their lifetimes, but Pam beat them all, hands down.

Bart finally managed to shake off the trance he found himself in. "Pam, everyone has been invited into the next building. That's where the museum is located. The one Fogg told us about."

Pam stepped out from behind the screen and, if possible, looked more stunning than when she had been naked. She wore a beautiful, full-length gown of violet-colored, quilted material with satin lapels and trim around the sleeves and hem. She smiled and Kong felt his feet warm up. His grin stretched from ear to ear, like a love-struck suitor. She placed an arm over each man's shoulder and they walked together. Bart was splendidly dressed in a flowing, black robe with royal purple trimmings and dark scarlet interior. Even in this ancient attire, he displayed knowledge of how to properly wear any clothing. Kong, on the other hand, was his usual mess. One collar was out and the other tucked in, and the arms of his robe had been rolled up to his elbows. The outfit was too long for his short, massive frame and dragged the floor, the shoulders were too tight and his hairy chest was exposed. Occasionally, he would trip as he stepped on the hem of the robe.

"Do you think Doc's okay, guys? I don't like being out of contact like this." Pam voiced her concerns.

Kong reassured her. "Heck, Pam, Doc can take care of himself. Wow, will you take a gander at this place?"

The view was, indeed, breathtaking to behold. Even though there was no gold or jewels evident, which would have been almost gaudy in this environment, every item in sight showed an incredible degree of craftsmanship and detail. Carvings adorned almost every surface and elegant statues lined the brick walkways. There were no signs of trash, refuse, or filth anywhere, as though the entire valley had been scrubbed clean. The skies were a blue rarely seen in the world, except from high in the mountains. Beds of wild flowers and gardens were neatly organized and the perfumed smells and rainbow of colors created an almost overwhelming assault to the senses.

Framing the entire valley was a circle of immense mountain peaks, soaring thousands of feet high. The upper edges were snow-covered and penetrated the soft clouds. The clouds did not seem to enter the skies over the middle of the bowl-shaped valley. It was perhaps ten or twelve miles across the large valley, from mountain base to mountain base. The circular canyon was basin-shaped, the center lower than the edges, allowing visibility across the entire valley.

Directly in the middle was a large lake, perhaps two miles across. From the rock faces a dozen waterfalls, ranging from one hundred feet high to over a thousand feet, poured their white-blue contents into the valley. The fine mists created a multitude of delicate rainbows. Less than one hundred man-made structures were evident. There were small gardens and vineyards everywhere. A rainbow of color saturated the eyes and the soft sounds of nature caressed the ears. Birds and butterflies darted lazily from flower to flower.

Xanadu, Eden, Utopia, Arcadia, Zion, Shangri-La, Elysium, all referred to paradises on Earth. But it was hard to believe that any of these were equal to this land that men called Sanctuary.

Bart noticed there were no doors at the exterior of any building. No need for security and apparently the temperature was a constant, comfortable level. They walked through an immense stone archway and discovered another incredible sight. The building they were approaching had a timeless architecture, combining several styles into one. It was impossible to tell if the structure was recently built or was five hundred years old. This was the building Phileas Fogg had described as the Museum, and it had been well-named. As they entered, their eyes were greeted by thousands of leather-bound volumes, lining handcrafted wooden shelves. The text works varied from journals, biographies, research materials, writings of well-known wordsmiths, and newspaper collections from around the world, in every known language. A silent monk bowed slightly at their approach and guided them with an outstretched hand.

Gibs, Megan, Cassie, Wall, and Mick were already in attendance. All were dressed in splendid robes and dresses. After greetings had been exchanged, a tall, solidly-built man entered. He was bent slightly with the weight of many years. His sandy-colored hair had hints of gray and his beard, although slightly darker, had the same. He possessed strong but slightly gnarled hands. His beautiful, blue-green eyes sparkled with life. When he spoke, his voice was a pleasant growl.

"Greetings, friends. My name is Ned. If you have any requirements, please feel free to ask. We want your stay in Sanctuary to be a comfortable one."

"Where are Doc and Simon? Are they going to …?" Pam started.

Ned held up one weathered hand. "Your friends have already visited the Museum and studied the information you need to review. Tomorrow you will meet them again, when the Council of Elders convenes. All of your questions will be answered then. But there is much you need to read about, before that time. The various books, photos, and journals have been laid out for your perusal."

Ned slowly walked to a large chair in the next room and sat down. He rested a large volume on his knees and slowly paged through it. The eight visitors walked around, looking at various articles and sometimes voicing surprise at some new discovery. The others would gather around to read the item and then slowly spread out again, until the next major treasure was found.

One such newspaper article mentioned the Baltimore Gun Club purchasing the North Pole, in hopes of finding coal and oil. Another announced the expedition, funded by Clarke Titan and his friends, Robert Hubertson and Professor George Edward Challenger, returning to the mysterious place known as Maple White Land, also referred to as The Lost World.

Kong tapped the bearded man in the picture. "That's Doc's father. And my Uncle George."

Bart looked incredulously at his old friend Kong. "Professor George Challenger is your uncle?"

"Yeah, he is." Kong replied defensively.

Bart smiled. "So he's a monkey's uncle?" Everyone chuckled at the jest.

Mick held up a photo and frowned. "Ach, Wall, Cassie, take a look at this."

He handed them a newspaper clipping and a photograph in a simple frame. It was from 1938 and showed the front facade of the Unsolved Mysteries, Incorporated buildings. Standing before the structures were Mick,

Wall, Cassie, Gabe, Isabelle, and Simon Blake. The caption below read, '*Simon Blake, known as The Guardian by the underworld of crime, is shown with his fellow private investigators, in front of their new headquarters located on Barren Street. Their organization is known as Unsolved Mysteries, Incorporated.*'

Cassie stared in amazement. "This was taken before Andrew Carter joined the group. But why would they have a copy of this here?"

Gibs frowned. "I have a feeling there will be many questions about what we find here today. Kong, Bart, take a gander at this photo." He handed them a framed picture with a handwritten notation on the back, describing the seven men in the photograph.

Bart stared closely at the yellowed picture. "That's us. We had recently returned from the war. The Great War. That was the day we first met Doc's father."

Chapter Forty-Six
Flashback to 1918 - The Reunion of Titans

April 6, 1945   8:30 pm

Beginning of Flashback to December 1ˢᵗ, 1918.

Newspapers worldwide announced the news in their boldest print. *THE WAR TO END ALL WARS ENDS! THE GREAT WAR IS OVER! TROOPS COMING HOME FROM EUROPE!* Unconditional surrender had been announced on the 11th hour of the 11th day of the 11th month. Twenty years later, they would start numbering the wars and it would be renamed World War I.

John Titan didn't know what to expect. He had not seen his father in three years. Soon after arriving in New York, he noticed the newspaper headline announcing that his father was opening a new wing to the city hospital. This was as good a time as any to reunite their broken family. His five new friends had volunteered to go with him. Actually, he was certain they were attending to make sure he didn't back out.

Now he stood in the crowd in front of the sparkling white new wing of the hospital. The new children's wing. His father had become quite the humanitarian. A hushed silence fell over the crowd. A tall, handsome middle-aged man stepped to the podium. He was neatly dressed in a nicely tailored suit that didn't hide his obviously well-built frame. Smooth, bronzed skin was the result of his exposure to tropical suns and artic winds. It had weathered to a soft, leathery appearance.

He spoke to the crowd of spectators and newspaper reporters in a clear, precise voice. While not loud, his voice carried to the furthest edges of the crowd. John glanced around and saw everyone was focused on the speaker.

Kong whispered to the tall man next to him. "Hey, John, is that your dad?"

John nodded, feeling a little proud. "Yes, it is."

Big Tom tilted his head to the right, motioning for John to look that way. "Looks like you have an admirer. Holy Cow, what a looker." Before he even turned his head, John knew this must be true. It was a rare feminine beauty that could attract Big Tom's eye. Unlike, of course, his friends Kong and Bart, who chased and fought over every piece of skirt that walked by.

The woman in question was, indeed, the most beautiful woman John had ever laid eyes on. Poise, hair, attire, everything was a pattern of perfection. He swore he could smell her perfume, even though she was thirty feet away, at the far edge of the crowd. She stared at John and he shifted uncomfortably. When he looked directly at her, she mouthed the word, "Hi." Without acknowledging her flirtations, he returned his attentions to the man at the podium. Her eyes reminded him of Iriana Noviskovaah, and he didn't want to think about her today. The memories were too fresh, too painful. This day was about reuniting John Titan and his father.

Kong gawked in surprise. "Geez, Doc, Sometimes I swear you must be made of stone. How can you ignore ... that?" He asked as he pointed toward the well-rounded woman in red.

John simply replied. "I have other business to attend to today."

Kong slowly slipped from his side and was soon lost in the attentive crowd.

During the majority of his speech, Doctor Titan had been directly addressing the reporters nearest the podium. As he glanced up, he immediately noticed John standing in the rear of the crowd. Actually, John was a hard figure to miss. At nearly seven feet tall and over two hundred and sixty pounds, he stood a head taller than nearly everyone else in front of the building. Their eyes met and locked, and for a minute John's heart skipped a beat. For an instant he considered turning on heel and running. No! He had come from nearly half way around the globe to have this meeting. Then he noticed the look on his father's face. Not anger or disappointment, it was the look of pride and happiness. John breathed a sigh of relief. Moments later, the crowd began to disperse as the reporters headed back to their offices, to write yet another story of the charity of the elder Titan.

"Johnny." His father proclaimed as he approached with open arms. Crushed in a bear hug, John simply smiled and patted his father's back.

"I go by John now, father. Only you call me Johnny." He said quietly, controlling his emotions as he had been taught to do since childhood.

Doctor Titan smiled an acknowledgement. "Yes, yes, of course. No grown man wants to be called 'Johnny.' Standing back, his father held his arms wide and stared at John, as if admiring a brightly decorated Christmas tree. He was smiling from ear to ear. This was *not* the welcoming he was expecting from his father. Had his years away colored his memories this much? Did he really remember his father as such an ogre? "My goodness," his father continued, "What did they feed you in Europe? You've become a giant!" John noticed for the first time he was actually taller than the senior Titan. As a youth he always remembered his father towering over him. Now he was several inches taller.

"Father ... I'm so happy to see you again." John finally spoke. For the first time he could remember, he felt tears well up in his eyes and did not even attempt to hold them back.

Doctor Titan also appeared to be fighting back tears. "Son, John, I am so happy you've finally come home to me. I hope you'll find it in your heart to forgive a selfish old man. I pushed you so hard as a child ... and I finally pushed you away. I always wanted the best for you ...." Doctor Titan faltered and seemed at a loss for words.

John nodded in understanding. "Actually, father, I have come back to continue my training. I realize that I have so much more to learn. When do you return back to Wilder Island? I can be ready by the end of the week. I want to spend a few days with some friends ..." John halted as the older man held up his hand.

"I shut down the island base and sold it. I decided it was time to stop hiding from the world." Doctor Titan spread his open arms toward the city of New York. "This country has many fine universities of learning. And more libraries than I could ever privately stock. It is time to set our roots in America. I feel this country, and the world at large, will face many trials in the upcoming years and I'm prepared to do my share. I traveled abroad, discovered lost treasures in far away countries, and amassed a small fortune. I have invested in oil and coal companies and multiplied that fortune a hundred times over. I raise funds through charities to finance projects to benefit mankind, such as this children's hospital wing." With a magnificent wave of his hand he motioned at the stunning, white marble structure added to the Manhattan City Hospital.

"I noticed you finally have your Medical Degree, father."

"Yes, finally. Seems like it took a hundred years to get it." The elder Titan smiled, as if acknowledging a private joke.

"Who is Simon Titan, father?" John asked quietly.

"Where have you heard that name?" The elder man remained calm, but John detected the slightest tremor in his voice.

"It is on the bronze dedication plaque of the new hospital wing. Are we related to him in some way?"

For a second the doctor hesitated, and then smiled warmly. "A distant relative, but for several years he was also my best friend. I met Colonel Simon Titan when I was a very young man. We hunted wild animals in Africa, charted rivers deep in the South American wilderness, even panned for gold in the Old West. Many years ago, after traveling the around globe several times, he was crossing the road and was struck by a wagon. He was the closest thing I had to a father. He was a good man ... a great man. And a great inspiration." There was a moment of silence between the two Titans and then the Doctor smiled. "You mentioned some friends … is this young fellow one of them?"

Before John could speak up, Big Tom approached and introduced himself. "Lieutenant Colonel Randolph Garnett Thompson, of the British Royal Air Force and a member of The Flying Knights, at your service. My friends call me 'Big Tom'." The Australian held out one of his massive hands. Doctor Titan felt like a child, placing his hand in that of a large adult. Big Tom's hands were nearly twice the size of his own. On one of the rare occasions that anyone could remember, Big Tom smiled. He was usually as somber as a mortician. He was also a large man, nearly as large as John. Six feet four inches tall and nearly two hundred and fifty pounds of hardened muscle and sinew, he created quite the imposing figure. His deep voice was like a growling bear in a very deep cave.

Doctor Clarke Titan wondered if Big Tom might suffer from a rare hormonal disorder called acromegaly, an enlarging of the extremities, specifically the hands, feet and jawbone. This was often caused by a tumorous mass on the pituitary gland. If this was true, Doctor Titan was certain he could prevent further damage, by surgically removing the tumor.

"Gilbert Elliot Maddox. The guys call me 'Gibs.' Military Intelligence." A small fellow who looked like the runt of the litter stepped up and shook hands vigorously. His looks, however, were deceiving. Despite his size, only four feet tall and one hundred pounds, he had been known to hold up his end of a fight in many a tough scrap. He was small but he fought like a wildcat. Gibs was a true midget, as opposed to a dwarf, the largest distinction being the normal-sized hands and fingers.

"My cog nominate is Kenneth Xavier Percival Pierce, 'Percy' to my five confederates. It is my esteemed pleasure to make your acquaintance, sir." This young man was also six feet tall, but was a striking opposite of Big Tom. It was doubtful he weighed a hundred pounds when soaking wet, and his skin had the same pale complexion possessed by mushrooms that grow in dark cellars. Doctor Titan noted that Percy had no military rank. He started to question this fact when a very sharply dressed young man, carrying a simple black walking cane, strolled up, smiled, and took his hand in a firm grip, shaking it smartly. He limped slightly, as though still recovering from a recent injury

Bart spoke in a clear, well-modulated voice. "Ignore the scarecrow there, he accidentally swallowed a thesaurus. As you surmised, he has no military rank; you might call what he did 'a non-military fact-gatherer.'"

Doctor Titan leaned close and whispered. "You mean he was a spy?"

"Spy? Good heavens no, my good man, A. S. S. - American Secret Service. Major Bartholomew J. Blackwell, at your service." The tall dapper man carried himself with the air of a proper English gentleman, although there was no hint of any accent in his clear voice.

From behind the Doctor's back came another deep voice. "Aaww, just call him 'Bart.' That's his nickname. Funny how his name and ass always follow one another, considering that's where he was shot."

"It most certainly is not my name, you anthropoidic mistake of nature!" Exclaimed Blackwell, temporarily losing his cool demeanor. "And I was shot in the thigh! I still think you did it, no matter how much you deny it."

"Major Henry Marmaduke Larson, sir. You can call me 'Kong'." When Doctor Titan turned to meet this last member of his son's friends, he was startled. Where Percy was two men tall and half a man thick, this man was the complete reverse. He was barely over five feet tall, but appeared to be nearly as wide! And nearly as thick as he was wide. A throwback to the caveman era. A small, bullet-shaped head, with almost no forehead to speak of, perched atop shoulders that resembled those of a low-land gorilla. The huge, apelike appendage held out to shake his hand seemed to belong to an entirely different species.

All of the other gentlemen he had just met were neatly dressed, in nicely tailored suits, but this fellow wore a short-sleeve sweatshirt in rather bright, and somewhat gaudy, colors. The sleeves of the sweatshirt did not seem long enough to cover the full length of this man's arms, chiefly because they reached past his knees. And the part of the arms not hidden by shirt sleeves were covered by a thick mat of coarse red hairs, resembling rusty nails. Doctor Titan had never met such a man in his entire life and was momentarily stunned by his simian appearance.

"Yes, he has that effect on most people, the first time they meet him." Laughed Bart, the lawyerly-looking young man with the black cane.

"How's that limp, Bart?" Kong teased.

Bart's face reddened but he kept silent.

"Hey, Kong, what's wrong with your eye?" Big Tom asked, as the ape-man approached.

"Ha. Hell hath no fury like a woman scorned, my friend." Kong grinned broadly. "I thought I would console that nice young lady John was ignorin'. Apparently, she got over him, but I think she took it out on me!"

"Ha! Serves you right, consorting outside your own species. Maybe I should talk to the young lady myself." Mocked Bart, at Kong's obvious pain.

"Hush, shyster! I already told her about you and your thirteen half-wit children. She's not buying today." Kong teased his friend.

Bart's face flushed. "Arguing with you is like wrestling with a pig in mud. Sooner or later you begin to realize the pig's enjoying himself."

Doctor Titan eyed his son and the other five gentlemen. "Well, John. You certainly have some very interesting friends. I have a proposition for you, son. If you want to go back to college, to further your education, I will sponsor full scholarships for you and your five friends, in your preferred fields of study."

"Hooyah!" exclaimed Percy happily.

The Titans shook hands, father and son. A newspaper photographer had been standing nearby, quietly eavesdropping on the gathering. Now he stepped forward.

"This seems to be a momentous occasion. How about a picture for the paper? Father welcoming his son and friends home from the war overseas?"

"Get lost, ragman." Kong shooed him with his long arms.

Doctor Titan held up one hand. "No, please wait, sir. If it's okay with you, John, I would like a keepsake of this day. Would you be willing ...?"

"Certainly. Why not, father." John placed an affectionate arm over his father's shoulder. His heart pounded hard in his chest. This was a great day, perhaps the first of many. He and his father were reunited.

Several hours later, a photograph of the seven men appeared in the New York Times. This would be the first article to feature the young man known as John 'Doc' Titan. Hundreds more would follow in the years to come. Doc Titan. The Ultimate Man. The Man of Tomorrow.

End of Flashback to December 1st, 1918.

Chapter Forty-Seven
Flashback to 1888 - Grey Eyes

April 6, 1945   9:00 pm

Pam was studying a faded photo of a well-dressed man standing in front of a large, brightly decorated balloon. On the back of the photo, in perfect script, was the notation, *Phileas Fogg and man-servant Passepartout 1872*. The word *'man-servant'* had been crossed through and the word *'friend'* had been written below.

Mick squinted at the small faces. "Ach, wasn't this the fellow who met us earlier at the entrance to Sanctuary?

"One and the same." Pam agreed with his assessment.

Wall read the inscription again. "According to the date written on the back, this photo was taken in 1872."

Pam nodded. "From what I remember reading, he was forty when he took the journey, so he really is 113."

Bart voiced admirably, "Sure is spry for such an old cuss."

Gibs cleared his throat. "Guys, you think that's an odd one, take a gander at this picture."

The photo he handed over was greatly weathered and the writing on the reverse was faded, but still legible. *Vingt mille lieues sous les mers 1867.* In English, a newer note had been added. *Professor Arronaxe, his faithful servant Conseil, the Canadian whaler Ned Land, and the mysterious Captain Nemo.* In the photo were four men, standing in front of a fantastic submarine, perhaps the most fabulous ever built. The name embossed on the hull read, *'Nautilus.'* As the description on the reverse side indicated, the third man was none other than Ned Land, the elderly man who had greeted them in this very building.

Kong frowned. "What does Vin ...? Vingt mille ... ?"

Bart stopped Kong before he could butcher the language further. "Twenty thousand leagues under the sea."

Kong's eyebrows rose. "Whoa, I thought that was just another story made up by Jules Verne. So this is some kinda science fiction museum?"

"Somehow, I think those stories were actually based on real events." Wall replied calmly.

Mick growled in his Scottish brogue. "Ach, how can such fables be true? It's a crock of …"

"Fables? Science fiction?" Gibs offered. "Folks might say the same thing about some of our adventures. But I've seen men turned into hulking monsters, and I've seen goblins, ghosts and spooks, and even vanishing men …"

Kong added. "… a thousand-headed man, a land of dinosaurs, flaming falcons, hundred foot daggers burning in the sky, …"

Bart joined in. "… men turned to stone, running skeletons, purple dragons, Kong in his underwear."

Kong scowled. "Ha ha. Keep it up and I'll have you stuffed and mounted and put in a display cabinet in this museum. I'll have a plaque made that reads *'Barthicus Blackasaurius. Do not feed the clothes-horse!'* Ha!"

As the battle of wits raged, the others continued discovering various treasures. The large-bore rifle that Allan Quatermain carried throughout Africa. Another article regarding Professor Challenger's initial discovery of the Lost World. A display of dinosaur bones. A heavy, badly worn, harpoon with Ned Land's name carved into the wooden handle. And a photo they initially mistook as Doc Titan and his father.

Kong wiped the glass. "Who is Professor Henry Jones? Says he was searching for the Holy Grail. There's a picture here, says it's him and his son, Henry Jones, Junior. The names Henry and Junior are scratched out and the word Indiana has been written above Henry. Why do they look so familiar?"

Bart raised one eyebrow. "Yes, they do, don't they? The boy reminds me of Doc for some reason."

"I believe he's an archaeologist." Cassie volunteered. "Percy might know him."

Kong smiled broadly. "Wow, who's the looker?" He was admiring the faded photograph of a beautiful woman. No name was written on the picture or on the flipside. "No name on the back or front."

Bart peered over his wide shoulder. "Hmm. I don't know."

"Guys, do you know a Simon Titan?" Cassie asked.

Gibs scratched his head. "I've heard that name before. Didn't Professor Titan dedicate that hospital addition to him?"

Bart's eyes twinkled. "Yes, that's correct. I remember Doc asking who he was and his father stated it was an old friend. Why do you ask, Cassie?"

"This newspaper clipping states that a Colonel Simon Titan aka Colonel Richard Henry Savage was run over by a wagon in Utica, New York on October 3, 1903 and died eight days later. Apparently, he wrote over 40 stories and Savage was his pen name."

"I wonder if Doc ever found out anything more about Colonel Titan." Gibs pondered. "Pam, did you ever hear the name?"

"No, but I never did meet too many members of our family." Pam confessed.

Bart held up another tintype photograph. "This is another one for the history books. Here's a picture of Professor Titan and Stephen Stone standing in front of a ship named *The Falcon*."

Wall shrugged his huge shoulders. "Who's Stephen Stone?"

Bart explained. "He was before your time, but you might have heard about his son, Henry Stone."

Megan looked up from her reading material. "The multi-millionaire, Bart?"

"That's right. Rumor was that Stephen Stone's wife ran away with another man. He was mortified. In 1898 he bought a large schooner, *The Falcon*, loaded it with everything he and his passengers would ever need and set off from New York City. He left his publishing empire in the hands of an old friend. It was worth half a million dollars. On November 3rd, 1898 he purposely grounded the ship on the reef of a small Pacific island. It was located somewhere in the triangle formed by Ceylon, Tasmania, and Madagascar, two hundred miles from any known shipping lane. Ships and vessels skirted the edges of that part of the ocean, but none penetrated the center, where the tiny island was located."

Cassie listened attentively. "How many were on board, Bart?"

"Stephen Stone, his infant son, a Scottish engineer named David McCobb and a huge Negro named Jack."

Cassie looked mortified. "He took a baby with him?"

"He didn't want his infant son to be raised around women. He raised his son, Henry, to be the perfect gentleman, well-versed in conversation, knowledgeable in all of the known sciences, a mental marvel. Henry also grew tall and strong, from a good diet and plenty of exercise."

"So how long where they on the island?" Pam studied the picture.

"That's the unintentionally sad part of the story. Stone carefully planned for every need they might have on the island, but he paid for his hubris. He forgot to make arrangements for any kind of rescue. They didn't see another human being for thirty-three years, until a small Scandinavian freighter named the Cjoda rescued the castaways. Stephen Stone never left the island. He died June 6th, 1929, about eleven months before the rescue ship landed."

Pam laid the photograph down. "Raised on an island, trained since birth, no women … sounds vaguely familiar, doesn't it?"

Cassie nodded. "Sounds like Doc's upbringing."

"I've made that connection myself, when I first heard the story." Bart agreed.

Cassie bit her lip. "And nobody ever went by the island in thirty-three years? Not even by accident?"

Gibs joined in. "The Pacific Ocean covers about forty-six percent of the Earth's water surface and about thirty-two percent of its total surface area, making it larger than all of the Earth's land area combined. An island that size would be less than a needle in a haystack. It would be like finding a pinhole in an area roughly the size of a city block."

"After returning to New York in 1931, they discovered the Stone fortune was now worth two hundred and eighty million dollars and included twenty-two newspapers and eleven banks." Kong added.

Gibs continued. "I distinctly remember the newspaper headlines touting him as the 'Savage Gentleman.' A naked savage who couldn't speak a word of English. They soon discovered that he was a magnificent young man of extraordinary intellect and strength. As rich as Rockefeller or Vanderbilt but raised like a wild man. A sort of Americanized version of Kan-Tar."

Cassie, Megan, and Pam exchanged knowing glances. A warm breeze blew in through one of the exterior openings. A broad and brilliantly colored butterfly gracefully passed by the gathering of men and women.

Kong looked around them and dropped into one on the leather chairs. "Man, I just thought of something. Percy would love this place. This museum and the entire valley. There must be thousands of ancient secrets buried in this one room alone."

Everyone was quiet for several minutes, remembering madmen, at some unknown location, were holding their friends captive.

Megan had been sitting in one of the large padded chairs, reading an ancient, musty journal and listening to the conversations. Her legs were tucked below her and the tome rested on her inclined thighs. She shifted in her chair and called to the others.

"Everyone, you might want to listen to this. I've been reading this journal and I think I've discovered something." Megan flipped several pages backward and started reading aloud to the group. They slowly gathered around her, sitting in chairs and reclining on the thick carpets on the stone floor. Megan had a great voice and she read very dramatically. Soon everyone felt themselves transported back in time, reliving the words on the page.

Beginning of Flashback to August 31ˢᵗ, 1888.

The small medical facility was located at the end of Prince William Street, Whitechapel, England. A small brass plaque on the door, bearing the name Wildman, M.D., was the only advertisement. The door bell clanged at the front entrance. First patient of the day. No matter how many times this happened, James Clarke Wildman always felt a nervous surge of adrenalin rush through his body. Everyday was a new challenge. Someone came to him to receive relief from whatever ailment might be plaguing them on that particular day. His challenge was to find that remedy, that powder or liquid that would put them back on their feet. Sometimes it was a tougher challenge. He would have to stitch up some cut or apply some ointment to a minor wound. Then, of course, there were the serious injuries. Stabbings, beatings, broken bones, and worse. Physical abuses that would twist his insides to look at. And not only from strangers. More often than not, husbands beating wives, fathers abusing their children, and so on.

Life in Whitechapel was cheap and nobody had much to speak of. Crime and lawlessness were the coin of the day. If men were lucky, they found jobs on the docks, but there simply weren't enough jobs to go around. And the women? Well, when all else failed and they were facing starvation in the streets, many turned to the world's oldest profession. Prostitutes, ladies of the night, or just plain whores, depending on who was describing that particular profession. The English royalty preferred the term 'unfortunates.' By any name, Clarke usually kept his distance. Venereal disease was commonplace. And there were other dangers as well.

A head appeared at the open doorway. A very concerned-looking young woman, wearing a rather bright hair bonnet, looked into the room and met his gaze. Her face was flushed, as if she had been running or excited by some … "Are you the Doctor, sir?" He could tell by her tone and diction that she was of servant class. And the 'sir' came out so reflexively she probably didn't even notice saying it anymore.

"Yes, I am the doctor. Please enter. Do you suffer an ailment?" He tried to project friendliness and professionalism, even though he knew it was lost on this … child. As his eyes focused on her, he realized she was certainly in her mid-teens, perhaps younger. As she took one step in his office, his eyes scanned her posture, clothing, and face; dissecting everything with a scrutiny, as he might a cadaver. She was clean-faced and well-dressed. The plain, pale-blue dress was well-maintained and pressed, but certainly one of the few dresses she owned. Possibly handed down from someone older and/or wealthier. In seconds, he finished his scrutiny and could have told you, with a certain degree of accuracy, everything about this young woman's life. Clarke always believed that knowing his patients was the first step to curing them.

"It's milady, sir. She fainted dead away. We were riding in the Hansom cab and she became pale and swooned." Before Clarke could respond, the cab driver pushed into the doorway, carrying a pale burden in his arms. Clarke waved toward an empty examining room and led the way to the operating table.

The tall man, wearing a pinstriped suit, lowered her gently onto the table and stepped back. Clarke's eyes quickly scanned over the attire of the clean and proper cabby and the woman reclined on his table. These folks were not from Whitechapel, that much was for certain. The lady wore a dress that cost more than anyone in this poor, dingy neighborhood could make in a year.

Wildman turned to her maid. "What is the patient's name?"

The young lady, named Caroline, spoke haltingly. "Milady's name is Alice Rutherton ... I'm sorry ... Alice Claybourne. She recently married John Claybourne, Lord Greyson. She is expecting her first child."

Wildman nodded and pried further. "How far along? How many months?"

Caroline hesitated, as if calculating the length of time, and then finally answered. "She is in her seventh month."

Wildman spoke slower, allowing his voice to soften. "And has she had any spells before this one?"

Caroline seemed more at ease. "No, sir. She mentioned feeling a bit warm; her face had flushed a little. Suddenly, her head fell backward and she passed out."

Clarke proceeded to do a brief, cursory examination. Nothing obvious was ailing the patient. He turned to the cab driver and politely asked him to step out into the waiting room. "I will have to check her heartbeat and that of her baby. Please unbutton her blouse and remove any garments covering her abdomen." He was so accustomed to patients doing as he said, Clarke nearly laughed as he turned and saw the startled face of the young girl.

"But, sir. I'm not sure if a proper lady ..."

Wildman smiled. "Rest assured, young ... what was your name, my dear?"

"Caro ... Caroline, milord." She stuttered nervously and swallowed hard, seemingly with great effort.

"My name is Doctor James Clarke Wildman. You may call me James, Caroline." He smiled at her and she seemed to comfort herself a little. He took her hand in his and said, using his best bedside manner, "Rest assured, young Caroline, that I am a doctor and a gentleman. I have seen and examined many women, of all ages, as completely naked as the day they were born. Your lady is in safe hands. If you would like, you may stay here in the room the entire time, to protect her honor. I am quite certain Alice Claybourne would place her honor in your hands. Alright?"

Caroline's face flushed red when he said the word 'naked' and he almost burst out laughing. "Yes, doct ... Sir ... James."

"Very well, Caroline. You may be my nurse for this examination. Please proceed to remove only enough garments so I can get an accurate heartbeat of the mother and fetus."

Caroline's eyes were wide. "The what?"

"The baby, Caroline." He had found that most patients felt more at ease when he called them by name.

Caroline nodded. "Oh, yes, of course." He noticed her hands were trembling as she undid the buttons and wrappings. Clarke swore he could hear her heartbeat, fluttering like that of a hummingbird, from the opposite side of the examining table. "I'm done, sir ... James."

"Well, Caroline, let's see what ails this young lady." He placed the small cup of the stethoscope on the bared top edge of the smooth breast of Lady Greyson and quietly counted. He smiled and comforted Caroline with, "Sounds fine. Let's check the infant's heartbeat now." Positioning the monitor on the small, bared patch of belly, he listened again. He looked up and saw Caroline leaning forward, as if expecting something to happen. "Would you like to hear the baby's heartbeat?"

"But, I'm not a doctor ...."

"You don't have to be a physician to hear something." Wildman gave her a broad, flirting smile.

She nervously smiled back at him and said, "Yes, I would like to." Clarke showed her how to place the earpieces and set the small cup back on the swollen abdomen. Her brow wrinkled in concentration for a moment and then her face lit up. "I hear it. I can hear the baby's heartbeat. It seems very fast."

"Actually, Caroline, if you listen closely you will notice there are two distinctly different beats. The faster, lighter beat is the baby's. The louder, slower beat belongs to the mother, Lady Greyson."

"I've never heard anything like this before, James. It is truly amazing." She smiled. Her face was very pure and fresh-looking. Clarke found himself blushing slightly as he realized how close they were standing to each other. Her nearness was intoxicating and he suddenly felt quite lightheaded. He smiled again, took the instrument from her hands and turned to place it back in the medical cabinet. He could feel her eyes on him and realized that he couldn't speak.

Then it happened. His eyes saw hers reflected in the glass of the medicine cabinet and he focused beyond her face. In the back of the glass-faced cabinet stood the small, glass vial filled with blue, shimmering liquid. Similar to mercury, the smooth, thick elixir glistened and reflected effervescent light from its depths. He could swear it called to him, like the temptation of alcohol or the powerful narcotic Opium, nicknamed the Dancing Dragon. He had witnessed many 'Lotus Eaters' wandering the dark streets of Whitechapel, experiencing hellish hallucinations, as their addiction slowly consumed them. As they 'chased the dragon.'

A twisted, evil face stared back at him from the reflection in the glass. It mouthed the words 'she is the one.' And it was right. He had the perfect subject for his experiments, here on his examining table. Not some wine-soaked prostitute, who would lay with a dozen different men in a single day. No venereal disease ridden drug addict, living in filth and human waste. This was a well-nourished, proper lady. She would eat well and sleep on clean sheets at night. He only needed two minutes alone with her.

"Caroline," Wildman turned, staring deeply into her young, blue irises. "Would your lady have carried a clutch or purse with her?"

"Yes, yes, James, I believe she did. I remember seeing it in the cab. It matched her gown. She placed it in the glove compartment."

"Would you mind retrieving it for me? She might have something in there that would explain the reason for her fainting."

Caroline glanced at her lady and hesitated. Clarke placed a modest, clean white cover over the Lady Greyson and smiled his most reassuring face at Caroline.

"Don't you worry; I won't leave her for a second while you are gone."

Smiling back, she left the room and went outside with the cab driver to search for the purse.

Clarke moved rapidly, knowing he had but one chance of success. He must do this quickly. Grabbing a syringe and the bottle filled with the blue mercury liquid, his hands calmly proceeded with practiced movement. Lifting a small area of the sheet, he exposed Alice Claybourne's bare belly. The long needle sank several inches beneath the skin, into the womb. He pushed slowly, steadily on the plunger until the needle was completely empty. The cover was pulled back down, the bottle and syringe replaced to their proper places in the cabinet. Clarke sat down on the stool next to the table. Even though his heart was pounding furiously, he was the picture of calmness when the cabby and Caroline re-entered the building. She was holding a woman's small clutch.

"Please allow me to examine the contents of the purse. Would you mind refastening Lady Greyson's clothes? I will keep my back turned." Wildman dumped the contents of the small clutch and examined them. He was relieved to discover the absence of narcotics and other such vices. He replaced the contents just as Caroline had finished.

"Good news, Caroline, I find nothing alarming in her purse. And she, and the baby, both seem quite healthy. I would be willing to bet she suffered from a simple fainting spell. No more than that. This sometimes happens in the latter months of a pregnancy. She should rest for a couple days and if she experiences no further spells, she should be just fine. Let's see if I can awaken her with some simple smelling salts."

Clarke waved the small brown bottle under Alice Claybourne's nose twice, and after a delicate cough, her eyes opened. She stared directly into Clarke's golden-brown eyes and seemed bewildered. He was lost in those light-grey eyes. They were the most beautiful eyes he had ever beheld. His professional, medical demeanor was gone. Vanished in an instant. He simply stared, and she returned his deep gaze. A long moment seemed to pass.

"Milady, are you okay?" Caroline interrupted. Lady Greyson, seemingly for the first time, realized she was not in familiar surroundings.

Alice Claybourne sat up. "Wha … What happened. Last I remember, we were in our Hansom cab."

Caroline quickly explained. "You fainted dead away. We brought you here and Jame … the doctor used smelling salts to wake you up."

Clarke noticed that Caroline had reverted back to calling him 'the doctor,' instead of James. He also noticed she failed to remark on the physical examination of her mistress. Probably to save her lady embarrassment.

Lady Greyson blushed slightly. "Thank you, doctor. It appears I am in your debt." Once more their eyes met and locked. With some effort Clarke was able to finally look away. "Do we owe you anything for your services?"

Wildman nodded his head. "No, ma'am. It is my pleasure to rescue damsels and ladies in distress. I would recommend a week or so of rest." He gave his brightest, full-faced smile.

"If only I could. My husband was recently informed that he has been assigned to help survey the western coastal jungles of equatorial Africa. We leave within the week." Claybourne smiled and one final time their eyes met. Then she turned and, with the assistance of the cabby and her maid, Lady Greyson climbed into the cab. "Thank you, again, Doctor."

He waved politely as the cab pulled away from the curb. Caroline gave him one last smile as they left him standing at the entrance of his medical offices. Those eyes. Those light-grey eyes would stay with him for the rest of his life. Little did he know he would be seeing those same eyes, but in a different face, in eleven short years. Eleven years that would seem like an entire lifetime.

Perhaps it was time to quit all of his other experiments. They had all resulted in failure, anyway. A voice in the back of his head spoke to him. The experiments failed because his subjects were dirty, filthy creatures who sold their bodies for a meal or a night's lodgings. They often indulged in narcotics and alcohol to the point of constant inebriation. How could his experiments possibly hope to succeed under those vile conditions?

As he turned to re-enter his offices, another face was reflected in the windows at the front of the building. Newspapermen and police would have immediately recognized that face from the descriptions they had received recently. The face belonged to the man known as Saucy Jack or Jack the

Ripper. James Clarke Wildman was unaware of the fact, but Saucy Jack would strike again tonight, in the Whitechapel district. The name Polly suddenly came to mind. He would have to pay pretty Polly a visit. And then, maybe Long Liz and Dark Annie. He always liked Dark Annie. A cruel, sadistic smile touched his lips. Under his breath he muttered, "One day men will look back and say I gave birth to the twentieth century."

End of Flashback to August 31ˢᵗ, 1888.

Chapter Forty-Eight
The Missing Page

April 6, 1945   9:00 am

Professor Randolph Schmidt stood at a distance from Black Skull, until the obsidian-masked man motioned for him to approach. Professor Walters followed close on Schmidt's footsteps. Of the half-dozen scientists involved in Project Gladiator, Walters and Schmidt were the leaders. Each was considered a genius in the advanced fields of microbiology and human physiology, the study of the mechanical, physical, and biochemical functions of living organisms.

Simply stated, this was a brain trust of modern-day magicians and wizards, who had mastered other major branches of scientific study of physiological research including biochemistry, biophysics, paleobiology, biomechanics, and pharmacology. Black Skull placed his faith in the intellectual genius of these mystics of science. Their incredible creations would be the weapons required to defeat Totenkopf's enemies.

Victor Kaine was relaxing in a nearby leather lounge chair. He was dressed in dark blue. Boots, pants, shirt, and gloves, all dark blue. Against the pale color of his skin and snow-white, shoulder-length hair, the blue was striking in appearance.

Schmidt whispered, "Herr Totenkopf?"

Black Skull acknowledged his presence. "Yes, Professor?"

"There is a problem with the last Danner notebook," Schmidt continued.

Black Skull eyed Kaine. "What is the problem?"

"There seems to be a page missing from the journal. It is the page that contains the chemical compounds required for the fourth and final phase. Without that missing page ..."

"I understand." Black Skull looked at the tall, lounging man. "Herr Kaine, I must request that you give us the missing page. We are nearly ready for the next phase."

"Me? I do not have any page ..." Victor stopped speaking and a realization spread across his thin face. "Doc Titan."

Totenkopf's eyes narrowed. "Excuse me?"

Kaine's face flushed with anger. "This is just like Doc Titan, to remove the firing pin from the gun. He must have studied the notebooks and removed the page as a precaution. Damn that man!"

Schmidt leaned forward and whispered into Totenkopf's ear. "Perhaps one of the prisoners would know where …?"

Totenkopf nodded. "Yes, you are correct, Professor. Thanks to Herr Kaine, we possess a resource to find the whereabouts of the missing page. I shall force his men to tell of the location."

Victor waved an open hand dismissively. "He would never have shared that kind of secret with any of his men."

Totenkopf's voice rose slightly, his patience was limited. "I must have that page, Kaine. Failure of this project is not an option. The future of the Third Reich is in my hands. My country has invested too much time and money to fail now."

Kaine bit his lip nervously. "Even if his men knew, they will never tell you. They'd sooner die. Torture will never work on them."

Totenkopf smiled evilly. "We have ways to make men talk, don't we, Professor Schmidt?"

Schmidt agreed without hesitation. "Yes, Mein Herr."

Totenkopf promptly stood and aggressively marched toward the door. "Kaine, prepare to leave immediately to find the missing page. I shall summon you when I have information on the location."

Victor, feeling perturbed at be given orders like a mere lackey, protested. "Totenkopf, do not presume to order me …"

Totenkopf, turning quickly, violently, his horrific obsidian face twisted with uncontrolled anger. "Do *not* question me on this point. Any other man would be dead for allowing this failure to happen. Our continued partnership depends on your ability to find the missing page. Do I make myself perfectly clear, Herr Kaine?"

Kaine, for the first time in his life feeling intimidated by another, answered cautiously. "Yes. I understand."

"Very good. Herr Professor, with me." Black Skull stalked away, his heavy footsteps reflecting his anger.

Hermia had been watching the Black Skull during this outburst and found herself trembling slightly. She did not like this horrible man. Victor Kaine noticed her nervous shaking and placed his hand upon hers. He had resumed his normal calm manner.

"Fear not, my dear Hermia." Victor said reassuringly. "I believe our partnership with this madman is nearly through. Very soon, we will no longer require his presence."

The London Gazzette

The Official Newspaper of the UK - Established 1665 ***Special Morning Tabloid Edition*** 1¢ September 30, 1888

JACK THE RIPPER STRIKES AGAIN!!

Artistic depiction of the notorious serial killer, Jack the Ripper.

By THOMAS ALLEN

The as-of-yet unidentified serial killer known only by his alias of Jack the Ripper aka 'Saucey Jack' struck again last night, this time committing what police are calling a 'double event' murder, claiming the lives of two known street prostitutes.

At 1:00 am this morning, the body of the first victim, Elizabeth Stride - as known by her street name as 'Long Liz', was discovered lying on the ground in Dutfield's Yard, off Berner Street in Whitechapel.

The second victim, Catherine Eddowes, who used the aliases 'Kate Conway' and 'Mary Ann Kelly,' was discovered at approximately 3:00 am. Her body was discovered in Mitre Square. There are rumors of a message from the killer on a nearby wall, written in white chalk, which was immediately removed by Police

Superintendent Thomas Arnold, before the evidence could be photographed and recorded.

The bodies of the two victims were found horribly mutilated in the same fashion as the previous slayings.

According to a confidential, but unnamed source, Scotland Yard has not ruled out that the notorious Jack the Ripper might be responsible for as many as a dozen other unsolved murders this year.

However, although the killer has been terrorizing the impoverished Whitechapel district of England for several months, only two others are positively identified as 'Ripper' slayings.

Mary Ann Nichols, nicknamed 'Polly', was the first victim. Her body was discovered at about 3:40 in the morning on Friday, August 31, 1888, on the ground in front of a gated stable entrance in Buck's Row, a back street in Whitechapel.

(This is only two hundred yards from the London Hospital, where the fabled 'Elephant Man' makes his home. Locals have spread slanderous rumors, speculating that Joseph 'John' Merrick might be sneaking from his rooms and committing these atrocities. However, this reporter has personally met Mr. Merrick and can assure the readers of this fine newspaper that he is definitely not the serial killer.)

The second of two 'unfortunates', as the royalty of Great Britain

so often call them, was Annie Chapman, nicknamed 'Dark Annie.' Chapman's body was discovered about 6:00 in the morning on Saturday, September 8, 1888, lying on the ground near a doorway in the back yard of 29 Hanbury Street, Spitalfields.

Recently, Chief Inspector Lestrade had requested that the great detective Sherlock Holmes investigate the grisly murders and study the various clues eft behind, including the 'Dear Boss' letter. Formerly considered a hoax, the letter, received on September 27, 1888, referred to 'clip the lady's ears off.' Upon a detailed examination of the corpse of Eddowes, it was discovered that one ear was partially cut off, just as the had letter promised.

Among the list of recent suspects was stage actor Richard Mansfield, currently performing a serious theatrical version of Robert Louis Stevenson's novel The Strange Case of Dr. Jekyll and Mr. Hyde to sold-out audiences.

The stories subject matter of horrific murder in the London streets drew much attention, even leading the star of the show to be accused by some members of the public of being the Ripper himself, although this theory was never taken seriously by the police or Scotland Yard.

The skillful removal of internal organs from some victims have led some officials to speculate that the killer might possess anatomical or surgical knowledge.

Continued on reverse side of page

Chapter Forty-Nine
Flashback to 1888 - The Last Stand of Saucey Jack

April 6, 1945 10:00 pm

Gibs shook his head. "Wow, that's a rather bizarre story. But what does this Wildman guy have to do with this place? Or Doc? Or us?"

"I suppose it's like the Doorknob in Alice in Wonderland said, *'Read the directions and directly you will be directed in the right direction.'*" Pam suggested.

Megan held up a finger. "Wait, there's more to this tale. Listen to this."

Pam motioned for Megan to wait a minute.

Ned was lightly snoring. His head was leaned forward and the book in his lap was perched precariously on one knee. Pam silently padded on tiptoe and approached the elderly man. Without disturbing his slumber, she carefully slid the heavy tome away from him.

The pages that were open to Pam's eyes captivated her attention. The left hand page contained an antique tintype of a very young-looking Ned Land, his arm around a beautiful woman. They were standing in front of a small, quaint house. The woman appeared to be holding an infant in her arms. They had the look of a recently married couple, both smiling happily. On the other side of Ned was a tall, handsome older man with a scholarly look to his face. Inscribed below the image was *Professor Pierre Arronaxe, Ned and Patricia Land and Baby Arronaxe. 1866.*

On the right page was another black and white tintype. This one was more recent and of better quality. A young woman knelt between two younger girls, possibly in their early teens. They were all smiling broadly, unusual for this time period, when having a photo taken was serious business. A young boy, perhaps four years old, sat on the dirt in front of the three women. Pam recognized the background as Canadian wilderness, since she had originated from that part of the world. In fact, the small cabin in the background even looked similar to the one where she had grown up.

In a fine, clear hand was written *Arronaxe Land and her daughters, Arronaxe and Patricia. 1896.* There was no inscription for the boy to be found. Pam closed the book and placed it on a nearby table.

Pam smiled at Megan. "Thanks. Please go ahead with the story."

Megan displayed a sliver of paper. "This is where I stopped and called you all over. Actually, at this point there is a note saying we should read from another journal. Cassie, I believe it's that book to your right."

Cassie lifted the thick tome and read the handwritten inscription on the leather cover. "The personal memoirs and reflections of Doctor James Hamish Watson 1888." She glanced at her friends and opened it to the page indicated by a black and gold bookmark. She began reading.

Journal entry - Fourth day of November, 1888.

Per Sherlock Holmes instructions, I am writing this in my personal journal and will not reference these incredible accounts to our biographer, Mr. Arthur Conan Doyle. Of the seven years that I have been acquainted with Holmes, the past several days have certainly been the oddest. And these are, bar none, the strangest, most extraordinary experiences I have ever scribed.

Inspector Lestrade of Scotland Yard came to visit our apartment rooms at 221B Baker Street early yesterday morning. His face was flushed from the cool morning air and something else. He dashed up the seventeen steps, barely pausing to acknowledge Mrs. Hudson's presence. Holmes, in his rather annoying fashion, was already standing at the doorway at the top of the stairs.

"Morning, Chief Inspector Lestrade. I've been anticipating your arrival." Holmes said quietly, with an air of confidence. Lestrade looked flustered. You would certainly think by now that he would have become accustomed to Sherlock's foreknowledge of events and actions.

"You have?"

"Yes. Absolutely. And by the color in your cheek, you've rushed here with the newest information on the Whitechapel slayings. Before you ask how I know … you already have your notebook in hand and I noticed your notations have been scribed somewhat hastily, rather than in your usual, precise handwriting. The local newspapers have been abuzz with the Ripper's recent exploits and horrible deeds. You've arrived on foot, so you obviously could not await a cab to bring you here. Thank God, it's simply a taunting note to the police and not another actual slaying."

"But how do you know …" Lestrade began.

"Too early. By my estimations we still have five more days before Jack strikes again. Five days to figure out his hidden identity."

"That's why I rushed over here, Mr. Holmes. He sent another letter, another hint." Lestrade said breathlessly. "This time he gave away too much. He told us where he lives!"

Holmes frowned and looked perplexed. "He gave you the actual address to his residence? Impossible."

Lestrade offered his notebook for Holmes perusal. I read the note from Holmes' right shoulder. The transcription read thus.

What fools the police are. I even give them the name of the street where I am living. Prince William Street.

Lestrade explained further, although Holmes was quite familiar with every street in Whitechapel, if not all of London. "Prince William Street is only yards from the main road between Aigburth and the office of the Cotton Exchange. The East end of England, where all the murders have occurred!"

"But what does that mean?" I displayed my ignorance, without hesitating to think. The chief inspector opened his mouth to elucidate but Holmes cut him off abruptly.

"It means absolutely nothing, Watson. If memory serves me correctly, you will find two butcher shops, several Jewish businesses, and a doctor's office. Doctor James Clarke Wildman, if I remember correctly. A polite gentleman and certainly not the Ripper. I might be wrong but I believe this message is simply another red herring. Naturally we would be fools not to question the residents and owners, but considering the emotional climate in Whitechapel, I would certainly use the utmost of discretion."

"You think he's trying to create hostility between the citizens and officers? Or against the Jewish population in Whitechapel? Like the September 30th message chalked on a wall at the Catherine Eddowes murder in Mitre Square?" I offered.

Lestrade nodded and referred to the notebook that Sherlock had returned to him. He cleared his throat and recited.

"The Juwes are the men That Will not be Blamed for nothing."

"Wrong!" Holmes stated loudly. "The correct inscription was *'The Juwes are not the men That Will be Blamed for nothing.'* By moving the word 'not', the meaning changes."

I once again displayed my ignorance. "But what does that mean? Either way it's read, it makes no since."

"It refers to an ancient tale about the assassination of the leader of the Freemasons and King Solomon's punishment ..." He stopped and glanced from Lestrade to myself. "... and is a utter waste of time." Holmes preferred not to pass his time discussing dead ends. "Mark my words Lestrade. These murders are not being committed by Jews, butchers, a member of royalty, or some mythical, Freemasonic Order. These slayings are neither the workings of a conspiracy or a satanic ritual."

The chief inspector raised an eyebrow. "Oh? And what are they? Why is he killing these prostitutes?"

Holmes was silent for a moment and finally confessed. "I honestly don't know. Because he enjoys it." Without another word, Sherlock turned and walked to his private room. The door slowly closed. Lestrade and I exchanged glances and I gave a sheepish shrug.

"This one is bothering him, isn't it?" Lestrade asked quietly.

I nodded in agreement. "Every death causes him to question his abilities further. Most killers are stupid, careless. This Ripper is different. Methodical. Fearless. Killing women only minutes and yards away from both witnesses and the police. And utterly lacking in motive, as far as can be determined."

"True. But of the estimated 80,000 or more prostitutes in London, these four victims personally knew and associated with each other, including routinely socializing with one another at the same pub. Moreover, the victim's bodies were found several miles apart from each other and yet they lived within the same, or adjoining, flats at a flop-house on Dorset Street. And Dorset Street is only a short, one block street. There must be a link to these slayings."

I quickly consulted my journal. "Have the police located the missing woman? Mary Jane Kelly, according to my notes."

Lestrade lowered his gaze and shook his head. "Stories vary, but it's possible she took a trip to Paris with an unnamed gentleman friend. I hope we don't find her body buried somewhere. However, that wouldn't be Jack's style. He wants to taunt us. Rub it in our faces that we can't catch him. It damned embarrassing, Watson."

"I have faith that you will bring him to justice, Lestrade."

The chief inspector nodded in agreement. "I hope you're right, Watson." He glanced towards Holmes' door. "Please let him know that we'll inform him if anything comes of the Prince William Street message. We'll be doing a door-to-door search today."

Lestrade left and I settled down in my chair near the front window. As I watched the inspector walking down the street, I noticed how the pressure of the recent murders had weighed heavily on his shoulders as well. Reviewing the notes I had taken for Holmes, I searched for some missing piece of the puzzle.

Mary Ann Nichols (maiden name Mary Ann Walker, nicknamed 'Polly'), born on August 26, 1845, and killed on Friday, August 31, 1888. Nichols' body was discovered at about 3:40 in the morning on the ground in front of a gated stable entrance in Buck's Row, a back street in Whitechapel two hundred yards from the London Hospital.

Annie Chapman (maiden name Eliza Ann Smith, nicknamed 'Dark Annie'), born in September 1841 and killed on Saturday, September 8, 1888. Chapman's body was discovered about 6:00 in the morning lying on the ground near a doorway in the back yard of 29 Hanbury Street, Spitalfields.

Elizabeth Stride (maiden name Elisabeth Gustafsdotter, nicknamed 'Long Liz'), born in Sweden on November 27, 1843, and killed on Sunday, September 30, 1888. Stride's body was discovered close to 1:00 in the morning, lying on the ground in Dutfield's Yard, off Berner Street in Whitechapel.

Catherine Eddowes (used the aliases 'Kate Conway' and 'Mary Ann Kelly,' from the surnames of her two common-law husbands Thomas Conway and John Kelly), born on April 14, 1842, and killed on Sunday, September 30, 1888, on the same day as the previous victim, Elizabeth Stride. Her body was found in Mitre Square, in the City of London.

I added the following, for Sherlock to read later,

Mary Jane Kelly (calling herself 'Marie Jeanette Kelly', nicknamed 'Ginger') believed to have left England, perhaps traveling to Paris, reportedly born 1863 in either the city of Limerick or County Limerick, Munster, Ireland.

I noticed the two kindred names Mary Ann Kelly and Mary Jane Kelly but dismissed the fact. Sometimes prostitutes took similar names, because clients would pay extra to have two women, especially sisters, at the same time. What horrible times we live in, where a woman is forced into such a nasty business or face starvation. And now, a man butchering prostitutes (Sorry, Holmes, I know the royalty prefers the terms *lost souls* or *unfortunates*) for some dastardly, unknown reason.

Morbidly, I found myself almost thankful that my fiancé Mary Morstan had left the country for several months and I wouldn't have to worry about her being stalked by a murdering madman. The image of a man slashing, tearing, and cutting some poor helpless … I tried to put the thought from my mind. I wished I were with Mary and away from this horror. We met in the first week of September and we were already discussing getting married next spring.

Back to business. Study the clues. That's what Holmes would do. Perhaps there was something in one of Jack's letters. I reread them again, for what seemed like the hundredth time in the past several weeks.

Received on September 27th, 1888:
Dear Boss,

I keep on hearing the police have caught me but they wont fix me just yet. I have laughed when they look so clever and talk about being on the right track. That joke about Leather Apron gave me real fits. I am down on whores and I shant quit ripping them till I do get buckled. Grand work the last job was. I gave the lady no time to squeal. How can they catch me now. I love my work and want to start again. You will soon hear of me with my funny little games. I saved some of the proper red stuff in a ginger beer bottle over the last job to write with but it went thick like glue and I cant use it. Red ink is fit enough I hope ha. ha. The next job I do I shall clip the ladys ears off and send to the police officers just for jolly wouldn't you. Keep this letter back till I do a bit more work, then give it out straight. My knife's so nice and sharp I want to get to work right away if I get a chance. Good Luck.

Yours truly
Jack the Ripper

Dont mind me giving the trade name

PS Wasnt good enough to post this before I got all the red ink off my hands curse it No luck yet. They say I'm a doctor now. ha ha

Received on October 1st, 1888:

I was not codding dear old Boss when I gave you the tip, you'll hear about Saucy Jacky's work tomorrow double event this time number one squealed a bit couldn't finish straight off. ha not the time to get ears for police. thanks for keeping last letter back till I got to work again.

Jack the Ripper

Received on October 16th, 1888:

From hell.
Mr Lusk,
Sor
I send you half the Kidne I took from one woman and prasarved it for you tother piece I fried and ate it was very nise. I may send you the bloody knif that took it out if you only wate a whil longer

signed
Catch me when you can Mishter Lusk

As I added the last letter to the list, from this mornings meeting with Lestrade, I had to agree with the Inspector. Jack the Ripper *was* taunting the police. The Chief Inspector had received other letters, but Holmes and the police agreed they were certainly fakes. Still, I found no hidden clues. Unfortunately, I had to confess to myself - as I have so often done since making the acquaintance of Sherlock Holmes - that I was no master detective.

Journal entry - Ninth day of November, 1888.

Sherlock Holmes awakened me at the hour of midnight, with a loud pounding at my door and shouting out my name. My first thought was … Jack has struck again! Mrs. Hudson, our devoted housekeeper, has left London to visit her aunt in Middlesex, so the rest of the house is vacant. Although a charming and tolerant woman, she would have certainly frowned at the hour of the night. Sherlock was rushing about the flat when I opened the door to my room. In one arm, he held my medical bag and in the other were several clean towels from the hall bath. He placed them on the floor near the doorway to his bedroom.

"Watson … James, I need your help." His manner was excited and his expression was worried, something I very rarely saw in Holmes.

"Of course, Sherlock. What is it?"

"Remember the telegram I received this morning?"

I had not forgotten. It was a short but strange message. It read: *'Arriving in London this evening. I need your help. Adam.'*

Over the years, Holmes had received many interesting messages. But this was the first time I ever saw his face pale after reading it. Despite my inquiry as to the sender, this 'Adam', Sherlock had quietly nodded his head and refused to answer. He began playing that infernal violin, some German melody he had been practicing, and smoking that thick grey-blue tobacco which filled the apartment with a billowing cloud. I finally had to open a window to catch my breath.

"Yes, Holmes, I remember."

"Well, Adam is here." He said this as though he were announcing the entrance of the King of England. "And we have need of your medical skills."

"God Lord, man. Is something wrong with him?"

Holmes drew himself up to his full six-foot height. He seemed to be searching for the words. "Watson, I need you to promise me that I have your complete confidence. What you are about to see must never be revealed, never spoken aloud. No hint of it can be placed in your memoirs to Conan Doyle." I nodded and gave him my solemn oath. He placed his hand on my shoulder and smiled. "Good man. Thank you, my friend." As he reached for the doorknob, he added, "Oh, one last thing. Try not to scream."

My heart beat madly as I stared into the dark abyss of the unlighted room. The dim illumination from the main sitting room behind me filtered in and outlined a dark silhouette. My mind kept replaying Sherlock's last words, 'Try not to scream.'

My nostrils were assaulted by the fetid stench of death and decay. This immediately rekindled memories of the battlefield, when I was a surgeon with the military and of the morgue, when I was in medical school. It was not a pleasant smell and they were not happy memories.

The man Sherlock had called Adam shifted and I realized that he was not a man of normal human proportions. I thought of the man named Joseph 'John' Merrick. The newspapers called him The Elephant Man. Holmes and I had met Mr. Merrick several months ago, during his stay at the Royal London Hospital. The unfortunate man was originally misdiagnosed with a disease called neuro-fribromotosis, which causes tumors to grow on the nerve endings, both on the skin and inside the body. Recently, however, it was discovered that he was actually suffering from something more malignant called Proteus Syndrome. Although he was still at the Royal London Hospital, it was doubtful he would live to see his twenty-fifth birthday. I had nearly forgotten about the stricken man until rumors began that Merrick was actually Jack the Ripper. Locals were certain that Joseph was sneaking out of the hospital grounds at night and killing prost … unfortunates. Little did they realize, the man could barely walk, much less attack and kill a healthy woman.

Sherlock struck a match and lit the lantern in the room. As the flame grew stronger, I could see Adam in its illumination. My head swam dizzily and then I realized that I had been holding my breath. Holmes has asked me not to write a description of the man and I am remaining true to my vow.

The local population and police of Whitechapel believe that Jack the Ripper must certainly look or act like a monster. A demon. So anyone, like Joseph Merrick or Adam, who do not fit the mold of 'normal' are suspect. Without warning, one such officer had pulled his revolver and shot Adam twice in the upper chest.

I stitched the yellowed leathery skin and bandaged the wounds. However, I noticed other, older wounds that had never quite healed correctly. The upper torso was a battlefield of injuries; many of them should have been mortal. Adam thanked me politely but his eyes projected a sadness that forced me to look away.

We left him to rest in Sherlock's room and talked in the main study. I couldn't restrain myself from asking the question.

"According to Mary Wollstonecraft Shelley's novel, he died. Nearly one hundred years ago. Lost on the Arctic ice. This is most …"

"Irregular, Watson? That's the word you usually use and it couldn't apply more in this particular instance."

"And you're certain he's not … that he couldn't be …?"

"Jack the Ripper? Absolutely certain. Adam has come to London to help me stop the Ripper from killing any more women."

The following morning the gruesomely mutilated body of Mary Jane Kelly was discovered lying on the bed in the single room where she lived at 13 Miller's Court, off Dorset Street, Spitalfields. Killed on November 9th, just as Sherlock Holmes had predicted.

Cassie stopped reading and closed the journal. She was trembling from what she had just read and appeared slightly pale. "I believe you're supposed to read the next entry from that book, Megan," She said weakly.

"Okay. Now, where was I? Oh, here it is …" Megan continued her narrative.

Kong listened as Megan continued. He glanced over at Bart, who was sitting quietly, staring at the floor. Bart had a faraway look in his dark eyes.

Beginning of Flashback to November 10th, 1888.

Mary Jeanette Kelly had escaped him for the last month. She had traveled to Paris, under the nickname 'Ginger,' and had only returned last night. But he soon learned of her return and had immediately hired her for a 'private sitting.' The police and the good folks of Whitechapel would not soon forget the results of that meeting. He had done her and done her up good. Admittedly, he got a bit carried away. The bloodlust had consumed him. Merely the memory of what he had done made him smile. A cruel, evil smile.

He had enough presence of mind to confirm that the experiment had failed with her, just like all of the others. All of the others. Eleven in total, thus far, including 'Ginger.' And not one had been pregnant. He knew, because he had thoroughly checked each one. Removed their filthy uteri and ripped open their wombs. Barren wombs. He had … had … oh, God … what had he done? Saucy Jack immediately fought down those feelings. That was James Clarke, trying to rise to the surface. But Jack couldn't allow that. Not yet. He had one more whore to find. And James Clarke couldn't do what had to be done. He was too weak, too spineless.

Jack was going to find the twelfth prostitute tonight. He even knew her name. Anna Marie Blake was number twelve. The things he would do to her. To the filthy whore. The sun would be going down soon and he would take his evening stroll. Pretty as you please and never mind to the police. He had walked right past them last night and they didn't even acknowledge him. Saucy Jack might as well be invisible. He was merely another middle-aged, well-to-do gentleman out for an evening stroll. They hadn't even found all of the bodies yet. And some would never be found, the advantage to intimately knowing the various dissecting rooms and slaughterhouses of Whitechapel.

He sneered nastily and grabbed for his hat, coat and cane. A bell rang in his ears. The front door! He had forgotten to lock the front door! No, James Clarke had forgotten. That damned fool. For a moment he was conflicted. Continue heading out of the back door as planned or re-enter his offices? He might have to let James Clarke take over for a short time. Jack couldn't hold a civilized conversation. Especially, when his blood was up, like it was now. He had always allowed his actions to speak for themselves.

"Doc'or James? 're you in, sir?" A woman's voice. Very Whitechapel in her vocalization. Sometimes he had to piece together what these idiots were saying, just to make sense of their butchered vocabulary. Jack smiled. Butchered. He glanced through the curtains, into the front parlor. His breath caught in his throat. It couldn't be. But it definitely was. Anna Marie Blake had just walked into his offices. His heart skipped a beat. Like a fly into his spiders web. He slowly released his hold on James Clarke.

James Clarke Wildman woke up in the doorway to his offices. Why had he been standing here? He was preparing to lock up for the night and … and … what? He had been daydreaming again. A sign he needed more sleep at night. Sleep without nightmares. He looked up as a young lady walked into the doorway at the opposite side of the room.

"Doc'or James? Sorry t' bother you sir. Ah've ha' need of your services." She was in great pain. He could see it from her expression. Gently guiding her to an examination table, he helped her to sit on the edge. "M' belly. Somethin' hurts inside. Crampin' worse than Ah've ever remembered. Please sir, take th' pain away."

"Of course, I'll do what I can. I'll be right back." James said, in a reassuring tone. Stepping into the vestibule he locked up the front door to the offices and pulled the shades. Stepping back into the exam room, he stood for a second in the doorway. A cruel smile played across his thin lips. "Now, m'dear, let's see wha' we can do 'bout stoppin' yer pain." Saucy Jack sneered evilly.

The terrified screams, echoing within the small doctors office, were never heard on the filthy streets of Whitechapel.

Several hours passed.

"Good Lord!" Sherlock Holmes exclaimed, as he perceived the butchered remains of what had once been a beautiful woman. Blood dripped from the operating table, the light suspended above, and the small pile of stainless steel surgical tools that had been used to utterly destroy this human victim. Even though he had been witness to many horrible things that one human being could do to another, Sherlock had never beheld anything like this before. He was not a man easily shocked, but now he was simply nauseous and disgusted. Then he heard the little sound. A tiny whimper. For one horrified second, he believed that the woman might still be alive, despite the mutilations. But no, nothing human could have survived that. She was certainly beyond this mortal plane. Turning to his companion, Sherlock inquired quietly. "Did you hear that, Adam?"

The other man who occupied the room with him was enormous. His long, black hair nearly touched the ceiling and his shoulders filled the doorway. His voice was the sound a large cave bear would make, a deep rumbling noise. "There." A monstrous, yellow-tinged hand, with mottled grayish flesh, stabbed out and pointed to a wardrobe closet. On the arm and hand of the gargantuan man were deep, horrible scars. Matching scars covered his exposed chest, neck and head. The fetid stench of the grave hung in the air around the cadaverous man. This would partly explain why the large man had been wearing a London fog coat, despite the abnormally warm evening.

The wardrobe closet doors were swung open and hid the occupants from view at first. Blood-soaked shoes extended out of the opening, and again could be heard a small animal-like whimper. Sherlock held his breath and looked into the closet, not really knowing what to expect. What he saw was the last thing he would have suspected. Pushed into the back corner was the figure of a man. Most would have considered the face handsome and kindly. At this moment, however, it reflected nothing but fear and anxiety. The face, hair, clothes were all covered in blood. Saturated with what seemed to be gallons of it. Held in the trembling arms of the man was a small bundle of white cloth. The whimpering noise was coming from this tiny parcel. The man leaned forward and moved aside the top layer of cloth, revealing the mysterious, unseen creature.

A baby. Swaddled in this makeshift blanket, the baby seemed content. As he took a step forward, Sherlock realized something was odd about this baby. The skin wasn't merely pale. It was pure white. As was the small patch of colorless hair on its head. Obviously, assuming from the human carnage scattered about the room, this must be a newborn infant. However, the eyes were wide open and staring at him with a strange awareness. Sherlock was certainly no expert on newborn infants, but he knew something was different about this child. He found himself almost hypnotically drawn to those pale, almost colorless eyes.

The man in the closet held out one trembling hand in their direction. "Please … please, help me. I've been ill. My head … there was someone … else … in my head. He's gone now. Please help me. Please …." Tears filled his eyes and his voice vanished but his quivering lips still moved.

The monstrous, misshapen mockery of humanity stepped forward and helped James Clarke Wildman from the closet. As he stood erect, Clarke looked up into the mis-matched eyes of the large man-mountain. "You. It is ironic that you should be the one to save me. I've once more fallen into sin … I need help to save my soul. Will you help me? Please help … me … help us." Saying this, he looked down on the tiny child in his blood-soaked arms. His eyes rolled back into his head and he fainted. The large man caught him and the infant, before either had moved far, displaying impressive speed, despite his hulking size.

"I will help you … Father."

End of Flashback to November 10th, 1888.

Chapter Fifty
Death Most Singular (The Death of Gabe Robinson)

April 6, 1945   10:30 am

The dungeon was in a filthy, unkept wing of the ancient structure that dated back over one hundred years. The island had housed several hundred prisoners at one time, mostly political in nature. Due to the unsanitary conditions, a plague had ravished the population and the island was labeled as condemned property. Gabe and Isabelle Robinson were housed in one cell, Rav Chandra and Whitney in the next, followed by Percy and Big Tom in the third. One last cell held the single prisoner. Despite efforts to coax the man to talk, he had remained silent. Whether mute or simply in shock, he ignored his inquiring neighbors. He simply sat on the cold, stone floor, without moving. At first they thought he might be dead, but Big Tom could see him slowly breathing, by looking at the reflection in a small piece of broken mirror, held outside the bars of the cell.

Two hours ago, Black Skull, his large, silent bodyguards, Ernst and Orban, and Professor Schmidt had entered the prison. Big Tom and Percy were shot with hypodermic needles, filled with a fast-acting drug. They had not cringed in a corner when the tranquilizer guns were aimed at them, but bravely and defiantly stood facing their jailors. They were dragged down the hallway to an empty room. Black Skull knew how demoralizing it would be for the remaining prisoners to listen to the sounds of torture from a distance. Ten minutes ago, Professor Schmidt and the two large guards emerged from the room, drugged Gabe, and dragged him away. Isabelle attacked one huge man, but she was easily shoved to the floor, and the cell was relocked.

Totenkopf paced the floor of the small room. "Herr Schmidt has suggested a different approach in obtaining information from you."

Big Tom had one black eye and blood trickled from a split lip into his thick beard. "I'll never tell you anything, you insane bastard."

Percy's forehead was bruised, as was his right check. "Goes double for me, fright-face. You Razis are finished."

Totenkopf's ghastly face-mask hid his evil intentions. "Your bravado and strong will is to be admired. But, I think you'll tell me exactly what I wish to know. I have broken far better men than you. It's a simple matter applying the right kind of leverage."

Percy laughed defiantly. "In your dreams, pal. I don't know anything about any Danner Journals. But even if I did, I would never tell you."

From their ragged appearance, it was obvious Big Tom and Percy had been thoroughly tortured and questioned for a length of time. They would not die from the torture, but they would bear scars for the rest of their lives. Black Skull was forced to hold back, he needed these men alive. At least, until he found the missing page of the journal. And they might have other secrets that Black Skull could use later.

Big Tom taunted his torturers. "Yeah, your truth serum tasted like mouthwash. If that's all you have …"

Totenkopf gritted his teeth. "I assure you, Mr. Thompson, I have merely begun. I understand your loyalty to Doc Titan and your ability to withstand torture is astounding. But I can now see that continuing in this fashion would simply be a waste of my time."

Percy spit venomously. "Damned straight, double-ugly!"

Totenkopf calmed himself. "The question is, are you willing to watch another man die, simply to keep your secrets?"

Black Skull's two silent bodyguards, Ernst and Orban, hauled a drugged Gabe Robinson into the room. He was tightly bound to a large chair with heavy leather straps. They dragged him closer, the metal chair scraping loudly across the concrete floor. Totenkopf pulled out his service revolver, a coal black Luger pistol, and without hesitation placed the barrel of the gun to Gabe's forehead. "You know how the Third Reich feels about these inferior races, Schwarzes in particular. I will not hesitate for a second to put a bullet into this … creature's brain, unless you comply immediately."

Gabe warned Big Tom and Percy. "Tell him to go to Hell. Don't tell him … "

Black Skull swung back and hit Gabe in the mouth with the revolver handle, drawing blood. Totenkopf barked. "Silence, animal!" His eyes blazing with madness as he turned back to Big Tom and Percy. "I *will* shoot this man, and then his Negro wife, and then all of the prisoners in the other cells. Give me your answer now or watch this man die. Where did Doc Titan hide the missing page of the sixth Danner Journal?"

Black Skull placed the revolver barrel at Gabe's temple and the trigger was slowly squeezed back.

Isabelle sat alone in her cold, dark prison. She could not see Rav Chandra or Whitney in the next cell; the walls between the cells were solid stone. The only opening to each cell was at the front and this was heavily barred. She tried to listen for sounds at the other end of the long hall, where the prisoners, including her husband Gabe, had been taken.

Whitney tried to reassure her. "Isabelle? Everything will be okay, dear. I've been in worse places than this and everything always works out in the end." Isabelle fought back her tears. "I'm not worried about me. It's Gabe."

Whitney reached her hand through the bars toward Isabelle. "Dear, your husband is a strong, brave man. He'll be just fine ..."

A man's scream of panic echoed from the room at the end of the corridor. Three shots rang out in rapid succession. Then total silence filled the dark prison.

Isabelle sank to the stone floor of the confining prison. "Oh, no. Gabe, please be okay."

Big Tom's face was pale. Percy seemed to have trouble breathing. What they had witnessed shocked them to their very core. These men thought they had been exposed to the worst of humanity. They believed nothing could ever shock them. They watched as blood dripped from a fingertip and pooled on the floor.

Big Tom couldn't pull his eyes away. "Oh, my God. I can't believe it."

Percy was in shock. "I never suspected ..."

Big Tom, looking up, asked the man who stood above him. "What ... what do you want ...?"

Isabelle sat silently, her head in her delicate, brown hands. The long silence was killing her. Several minutes had passed since the gunshots were heard. What had happened? She refused to cry. Whitney was whispering something about everything being okay, but the voice seemed very far away. Her focus was at the other end of the corridor. An eternity later, she heard the heavy, steel door creak open on old, rusty hinges. Pushing her face against the bars, Isabelle could see Black Skull, followed by Professor Schmidt. She cringed at the sight of Totenkopf's leering mask, but he appeared completely oblivious to her. What a horribly evil man he was. She shivered, as if someone had walked across her grave. As the two men strolled past her cage, she heard them discussing information about a missing page from a journal. But her full attention was focused elsewhere. She heard a dragging noise coming from the other end of the corridor.

Placing her hand over her mouth, Isabelle managed to stifle a scream of horror. Totenkopf's giant bodyguards, Ernst and Orban, were dragging three inert figures. Two men had their faces covered with hoods and displayed obvious signs of having been tortured. They must be Doc Titan's men, Big Tom and Percy. One of the two groaned beneath the hood, he was still alive. The other man didn't move, but it was obvious he was only unconscious; she could see he was still breathing.

It was the third figure that had caused her pitiful scream. His jacket had fallen over his head so she couldn't make out his features, but his hands were an ebony brown color. She knew on an island of true Nazis, there was little chance of them indoctrinating a member of her race. The jacket over the man's face was covered in blood and there were two bullet holes in the white shirt. As the body was dragged past her cell, a trail of blood exited the wounds and painted the floor with a wide brush of gore. Isabelle slumped to the floor; her trembling legs unable to support her weight. She wished this was a dream or that she would faint, but no relief came. Her entire body shook, her breasts heaving with the force of her sobs as she cried out.

The two hooded prisoners were handcuffed to the bars of the cell where Percy and Big Tom had been confined. They were chained spread-eagle, hanging suspended, their feet several inches above the dirty floor. She heard her husband's body drop heavily onto the hard, stone floor. It made a sound she would never forget. She felt her stomach turn and she became ill.

Whitney quietly said, almost to herself, because she knew there was no true relief for this woman who had just lost her husband. "I'm so sorry, Isabelle."

"He can't be dead. We're going to have a baby. The baby needs his father."

Whitney tried to respond to Isabelle's comment but her throat froze and she found she couldn't speak. The sobs from the adjoining cell tore at her heart.

Black Skull turned before exiting the room and instructed the two guards at the outer door. "Nobody is to enter this room or talk to these prisoners except myself or the Professor. Do you understand?"

The guards were intelligent enough to catch the veiled, unspoken threat in their commanding officer's voice. *'Fail me and you shall die horribly.'* In unison, they replied, "Jawohl, Herr Totenkopf!"

Chapter Fifty-One
Flashback to 1899 - Wilder and the Savage

April 6, 1945 11:00 pm

Cassie's eyes were filled with tears. "That was horrible. That poor infant." Mick silently nodded in agreement. "Aye, what happens next, Megan?" "The next journal is dated 1899. Eleven years after the last one. This one begins in Africa."

Beginning of Flashback to September 12th, 1899.

Clarke Wilder breathed in the warm dry air. Life was good. Only six short months ago, he might never have believed that he would ever be standing on the dry, arid savanna of Africa. Here, where life had begun. Out of the primordial ooze, had climbed the first creatures that would eventually evolve into mankind. After ten years of living at the frigid North Pole, it was nice to bask in the warmth of the radiant sun. His friends, Allan Quatermain, Robert Hubertson, Professor Challenger, and Hareton Ironcastle had accompanied him on this expedition to the wilds of this ancient continent. So had Ned Land and his grand-daughter, now Clarke's beautiful wife, Arronaxe Larsen ... Wilder. Still took some getting use to, his being married. During the last few years since ... Lord, would he ever truly forget that nightmare? Whitechapel. Even the name made his skin crawl. During his recovery at the North Pole, Arronaxe had been his constant companion. And when he announced that he wanted to travel the globe, she agreed to go with him.

Slap! Damn mosquitoes.

Wilder returned to America, for the first time in several years. He soon purchased an eighty-foot schooner, which he renamed *Prometheus*. They stopped in New York for provisions, in preparation of an extended journey to Europe and the African continent. Much to his surprise and elation he ran into, quite figuratively, an old friend, Stephen Stone. The man was preparing to embark on his own lengthily journey. Stone took Wilder into his confidence, showing him a map to an uncharted island in the Pacific Ocean. His intent was to raise his son as a proper gentleman and away from the evil temptations of the female of the species. Wilder was intrigued by Stone's passionate beliefs, and about how he intended to provide training for his son, both mentally and physically. They spent hours discussing what provisions and preparations would be required to make a successful expedition. Wilder wished his old friend well and returned to his own ship and his loving wife. They left for the wilds of Africa the following day. He was in the mood for bold, manly, adventures.

Of course, Arronaxe wasn't much for roughing it. She enjoyed relaxing on the *Prometheus*, while he and his friends roamed through the dense brush, sightseeing, and occasionally hunting wild animals. She would lounge beneath the shaded canopy on the boat, reading or knitting or playing solitaire. Naturally, he couldn't blame her. Only men would enjoy hot, dirty conditions with no return for their efforts, other than to know what was beyond the next hill. Men were such silly creatures sometimes. Besides, she proudly announced a few months ago that she was with child. Pregnant women had no business exerting themselves on such meaningless adventures. As he wiped the beaded sweat from his bronzed brow, he smiled to himself. He was going to be a father. He would have a son. A son! Together, they would travel the world, righting wrongs and helping those less fortunate. He had done many … horrible deeds, many questionable things in his life and had many sins to redeem.

Slap! Damn mosquitoes.

Filthy, little plague-carriers. The northern winds and tropical sun had given his skin a healthy glow, however, it leathered his skin a little. Yet, they would bite even through his weathered, bronzed skin. In this back-world country, the mosquitoes spread malaria and other diseases. Malaria parasites were transmitted by the female Anopheles mosquitoes. The parasites multiplied within the red blood cells, causing ailments similar to anemia (light-headedness, shortness of breath, tachycardia etc.), as well as other general symptoms such as fever, chills, nausea, flu-like illness, and in severe cases, coma and death. Thousands suffered and died from this pestilence. Unfortunately, no vaccine was currently available for malaria.

He sat down on a flat, tan-colored rock, warmed by the morning sun. Only ten o'clock or so and already the temperature was nearly one hundred degrees. Today would be another scorcher. When he first told Adam he wanted to come to Africa, well, the idea was met with skepticism, to say the least. Not that Adam would have stopped him. That was not his way. Adam was a unique individual, in so many ways. Clarke was glad that Adam had found a place in the world for himself. But Clarke couldn't stay there with him. He had trouble even calling him by that name, Adam. He found it difficult to look into those mismatched eyes, without feeling terrible guilt over his part in giving Adam life, those many years ago. He had simply been a science experiment, a collection of pieces and parts. An inanimate object. Suddenly, there he was, a living, breathing ... collection of pieces and parts. Clarke smiled to himself at the poor jest.

Clarke had been so caught up in the question of *could* he create life from the un-living, he didn't bother to ask himself *should* he. And then Adam was there. Too late to turn back now. Poor creature. Called wretch, monster, daemon, horror, and more, he was shunned by the world of men and even by his own ... father. That is what Adam still called him to this day. But try as he might, Clarke simply could not find it in himself to call Adam his son. Not even after Adam had traveled from the North Pole, eleven years ago, to save Clarke from himself. And saved the life of the infant born to the prostitute, Anna Marie Blake, such as it was. Another unfortunate creature born of Clarke's experiments. Even though it appeared normal at first, other than the white skin and hair, he soon discovered that the infant had suffered many physical ailments and traumas. Apparently, his mother had imbibed in large doses of alcohol and hallucinogenic drugs, principally cocaine and opium. Those drugs, combined with the formula that Clarke had injected into her unborn fetus, created a lethal mixture. The council members of the Illuminati had debated putting the child out of its misery. Clarke had convinced them that he could cryogenically freeze the infant, until the technology could be discovered to reverse the birth defects. Reluctantly, the Council of Elders had agreed to his request.

Ten years had passed. Clarke wished to leave the North Pole again. He discussed this with Adam and the Council. He had stayed there from 1799 until 1809, when he and Adam had first discovered Sanctuary. That was before the 'Elders' had even been born! Clarke spent from 1888 until 1898 at Sanctuary but wanted to rejoin mankind before the turn of the century. The world of man, as Adam stated it. The world was getting smaller and Clarke wanted to experience it, embrace it, explore it, before all of its mysteries were discovered. Several of his friends on the Council had agreed to accompany him on his travels. Although, sometimes, he felt it was actually to watch him. Or perhaps he was merely paranoid. He had known a few of these men for several years. Decades. Some days he felt the years press down on him, suffocating him. He had lived a long life, by many names.

How many names had he used over the years? He was born and christened Victor Frankenstein and kept the name until he found Sanctuary. That was 1772 - 1799. Then he used the name Victor Clarke from 1800 - 1824. From 1824 - 1854 he changed his alias to Clarke Franks. And Frank Wildeman from 1854 - 1884. James Clarke Wildman was the shortest 1884 - 1888, but for good reasons. And now he was traveling the world as Clarke Wilder.

He first saw the entrance to Sanctuary in 1799, after chasing Adam across the world for nearly ten years. Hatred and anger were burning a hole through his heart. He and Adam had left a wake of destruction behind them. There was nothing left in their hearts but hatred for one another. Their trek crossed Europe and then the frozen wastelands of Siberia, and finally penetrated the windswept ice-fields of the Arctic. They had traveled to the top of the Earth, to embrace each other in one final battle. The creature appeared to have unlimited reservoirs of strength, derived from the chemicals and formulas force-fed into his body, before the life-spark had been re-ignited. It was possible he was even immortal, or as close to immortal as mankind had ever been. He had been the sole recipient of a Lazarus Formula. And like Lazarus from the biblical tales, he too had risen from beyond the land of the dead.

Doctor Victor Frankenstein realized that his strength had reached its end. His hatred had fueled him past human endurance and now he had no reserves left. He knew the daemon was only a few miles ahead of him, but Death's frigid embrace was even closer. The bitter cold of the North enveloped him like a lover and he could not break its ever-tightening grip. He had only one choice. In one fur-lined pocket, he carried a syringe filled with an experimental mixture, similar to the formula that had been used on the Monster, to infuse it with life. The blue mercury fluid glowed with an effervescent phosphorescence. Without hesitation, he plunged the needle deep into his chest and pressed down on the plunger. Liquid fire coursed through his constricted veins and a primal scream erupted from his chapped lips. His body contorted and squirmed in the knee-deep snow. Victor's heart beat so fast, he was certain it would burst and his temples throbbed from the overexertion. Finally, his eyes rolled up into his head and he plunged face-first into a hard-packed snow bank.

How long Victor lay in the freezing snow, he was not certain. However, when he awoke, he was surprised to find out he was no longer freezing cold. Or exhausted. In fact, new energy coursed through his veins like he had never known before. For the first time in ten years, his emotions were not controlled by molten anger. Victor felt, for lack of a better word, reborn. When he and Adam finally met near the North Pole, they were able to make peace between them. As the sun lit the frozen valley, they saw the portal to the magical place known as Sanctuary. That was one hundred years ago.

And here Clarke Wilder was, one hundred years later, standing in the western coastal jungles of French Equatorial Africa. Next year, he would turn one hundred and thirty years old! Yet he only looked, and felt, about forty-five. Amazing. Simply amazing. Wanting to get back to the schooner before the blistering heat of the noonday sun, he stood up and started walking along the small streambed. This should lead him back to the area where they had anchored the boat.

Today, he was on his own. The other men had decided to sit under the canopy on the rear of the ship and play poker. During the slow days of dead calm on the ocean or when they were waiting for supplies at one of the outposts, these men of action had to find something to fill their days and evenings. Games of chance were at the top of the entertainment list. They enjoyed competing against each other, even mentally. Clarke became restless during these periods of inactivity, being the consummate explorer. As a youth, he enjoyed wandering the beautiful hills and mountains that surrounded his family estates. It was never recommended to travel alone through the dense underbrush of Africa but here he was. Fearless. Or just plain stupid. It was hard to tell the difference sometimes.

A slight movement in his peripheral vision caught his attention and he was immediately on alert. Always expect the unexpected. That's what every expert survival guide had drilled into him. It only took a second to become the meal of a larger predator. He remained completely motionless as a large black mosquito buzzed past his ear and landed on his forearm. The mosquito bit deep, but this time Clarke did not slap the miniature vampire. Instead, he slid the large-bore rifle from his shoulder and tensed, waiting for the next movement. When it came, he was almost disappointed.

It was not some predatorial creature stalking him as prey. A small piece of dirty, white cloth was waving and fluttering in the warm breeze. Clarke tensed again when he noticed that the small flag had been tied to a post. Quietly studying it, he realized the cloth was not truly white, merely bleached by long exposure to the sun. There was a pattern that could be barely distinguished … it was a British flag! And just beyond, almost completely overgrown and nearly hidden from sight, was a small wooden cabin. The weeds were several feet high around the building and jungle vines intertwined through the window and door openings.

Obviously, this habitat had been abandoned for several years. Slowly, Clarke released his breath. Glancing around one last time, wary of traps, he walked across the small open area that surrounded the cabin. The elephant grass was waist-high now but had apparently been burned to the ground sometime in the past ten years. The decrepit building had been set up like a small fort, with a view of the surrounding razed area. No animal could have approached within two hundred and fifty feet of the cabin without having to cross the surrounding open space. The windows could be shuttered at night, as protection from the fierce night creatures that prowled the underbrush. The door could be bolted from both sides and, although neglected from disuse, the little cabin appeared to be of quite sturdy construction. Clarke was impressed.

Turning sideways, he squeezed through the door opening and caught his breath. He had been prepared for nearly anything but the sight that greeted him still caused him to hesitate. Two human skeletons flashed wide-open smiles in his direction. One was lying near the entrance; the other was reclined on what must have been a bed. There was no obvious trauma to the skull or main bones of the female on the bed. The male on the floor had a damaged skull, but this could easily have been caused after death had occurred. Not caused by a bullet, of this Clarke was certain. So, not killed by man nor beast. Starvation? Doubtful, too many fish in the creek and other slow prey were nearby. Sickness? Possible. More humans died in Africa from malaria, dysentery, and so on, than any other continent in the world. Another mystery of the African continent.

Slap! Damn mosquitoes.

Creak. Clarke was surprised when he spun around and faced a … young boy. At first he had thought the dirty and sun-bronzed child was an ape of some sort. Crouched low to the ground, body posture and facial features mimicking those of the great apes that Clarke had seen in the nearby jungle, only two days prior. The apes or gorillas had kept their distance from Clarke's party and eyed them cautiously. Clarke slowly stood erect and faced the young man, trying not to startle him. The boy didn't move. Brave or stupid, Clarke couldn't tell which yet. Blood had dried and caked on one shoulder and flies were swarming the injury. Through the thick, long black hair, Clarke could see deep claw marks on the forehead that would become permanent scars someday.

The boy's face was hidden in darkness and black hair. He took one step forward and the sunlight pouring through a hole in the thatched roof caught his eyes. They stared straight at Clarke. At him and through him. They penetrated his very core. Hauntingly light-grey eyes. Clarke was lost in the depths of those eyes. The most beautiful eyes he had ever seen. No. That was not quite true. Actually, he had seen eyes exactly like them … where? Hidden memories poured back into his head and his brain reeled from the unexpected flood.

"Your eyes, I know your eyes. Lady Greyson … Alice Claybourne. She was pregnant. Her husband had been assigned to survey Africa … the western coastal jungles of French Equatorial Africa. This area is no longer under French rule, but this must be where they landed. Marooned, from the looks of it. Pirates, more than likely. You must be her … son. Amazing. Astounding. But these skeletons are a decade or more old. How could you have survived … alone … in this wilderness? Alone. Just an infant …" He stopped talking when he realized the boy was swaying. The injuries had taken their toll and the lad was feverish. Like a puppet with its strings cut, he dropped to the ground in a faint.

Clarke had a small medical bag that he carried with him at all times. Antibiotics, gauze, and a stitching kit. Just enough to stop bleeding and prevent illness, in the event of an animal attack. Using this, he cleaned and stitched the open wounds on the boy's shoulder and head.

"How could an infant have survived out here?" Flash. A memory. A face in a medicine cabinet glass. A face not his … and yet, the same. A small vial filled with blue, liquid mercury. "Oh, no! He did it, didn't he? Jack injected this poor boy's mother. Will I never escape that demon?! Shall I be forever tortured for the things I've done in my past?" Clarke cried out in disgust and horror.

Clarke Wilder had a fleeting image of the infant Anna Marie Blake gave birth to. Horribly stricken. But this boy wasn't. He seemed to be a picture of perfect health. He was ten or eleven years of age and even crouched down, apelike, he had been nearly as tall as Clarke. The muscular development of an athlete. A young Greek god. These were the very results James Clarke Wildman had been trying to accomplish. Creating a formula that would allow all men and women to live fuller, healthier lives. Disease and plague would be wiped from the Earth. And then what? Would men stop being greedy, selfish bastards? Would it stop wars, brother killing brother, over religious differences? Or fighting over a line drawn on a map? Adam had voiced these questions during one of their heated debates. And he was quite correct. It was a sad realization. Man was a petty, selfish creature.

Clarke finally forced himself to admit that Adam was correct. Pursuit of a utopian society was a childish fantasy, an utter waste of time. Life is conflict. The strong grow through adversity. Eliminating hunger, famine, and disease would not bring peace or harmony to mankind. Surprising enough, Sherlock had explained this with a joke. Never try to teach a pig to sing. It wastes your time and annoys the pig. Clarke smiled and shook his head.

Tampering in God's domain was foolish and irresponsible. And immoral. And disastrous. Of all people, shouldn't he have learned this lesson by now? Single-handedly, he had unleashed horrors upon this world that would be discussed for centuries to come. While in New York, he had gone to a theatre to watch a new play, entitled *A Modern Prometheus*.

Clarke had expected a production about the Titan who stole fire from the Gods and gave it to man. In the Greek tragedy, Zeus was enraged because the giving of fire began an era of enlightenment for Man. He had Prometheus carried to Mount Caucasus, where an eagle (often mistaken as a vulture) by the name of Ethon (the offspring of the monsters Typhon and Echidna) would pick at his liver. It would grow back each day and the eagle would eat it again.

In the modern context, Clarke knew this legend led scientists to theorize that the ancient Greeks had discovered that the liver is one of the rare human organs to regenerate itself spontaneously in the case of lesion.

However, much to his surprise, the story was about his own life. Victor Frankenstein's life. He watched the play with a mixture of amazement and horror. Before leaving New York, he purchased a copy of the popular book, *Frankenstein, or the Modern Prometheus*. It was a sensationalized version of the true events, but still accurate enough to strike close to heart.

The young man moaned lightly and stirred, but his eyes did not open. The wounds were cleaned and would heal nicely. Clarke inserted the hypodermic needle into an arm vein and injected the antibiotic. He started to pull out the needle and hesitated. This child represented the single greatest success of over one hundred years of research. Could he really just walk away without ever knowing how close he had gotten? A moment passed. With a heavy sigh, he pulled on the plunger and drew a sample of blood with the syringe. He had to know. Damn his soul, he had to know.

The boy had already stopped trembling, the fever broken in a matter of minutes. Impossible. His metabolism must be incredible. Placing his hand on the child's chest, Clarke smiled and stood up. "Take care, young man." Placing the hypodermic back in its protective sheath and slinging his rifle over one shoulder, he walked back in the direction of the schooner *Prometheus*. He felt better than he had in years. All of his accumulated years of scientific study had finally resulted in a success. He had lost his way so many times. Even though the price had been high, perhaps, in some small way, it had been worth all the hardships. But how would he use this knowledge? This is the question that plagued him for the next month.

Slap! Damn mosquitoes.

End of Flashback to September 12th, 1899.

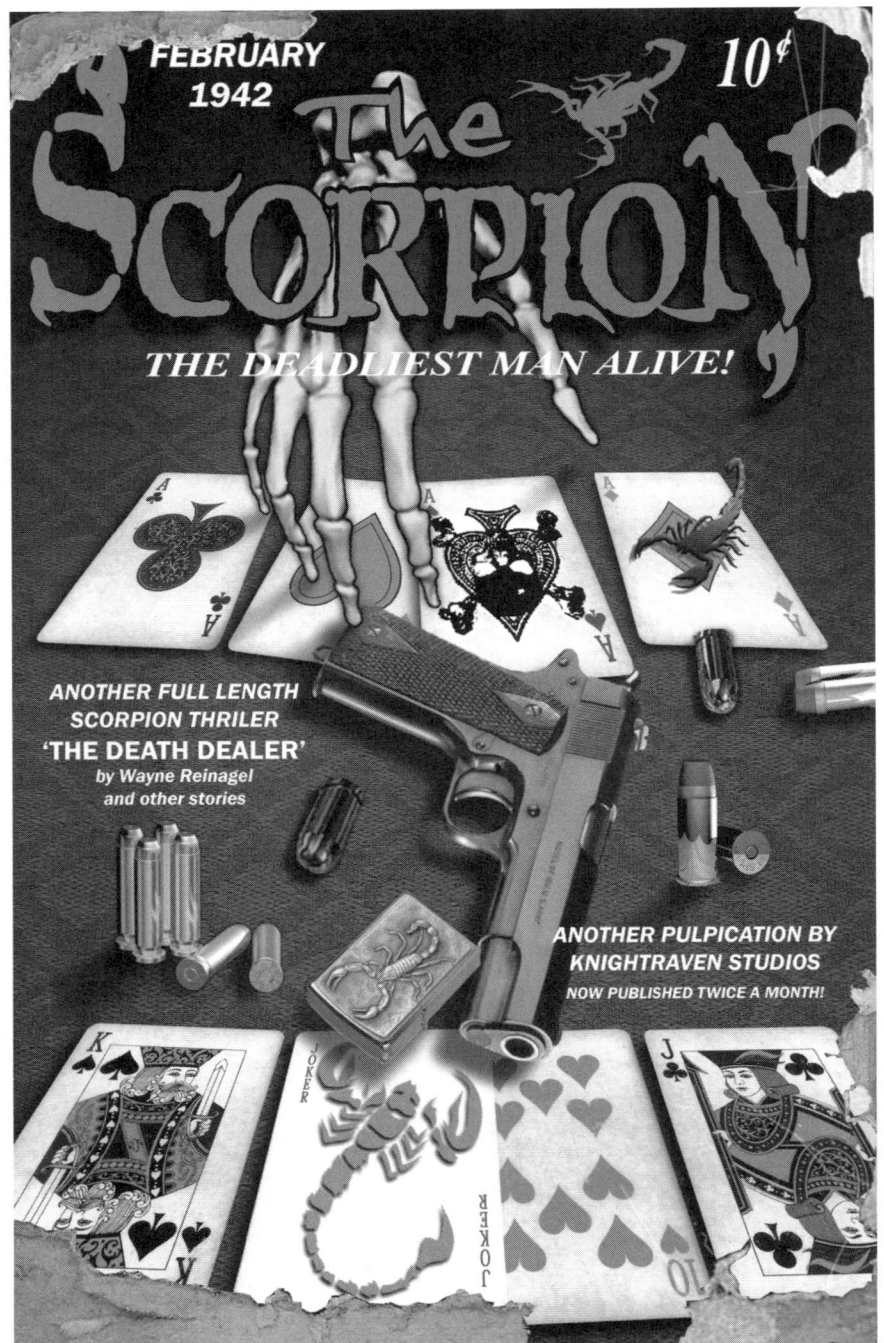

Chapter Fifty-Two
Return to the Hidden Acropolis

April 7, 1945 12:15 am

Luthor Gibson angled the plane downward, toward the drifting white snow. It was dusk but the visibility was still reasonable. He had been able to make out the silhouette of the light-blue domed roof from a distance. Preston Stockbridge relaxed in the seat next to him. A small monk, wearing a warm robe and fur footings, was staring out of the windows from one of the passenger seats. It was obvious that he had never been up in the air before, but he was reacting bravely to the experience. When the little man waddled up to them at the runway, Stockbridge's first impression of the short, heavy-set monk was an innocent, young penguin. He had smiled at them and boarded the plane without hesitation.

Luthor planned on landing a mile or more from the dome and walking to it, in case there was trouble waiting for them. It was a good plan, but he didn't take into account the rocket launcher. The missile struck the plane near the rear cargo bay. The explosion did enough damage that controlling the craft was impossible; a crash landing was certain.

Luthor warned his passengers. "We're going down. We're going to crash."

Stockbridge smiled, despite the danger. "Not if the fuel catches on fire and we explode first."

Both men were already a blur of motion as they each grabbed a parachute and released the emergency hatch. Stockbridge picked up the monk, as though he weighed nothing, and dove out of the opening. Without hesitation, Gibson followed him. Half a second later, the plane ignited into a fiery comet. It plummeted to the ground and exploded into a million fragments. From two hundred feet away they could feel the intense heat from the flames. Both men pulled their parachutes only seconds before hitting the ground. The deep snow softened the impact. The wind was driven from their lungs and it took a few seconds to recover. But they would all live.

Preston rationalized. "Well, they say any landing you can walk away from ..."

Gibson indicated the small monk with his thumb. "Well, at least you managed to save 'the treasure'."

Luthor smiled, despite their predicament. They were hundreds of miles from civilization, without food or transportation. The monk quietly dug himself out of the snow and brushed the flakes from his clothes. His order did not believe in speaking, so he simply stood, patiently waiting, as the men decided a course of action. Obviously, someone did not want them near the blue dome. So, naturally, they walked in that direction.

"What was that domed building I saw from the sky? It appeared to be half buried in the snow." Stockbridge asked Gibson.

"That was Doc's Hidden Acropolis."

"He didn't hide it very well, did he? How do you know about it? Never mind." Preston silently mimicked Gibson. "The Darkness knows all."

Gibson looked from behind a snowdrift and saw the top of the dome in the distance. "What I would like to know is, who shot at us? And why?" He pondered.

"I'd like to know why we're here and Doc isn't. This is *his* Hidden Acropolis. I feel like I'm being used. Being manipulated. Of course, as long as I get to shoot something soon, I'm okay with it."

Kaine handed the field glasses to Egorov. He did not see any parachutes or other signs of survivors from the plane, but a ridge of snow rose between him and the crashed craft, impeding his vision. The airplane had exploded almost instantly, so he doubted that there would be any chance of survivors. He stood for a few more seconds staring into the whiteness of the landscape and then turned back to the task at hand. Finding the missing page to the Danner Journal. The large blue domed roof stood before him once more. This was a frosted glass-like skylight that allowed the suns rays to illuminate the large, underground structure.

Several years ago he had found this structure, after escaping from the Russian Gulag prison. He led a band of criminals, fleeing to a new life on board an ice-cutter ship, the *Oldendorf*. They were running out of food and supplies and landed on this deserted isle of snow, ice, and rock. Surprisingly enough, they had discovered, in the middle of nowhere, this strange, glistening blue half-sphere. Poorly equipped for such work and exhausted to boot, Victor Kaine spent several days attempting to find the entrance. It baffled him, it daunted him, and he would not have that.

Once inside, Victor found a treasure trove of devices and weapons, such as the world had never seen before. It was not until much later, that he discovered the mysterious blue dome belonged to the man known as Doc

Titan. After a game of cat and mouse, Doc chased Kaine back to this location. He sought to escape across the ice, but Titan hounded him. Finally, a monstrous polar bear barred Kaine's path, and he struggled for his very life, and won. Hours later, when Doc arrived at the sight of the struggle, he discovered signs of the encounter and subsequent battle. He assumed Kaine had met his end.

Months later, Kaine emerged in far off Mongolia. Attempting to gather a force of warriors, in the tradition of the infamous conqueror, Genghis Khan. He was, once again, thwarted by Doc Titan. His men turned against him and in the ensuing melee, one of his lieutenants was mistaken for Kaine and was summarily, and horribly, dismembered. Kaine escaped death again. Months later, Kaine met Titan for a third encounter, this time in Tibet.

Victor Kaine placed a large, open palm against the smooth, glass-like surface of the enormous blue dome and stroked it affectionately.

"Hello, precious. I'm back to plunder your hidden treasures again." He spoke to the structure as he would a passionate lover. "I wish I could be gentle and take my time, but the clock is ticking." He placed a blob of clay-like substance, roughly the size of two fists, on the smooth surface and began walking away. A small timer in the clay counted down seconds. The resulting explosion seemed to rock the entire landscape.

A large, broken hole gaped on the surface of the half-buried globe. Victor stepped inside, followed by Egorov, Professor Walters - Professor Schmidt's second-in-command, and Black Skull's two large, silent bodyguards, Ernst and Orban. Totenkopf had insisted Schmidt was to remain safe at Skull Island. He also insisted that his two personal bodyguards accompany them, to make sure of Walters' safety. And, Kaine knew, to also watch him and Egorov. This was an uneasy alliance, to say the least. Victor stood aside as Walters wandered through aisles of shelves and tables, littered with various scientific paraphernalia and half-completed projects.

Victor spoke quietly to Egorov. "When Doc Titan is dead, I intend to come back here and ransack this structure. There might still be weapons here that could destroy entire armies, entire countries. Let Germany and the Nazis win their war. Then, when they are at their weakest, I will destroy them all. My goal of world domination will be a dream realized. And I shall not forget the loyalty of those closest to me, my faithful friend, Konstantin."

From the corner of his eye Kaine detected a movement. Perhaps merely a shadow, dancing across the surface of the dimly lit snow, and nothing more. But Victor Kaine was not a careless or stupid man.

Kaine whispered to Egorov. "Let's, you and I, step outside for a moment. I believe there might still be survivors from that plane wreck. Keep your eyes on the snow bank on the left. I saw something moving."

Egorov smiled cruelly. "Perhaps a snow rat, Viktor. We'll roast him and have him for dinner." Sometimes the large Russian man was still a mystery to Kaine, but he didn't say anything in response to Egorov's comment. He knew the barrel-chested Siberian both feared and respected Kaine and that was all that mattered.

Victor allowed a hand grenade to slowly slide into his large hand and he pulled the pin ring with one long finger, still holding the trigger. Again, from the corner of his eye, he saw a dark form moving in the overcast evening. Immediately, the hand released the trigger and flipped the grenade in the direction taken by the shadow. The explosion kicked up snow and ice, hurtling it in all directions. Kaine peered back into the dome and shouted at Professor Walters and the mute guards to stay inside the structure until he returned.

Egorov and Kaine climbed over the mound of snow, guns drawn and ready for combat. A dark, cloaked human form lay in the snow. Kaine approached slowly, wearily.

Kaine barked at the shadow. "Stand up and make no sudden moves. We have you covered." The ebony-clad man shifted and slowly stood, turned, and faced Kaine. As if a director in a Hollywood movie had requested a lighting change, the sunlight spilled through a small crack between the clouds. It fell on the face of Luthor Gibson. His hat still lay on the ground behind him and his collar was pulled aside, revealing his face. From behind the dark lenses of his glasses, his gaze met Kaine's and there was a sudden moment of mutual recognition. They had met before. Years ago, in Russia, they had stood facing one another at a distance, just as they did now. Victor allowed his gun, and lower jaw, to drop in surprise. Egorov could not see Gibson because Kaine stood between them. He took several steps to one side to improve his view.

Scorpion whispered. "Stay here and I'll come back for you …" He stopped speaking when he realized the short, quiet monk had vanished. "Damn."

Scorpion stood up on the small stone projection. He watched as Egorov stepped around Kaine. "Everyone stand right where …" Stockbridge did not have a chance to finish his instructions as Egorov spun around and began firing. Scorpion was caught off guard, and even though he fired without aiming, the first four bullets struck Egorov center mass, square in the chest. Egorov coughed blood and dropped face first into the snow bank. Victor Kaine turned in time to see his old friend fall. His gun leapt into his hand and he fired all six rounds at the Scorpion. The first bullet struck the icy stone ledge to his left, the next clipped his right arm and he dropped his automatic into the billowy snow.

The next three bullets ripped holes in his parka and struck him in the chest and abdomen. The last whistled past his head as Scorpion fell onto the hard rock ledge.

Victor spun around to confront the Darkness but the caped man had disappeared. He ran to Egorov and lifted the dying man's head in his arms. Egorov's eyes opened slightly, he coughed again, and blood dripped from his bearded chin. His powerful, large hand grasped Kaine's light blue suit and left a bloody print.

"Viktor ... you must ... fulfill your destiny ... old ... friend ...." Egorov's head dropped to the side, and he was dead.

Kaine emitted a primal scream of anger into the half-lit skies. He dropped the body of Egorov and spun around, looking for any signs of the Darkness. Professor Walters called to him and Kaine nearly shot him by mistake.

"Herr Kaine. I found the missing page we are looking for. We must leave right away." Victor made one last attempt to spot the Darkness and then he followed Professor Walters and the two hulking silent bodyguards back to the airplane. A minute later, they were gone.

Gibson stepped out from behind a drifted snow bank and walked to where he had fallen. He picked up his hat and dug into the deep snow and found his firearms. He noticed Egorov lying dead in the snow and beyond him Stockbridge's arm dangled over the cliff's edge. Blood dripped from the opening of his coat sleeve. Gibson ran up the embankment and knelt next to his friend's still body. Three large holes had been ripped through the parka. Gibson bowed his head in sorrow. Today a hero had fallen ...

Suddenly, Scorpion's body was racked by a cough and his eyelids flickered. He looked up at Gibson and smiled weakly. He reached to the center of his coat and pulled the fabric aside, to expose the bulletproof undergarment of alloy, chain-mesh below. And the three bullets flattened against it.

Scorpion winced in pain as he sat up. "Guess Doc was right ... about using these bulletproof vests. They can save your life."

Gibson sneered. "Yeah, but I noticed you still managed to get shot in the arm. Can't you get through one fight without getting shot, or stabbed, or ..."

"Yeah, yeah ... why don't you help me up, old man?"

Gibson assisted Stockbridge until he could support himself. They stood looking out at the destruction surrounding the Hidden Acropolis. A large hole gaped on one side of the blue domed roof.

Scorpion laughed. "You do know Doc is going to blame us for this mess."

Darkness shrugged. "You have to admit, we do leave a wake of destruction behind us."

Scorpion snapped his fingers as he remembered something. "Damn, we have to find that little monk guy. He disappeared right before the gunfight."

As if on cue, the small, quiet monk stepped into view. He motioned for the two men to follow him.

Scorpion walked along slowly. "Wonder where he's leading us. You know, we're out in the middle of a thousand square miles of ice and rock with no provisions, limited protection from the elements and ..."

Before he could finish his sentence, the monk removed the icy cover from a large global radio system, buried inside a hollowed-out drift of snow.

"... only a deluxe radio transmitter/receiver to use to call for help." Scorpion finished, chuckling.

Darkness frowned. "Do you feel this was some kind of set-up? I believe we were manipulated into participating in some grander scheme. Like pawns on a chess board."

Scorpion waved the notion away. "Nah, I'm sure you're only being paranoid. Of course, that may be exactly what they *want* us to think."

If Darkness and Scorpion had been inside the blue dome ten minutes earlier, and witnessed several events that occurred, they might have had more than a simple suspicion.

Professor Walters was systematically searching the contents of each workbench and container. He dragged a large crate out from under a table and glanced behind where it had dwelt. A small man, dressed in the simple vestments of a monk, sat quietly under the table. He smiled up at Professor Walters and handed him a cigar-sized, flat box that he had pulled from his fur coat. The professor heard the noises of gunfire outside and knew he must move quickly before Kaine could return. Walters opened the box and saw an aged parchment that had been torn from a ledger or journal. The professor nodded a thank you and the monk smiled and mutely nodded back.

Walters glanced around. "It is time to go, gentlemen."

The two large, mute guards, Orban and Ernst, stared down at the little man, and then glanced at one other. One reached forward, and seemingly without effort, moved the crate back to its original position, in front of the monk's hiding place. Several minutes passed after the three had left. Finally, the small man emerged from his hiding place and sought out Gibson and Stockbridge.

When he had recovered from the impact of the bullets, Scorpion left the Darkness for a few minutes. Gibson was using the radio to call for help. Stockbridge placed his crimson seal, depicting a hairy-legged scorpion with it's curved, barbed tail, on the forehead of the deceased Egorov. The blood-splashed form was already stiffening from the freezing temperatures. He stood up and began walking away. He stopped, turned around, and walked back to the dead man. He pulled out one of his automatics and emptied the clip of bullets into the still form.

Gibson appeared next to Stockbridge. "Feel better now?"

Stockbridge cursed. His jaw was set firmly and his eyes burned with anger. "No. He was the man who kidnapped Whitney. I wish he was alive, so I could kill him again. Until she's safely back in my arms, I fully intend to cry havoc and let slip the dogs of war."

Chapter Fifty-Three
Flashback to 1899 - The Titanic Choice

April 7, 1945   12:30 am

Kong dropped into one of the large leather chairs, exhausted. "I simply can't believe this Clarke Wilder fellow was Jack the Ripper. And Victor Frankenstein."

Gibs agreed. "This is like something out of one of those science fiction pulps you read, Kong. Where a man, through a strange series of events, winds up being his own grandfather."

Megan flipped through the journal pages. "There's one more entry in this book. Want me to read it?"

"Heck, yes!" Cassie was perched on the edge of her seat. "You can't stop now. This is getting stranger by the minute."

Kong noticed Bart still hadn't spoken since Megan began reading from the journals. He appeared distant and withdrawn. He knew his old friend as well as he knew himself. Something was troubling him.

Beginning of Flashback to November 12th, 1899.

Malaria. Clarke Wilder recognized the signs immediately. Arronaxe had complained of dizziness and started toward their private cabin when she fainted. She quickly succumbed to a high fever and took a turn for the worse. She was fading fast. Even if she survived, which was becoming more doubtful every hour, she would certainly lose the child. His son. And even if mother and child survived, chances were certain that the infant would be born with genetic defects. He couldn't allow that. Not again. He had only one choice.

Aboard the small ship he had set up a cramped laboratory. More of a catalog room for the various species of insects and the flora and fauna he had agreed to bring back to a museum in the United States. In fact, the museum had agreed to pay some of his expenses in return for his services. However, in the rear of this small room he had set up a chemical laboratory. When his friends, Robert Hubertson and George Challenger had questioned him on the need for such a lab, they had looked concerned. Even after his explanation, they made sure he didn't spend an abnormal amount of time in the ship's hold. Since none of them were scientists or chemists, they didn't know exactly what was contained within the beakers and vials. Obviously, they knew of his past association with such ventures and wanted to make sure he had not reverted back to his 'evil' ways.

He stared through the microscope lens for the twentieth time in the past few minutes, hoping for some change in the results. His wife's white blood count was low and this accounted for her quick descent into fever and weakness. So far, every medicine he had tested had the same results. Her system was so weakened, that to administer a dosage strong enough to fight the illness, would certainly kill her in the process. Time was running out. He had only one choice.

It kept coming back to this. He would have to break his vow of never experimenting on another human being, with the lives of his wife and unborn child hanging in the balance. The vow he had made to Sherlock Holmes, to Adam … and to himself. But he had no choice, if his wife and son were to live.

Even if it damned his soul. Again.

Allan Quatermain had stayed behind in Africa. Although a loyal subject of the land of his birth, England, Allan truly loved his adopted country of Africa. Its tan-colored plains and wild creatures called to him. They had shouted their final fair-thee-wells several weeks ago and headed across the ocean. The voyage was without incident and the schooner *Prometheus* made good time. They landed on the eastern shores of South America and Professor George Edward Challenger had disembarked. He claimed to be following a lead to discover a plateau deep in the treacherous South American Amazon area, where extinct creatures from prehistoric ages might still live. Sounded a trifle insane, but most great discoveries did sound crazy. Hareton Ironcastle was intrigued by the idea of such a monumental adventure and agreed to accompany Professor Challenger on his travels.

As Robert Hubertson, Ned Land, Arronaxe, and Clarke Wilder relaxed in the shade of the ship's canopy, they had been bitten several times by a gathering of mosquitoes. After suffering bites from the monstrous black mosquitoes off the Eastern shores of Africa, these smaller creatures were mild in comparison. Unfortunately, Robert and Arronaxe soon showed symptoms of illness. Malaria. They both suffered the effects for several days, while Ned Land and Clarke watched them closely and administered the prescribed medicines. Robert was still weak but already recovering. His fever had broken and he was resting comfortably. Arronaxe, unfortunately, was not doing as well. Two nights ago she had fainted and, despite the efforts of Clarke and Ned, she seemed weaker every minute. Other than fevered dreams, she did not wake or speak to them.

Glancing around the room, Clarke made certain everyone had gone back upstairs. Ned rarely left his granddaughter's bedside and the nurse they had hired was currently helping Robert. Clarke pulled the small vial from its hiding place in the refrigerator under the counter. The golden mercury fluid glistened like small pieces of metal suspended in a thick liquid. Always, in the past, the chemical had glowed blue, with a radiance of its own. Now the color was a bronzed, copper color. He had studied the blood sample from the Claybourne child, stolen while the boy lay passed out on the matted floor of the small cabin in Africa. It was more than normal human blood, beyond any accurate description. Clarke subjected the sample to various viruses and the results were fantastic. The blood was able to combat any illness or contamination quite rapidly. He had been able to synthesize many aspects of the blood and enhance the formula that he had created years ago. But until tonight, Clarke had resolved to never use this ... 'superman' formula. He had made a vow and intended to steadfastly keep it.

Time was running out, though. This was risky. His formula had never been tested on lab animals, much less a human being. His wife and child. The results were unknown, the outcome ... uncertain. His heart beat fast and threatened to burst from his chest. One last minute of doubt. Inject his wife and unborn son with a foreign substance or keep his vow of noninterference? Really no choice at all. He couldn't let them die. Driving the needle into the vial, he pulled the plunger and filled the syringe with the golden mercury. A minute later, he stood beside his bed, looking down at his suffering wife. Ned Land was sleeping soundly in a chair nearby, his head was tilted forward and a light snoring noise came from deep within him. Poor Ned, watching his only granddaughter sliding toward death, knowing there was nothing he could do to help her. His weathered face had taken on a haggard appearance from lack of sleep and stress.

Clarke could not hesitate. It was now or never. Pulling aside a small flap of clothes he exposed his wife's swollen stomach. Gently, he inserted the needle into the flesh of her naked belly. The entire contents of the hypodermic disappeared into her body. His hands shook as he removed the needle and covered her again. He quickly disposed of the syringe and sat in the soft lounge chair next to Ned's. Other than a light snort, Ned did not move. Clarke laid his head back on the cushion and within moments he was fast asleep. All in God's hands now, he thought.

Clarke dreamed about his son. The boy was a tall, well-built Greek God, with lean features. A titan. That was what they called the children of the Greek Gods, Titans. Men gathered around him with respect and women admired him.

He was the perfect human, the first of a new race of supermen. This young man would be trained in every physical and mental vocation known to man. And for every questionable thing Clarke Wilder had done during his long life? Well, this son of his would never know such failures. He would understand the difference between right and wrong and never cross over that line.

For the first time in months, Clarke thought about Stephen Stone, raising his son on an island, away from evil influences. Training him from birth to do right. Stone had the right idea, but Clarke's son would not learn from books. He would hire the best minds in the world, the smartest men in each vocation. They would show this child everything they knew and one day he would surpass them all. He would be a physician, an engineer, a chemist, he would be taught every known profession. His son would be more than mere mortal. He would be a superman.

Clarke smiled. His entire life's work had brought him to this place, this realization. And Clarke knew of an island. Away from shipping lanes, marked as a quarantined zone for the last hundred years. The last person to buy it had built a castle or mansion on the property, ignoring the rumors of the island being haunted. But that was a hundred years ago and now it was vacated again.

Clarke dreamed that Arronaxe gently touched the side of his face and quietly spoke his name. She was so beautiful, truly stunning. Her family descended from a respected background, men and women of strength of character, mind, and body. Her grandfather, Ned Land, was a perfect example. The man had to be in his nineties and was traveling around the world with his granddaughter. Clarke was impressed. Arronaxe spoke his name again. As she repeated it a third time, Clarke realized he was no longer dreaming. His lovely wife was standing in front of the soft chair where he had fallen asleep.

Ned Land was rousing nearby and cried out in happy surprise. After such a long bout of illness, she should have looked haggard and very tired. Instead, she appeared to have awakened from a long sleep, obviously well rested and alert. Clarke jumped to his feet and placed his powerful arms around her no-longer-slender waist. She smiled and touched the side of his face.

Arronaxe laughed and stroked Clarke's unshaven face. "Poor darling, were you worried about me? You look absolutely exhausted."

"We were all concerned. You were … not well." Ned said. His face seemed to relax and he appeared ten years younger.

"I feel fine, now. My fever must have broken during the night." Arronaxe smiled brightly, as if she had never been sick.

During the following month, Arronaxe gave birth to a baby boy, with copper-hued skin, so healthy he appeared to glow. Arronaxe looked into her sons face and stated confidently. "We shall call him Johnathon." His eyes were deep pools of brass, always a reminder to Clarke of the golden elixir formula that he had injected into his wife that night.

And Clarke decided that he would never tell her the truth of what he had done to save her and his unborn child. Their son.

But he thought about the dream of his son. A world traveler. Righting wrongs, battling injustice. A new life, a new beginning. Perhaps it was time to say goodbye to Clarke Wilder. He liked the name Clarke, but maybe it was time for a new last name. What had he called his son during his dream? A titan. Like one of the children of the Greek Gods. Clarke Titan and John Titan. Father and son. His old friend Simon would certainly approve.

One day the name John Titan would be known to the entire world. What were those prophetic words that he had spoken all of those years ago in Whitechapel? "One day men will look back and say I gave birth to the twentieth century."

End of Flashback to November 12th, 1899.

Nobody spoke for a long time. They were still trying to digest the stories that they had just been read.

Pam shook her head in disbelief. "This is incredible. All of these men were Doc's father? Clarke Titan? My uncle Clarke?"

Bart frowned. "Unbelievable is more like it."

"Somebody's pulling our legs, right?" Gibs paced the floor.

Kong raised his hands in the air. "Yeah, but why?"

Cassie calmly added her thoughts. "Maybe, but if everything else here is the real article, why fake this?"

Ned Land slowly walked back into the room. "I can assure you all that everything in this museum is real. What you read is real. This is the reason you were all called here. To reveal secrets long hidden from the world."

Pam needed something more than mere hints. "But why …?"

Ned Land continued walking away. "Forgive me, but all of your questions will be answered tomorrow. For now, I recommend you all get a good night's sleep."

Kong grumbled. "Yeah, like I can sleep after all of this?"

Megan yawned. "I don't know about y'all, but I could sleep for a week. That trek across the snow wiped me out. I'm exhausted."

Cassie nodded in agreement. "Yeah, I agree. Let's wait until tomorrow, after we've rested."

The entire group began walking toward the other building, where quarters had been set up for their comfort. Each person had been given his or her own private rooms. Half an hour later, Bart, Mick, Cassie, Megan, and Wall, despite earlier protests, were sleeping like the dead.

Pam paced the floor of her room. She walked back to the museum and looked around some more, carrying a picture in one hand. She strolled between the tall shelves, filled with hundreds of ancient tomes and personal journals throughout history. They had only read from a tiny selection and she considered everything that they had discovered. Imagine what someone might unearth by reading from a single shelf? Or an entire bookcase? It would take a lifetime to read every book in the enormous museum. A very, very long lifetime.

A realization suddenly struck her. Ned Land was her great-grandfather! Once more, she closely scrutinized the photograph of Arronaxe Land and her daughters, Arronaxe and Patricia from 1896. Pam's mother had died during childbirth, but she remembered seeing a picture of her, among her father's belongings. She now saw the family resemblance between herself and the little girl named Patricia. And the cabin in the background wasn't just similar to the home where she had grown up. It was the same cabin! Tracing a finger along the face in the picture, a tear welled up in her eye. Pam held the book tightly against her breast, as if hugging her mother.

Still holding the tome, she paced around the Museum. Pam was leafing through a large journal, when she noticed a woman outside the window, dressed completely in white, watching her from a distance. She glanced away for an instant and the ghostlike figure had vanished. Rubbing her tired eyes, Pam convinced herself that she was hallucinating from lack of sleep. Finally, she strolled back toward the building that housed the sleeping quarters, holding a small, framed photograph. She looked up into the skies.

The sun was still quite bright. For the next six months, the valley would remain lit twenty-four hours a day. The Northern Lights, also known as the Aurora Borealis, lit up the skies with a rainbow of colors. It pranced and cavorted to some unheard melody. Even though Pam knew that the aurora was simply an electro-static phenomenon, characterized by a bright glow and caused by the collision of charged particles in the magnetosphere with atoms in the Earth's upper atmosphere, she still found the view breathtaking. It was like magic. This whole place was like a fairy tale. It was as though they had traveled to another planet. A world without war, without crime, without borders. She sighed dreamily and went inside.

Pam tapped at Kong's door. He was still awake and allowed her to enter. She yawned and smiled. "Hi, Kong. Mind if I come in? I can't sleep."

"I know what you mean. I've been sitting here thinking about … well, everything. Can you imagine how Doc feels? Finding out your old man is quite literally Frankenstein and Jack the Ripper, all rolled into one? Wow. That's gotta make you feel … I don't have the words."

Pam nodded. "Yes, I agree. I only met Doc's father one time, but this sheds a whole new light on things, doesn't it? Here's what I haven't figured out yet. Why were we asked to read from those particular journals? What is it that they are going to tell us tomorrow? Ned mentioned secrets being revealed. Secrets even beyond what we've found out today?"

Kong cracked his large, hairy knuckles. "That's what I've been sitting here pondering."

Pam lay on the bed next to Kong and rested her head in his arms. She relaxed against his solid frame, feeling safe in his Herculean arms. They continued talking for several minutes, each taking turns yawning, but enjoying the company too much to call it a night. Pam took one of Kong's large callused hands in her smaller smooth one. She had always felt close to Kong, maybe because he treated her as an equal.

"Y'know, Kong. I like hanging out with you. Truth be known, you're my closest friend. I mean, I know I hang out with the girls a lot and they can be fun, but you're the one person I feel I can tell anything. If things were different, I think maybe you and I would … we might be …"

Kong's loud snore cut her off. She smiled and stroked his homely face with her smooth hand. He snorted but didn't wake up.

"My handsome Prince Charming. Well, not actually handsome …"

Her eyes drooped and she also nodded off to sleep. In her hands was the framed picture that she had brought over from the museum. It dropped onto the mattress. In the picture were several men gathered together for a photograph. She had recognized Phileas Fogg and Ned Land from their earlier meetings. From the caption on the back, and the other photos at the museum, she was able to figure out a few others. Sherlock Holmes, Professor George Challenger, Allan Quatermain, Hareton Ironcastle, Robert Hubertson, and Professor Clarke Titan were also in the photo. In the background stood a hooded figure, much taller than the other men. She could not make out a face, and there were no other references, except the name on the picture. *Adam.* On a whim, she had re-read the final chapter of the Jack the Ripper story. This was almost certainly the large man who had accompanied Sherlock Holmes and helped James Clarke Wildman that night in 1888. The man who had called Wildman 'father.'

The inscription on the back of the photo simply read, *1888 - Founding of the New Illuminati, members of the Council of Elders of the People of the Light.*

Chapter Fifty-Four
The Illuminati

April 7, 1945   9:00 am

On the following morning, the group of eight intrepid explorers followed a silent monk, one of the Order of the Brotherhood of Silence. He guided them through the streets of Sanctuary. It was a slow walk, constantly interrupted by one of the eight stopping to admire some new artifact or sight. The monk would wait patiently until they were all ready to proceed again. As they walked, several monks wearing simple brown robes, with the hoods pulled up to cover their faces, strolled past. Pam, Kong, Cassie, Bart, Wall, Megan, Gibs, and Mick would have attracted many eyes if they had walked down any street in Manhattan. Especially, Wall and Kong, with their massive physiques, and Pam, the tall, stunningly beautiful Amazon warrior. However, here in Sanctuary, the presence of the group of strangers was completely ignored.

An hour after starting, they approached a massive lodge. The structure seemed to tower over them, even though it was actually only three stories tall. Like the other buildings in Sanctuary, this one was well designed and constructed, offering a multitude of carvings and accents along its face. Phileas Fogg walked down the stone steps at the entrance and welcomed them with open arms.

"Greetings. Thank you, brother. I can guide them from here." The monk bowed slightly and was gone. "I trust you have all had a good night's sleep and are well-rested?"

Doc Titan and Simon Blake walked among the alabaster tombstones. The graveyard was immaculately groomed and well-tended. Small, carved angelic shapes topped several markers. They both recognized many of the names engraved on the various stones. It was a virtual Who's Who of adventurers and explorers from the last hundred years. They had talked very little after visiting the Museum the day before. Each man was in the habit of keeping his own council, until they completely understood the facts. They were not the type of men to share their speculations.

Blake noticed a woman watching them from a distance. She was dressed in a full-length robe of absolute white, with the hood completely covering her face. She was a stunningly angelic figure. Her face, however, showed no emotion, as if it were a mask.

"Doc, have you noticed …?" Blake started.

Doc nodded in acknowledgement. "She's been watching us from a distance for the last day. Never close enough to see her face."

"At first I thought it was a coincidence. Another mystery."

"Boxes within boxes." Doc pretended to stroke his beard and whispered, barely loud enough for Blake to hear.

The white, snow-capped mountains that surrounded the valley were so high they touched the clouds. Small birds darted about in the clear sky, whistling merry tunes as they passed. The smell of honeysuckle and freshly cut grass permeated the air. Doc and Blake had watched as the silent monks tended the small gardens, orchards, and lawns, equipped with only the simplest of hand tools. There was absolutely no evidence of modern equipment or even basic electricity. It was like stepping back two hundred years in time.

Doc finally commented, "From all appearances, it's almost a utopian society."

"Amazing, isn't it, Doc? No fighting, no greed, no crime. Mankind at its best. Almost too good to believe, isn't it?"

Doc smiled. "I've been fighting evil masterminds, mad scientists, and unscrupulous gangsters for so long …"

Blake laughed lightly. "You keep waiting for the villains to show up?"

"Yes."

"Me, too." Blake's cold, frozen face did not smile but Doc could see it in his pale eyes.

They walked in silence for several minutes. The woman in white had vanished again, as she had done several times in the past day. Blake noticed an elderly man walking in their direction. He was slightly bent with age but seemed to walk without difficulty. He made his way along the clean paths between the headstones. His face brightened when he looked at Doc Titan. Doc sensed the man's approach and turned to face him. Blake had known Doc for several years and had never seen the look of pleasure that now filled his eyes.

"Ned? Is that really you? What are you doing here?"

"I've lived here for the last thirty years or so, John."

"But … I don't …." Doc stammered, at a loss for words.

Ned nodded. "I understand your confusion. You're wondering what a simple groundskeeper is doing here? I suppose your father never told you the full story."

Doc frowned. "No, he did not. But I found out yesterday, when I read my father's journals."

Ned's ancient face wrinkled into a smile. "Ah, good. I've always hated keeping secrets. John, my name is Ned Land. My daughter was Arronaxe Land, named after a close friend of mine. Her daughter was Arronaxe Larson, your mother. I am your great-grandfather."

They embraced in greeting. Doc was happy that his old friend was here. He had always had a warm place in his heart for this elderly man, even when he thought he was only a simple groundskeeper.

"It's so good to have you here." Ned glanced in Blake's direction and added, "Both of you. You've each changed quite a bit since I last saw you."

Blake glanced questioningly at Doc, who seemed equally surprised by Ned's comment.

"I'm not certain I remember meeting you before."

"Oops. Guess I let the cat out of the bag. Always doing that. Guess that's why I'm never trusted with important secrets." Ned laughed, placed a weathered hand on each of their shoulders and smiled broadly, his old, leathery face displaying deep cracks. "Listen, boys. You're going to hear a lot of things today about Doc's father. Some things you won't like. Please remember one thing. Clarke Titan, for all his faults, was a great and noble man. Doc, he loved you and your mother more than life itself. It nearly killed him when she died. He pushed you to the edge of perfection, at the cost of allowing himself to be close to you. I'm proud of how you turned out. Both of you."

He glanced over Blake's shoulder and his eyes fixed on something in the distance. The woman in white had returned and was watching the three men. When Doc and Blake turned in that direction, however, she had already vanished.

Ned strolled slowly with the two men on either side of him. "I know you both have many questions. And that's why you've been summoned to the great hall. The Council of Elders will explain everything. Come along, Ol' Phileas will be waiting. He's a stickler for maintaining schedules."

As they ascended the stone steps, Pam noticed a small graveyard on one side of the building. There were perhaps one hundred tombstones, mostly simple in design. There were a few elaborate grave markers and Pam decided she would like to check these out, perhaps after the gathering. On the far side of the graveyard stood a woman, dressed completely in white. The woman Pam had seen from the museum window last night. Her hood was pulled over her head and hid her features from Pam's searching eyes. She watched intently as those already gathered talked with Fogg. This woman was another mystery Pam would have to investigate.

Fogg continued. He was a friendly and amiable host. "I believe we will be sitting outside today, if no one has any objections. The valley is so pleasant this time of year, it's a shame to spend any part of the day indoors."

Bart smiled. "I think that would be nice. We've enjoyed the walk up here today. The panoramic view is simply breathtaking."

"Yes. I never tire of the simple life this place affords us. The monks insist on growing gardens full of food and gladly prepare enough for everyone. We need to proceed to the meeting, we are five minutes late." Fogg stopped and looked at them apologetically. "Sorry, old habits."

Cassie breathed deeply and raised her small hands skywards. "It's so clean here. The air feels fresh." She watched dreamily as a tiny butterfly floated by on the light breeze.

Fogg smiled and waved them toward a simple circle of chairs set around a giant wooden table. All of the seats were equal in height and size, except the one located at what appeared to be the head of the table. It was one foot wider and two feet taller than the others. It was so large that it would have made anyone, except perhaps Wall; appear as small as a child. Several fireplace stoves were set outside the ring of chairs, but they were not in use this morning.

Before the eight sat down, Doc Titan and Simon Blake entered the courtyard from another direction. They greeted their friends warmly and agreed to discuss many things after meeting with the Elders. Megan was the lone wallflower, with the Darkness off on an assignment, but received quick, warm greetings from both Doc and Blake. Fogg motioned for everyone to take their seats.

Several other elderly men had entered the patio area. When everyone was seated, Doc Titan noticed the largest chair remained empty. He glanced at Blake and he acknowledged this fact with a slight nod of the head. Phileas requested that each member of the Illuminati introduce themselves. Not since the ancient days of King Arthur aka Uthur Pendragon, and his round table, had so many legendary and powerful men and women gathered together in one place at the same time. Pam recognized each man from various photographs at the museum.

The first man gave the appearance of an aggressive, dominating figure. Even in this simple gathering, he displayed an almost overpowering personality.

His head was enormous, certainly the largest Pam had ever seen on a human being. He had the face and beard one might associate with an Assyrian bull. The beard was so black that it appeared nearly blue, with a long stripe of gray-white starting at the right edge of his lower lip, proceeding south. The entire affair was spade shaped and rippled down his chest. The hair atop his head was the same color, but his hairline had apparently receded over the years. His eyes were blue-gray under great tufts of bushy eyebrows that grew wild across his massive forehead. His shoulders were wide spread and he possessed a great barrel chest. He rested his monstrous hands, almost as large as Big Tom's prodigious paws, on the wooden table. He spoke quietly, but his voice was still a roaring, rumbling sound.

"Good day. My name is Professor George Edward Challenger. An Englishman wrote of a few of my adventures at the turn of the century. I am perhaps best known for discovering a lost land of prehistoric dinosaurs in the wilds of South America. Years later, I returned there with Hareton Ironcastle and your father, Professor Titan." Challenger nodded his great head in Doc's direction. "And I am also Kong Larson's uncle, from his mother's side."

Kong nudged Bart. "See, I told you that he was my Uncle George."

The next man at the table was a direct opposite in appearance to the large, bearded professor. He was of average build, clean-shaven and well-groomed. His hair was short and combed; his clothing was clean and well-fitted. Several evenly spaced scars, caused by the sharp claws of a wild animal, started above one brow and disappeared into his hairline. His eyes were crisp and alert, glancing about the table. He spoke clearly, but with the tinge of a French accent.

"My name is Hareton Ironcastle. I am also an old friend of your father's." He nodded at Doc. "We explored nearly every continent, seeking wealth and adventure. Fortunately, we found an abundance of both. Several of us at this table were the founding members of the Baltimore Gun Club. I am the late Professor Archimedes Q. Portman's uncle, which means we are family." He smiled broadly at the petite blond Cassie. Others at the table turned in her direction and she began flushing. She looked around the table at her close friends and then at Blake.

Cassie shrugged lightly. "I'll explain it later."

The third man had the watchful eyes of a hunter. His skin was leathered from years of exposure to stifling heat and the relentless sun. At first glance, his age might be estimated at mid-sixties.

"Greetings. Like these other men at this gathering, I am an old friend of your father's, John. My name is Allan Quatermain. I spent nearly my entire life on the continent of Africa. Legends have it that I was blessed, or cursed, depending on your point of view, by a tribal shaman, or witchdoctor. He claimed Africa would never let me die. I'm not certain that this is true, but I have seen one hundred and twenty-eight years of life."

Phileas Fogg was next. He merely greeted everyone once more and looked to the man at the opposite side of the table.

Ned Land nodded at the assembly. "I have met all of you in the past day. Again, I welcome you all to Sanctuary."

Sherlock Holmes walked out of the building and took his place next to Ned Land. The largest chair, obviously reserved for the leader of the group, still remained empty. In Sherlock's hand was a thick journal, much like the ones from the Museum.

"I apologize for my tardiness. Adam and I were discussing ... current events. He will join us shortly. I am happy to announce that Luthor Gibson and Preston Stockbridge were successful in their mission and will be returning here soon. For those I have not already met, my name is Sherlock Holmes." There was a moment of revered silence from the visitors. They had all grown up reading or listening to tales about the world famous detective. "I shall not beat around the bush. We have asked you to come here in hopes of lying bare decades of secrets. We feel the time has arrived. There are things each of you should know. Am I assuming correctly that you have all read the journals and papers left for you at the museum?" He was met with affirmative nods from the group. "Very good. I have something to read to you. But first, do you have any questions?"

Doc was the first. "This gathering of men was called The Council of Elders by the men guarding the entrance. To what purpose have you called us here? Are you the so-called Illuminati or People of the Light?"

Sherlock lit his pipe and puffed. "Legends over the years have given this group many names. We've been mistakenly called the Nine Unknown; I believe they actually reside in India. Some think we are linked to the Order of Free-Masons. Realistically, we don't care what label men place on us, it does not change our final goals."

Challenger growled, "Perhaps not. But, personally, I prefer the title Illuminati, rather than Council of Elders. Sounds rather mysterious as opposed to ... well, a bunch of old farts." Many around the table smiled at Challenger's observation.

Bart polished his cane with his sleeve. "I have heard rumors of the Illuminati. They are suppose to believe in the end of the world prophecies and allegedly ..."

Fogg quietly interrupted Bart, "There are many rumors of our goals. Mostly, they are conspiracy theories and rumors of secret societies, hell-bent on ruling, or destroying, the world. We could argue for hours over courses of action and differing beliefs. Simply stated, this gathering of men before you do *not* interfere in the ways and lives of man. We never leave this valley. We will sometimes enlighten 'men of good conscience' about events that might be happening around the world. The final course of action remains in their hands. This is the first time in many years we have had direct congress with members of the outside world."

Challenger added gruffly. "And quite frankly, we have absolutely no desire for world domination. What would we do with it? The world is usually a mess. Who needs the grief of that constant state of chaos? We have resigned ourselves to merely council others. As Fogg stated - men of good conscience."

"Our membership has grown and waned over the decades. You have visited the graveyard." Ned Land nodded his head at Blake and Doc as he spoke. "Many great men have joined and aided us in our quest."

Blake joined the questioning. "And the objective of this quest is?"

Ironcastle leaned his elbows on the round table and placed his fingertips together. "World peace seems too vast an aim. Let's simply describe it as a balance of power. Order versus Chaos. When some madman decides to create a weapon of mass destruction, we allow that information to reach certain qualified men who can, simply put, save the world. Or, at the very least, restore the balance."

Doc frowned. "But you never directly battle this evil yourselves?"

Sherlock puffed a billow of gray smoke. "Experience has taught us all one very important lesson. What is true evil? What is right, what is wrong? Is there ever absolute black and white? Or are there simply a hundred shades of gray?"

"'All that's required for evil men to succeed, is for good men of conscience to do nothing.'" Doc Titan quoted.

Fogg nodded. "Yes. Perhaps, this sounds noble and sane when first spoken. Unfortunately, everybody thinks that they're on the proper side. Men like Victor Kaine believe they are on the side of good, against a world that wages war over borders and religions. Adolf Hitler thinks that he is on the side of good by unleashing a supposedly genetically superior German race and allowing it to rightfully supplant the rest of humanity. As far as I'm concerned, 'good men' doing something they believe in their hearts to be right and true, is at the root of all evil in this world."

Bart, who had once studied law in college, defended this vocation. "That's why mankind developed laws."

Quatermain raised one eyebrow. "Laws that are bent and broken everyday, when they become an inconvenience. Nothing in law is absolute. Law is too easily corrupted. As long as the end justifies the means."

"That's a rather negative outlook," Blake observed.

Sherlock removed the pipe from his thin lips. "So, then, I put this question to you. If a man was guilty of kidnapping, torturing, drugging, stealing and even murder, what would be your course of action? Would you appeal to the courts to convict him? No matter the circumstances?"

Bart rebutted, an expert with this kind of cross-examination. "Absolutely. He should be imprisoned for any one of those offenses. We've dedicated our lifes to upholding the letter of the law."

Sherlock smiled and spoke softly. "And yet John Titan and Simon Blake are guilty of repeatedly committing these very offenses. And many more. All in the name of justice. And we won't even discuss the careers of Preston Stockbridge and Luthor Gibson."

Megan jumped to their defense. "But they are trying to fight evil, to save innocent people."

Sherlock pointed the mouthpiece of his fabled calabash pipe at Megan. "Perhaps, but the letter of the law, as Mr. Blackwell so righteously noted, should convict these men. Not black and white, simply more shades of gray. The question becomes, what are you willing to do, how far are you willing to go, to see justice prevail?"

Doc nodded in agreement. "Your point is well made."

Kong interrupted, his face becoming flushed with anger. "So you're saying Doc is as evil as the men he stops?"

Sherlock shook his head side to side. "Not at all. But, obviously, the true letter of the law should not apply under certain circumstances. Laws were created for keeping the truly lawless in check. Checks and balances. Order and chaos. Agreed?"

Gibs quoted his favorite scientist. "*The world is a dangerous place. Not because of those who do evil; but because of those who look on and do nothing.*"

Sherlock smiled. "I've also read the quotes of Albert Einstein. *'Whoever undertakes to set himself up as a judge of Truth and Knowledge is shipwrecked by the laughter of the gods.'* This is certainly something that could be debated for days, without complete agreement. Are there any other questions you would like to ask?"

Blake narrowed his eyes, glancing from one elder adventurer to another. "If we are to assume the journals in the Museum are real and not an elaborate fabrication, the man known to the world as Professor Clarke Titan was nearly one hundred and fifty years old at the time of his death in 1930. Everyone here is rather healthy, considering your ages. Have you discovered a way to extend your lifespan?"

Sherlock smiled again. "Ahh, this is good question and a step in the right direction."

Ironcastle offered, "All of us, at one time in our lives, have discovered some elixir or potion believed to extend one's lifespan."

Wall added his opinion. "But, surely, like the changing of lead to gold, this is merely the stuff of legends, right?"

"Sorcerers of ancient Egypt called it the Infinity Formula. Or the Lazarus Formula, if resurrection was the goal." Doc volunteered.

Bart frowned. "The what?"

Kong piped in with his deep voice. "The Infinity Formula, shyster! Ponce de Leon's bubble bath. The damned Fountain of Youth. And don'tcha remember when Doc resurrected that old, moldy mummy? That was a Lazarus Formula."

Gibs shook his head. "I remember. Doc was going to bring back King Solomon. Crooks switched mummies and Doc accidentally resurrected that murderous tyrant pharaoh named Pah-dar-wah-khan."

Wall looked doubtful. "You're kidding, right?"

Mick dourly offered his insight. "Na, mon. Alchemy twas more than changing enemies to newts and the conversion of lead to gold. It was the search for immorality, making one impervious to harm, with increased strength."

"Better living through chemistry, indeed!" Bart muttered loudly.

Fogg continued. "There are several people who believe they have stumbled onto the Infinity Formula throughout mankind's history. Fu Manchu, Professor Moriarity, and Rama Tut, just to name a few. To our knowledge they have all simply managed to *extend* their lifespans, but have not discovered true immortality. Kan-Tar was given a potion by a witch doctor, Sherlock Holmes discovered a royal bee pollen extract, Quatermain was told Africa would never let him die. Dorian Gray has his painting. And some rumors of immortals have never been confirmed, such as the elusive Count de Saint-Germain, supposedly born in the late 1600's. Allegedly, he was, or is, a master alchemist and knew the secret key to the philosopher's stone, a potent substance also known as the universal solvent and identified with the elixir of life, and immortality. Charlatan? Pretender?" Fogg shrugged his shoulders and then motioned in Doc's direction. "But your father might have been the only human to discover anything close to achieving true immortality."

"Until he got killed by that damned scarlet plague disease thing." Kong added.

Phileas finished his thought. "And nobody has been able to perfect the super human formula successfully, until recently."

Blake picked up on Fogg's change of subject. "So you're not only talking about the Infinity Formula anymore. You're also referring to the Super-Soldier Formula. Like the one that created The Sentry."

Bart nudged Kong. "Do you remember the legendary Mysterious Scroll of the Khan Dynasty?"

Kong shivered. "I still can't look at shrimp, after that adventure. They remind me of those disgusting, black scorpions. Brrr. Nasty critters."

Sherlock dragged deeply on his pipe. "Actually, There has been one man who exceeded Professor Kirskine's ambitions in creating a superman."

Doc volunteered. "Professor Abednego Danner."

Pam turned to her cousin. "Who is that, Doc?"

"Years ago, my father met a brilliant professor, decades ahead of his time in genetic research. He was a mild, timid man who lived with his overbearing wife in Colorado. He had injected his pregnant wife with a formula, designed to alter the DNA of his unborn son." Doc stopped for a few seconds as he remembered the story he had recently read about his own father, injecting his pregnant mother. "The child, Hugo Danner, grew into a supra-human adult. He displayed abilities far beyond any possessed by mere mortal man. He also became isolated and depressed because he had no peers among mankind." He stopped again as he noted the similarities between his life and Hugo Danner's. "My father was there when Hugo was killed by a lightning bolt from the heavens. He was entrusted with the Danner Journals that contained detailed descriptions of the formulas used to create Hugo's genetic … mutation. My father brought these journals to me in 1930 and asked me to hide them in a safe place, away from the prying eyes of mankind. I took them to the Hidden Acropolis. When I returned, I was told of my father's death."

"Well I can't think of a safer person with whom to leave such a monstrous secret. If you can't safeguard this secret …" Bart began.

Doc cut him off. "Victor Kaine stole the six notebooks of formulas from my Hidden Acropolis."

Kong's eyes grew large. "Holy Geez! The man you once described as the most dangerous man alive!? Oh, that's just great!"

Bart reassured himself. "It's a good thing we're certain he's dead."

Sherlock warned. "Actually, we know for certain that Victor Kaine is still alive."

Doc added, "Konstatin Egorov, Kaine's lieutenant, helped him kidnap our friends in New York."

Kong gritted his teeth. "Oh great. At least it can't get worse than this."

Quatermain offered more bad news. "We've recently discovered that he is in league with the Nazi madman, Black Skull."

Bart slapped Kong on the shoulder. "You had to jinx it, didn't you?"

Kong placed his face in his hands. "Oh, this just keeps getting better!"

Gibs asked his leader. "Did you ever meet this Hugo Danner, Doc?"

"Three times. Once after his alleged death in Central America in 1926."

Cassie raised an eyebrow. "So he's still alive?"

"I'm not certain. Last time we met was several years ago."

Ned Land prophesized. "There is a great evil about to be unleashed on the world. A horrible secret about to be rediscovered, one that should remain forever hidden from mankind. This could cause the destruction of mankind, as we know it. Now you understand why we requested your presence."

Pam's keen mind was reviewing what she had heard so far. "Doc, you were talking about Danner tampering with human DNA?"

Bart frowned again. "And in English that would be …?"

Blake volunteered. "DNA - the building blocks of all life on Earth."

Mick was glad to 'flex' his brain and contribute to the conversation. "Deoxyribonucleic acid (DNA) is a nucleic acid that contains the genetic instructions for the development and function of living organisms. All living things contain DNA, with the exception of some viruses with RNA genomes. The main role of DNA in the cell is the long term storage of information. It is often compared to a blueprint, since it contains the instructions to construct other components of the cell, such as proteins and RNA molecules. The DNA segments that carry genetic information are called genes, but other DNA sequences have structural purposes, or are involved in regulating the expression of genetic information."

Kong smiled and added. "DNA is a long polymer of simple units called nucleotides, which are held together by a backbone made of sugars and phosphate groups. This backbone carries four types of molecules called bases and it is the sequence of these four bases that encodes information. The major function of DNA is to encode the sequence of amino acid residues in proteins, using the genetic code. To read the genetic code, cells make a copy of a stretch of DNA in the nucleic acid RNA. But, there are billions of codes in a single strand of DNA. It would be impossible to 'read' these codes." Shrugging his broad shoulders at Bart's amazed face, he added. "I read about it in a scientific journal last year."

"Wow. That was a mouthful. Does your brain hurt from using all those big words? So, it's what gave me these incredibly handsome features … and made you as homely as a jungle ape, an evolutionary mistake," Bart taunted his verbal sparring partner.

Blake nodded. "Essentially, yes."

"Hey!" Kong exclaimed. "Don't encourage him!"

Pam ignored Kong's objections. "But we're back to the stuff of legends. All of this is impossible, right?"

A deep voice joined the conversation. "You could say the same thing about me. The stuff of legends. However, the best lies, after all, have a shred of truth at their foundation."

Sherlock smiled and stood up. "Ah, Adam. I am glad you arrived at this particular moment."

Adam approached the assembled group and stood next to his chair, the large one that had remained unused, until now. His face was concealed in the depths of the large hood over his head. For a pregnant moment, he stood next to his chair and glanced around the table. He raised huge, grotesquely scarred hands and lowered his hood, revealing his cadaverous face. The fetid smell from beyond the grave assaulted the senses, in contrast to the sweet scent of flowers in the air. His flesh was a mottled grayish color, his lips thin and nearly black. Doc recognized this as the man from his childhood flashback. This misshapen mockery of humanity was the man from Wilder Island, when Doc was sixteen. The gargantuan golem had spoken only one word, but Doc would never forget that deep, guttural tone. *"Enough."*

Mick leapt to his feet. "Ach, it's the Frankenstein monster!"

Adam moved so quickly that it caught everyone off guard. He stood face to face with Mick, towering several feet overhead. His scarred face was a mask of horror. His mismatched eyes bored into Mick's unflinching face, the massive jaw muscles flexing, and his straight white teeth clenched tightly together.

Adam growled venomously. "There was a time when I would have killed someone for calling me that. These days I prefer the name *Adam*." Adam was impressed that Mick had not flinched. "I don't scare you?"

Mick chuckled boldly. "Me own mother-in-law was scarier than you ... and a damned sight uglier."

Adam laughed. "Hah! I like you Scotsman!"

Doc addressed the newcomer. "You mentioned legends about DNA manipulation."

"Stand up. And you as well, Mr. Walker." Adam instructed.

They obediently stood up as Adam instructed and he approached them. Usually Wall and Doc dwarfed any person standing near them. The towering behemoth named Adam stood more than a foot taller than either of the large men. The hulking man-monster looked down into Doc's golden-brown eyes and asked him earnestly.

"If you are both considered to be the largest of men, then how could Doctor Frankenstein have created me, patched and cobbled together from the simple body parts of corpses? Where would he have found the parts to create an eight foot tall ... creature?"

Doc shook his head in disagreement. "Not a creature ... a man."

Frankenstein's patchwork monster was obviously touched by this word. "Thank you for the kind thought, John. But when we first met, years ago, your eyes spoke volumes. McGrath is correct, I am a monster. Victor Frankenstein, my 'father,' might have solved the mysterious secrets of life and death, but he still returned life to a soulless creature."

Sherlock shook his head. "Adam and I have had this debate for many years. On the properties and substance of the human soul. I believe Adam possesses one of the greatest souls known to mankind. The tortured soul of a sculptor or poet or painter."

Doc defended himself. "I was a young, inexperienced boy when I first saw you, Adam. *'When I was a child, I spake as a child, I understood as a child, I thought as a child; but when I became a man, I put away childish things.'* I have always regretted not going back into that room and talking to you, man to man. At the time, I probably feared my father more than I did you."

Sherlock spoke lowly, almost to himself. "A biblical quote. How interesting."

Adam was quiet for a moment and then continued. "Your father was experimenting, searching for various results. His main goal had always been to create a new, improved man. A man who could withstand the elements and ailments that have plagued mankind since he first climbed from the primordial ooze. A superman. I was merely an experimental prototype. His greatest achievement and his worse nightmare, all rolled into one. Mary Shelley sensationalized certain parts of the story. Frankenstein was not creating a mate for me, which he destroyed in a saner moment. He was hell-bent on creating an army of patchwork men. I heard him whispering to himself. *'I must create legions of perfect men.'* I destroyed his laboratory and the soulless creatures that he had robbed from their eternal rest. Sewn and cobbled together like old boots. He had become insane, lost all reason and the ability to tell right from wrong. He fell into the pit of madness. He had lost the capacity to ask himself that one very important question. *Should* I do this, instead of *can* I do this?"

Cassie was fascinated. "So he was manipulating DNA before he even understood how it truly worked? And DNA determines how we look, the color of our eyes, and so on? Is that correct?"

Doc continued. "Yes, it is what gives one person red hair and another black." He stopped for a second and continued again. "Or manipulation of the DNA could cause someone to have white hair and features."

"I see you are catching on." Frankenstein's creature turned to look at Blake. "Deep down you always knew that the loss of your wife and child could not have been the cause of your 'change.' Otherwise, thousands of people who experienced a tragedy in their life would have a similar appearance."

Mick, a biochemical expert, agreed. "Such a radical alteration could only have occurred with a manipulation of your base DNA. But, such a thing would be difficult, or even impossible, to do after puberty, when the DNA basically locks itself in place. Unless ..."

Blake nodded in realization. "Unless I was born with this genetic defect."

"Exactly!" Adam exclaimed loudly.

Blake appeared confused. "But how can that be?"

Pam interrupted. "You just talked about how Kirskine altered the genetic makeup of The Sentry and he was not an infant. So how was that accomplished? What did Kirskine do that made the outcome differerent?"

Ironcastle explained. "It was not the formula that altered the outcome, it was the individual. James Adams has a one in a million mutation in his genetic makeup. This makes him completely unique. This is why, despite the efforts of your country, they have all failed to repeat the process. And they are not the only ones. The Russians, Germans, and even the Chinese are experimenting along these lines. Sooner or later, they will stop analyzing the formula and start looking at the test subject. When they discover James Adams genetic mutation …." He left the thought unfinished.

Adam continued. "Failure to replicate the results of Kirskine's experiment has nothing to do with the formula and everything to do with the fragile human condition. It simply cannot tolerate the radical extreme of change. The rewriting of a complete base DNA, that has already been locked in place, is impossible. To put it simply, Adams DNA was missing parts that the Kirskine formula 'filled in.' Scientists will soon figure this out."

Sherlock expelled a small cloud of smoke. "Adams is only the first of a new breed. Perhaps, even the next step in human evolution. We have noticed a growing trend of similar abnormalities. Men who can breathe beneath the surface of the ocean, androids who burn when exposed to oxygen, men possessing superhuman strength. A new generation of heroes is being born. The Sentry is merely the first of his kind.

"During the thirties, men such as yourselves and even vigilante heroes such as Darkness and Scorpion were needed to battle the lawless gangster elements, help enforce prohibition, and help your fellow man survive the changing, evolving world around them. You were needed, to serve as an inspiration to those less unfortunate during the Depression. But the world continues to evolve, replacing the old with the new, the so-called 'circle of life.'

"First, however, the world will turn its gaze toward other heroes, the soldiers who will come home from the war. Then, in five years, ten at the most, the American public will demand a time of security, of peace and quiet. They will start with vigilantes like Stockbridge and Gibson, but it will not end there. Whether the world needs you or not, the authorities will hunt down the vigilantes and the public will turn a blind eye toward you. It's a cold, hard fact. Nothing lasts forever.

"Trust me, ladies and gentlemen, we know of which we speak. We were part of the last generation of heroes. The so-called Victorian era. The heroic baton was passed from our own generation to yours. And soon, you will be forced to do the same, whether you want to or not."

There was a long moment of silence as the gathering considered Sherlock's prophetic words. Holmes had gazed into his crystal ball and read their futures. And they couldn't disagree with his analysis.

Adam finally broke the silence. "Sherlock, perhaps this is the appropriate time to reveal the final secret."

Sherlock nodded in agreement and turned his gaze toward Blake. "Do you remember your parents, Simon?"

Blake started to reply and then stopped.

Cassie turned to Blake. "You've never talked about your parents."

Sherlock offered his explanation. "Because he never knew them. Just as he never truly knew his wife and child."

"That's not true. I can remember their names, their faces …" Blake replied angrily in protest and then grew quiet.

Sherlock asked Blake. "Can you see their faces? Do you *truly* remember what your wife and son looked like?"

Guardian slowly shook his head and looked down shamefully. "No, I don't."

Sherlock nodded. "I believe now would be the appropriate time to read to you from Clarke Titan's last journal entry."

Sherlock opened the book and slowly began reading. Adam took his place in the large seat at the head of the table. Now everyone understood why the chair was so large, to accommodate his massive frame. A giant butterfly, elegantly painted with a rainbow of luminous colors, flew near Adam and finally settled on one of his scarred hands. While Sherlock read, the gentle monarch slowly flapped its sail-like wings.

Chapter Fifty-Five
Flashback to 1938 - The Guardian's Secret Revealed

April 7, 1945 11:00 am

Beginning of Flashback to May, 1938. The Introduction of the Guardian.

Clarke Titan stood before the large cylinder filled with bright blue fluids. Bubbles rose to the surface and pranced along the floating human form housed within the container. Even with the subdued lighting of the laboratory, it was evident that the man was not normal. A breathing apparatus covered most of his head and concealed the majority of his facial features. A long shock of snow-white hair floated above the bobbing head, resembling the movement of seaweed dancing in the ocean currents. The pale skin was barely a shade lighter than the hair, completely lacking pigmentation.

Outfitted with a pair of swimming trunks, simple modesty the sole reason, the man was otherwise completely naked. He appeared to be the average height and weight of a normal human male but his musculature was much more developed. Tendons and sinews on the arms and legs were well-defined.

Robert Hubertson walked up and stood next to Clarke. "He's ready. I think it's time the world met Simon, don't you, Clarke?"

Clarke nodded. "You're right, Robert. We've done everything we can for him. We can leave tomorrow and head to upstate New York. I chartered a private airplane to fly Simon there."

"You're still thinking of having him wake up on the plane during the landing?"

"That's where his programming ends. Once he lands, he will meet an agent I've requested especially for this assignment, a biochemist named Conall McGrath. McGrath will meet him at the airport. He knows about Simon's unique appearance and that he is suffering from a rare form of amnesia, but nothing more. McGrath doesn't know about myself or the Council of Elders."

Robert tapped a gauge on the container. "And McGrath will guide him toward a meeting with your son? To help him?"

"He has been instructed to drop hints about Johnny's goals to help those in trouble, and those less fortunate." Clarke confirmed. "I was purposely vague in my instructions. Things will unfold, as they must. I can't control this situation entirely. And McGrath is a decent fellow. I knew his father, Dugan McGrath.

Conall lost his wife and daughter in an automobile accident a few months ago and helping Simon will be good for him."

Robert looked concerned. "This will be very traumatic for Simon."

Clarke nodded. "Yes. But he's tough, he'll survive. Simon's come a long way in the past eight years. It's like he has been trying to make up for lost time. He's aged about twenty-five years in only five."

"Well, he *was* cryogenically frozen for nearly forty-five years. He's nearly as old as I am, Clarke."

Clarke closed his eyes and sighed. "It was necessary. His bones would not hold up the weight of his body. They were flexible, like hard taffy. Fortunately, he seems to have stabilized and appears to be aging normally now. His bones have hardened to an incredible degree; his muscles are tougher and stronger than those of an average man. He still has the white hair and skin, a simple lack of melanin pigment. Albinism is rare but publicly accepted these days as a genetic disorder.

"One hundred years ago, they might have burned him at the stake as a warlock or demon. And he can always resort to using hair dye and actors makeup. My only true concern is the paralyzed skin on his face. I haven't been able to confirm whether it was a side effect of the Danner Formula, or if it was from being frozen for all of those years, or from his mother ingesting various drugs, along with the original formula."

"I'm surprised you never gave up hope, Clarke."

"It was my fault, Robert. I was the one who injected his mother with that original formula. I owed him, and all of the other unfortunates who died at my hands, to make this work. This is my absolution for past sins and protection from eternal damnation."

"Clarke, that was a long time ago. You have redeemed yourself with a hundred selfless acts since that time. Your charities to hospitals, schools, and shelters alone should earn you a position among the Saints. You even raised your only son to carry on that tradition."

"Perhaps, Robert. But some sins can never be forgotten … or forgiven. I'm not certain I have done right by Johnny, either. I stole his childhood, raised him to be a superman. I pushed him too hard. A lesser man would have broken. Somehow, I never saw that, until I met Hugo Danner. It opened my eyes."

"Since you brought it up, what about your son? Will you let him know you're still alive? That you faked your own death eight years ago to come back to this island to help Simon? What about the Danner Formula? Did your son ever recover the journals stolen by Victor Kaine?"

Clarke frowned and responded negatively. "I can't return to the world of the living until the six Danner Journals are found and, if necessary, destroyed. I gave Hugo Danner my solemn oath that no one would ever use his father's formulas for evil purposes."

"Well then, Clarke, old friend. Let's see Simon off and start searching for those missing journals."

"You're planning on going with me?"

Robert laughed. "Don't forget, your son thinks I'm dead, too. I can't very well show up without him starting to question things. Things we might not want him to know about."

Clarke Titan jabbed the intravenous line and pressed down on the plunger of the syringe. The amber fluid from the hypodermic mixed with the clear liquid and slowly crawled towards Simon's right arm.

"This anesthetic should keep him asleep until he arrives in New York." Clarke affectionately placed one hand against the thick glass separating him from Simon's floating body. "Good luck, son."

Simon Blake's eyes opened a fraction of an inch. Floating weightlessly in the cold steel and glass womb, he could dimly make out the two faces that peered at him through the thick glass. His eyes slowly focused on a third face, visible through the blue-tinged waters that surrounded him. The face did not move. He did not have the knowledge to recognize this as a photograph. The sepia-toned picture was that of a woman's face. A beautiful woman. Years later, he could still close his eyes and remember this face. The image he believed to be the face of his departed wife. The amber-colored anesthetic began to take affect. Blake's eyes slowly glazed over and closed. He dreamed. His next memory would be as he staggered away from an airplane crash. His first true memory.

End of Flashback to May, 1938. The Introduction of the Guardian.

Chapter Fifty-Six
New Blood

April 7, 1945 12:30 pm

Sherlock Holmes slowly closed the journal and gazed around the table. He read confusion, amazement, and anger in the eyes of the men and women. Doc Titan said nothing, merely observed the others. Blake appeared to be in a state of shock. Not surprising, considering he had just been informed that his entire life had been a farce.

Kong whistled and scratched his scalp furiously. "Wow, that's some fairy tale."

Adam spoke quietly. "I assure you, it is all quite true."

Blake closed his eyes, looking exhausted. "Is there any proof to the validity of this ... story?"

"I'm sorry to do this to you, child." Sherlock apologized and then recited, *"'Nosce te ipsum. itaque Veritas vos liberabit'."*

Kong scrunched his homely face. "Huh? What the hell does that mean?"

"It's Latin. *'Know thyself and the truth shall set you free.'* " Bart explained.

"Ach. This is all a kettle of ..." Mick stopped short when he noticed Simon Blake was crying. He had never witnessed this man display a single emotion, but he could see the pain of a broken heart, reflected in Blake's pale eyes.

Cassie placed her small hands on Blake's heaving shoulders and looked into his moist eyes. "Chief ... Simon, it's true, isn't it?" Simon nodded his head, but couldn't find the words to speak.

Sherlock explained. "It was a secret phrase that we knew nobody else would speak by mistake. By saying these words, it has allowed him to have access to memories long hidden. It was part of his 'programming.'"

"Programming? Like brainwashing?" Kong asked.

Quatermain nodded. "In a manner of speaking, yes. For his own sake, he was given certain memory blocks."

Cassie looked around at the elder men at the table. "How?"

Ironcastle offered an explanation. "Professor Titan hired a scientist to create, for lack of a better term, a mental wave projector. Lando Manchester was a genius, years ahead of his time. His apparatus was almost telepathic in nature, allowing someone to pick up another person's thoughts."

Kong's mouth dropped open. "Lando Manchester? The Mental Man? He was a nut case. And his telepathic helmet device looked like an oversized colander with wires, light bulbs, and screws poking out of it."

Bart agreed. "He truly had 'Mad Scientist' written all over him."

Blake raised his head. "But I have memories. Silver mining in the American Southwest, oil drilling in Alaska, amethyst ventures in Australia, diamond mining in Africa ...."

Sherlock smiled. "Each of the Illuminati shared with you several memories of their own past adventures. After you were released from your cryogenic chamber in 1930, and Professor Titan began injecting you with Danner's formula compound, we discovered that you never slept. There was a concern that being trapped in the confines of the isolation tank would cause great psychological trauma. So we shared memories of our own adventures to keep your mind active. Professor Titan also hired the same men who trained Doc, to return to Wilder Island and instruct you in the sciences. All using the mental wave projector."

Kong whistled. "That would explain your expertise in so many professional fields of study."

"Gives a whole new image to the phrase 'home schooling.'" Gibs added.

While the others talked, Mick turned to Blake.

"Lad, I'm sorry. I didn't realize ..." He swallowed hard. "I had been asked to meet you at the airport. That was all. I never lied to you about anything."

"It's all right, Mick. I wouldn't be here today if it weren't for you. You've been a good friend." Blake turned back to Sherlock. "What about the airplanes? The mid-air collision? The missing passengers?"

"The accident was completely unplanned. A simple twist of fate. The only fatalities were the two pilots. Neither plane had co-pilots, crews or passengers."

"Then why take the bodies away? Why create a mystery?" Mick asked.

Sherlock sighed. "Because the pilots were men that Doc had operated on. Gradutes of his Rehabilitation Institute. If McGrath had convinced Simon to seek out John's aid and the metal tags at the base of their necks were discovered ..."

Doc concluded the thought. "... I would have started asking questions. The wrong kind of questions. And having only the two pilots disappear would have aroused other types of suspicions. But if the entire crews and passengers of both flights had vanished, it would have been the kind of unsolved mystery that would have drawn Simon and I together."

Mick added. "But you didn't take into account that Simon would decide to solve the mystery by himself. I do remember hinting to Simon for us to seek Doc's assistance but I don't remember being 'instructed' by anyone."

Ironcastle explained. "Clarke mentioned 'instructions' but it was more like subliminal suggestions. Newspapers with articles about Doc were left where you could see them. Discussions were carried out where you could overhear them. That sort of thing. You probably never even noticed at the time."

Blake nodded. "Except, I was more headstrong that Clarke Titan thought I'd be. No doubt, a trait I inherited from the men at this very table when they used the mental wave helmet."

Doc quietly asked the question that he had wanted to since Sherlock had finished reading from the journal. "When was this journal entry written?"

Sherlock glanced at the date. "April, 1938."

Gibs shook his head side to side. "That's impossible. We know for a fact that Doc's father died in 1930."

Quatermain raised a bushy eyebrow. "Did he? Are you quite certain?"

"Yes," Gibs stated emphatically. "We were at the hospital the day he died."

"But did you actually see him die?" Ironcastle queried. "Were you in the room with him?"

Bart looked at Doc apologetically. "No. The doctor came out and told us he had passed away. We only saw his sheet-covered body. We had no reason to doubt, especially after Robert Hubertson had recently died the same way."

Doc sighed deeply. "I always suspected something was odd about his death. I purposely never looked into my father's past or his business dealings. I always felt I was better off not knowing."

Bart glanced around the table. His gaze fixed on Adam. "So is he still alive?"

"He left Sanctuary years ago. We have had only sporadic communication with him since that time. One of the reasons I created this Illuminati was to watch over my father and men like him. I failed him when he succumbed to another bought of madness in Whitechapel in 1888. I promised myself that that would never happen again. I believe he is in need of our assistance again."

Wall stroked his thick beard. "So you know where he is?"

Frankenstein's creature stared at Doc Titan for several seconds, without speaking. Doc closed his eyes. "I know. He's returned to an island that doesn't exist on any nautical map. Wilder Island."

Adam nodded. "Yes. We fear he might have been taken prisoner by Black Skull. He might have been tortured and forced to reveal the secrets of the Danner Journals. According to my last communication with the island, he is being held in a cell block with your friends."

Megan felt emotionally drained. "You want us to stop this? Are you willing to provide assistance?"

"As we've explained, that is not our way." Adam responded quietly.

Wall spoke aloud, as much to himself as the others at the table. "We might need help before this battle is finished. We're facing some rather heavy odds."

"As I have stated many times in the past, I am done with the world of man. I am truly sorry."

"Suppose we do nothing? We simply return to New York? Has anyone ever refused to follow your advice? Or failed to fulfill a mission?" Cassie asked earnestly.

"If you simply did nothing? Well, that would make us extremely poor judges of character, indeed, wouldn't it? And yes, we have had failures over the years.' Sherlock glanced across the table and made eye contact with Fogg. "Phileas, if you please. Enlighten our guests."

Phileas Fogg nodded his head solemnly. "In 1914, we informed two men about a group of Serbian nationalists known as the Black Hand Secret Society. The men, half-brothers, were warned about a possible assassination attempt and our reasons for wanting it prevented. Early members of the Black Hand group included Colonel Dragutin Dimitrijevic, the chief of the Intelligence Department of the Serbian General Staff, Major Voja Tankosic and Milan Ciganovic. Their dream was to create a Greater Serbia. Naturally, their goal of unification and peace could only be attained through the extreme use of violence and terrorism. Dragutin Dimitrijevic, who used the codename Apis, established himself as the leader of the Black Hand. From over 2000 men, he selected three for a special assignment. Muhamed Mehmedbasic, Gavrilo Princip, and Nedjelko Cabrinovic were all suffering from tuberculosis and knew they would not live long. Therefore, they were willing to give their lives for what they believed was a great cause, Bosnia-Herzegovina achieving independence from Austro-Hungary.

"Each of the three men was given a revolver, two bombs and small vial of cyanide. They were instructed to commit suicide after accomplishing their mission, the assassination of Franz Ferdinand.

"On Sunday, June 28, 1914, Archduke Franz Ferdinand and Duchess Sophie von Chotkovato arrived in Sarajevo by train. General Oskar Potiorek, Governor of the Austrian provinces of Bosnia-Herzegovina, was waiting to take the royal party to the City Hall for the official reception.

"The first conspirator on the route to see the royal car was Muhamed Mehmedbasic. Standing by the Austro-Hungarian Bank, Mehmedbasic lost his nerve and allowed the car to pass without taking action. Mehmedbasic later said that a policeman was standing behind him and feared he would be arrested before he had a chance to throw his bomb.

"The next man on the route was Nedjelko Cabrinovic. He stepped forward and hurled his bomb at the archduke's car. The driver accelerated when he saw the flying object hurtling toward him and the bomb exploded beneath the wheel of the second car. Two of the occupants, Eric von Merizzi and Count Boos-Waldeck were seriously wounded. About a dozen spectators were also hit by bomb splinters. After throwing his bomb, Nedjelko Cabrinovic swallowed the cyanide he was carrying and jumped into the River Miljacka. Four men, including two detectives, followed him into the water and managed to arrest him. The poison failed to kill him and he was taken to the local police station. Franz Ferdinand's driver, Franz Urban, drove away quickly and the other members of the Black Hand decided that it was futile to attempt to kill the archduke in the speeding car.

"After attending the official reception at the City Hall, Franz Ferdinand asked about the members of his party who had been wounded by the bomb. When the archduke was told that they had been badly injured and were taken to a local hospital, he insisted upon seeing them. A member of the archduke's staff, Baron Morsey, suggested this might be dangerous, but Oskar Potiorek, who was responsible for the safety of the royal party, replied, "Do you think Sarajevo is full of assassins?" However, Potiorek did accept the advice that it would be better if Duchess Sophie remained behind at the City Hall. When Baron Morsey told Sophie about the revised plans, she refused to stay, arguing, 'As long as the Archduke shows himself in public today, I will not leave his side.'

"In order to avoid the city centre, General Oskar Potiorek decided that the royal car should travel straight along the Appel Quay to the Sarajevo Hospital. However, Potiorek forgot to tell the driver, Franz Urban, about this decision. On the way to the hospital, Urban took a right turn onto Franz Joseph Street. Gavrilo Princip happened to be was standing at that very street corner! Oskar Potiorek immediately realized the driver had taken the wrong route and shouted, "What is this? This is the wrong way! We're supposed to take the Appel Quay!" The driver put his foot on the brake, and began to back up. In doing so, he slowly moved past the awaiting Princip. The assassin stepped forward, drew his gun, and at a distance of about five feet, fired several times into the open car. Franz Ferdinand was hit in the neck, the bullet piercing the archduke's jugular, and Sophie von Chotkovato was shot in the abdomen. Franz Urban drove the royal couple to Konak, the governor's residence. Both were still alive when they arrived but they died from their wounds soon afterwards.

"After shooting Franz Ferdinand and Sophie von Chotkovato, Princip, following instructions, turned his gun on himself. A man behind him saw what he was doing, and seized Princip's right arm. A couple of policeman joined the struggle and the assassin was arrested. Princip and Nedjelko Cabrinovic were both interrogated by the police. They eventually gave the names of their fellow conspirators. Muhamed Mehmedbasic managed to escape to Serbia but was arrested and charged with treason and murder. Eight members of the Black Hand were arrested and charged with treason and found guilty of conspiracy in the murders of Archduke Franz Ferdinand and Duchess Sophie von Chotkovato.

"On July 25, 1914, the Austro-Hungarian government demanded that the Serbian government send the men to face trial in Vienna. Nikola Pasic, the prime minister of Serbia, told the Austro-Hungarian government that he was unable to hand over these three men, as it 'would be a violation of Serbia's Constitution.' The following day the Austro-Hungarian officials issued an ultimatum, containing five major concessions, to the Serbian government. After the time limit on the ultimatum had expired, Austro-Hungary declared war on Serbia. Germany supported Austro-Hungary in the war effort while Russia supported Serbia.

"Germany therefore declared war on Russia on August 1, 1914 and on their ally, France, on August 3, 1914. On August 4, 1914, German troops were sent into Belgium, defying the neutrality that Belgium was promised. Great Britain declared war against Germany that same day. The major European powers were at war within weeks because of overlapping agreements for collective defense and the complex nature of international alliances.

"The resulting casualties, both military and civilian, were over 40 million - 20 million deaths and 21 million wounded." Phileas finished his story and glanced around the table.

Sherlock tapped the ashes from his large pipe bowl and smiled. "If you haven't noticed, Phileas Fogg is very detail-oriented. Simply stated, World War I began because the two men, despite our warnings, failed to stop the Black Hand and a young man named Gavrilo Princip."

Wall studied Holmes through narrowed eyes. "By 'stopping' these men, do you mean killing them?"

"We mean, by whatever means you deem necessary. If Gavrilo Princip had been arrested and held in jail for even one day, a war could have been avoided. This is what is known as a *'butterfly effect.'*" Ironcastle responded.

Kong wrinkled his nose and gave Ironcastle a confused glance. "Huh? You're saying a butterfly caused World War I?"

Sherlock explained. "The butterfly effect is a phrase that encapsulates the more technical notion of sensitive dependence on initial conditions in chaos theory. Small variations of the initial condition of a nonlinear dynamical system may produce large variations in the long term behavior of the system. The 'butterfly effect' refers to the idea that a butterfly's wings might create tiny changes in the atmosphere that will ultimately cause a tornado to appear or prevent a tornado from appearing.

"The flapping wings represent a small change in the initial condition of the system, seemingly innocuous, but which ultimately begins a chain of events that will eventually lead to a large-scale phenomena. Had the butterfly not flapped its wings, the trajectory of the system might be vastly different. This theory was first described in the literature written by chaotician Jacques Hadamard in 1890. His book is at the Museum, if you are interested in reading more about it."

"Wow. This is all way beyond me," Kong confessed, scratching the back of his neck. "I'm just a good ol' boy from the backwoods of Oklahoma."

Pam glanced around at the Illuminati members. She was impressed on how well-read they all appeared to be. "But you're suggesting that if we fail to stop Black Skull and his experiments, we could be looking at something that could alter the world as we know it."

"Yes." Ironcastle replied emphatically.

Kong gave a lopsided smile. "Okay, that I understand. Stop Black Skull or bad things could happen. Short and simple."

Bart jibed, "Yeah, just like you."

"If you are so well informed, why didn't you stop World War II from starting?" Gibs joined in.

Challenger volunteered, "Actually, we tried. Twice. The first time, a man was sent to Germany in 1919 to prevent Adolf Hitler from joining the secret legions of the Thule Society."

"The who society?" Kong asked.

Quatermain explained. "The Thule Society was an occult group of satanic worshippers and became the foundation of the New German Worker's Party. This was renamed the National Socialist German Workers' Party or the Nazi Party. This group was responsible for supporting Hitler and propelling him to the post of Fuehrer, or leader. From his post as absolute ruler, Hitler saw the Jewish people, with their black hair and swarthy complexions, as the darker side of the human species, whilst the blond and blue-eyed Aryans constituted the light side of humanity. The so-called master race. This comes directly from the teachings of the Thule Society."

"So what happened?" Doc asked.

"One of the founders of both groups, the Nazi Party and the Thule Society, was Dietrich Eckart. He was a dedicated Satanist, the supreme adept at the arts and rituals of Black Magic and the central figure in a powerful and widespread circle of occultists, the Thule Group. He was also one of the seven founding members of the Nazi Party. We believe he murdered the man we sent to stop Hitler."

"I've never even heard of Dietrich Eckart," Bart confessed.

Quatermain's eyes met Bart's. "He died of a heart attack December 26, 1923 and was buried in small town in the German Bavarian Alps called Berchtesgaden."

"Heart attack or did the Illuminati sent someone to *stop* him?"

"Let's just say if he were still alive today, Adolf Hitler and Black Skull would be the least of our problems." Quatermain responded solemnly.

"So did you ever send anyone else after Hitler?" Cassie probed.

Sherlock rejoined the discussion. "Sometimes, care must be taken not to create a martyr." There was a moment of silence before Sherlock continued, nodding his head. "But, the answer to your question is yes. Another man was sent in August of 1939. He failed. Two days later, Hitler ordered German SS troops to stage on a false attack on a German radio station at Gliewitz, Poland. The soldiers were dressed in Polish uniforms to convince the world that Poland was the aggressor nation. And to justify their future invasion of Poland. When Gestapo officers arrived at the transmitter to investigate, they found the bullet-riddled body one of the alleged Polish attackers.

"In the morning, there were faked reports of numerous other incidents of Polish aggression along the border. In response, Nazi leader Adolf Hitler issued his 'final directive' to attack Poland, compelling the United Kingdom and France to declare war on Germany. Thus began World War II."

"I didn't know that was how the war started." Pam said, studying Sherlock but seeing no reason to doubt the great detective.

"Very few people do."

"Did you ever find out what happened to that agent?"

"Months later, we received a short message that we believe was sent by him."

Kong fidgeted in his seat. "Well, don't keep us in suspense. What did it say?"

"It was a quote from John Milton, *'Tis far better to reign in hell, than to serve in heaven.'*"

"Apparently your agent didn't like to be told what to do. So he joined up with Hitler, instead of killing him?" Gibs surmised. "What was that you were saying about being a good judges of character?"

"Unfortunately, it's far worse than you can image. The message was signed; using the codename we had assigned the agent. Totenkopf."

Kong's jaw dropped open. "You introduced Totenkopf, the Black Skull, to Hitler? Yeah, I believe you made a rather large error in judging character there."

"As you can see, failures can have great repercussions. However, it can be equally dangerous to act too rashly. That is why all of the Illuminati members *must* agree that it is the proper time to act." Phileas stared into Doc's deep eyes. "That is one of the reasons your father left here. He lacked the patience to wait for the appropriate moment."

Doc spoke quietly, summing up what he had heard. "So your position is like that of the two samurai warriors who are sworn enemies, standing in the rain, swords drawn, each ready to strike. According to the ancient story, they face one another for several days, neither moving. Poised. Waiting."

"Why don't they move?" Kong asked.

"Because whoever moves first, loses the advantage. So they both stand there, waiting for the perfect opportunity to strike. Searching for some small sign of weakness from their opponent."

"So they both stand there in the rain, getting soaked, and accomplishing nothing? Stupid way to make a living, ain't it?"

"It's a lesson about patience. About not rushing headlong into danger." Doc explained.

Kong shook his head. "That's not my way of doing things."

"That's why Doc is always having to rescue you." Bart ribbed his old verbal sparring partner.

Megan addressed Holmes. "Maybe you need to send more than one person, if these events are so important. If you could have stopped a war and saved millions of innocent lives ..."

"As we stated earlier, we are not the world's police force. We have no uniforms, no banner to rally around. And besides, sadly enough, mankind thrives on war. Sooner or later, there will always be a conflict, a battle over borders, religion, or skin color. We can't stop that from happening every time. We don't seek to lead, but we also don't want to see mankind destroy itself, either." Sherlock rubbed along his nose, between his eyes, as if battling a headache. "And this time we are sending more than one person. It's truly that important."

"You walk a fine line. Watching, but never getting directly involved. It must be hard to remain neutral." Doc said calmly.

Hareton Ironcastle leaned forward and said quietly. "You have no idea. I'm a man of action. An adventurer, a hunter. But what we do, we do for the betterment of all mankind. We all believe in the path that we are following. That was the premise upon which the Illuminati was founded."

Bart eyed the Council of Elders and met Fogg's gaze. "So, is there another reason you summoned us to Sanctuary?"

"Yes. You who have been gathered here today represent a new era, a new century. The Illuminati is a gathering of old men, with old ways of thinking. Perhaps it is time for us to step aside, to make way for new blood. We are inviting you ten men and women to consider joining the Council of Elders. After this matter involving Black Skull and Victor Kaine is cleared up, of course. Naturally, we do not require an immediate answer. Please, simply consider the offer."

Sherlock stood up. "There has been much discussed here this morning. We might consider adjourning to allow everyone some time to consider what has been revealed today."

The elderly men excused themselves and left the outdoor patio. Adam approached Doc and placed a massive hand on his shoulder.

"Doc, … John, … please do not hate us for standing our ground. Please do not hate me."

Doc smiled at the giant man. "Even though you were not born like mortal men, we call the same man father. How could I possibly hate my own brother?"

Adam's face showed a slight shock and his eyes welled with tears. Nobody, except the citizens of Sanctuary, had ever treated him with such respect. And he had never experienced the heartfelt companionship of a sibling.

"Thank you."

Adam turned and walked away quickly, before the tears falling from his mismatched orbs could be witnessed. The woman in white was watching from a nearby rooftop. If anyone had been standing close to her, they would have seen her own eyes overflowing with tears.

Kong found Bart sitting by himself at the edge of a cascading water fountain. The small, oval-shaped garden was surrounded by beds of flowers and stone benches. The apelike man quietly approached his old friend. They usually sounded like they would be willing to kill one another but, in reality, they were the closest of friends. Either would lay down their life for the other, without a second's hesitation.

"Bart. What's happenin', old buddy?"

"Merely thinking. A lot has occurred in the last two days. Certain facts and events, that we've based our entire lives on, have turned out to be false. Sort of takes the wind out of your sails."

"You can say that again. I'd hate to be in Blake's shoes right now. And Doc's, finding out his father is still alive. That had to be a shock."

Bart agreed. "And the fact that he's being held prisoner by Black Skull."

"So, what are you doing, sitting out here all by yourself?"

Bart seemed to gather his strength before answering. "You remember when I told you that I was born and raised in New England? That wasn't the entire truth. I was born in Whitechapel, England in 1888. People were dirt poor and life was cheap. My father was shot in the throat by street thugs when I was only two years old. He bled to death before a doctor arrived. When I was four, my mother was stabbed to death. Kids use to warn me that Jack the Ripper killed my mother and would get me too, if I misbehaved. I had nightmares nearly every night for years that Ol' Saucey Jack was coming to get me. After my mother's murder, I was tossed into an orphanage for an entire year.

"My uncle Chester in the United States finally came for me and brought me back to New England. I worked hard to get rid of my cockney accent and forget about my childhood in Whitechapel. But the nightmares continued to plague me for several years. At nineteen, I applied to Princeton. Four years later, I graduated at the top of my class in Math Sciences. I swore to myself to never look back at the days of my youth. At twenty-six years old, I ran off to join the war and met you guys. I had completely forgotten those years in Whitechapel, they were finally lost in the distant past. But now I find out that Doc's father was Jack the Ripper. I feel the days of my youth flooding back into my fevered brain. Last night I dreamt of Jack again. Seems silly for a man of my age, doesn't it?"

Kong's mouth gaped open. "Wow. I never would have guessed. Guess we all have our ghosts that haunt us."

Bart smiled and patted Kong on his thick shoulder. "Thanks, pal."

"For what?"

"Just for listening to me ramble. I feel better after talking about this."

"No problem, Bart, old chum. We better get some sleep. We have to fight Victor Kaine and the entire Nazi military tomorrow, and we're not as young as we use to be."

Bart and Kong placed their arms on each other's shoulders and walked down the path.

Bart began reciting from Shakespeare's Henry V.

"From this day to the ending of the world,
But we in it shall be remembered-
We few, we happy few, we band of brothers.'"

Kong finished the phrase that he had first learned in the Great War.

"For he to-day that sheds his blood with me
Shall be my brother; be he ne'er so vile,
This day shall gentle his condition.'"

Doc Titan and his lovely cousin Pam had been walking along a clean, well-maintained, brick-paved path. Doc and the others had conversed for several hours after they left the meeting with the Council of Elders, but now it was only the two of them.

"Thanks for walking with me, Pam. I sincerely wanted to apologize for what I did to you in New York City. I should not have left you, or the others, behind. Perhaps, I was being a little overprotective."

"Yeah, I suppose. But it's okay. Really. I never had a big brother when I was growing up, to watch over me and keep me out of trouble. And sometimes I *do* need watching over."

"I was concerned … actually, to be honest, I was scared. Nobody ever came so close to our personal lives before. I don't care about the danger to myself, but I … worry about those close to me. Sooner or later our luck will run out."

"Yeah, Doc, but this is what we do. We live adventurous lives. If we weren't chasing criminals and madmen, we'd be climbing mountains, storming barns, racing cars, or jumping off of cliffs. It's the danger and risk of death that makes our lives worth living. I can't even imagine my life without it. Look around, Doc. How many people have the opportunity to travel to the ends of the Earth? Adventure and excitement are our lives."

"She's right, you know." A man's voice added.

Simon Blake and Cassie Greyson walked up alongside the copper-hued giants. They had been strolling and discussing their own lives, when they saw Doc and Pam.

Cassie looked tired. "It's been quite a day, hasn't it?"

Doc agreed, "You can say that again. How are you doing, Simon?"

"Honestly? I'm doing good … great, even. Admittedly, it was a shock at first, but it explains so many things. Why I remembered attending colleges, studying professions, but couldn't remember when or where. Now I know why I am … the way I am."

Doc smiled. "I never really believed that makeup prevented the Death's-Head Virus from killing you."

Blake nodded. "Yeah. Trust me, it surprised me as much as anyone. I think I'm immune to most diseases and viruses. I can't remember ever being sick or even seriously injured. It explains my appearance. This might also explain my unnatural strength."

"I have to admit, I always wondered about that." Cassie said.

Doc looked at the other three. "So, what do you think we should do tomorrow?"

Blake's eyes twinkled. "What we always do. Storm the island, save our friends, defeat the bad guys, save the world."

Pam chuckled. "You make it sound easy."

Cassie smiled. "Hey, we're the good guys. We always win."

Blake turned to Doc. "What do you think about Sherlock's offer? For us to return here?"

"I'll think about that, after we rescue the world."

Pam added, "And your father. They said Uncle Clarke's also being held prisoner on the island."

"Yes, my father," Doc said quietly.

"That had to be a shock," Cassie said. "To find out he is still alive. To find out what kind of life he's lived."

"Yes, but it, too, answers a lot of questions. Such as why he pushed me so hard when I was young. Why he always had that haunted, guilty look in his eyes. He had me trained in psycho-analysis and psychology; he couldn't hide everything from me. I always understood that he was a deeply troubled man."

Pam looked to the sunlit skies. "He did many 'questionable things' in his lifetime. I believe that's the phrase written in the journals."

Doc made a fist, the tendons flexing across the back of his hand. "Perhaps. But don't we all? We cross over that line in the sand. The one we swear we'll never violate. When my father died … when I thought my father had died, and when my instructor and surrogate father, Gerald Coffmann, was murdered, I killed many men. In my search for justice and revenge, I allowed the dark side of my personality to assume control. And it was easy. Too easy.

"I remember Ned and my father arguing about my self-control. Whether or not I would have the ability, and the spirit, to keep the raging beast caged. To rebind it, after it had been released. After it had tasted its first blood. To understand the true difference between retribution and rehabilitation. I dread to think what would have happened if I hadn't had that inner strength of character."

Blake nodded in agreement. "It's something that haunts you. It's a hell of a thing, killing a man … to take away his life. I even warn them. I try to save them. I am sometimes tortured at night with visions of the men who have died by my hand."

Cassie placed Blake's hand in her tiny grasp. "Makes you wonder how Stockbridge and Gibson deal with their ghosts."

They were all silent for several minutes. Overhead, the Aurora Borealis danced wildly in the Earth's upper atmosphere. The view of the white-capped mountains surrounding the hidden valley, rising high into the soft clouds, was breathtaking. The sights and smells permeating everything was almost intoxicating. Pam yawned and stretched.

"It's late and we should get some rest. We have a long journey ahead of us."

Adam stopped at the sound of Sherlock Holmes' voice. The giant, patchwork man was beginning his ascent along the path leading to his private mountain aerie. His heavy, leather, ankle-length coat was open in front but the hood was raised to cover his abominable features. The evening light illuminated his mismatched eyes, one green and one blue. The stone path he was taking passed the ancient cemetery near the gathering hall, where he had met the visitors this morning.

"Leaving us so soon, Adam?" Sherlock asked.

"I have said all that needs to be said. Staying longer will accomplish nothing."

Sherlock was reclined against a giant tombstone, puffing his fabled calabash pipe. His shadow lay across the cold, hard stone, displaying the silhouette of his curved hooked nose and the pipe clenched in his teeth.

The Lady in White appeared from behind the headstone. Her polished, golden mask covered her features, but her exposed eyes were bright and alive. She rarely faced Adam or Sherlock head-on, only her silhouette or glimpses of her mask were visible. Her hood was raised and the pure white robe covered most of her head. Her beautiful, delicate hands appeared to be carved from pale alabaster. Her long, blonde silky hair cascaded down from the fur-lined opening in the hood and covered the upper portion of her chest. Every indication was given that she must be a stunningly beautiful woman. So why did the mysterious Lady in White hide her face?

The Lady in White glided toward Adam. "Our guests will be leaving tomorrow. You could stay with us for a while, after they have gone."

Adam sighed softly. "I have borrowed several books, I will return them soon. I have much to ponder."

Sherlock puffed deeply. "We're not concerned with your borrowing books from the Museum. Don't you wish to say goodbye to your … brothers?"

"Brothers." Adam touched his lips with a scarred index finger, as he quietly said the word to himself. "Brothers. Not a word I ever thought I would say." He pulled the finger from his face and stared at the black nails on his mismatched fingers. The thumb and the two fingers on the end of the right hand had been replaced with parts from other cadavers. The size and color of these were different from the middle two fingers.

The Lady in White's impassive masked face studied Adam. "John Titan, Simon Blake, and you were all brought into the world by the same man."

"Yes. Yes, we were. Unfortunately, I have other … obligations."

Sherlock puffed at his pipe, sending up gray tuffs of smoke. "Your friend on the mountain will wait, Adam."

"I might stay longer, but she will be wondering where I've been. She … worries when I'm gone very long." He was now staring at his left hand, with the missing ring finger. But his attention was drawn to the simple metal band on his little finger. They could tell he was reminiscing about Lady Megan, his late wife.

Sherlock sat quietly for several seconds. Leaning forward, he removed the mouthpiece from his thin-set lips and tapped the bowl of the intricately carved pipe against a broken stone, to empty the spent ashes. He studied the signature curve of the chamber of his pipe as he stuffed more umber-colored tobacco into the deep bowl. He puffed hard to ignite the new tender. Finally satisfied with his efforts, he reclined again.

"Does she still guard the entrance?" Sherlock asked.

"Yes. She protects and serves as she always has."

The white-clad woman turned to Sherlock. "Did any of our guests ask about the polar opening to the other world below?"

"No. I suppose they had much to digest, with the secrets we revealed today."

The Lady in White agreed. "And … did they ask about … me?"

"No, milady. But you did a poor job of blending into the background. I know for certain John Titan and Simon Blake saw you." Sherlock chided her.

"I had to see him. He might never return here again. Especially, where he's going. I had to see his face again."

Adam asked the woman. "Would you have revealed yourself to him, if he had approached you?"

"No." The Lady in White pondered this for many seconds. "No. He's better off thinking I'm dead."

"You could have let him make that choice." The large man said.

The Lady in White removed the gold-colored mask from her face. Delicate, trembling fingers traced a scar on one ivory cheek. The balance of her features remained hidden in the depths of the snow-white hood. "I would not want him to see me like this. I would rather have him remember me the way I was. He has enough scars in his life to bear."

Adam pulled back his long black hair and exposed his face. "We all have scars to bear in our lives. Some are simply more evident than others."

"Oh, Adam, I'm very sorry. Please forgive an old woman's vanity."

"There's nothing to forgive, milady. I understood your inference." Adam replied quietly, regretting his outburst.

She placed a soothing hand on Adam's arm and looked into his cadaverous features, framed by his coal-black hair. When Sherlock spoke again, she released the large arm and replaced the mask over her exposed face.

"Thank you for attending our meeting today, Adam."

Adam wrapped his dark cloak tightly about his monstrous, grotesque form, as if to keep out the chill. The rainbow colors of the Aurora Borealis played across Adam's solemn features.

"I would not have missed it for the world. But I must go now."

The Lady in White asked timidly. "Will you return soon? I miss our talks, Adam."

"Yes, soon. If you, or any of the others, ever have need of me …"

Sherlock smiled and finished Adam's statement. "… we'll know where to find you. Say 'hello' to your friend for us."

Adam started to walk away, stopped and turned to his friends. "Did we do the right thing today?"

"Of course. It was time to put an end to secrets." Sherlock said with absolute certainty. "Long past that time."

Adam raised one brow. "And what of the secrets we did not reveal?"

The Lady in White waved a small hand through the air. "Isn't that the way of life? The more secrets that are revealed, the more secrets there are to be revealed?"

Adam's face became dark and solemn. "Perhaps. I suppose only time will tell."

"*'Oh! What a tangled web we weave, when first we practice to deceive.'*" Sherlock quoted and then confided in them, "I've always enjoyed Sir Walter Scott."

The Lady in White waved at Adam as he walked away. "Be well, my friend."

"And you as well, milady." Without another word, the gargantuan behemoth who claimed himself soulless walked away, ascending the mountain path. Leaving behind the world of man once more.

Sherlock sat for several minutes, puffing heavily on his calabash pipe. He watched as the beautiful woman without a name walked toward the small building that housed her quarters. The retired detective forced down the thoughts of solving her mysterious identity. It was an old habit, playing the great detective. Finally, he stood up and patted the large headstone he had been reclining against. Brushing at imaginary dust, he read the inscription, as he had a thousand times before.

Doctor John Hamish Watson. Born August 7, 1852. Died 1939.
A good friend and confidante. May he find peace.

"Well, Watson, my old friend, what do you think? Hmm? Yes, yes, I quite agree, wholeheartedly. It is time for this old man to retire for the night. Confounded sun never sets during the spring and summer up here. I miss spring in London. I miss the changing of the seasons. I miss our adventures. And I miss you, old friend. I wish you were still here with me."

A single tear ran down his cheek as he slowly walked down the clean, stone path. Pillars of gray smoke billowed over his narrow shoulders. A minute later he was out of sight. The cool, evening breeze blew through the headstones, carrying the scent of honeysuckle and pipe tobacco. Several more minutes passed. From behind one of the largest tombstones, close to where Sherlock had been reclined, stepped a human-shaped shadow. The eavesdropper had been close enough to listen to the entire conversation. After a moment's hesitation, the figure quietly exited the graveyard.

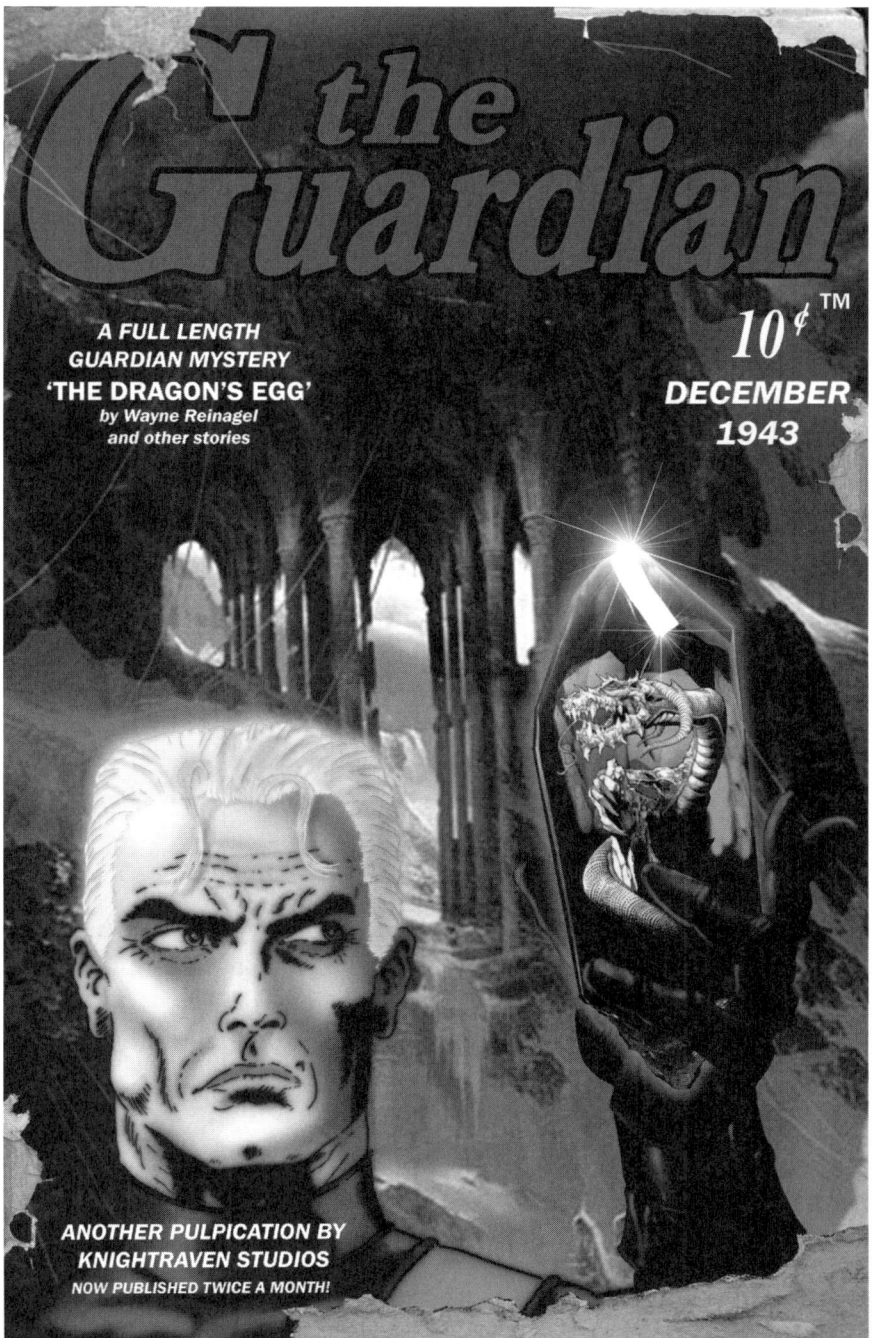

Chapter Fifty-Seven
Conspiracy Theories

April 8, 1945 2:00 pm

Victor Kaine was quite displeased. He had recently returned from Doc Titan's Hidden Acropolis. His old friend Konstantin Egorov lay dead in the snow. He had battled with two mysterious unknown men and was convinced to leave before investigating further. That had been a mistake. Now he had returned to Skull Island and heard rumors of his prisoners being tortured and one had even been killed. He wanted answers.

He stormed quickly through the lower levels of the old building. His long legs carried him along so rapidly that the two large sisters, Hermia and Xena Reeves, had to trot to keep up. Despite their larger size, both women feared the dominating man. Not only was he a tall, imposing figure, possessing unbelievable strength, he feared nothing and no one. It was said that he would storm Hell itself and shove old Satan off of his throne, if Kaine wanted to sit down.

Today, he was dressed to match his mood. All black. He even had a black scarf around his neck and as he moved forward it resembled a flag, waving over his broad shoulders. When the two women first met Kaine, he had long, straight, jet-black hair. Now, years later, the flowing mane was snow-white, greatly contrasting with his black outfit.

Two large guards, in full-dress, black Nazi SS uniforms, complete with insignias and side-arms, stood guard in front of the prison door. On the opposite side of the door, inside the room, two more men were on guard. Black Skull insisted all of his men remain in uniform at all times. The only variation from standard Nazi uniforms was the collar, which had been modified to accommodate the bright red skull at the neck. Black Skull had also insisted that each of his men, as a sign of loyalty to him and the Third Reich; have this crimson deaths-head epoxied to their throats. After seeing what these skull bombs could do to a man, Kaine had to respect the dedication to, and faith in, their leader that these men possessed.

Victor planted his feet firmly in front of the two guards. "Remove yourselves from my path. I wish to speak to my prisoners." The men did not move, or even flinch. "Did you hear what I said? Out of my way."

The guard on the left stayed at attention, but turned his head toward Kaine. "Sir, we have orders that nobody is to enter this room except Herr Totenkopf himself." After stating this, he turned his head back to full attention.

Color flushed into Kaine's usually pale features. Fear and intimidation would not work with men like these two. Their loyalty to, and perhaps fear of, Black Skull was very powerful. Even as upset as he was, Victor Kaine had to admire that Totenkopf could inspire such feelings in his men. He *did*, however, have death-wielding bombs glued to each man's neck. Kaine braced himself to attack the guards, and have his large female bodyguards assist if needed, when a distant voice halted him.

Professor Schmidt stood twenty feet away. His voice carried well in the dim corridor. "They will not disobey the direct orders of Black Skull."

Victor motioned for Hermia and Xena to remain where they were and, in several long strides, stood face to face with Schmidt. The old man did not look away as Kaine glared at him. Victor was not accustomed to such bravery in a man. He had witnessed that the old man also had no fear of Totenkopf. Of course, Black Skull was only a man in a Halloween fright mask. There were very few men that Kaine could not intimidate and this was becoming an irritant.

"I wish to speak to my prisoners. Something is ... I feel that ... " Kaine flushed with anger, unable to put into words his suspicions. All he truly had was a feeling that something wasn't quite right.

Schmidt spoke softly. "This is the wrong time and the wrong place to start having doubts. Project Gladiator is close to completion and Black Skull will not allow anything to interfere."

Kaine felt like shouting at the mild-mannered professor but did not want the other four people to overhear their conversation.

Victor whispered. "You've been manipulating things since the beginning. Why have me capture and kidnap these prisoners, then deny me access to them? It was your idea for me to send my people to New York and snatch them before Black Skull's forces could murder them. Why? What are you planning, Schmidt?"

"All in good time, Herr Kaine."

Kaine reached out and wrapped his long fingers around Schmidt's neck, effortlessly lifting him from the ground. He brought his face within inches of the professor's and stared into his eyes. Kaine possessed some smattering of hypnotism and tried to apply that knowledge now. But, even though the elderly man's face became red from the constricting fingers, the professor retained control of his will and his mind.

"You will tell me what I want to know, right now, or you will ..." Kaine's threat was interrupted by a new arrival in the corridor.

Black Skull approached. "Put Professor Schmidt down, Kaine. Now." Victor growled deep in his throat and turned his gaze toward the Nazi leader. "I will not repeat myself." He motioned and a dozen men on either flank lifted their machine guns and pointed them at Kaine.

For a long moment, the two men faced one another. Kaine reasoned with himself. Totenkopf had the superior firepower. While Kaine and the two large female bodyguards would certainly be able to charge, there was no possibility of surviving a battle against a dozen well-armed soldiers. Deciding that discretion was the better part of valor, Kaine slowly lowered the professor back to his feet. Victor, his incredible strength concealed by a gentle facade, smiled and bowed slightly to Professor Schmidt and Totenkopf.

"My apologies, sirs. I lost control of my temper." Flames of anger still burned at his core but only politeness showed on the surface. Kaine had the ability to make good judgments and enough discretion to keep secret information ... secret. His was the trait of utilizing knowledge and experience, combined with common sense and insight, to turn events to his favor. He simply had to bide his time. "I only wanted to speak with the prisoners and things got out of hand. My fault."

Totenkopf ignored Victor's apology. "I understand Professor Walters found the missing page of the Danner Journal."

Kaine nodded in agreement. "Yes. But there were two men who attacked us while we were there. I did not recognize them." This was a lie. Victor had recognized the man who had disappeared. The man known as Max Grant, the Dark Eagle. The man who had killed his father. Kaine did not understand why Grant was at Doc Titan's Hidden Acropolis, but he swore to himself that Grant would not survive their next encounter.

"Will they be a problem?" Totenkopf asked quietly.

"No, they are both dead." Another lie. Kaine was still not satisfied with the way he was being treated. "Totenkopf, I would like to speak to the prisoners."

Totenkopf looked at Kaine sternly and pronounced emotionlessly. "The prisoners are off limits." Kaine appeared to start to verbally question this dictate. Totenkopf approached him and stated emphatically. "Do not presume to question my orders. You will receive your payment of ten million dollars in diamonds tomorrow. Meanwhile, I will countenance no further delays and brook no failures. Project Gladiator will proceed as scheduled. At this point, you are merely my guest. I am in complete charge of this situation."

Without awaiting a response, Totenkopf simply turned his back to Kaine and walked away. This was how you dismissed a subordinate; Victor had often used the same technique. Totenkopf was certainly a master at the art of intimidation, and the tall man respected him for that ability. Any moron could kill another man, but to bend him to your will was infinitely harder and far more pleasurable.

When they were out of earshot of Kaine, Black Skull quietly asked Professor Schmidt. "Are you okay? Did he harm you?"

"No, I'm fine. Herr Totenkopf, I do not trust that man. He will need to be watched very carefully."

"I agree. I shall place another set of guards at the door outside the prison cells. Is everything ready for Project Gladiator, Herr Schmidt?"

"Yes. We will soon harvest the fruit from all of these years of labor."

"In the meantime, stay away from Kaine. He is a dangerous man. If he understood what will soon take place ...." Totenkopf left the sentence unfinished.

Schmidt nodded and a minute smile played on his lips. "I agree."

Black Skull walked away; followed by his two large, mute bodyguards, Ernst and Orban. They were always present but never uttered a word. Schmidt always wondered if Totenkopf had had their tongues removed. Seemed like something he would do, simply to keep them from talking. The professor also realized that his own life was forfeit, if Project Gladiator should fail in any way. Black Skull was a very dangerous man and took failure very badly.

Victor Kaine walked slowly down the corridor, the two large women following. He spoke loudly enough that the two could hear him, but he was actually talking aloud to himself. "Schmidt is up to something. I can see it in his eyes." He paused for a minute, and then continued. "He's not who he appears to be. But then, who is he?" Kaine pulled his long, snow-white hair back from his face and breathed deeply. He apparently decided on a course of action. "I shall take Totenkopf's advice and simply watch and wait. Sooner or later, the wolverine must come out of his hole to feed. The hunter simply needs to wait, with club in hand." He smiled at his analogy and strolled back to his quarters, the two women following silently behind.

When he entered his rooms, Victor instructed the sisters to remain on guard outside the door and told them he was not to be disturbed. The door closed and they stood silently for a full minute. Finally, they stepped several feet away from the door and silently whispered to one another.

Hermia glanced around nervously. "We are surrounded by madmen, sister. What are we to do?"

Xena returned the whisper. "The one called Doc Titan will certainly come to save his friends. He is our only hope. He saved us last time."

"Unless he is already dead. Do you believe that Totenkopf might have killed all of the prisoners? Why else would he not want Kaine to enter the prison? And who is that strange prisoner Totenkopf keeps locked up? I heard he beats him like a dog, every day."

"I don't know. I long for the days when we were merely circus performers. Life was so simple then."

"We shall have to bide our time until an opportunity of escape presents itself." Hermia bit her lower lip.

Xena frowned. "What about our poor sister, Ariel? Kaine says he has spies who will do her harm, if we should ever leave him again."

Hermia tried to comfort her large sibling. "Do not give up hope, sister. We will find a way out of this."

Victor Kaine stared out of the windows in his quarters. His breathing was slow and shallow. He was so still that he appeared to be carved of marble. He had changed into an different outfit but still of all black; it always calmed him when he changed his attire. Raised a poor beggar child, he often had only one set of clothing. He was trying to focus, but his mind was in turmoil. Something was wrong, he knew this instinctively, but he simply could not put his thumb on the problem. Perhaps it was merely the stress of dealing with Black Skull. He suddenly realized that he was growling, something he did unconsciously, in moments of apprehension and surprise.

He had studied under Arabian fakirs, Tibetan mystics, and Indian yogis. They had tried to show him ways to calm his inner soul. They had all failed. There was a fire burning within him, consuming everything in its path. He turned away from the window and stormed across the large room. His eyes lifted and he found himself staring into the giant mirror. He had requested this room because of this mirror. He would change his clothing and study his own reflection, before walking amongst his peers. Now his gaze was captivated by the pitch-black reflection. The Marquis De Sade scar at his left eye gave his face character. But, before his eyes, the obsidian image changed, until all he could see was the face of Totenkopf, taunting him. Laughing at him. Mocking him.

His long-fingered fist lashed out and struck the reflective surface. He half expected the mirror to smash into a million fragments. Instead, his hand abruptly stopped upon hitting the thick quicksilver surface. A lesser man would have broken the bones in his hand. Victor Kaine did not. Much to his surprise, however, a hollow sound, like a monstrous bass drum, echoed back. There was nothing behind the mirror. He studied the frame for a minute before discovering a hidden catch, almost beyond the reach of his long fingers. There was a 'snap' sound and the mirror hinged away from the wall, revealing a dark doorway beyond. Decades of dust and cobwebs filled the opening. Using his short, black cape he wiped the webs away and stepped through the opening.

It took several seconds for his eyes to adjust to the near total darkness. The light from his rooms filtered through, outlining odd and distorted objects. Slowly, his mind was able to decipher the shadows as scientific equipment. A hidden laboratory. Curiouser and curiouser, as Alice's rabbit had recited. Much to Victor's surprise, the light from his room was not providing the only illumination. From a glass cabinet against one wall, came an eerie, blue luminescence. He couldn't tell if it was enhancing and amplifying the light from his room or providing its own icy fire. The blue mercury liquid in the sealed container seemed to move and whirl, as though it were alive. The blue fluid cast an eerie, unnatural light on Kaine's leering face.

"Well, precious, what have we got here?"

Act III: The Battle

Chapter Fifty-Eight
The Calm Before the Storm

April 11, 1945   10:00 am

After leaving the Sanctuary at the North Pole, the group stopped in New York and picked up supplies and equipment. Doc, Kong, and Simon Blake returned to the skyscraper laboratories and spent several hours mixing three separate concoctions. Pam, Cassie, and Megan made a brief detour in the *Pamela* to pick up Preston Stockbridge and Luthor Gibson from an airstrip in Greenland. The Council of Elders had already sent a plane to rescue the stranded men at the Hidden Acropolis and this was the closest intersecting point on the return to New York. When they arrived at the Global Navigator Consortium, the Windjammer was ready for action. The *Pamela* was left at the enormous warehouse and everyone piled into the gargantuan zeppelin.

Much later, Cassie sighed with boredom. She was ready for action and it would take several more hours to reach their destination. Megan was sipping a watered down gin-fizz and was studying the layout of the immense main cabin of the Windjammer. Bart was lightly napping in one of the comfortable lounge chairs.

Megan eyed the large main room with amazement. "I didn't realize that blimps were this big."

Kong could not resist the temptation of flirting with the nearest female. "This isn't a blimp, Megan, it's a zeppelin."

"I didn't know there was a difference."

Kong broke into a lengthy explanation. "Non-rigid airships, commonly known as blimps, simply rely on a slight overpressure within the single gasbag to maintain their shape. The most important feature of the zeppelin's design is a rigid aluminum alloy skeleton, made of rings and longitudinal girders. The advantage of this concept is that the ships can be built much larger, which enables them to lift heavier loads and be equipped with more powerful engines. Zeppelins are larger, faster, and stronger."

Megan sipped her drink and frowned. "But don't they catch on fire? I remember the Hindenburg disaster in 1937. All of those poor people."

Kong smiled and nodded. "They originally filled these huge dinosaurs with hydrogen gas. After the Hindenburg disaster, they converted to an inert gas called helium. Doc and I brewed up a mixture of gases that have greater lifting power and are completely fire-proof. The skin is coated with a lightweight metallic fabric that is nearly bulletproof. The Windjammer was one of the last of these airships built. We've taken it around the world several times. With its reinforced framework, we can haul over one hundred tons and still reach nearly three hundred miles per hour. We are using eight modified Maybach engines of around three hundred and twenty horsepower each. There has never been an airship like the Windjammer and probably never will be again. It's one of a kind."

Megan liked the homely apeman. "Huh. I'm impressed. Doc Titan likes his toys, doesn't he?"

Kong frowned and looked hurt. "Toy?!"

Bart stirred from his nap at Kong's excited exclamation. "Ignore this mistake of nature, Megan. He has a half-witted wife and thirteen ugly children waiting for him at home. Or is it the other way around?"

Kong shook his hairy fist at the well-dressed man. "Listen you overdressed shyster, I'm going to hit you on the head so hard, you'll have to untie your shoes to brush you teeth."

Bart yawned and stretched. "I would have a battle of wits with you, but I refuse to fight with an unarmed man."

Kong's eyes narrowed. "Why I have half a mind …"

Bart waved his hand dismissively. "Ignore him, he's just bragging."

"You keep this up and I'll make you wish you were never born," Kong warned.

Bart countered, "When I'm around you, that's every day."

"Keep it up and things will get ugly around here, shyster."

"Too late. You were born that way. Want some advice, double-ugly?"

Kong leaned forward. "I'm all ears."

"Yeah, so's a jackass."

"You're asking for a bruising, fella," Kong threatened mockingly.

Bart flourished his slim, black cane menacingly. "I'll pick your teeth with this thing if you lay a hand on me, you missing link! Besides, I still have a lump on my head from your aerial acrobatics."

Kong growled, "Want a matching lump?"

As they continued their friendly bickering, Kong soon forgot about flirting with Megan.

❧ ❖ ❖ ❧

Phileas Fogg was an absolute stickler for schedules, details, and organization. Long ago, he had volunteered his services toward the care and maintenance of the museum. *'A place for everything and everything in its place'* was the motto he lived by. He even had a plaque created and hung over his small desk. Adam had come to him earlier with a request to borrow certain books. Much to Adam's chagrin, Fogg carefully notated the time, date, the titles of each book, and so on.

This afternoon, Fogg was filing the private journals that the visitors had perused. The writings of James Clarke Wildman, of Clarke Wilder, and others. Sherlock had returned Professor Titan's notebook, as well. Photographs were restored to their places on the walls or filed in their respective drawers. He breathed a deep sigh as he completed the job. Everything was where it belonged once more.

A tiny butterfly, certainly one of the smallest Phileas had ever seen, fluttered by quietly. He watched the miniature creature rise and fall on delicate wings. It passed by a bookshelf. Phileas was no longer watching the colorful insect. His fixed gaze was on the empty space on the bookshelf. A volume was missing! He glanced around, but everything was filed away. Consulting his catalog key, he soon discovered the name of the missing volume. He pressed his lips together nervously.

Fogg spent the next hour carefully examining each shelf, visually confirming the presence of every volume. Six journals were missing. Phileas sat at his desk as he referenced the catalog key and compiled an accurate list of the missing tomes. A bead of perspiration gathered on his brow.

Sherlock Holmes must be informed about this as soon as possible.

As Phileas left the building, he failed to notice the small butterfly, struggling for its very life. It had become trapped in a gossamer web and a predatory spider was slowly reeling it in. As the eight bulbous eyes studied its helpless prey, the arachnid's fangs drooled in anticipation. Anywhere else in the world, these events would be quite commonplace. But Sanctuary was unique in this aspect. It was completely devoid of any predator. Until now.

Chapter Fifty-Nine
Rendezvous Trap and *Peril's Stowaways*

April 12, 1945 5:00 am

Count Drakoft could feel the heat from half a mile away. He watched impassively as the fire spread out of control. The massive explosions at the military base were catastrophic. They quickly spread to the fuel dumps and threatened the large Army hospital located at the far end of the base. Fire departments struggled to fight the fires with every available man. Men abandoned their guard posts to assist the firefighters in battling the blaze.

Two men were left guarding the structure that Drakoft wanted.

"Should we help …?" The first guard asked.

The second guard shook his head. "No. We were assigned to guard this building."

Count Drakoft casually strolled to the rear of a large hanger, a metal-roofed quonset hut. He signaled one of the three powerful androids that followed him. The ten foot tall giant stepped up to the building, squatted low, dug unfeeling fingers into the structures corrugated skin and effortlessly lifted. The corner of the building had become an entrance. Drakoft quickly stepped through the opening, followed by his mindless automatons. He had to move quickly if he was to succeed in his mission. The distraction and noise of the fire would not last forever. The two guards outside did not notice Drakoft or his androids; their attention was drawn to the raging flames.

He approached the small, experimental drone plane. It was an unmanned unit, designed for surveillance and sabotage. It was roughly a third the size of a small airplane. Two of his robots could easily lift the craft. He had a boat waiting nearby for a quick escape. Despite this, Drakoft took his time and thoroughly examined the ship. It would be a simple matter to reset coordinates and send it winging its way toward Germany. He could easily program the drone to land in Berlin, at the very entrance to Hitler's bunker, if he desired. One of the androids opened the doors and another began pushing the drone toward the opening.

"That's far enough, Count Drakoft." Sentry's voice came from behind him.

Count Drakoft smiled beneath his black leather mask and turned to face his nemesis. This could only mean Black Skull had sabotaged the mission to steal the drone. Count Drakoft would deal with that traitorous bastard later. One of the guards from the front of the building stepped through the doorway. He was wearing a disguise over his face and a military uniform but Drakoft recognized Sentry's bold stance. The smaller guard stepped from behind Sentry and Kid Sentry spoke.

"You didn't think we would let you waltz in here and steal the prototype drone, did you, Count Drakoft?" Kid Sentry asked.

Drakoft surprised them with his reply. "Actually, I've been waiting for you gentlemen."

"Cody, watch out!" Sentry warned his young sidekick.

The words had scarcely left his mouth, when the three towering androids silently attacked. The battle was surprisingly short. The two humans, even though highly-trained, did not stand a chance against such ruthless machine-men. Metallic fists pummeled the two heroes until they were unconscious.

James Adams' jaw was swollen and stiff and his mouth was filled with the taste of copper. Blood. He tried to move but discovered he was tightly bound. He felt movement and turned his head. Kid Sentry was held captive next to him. They were tightly chained to a smooth, metallic surface. They still had on the military uniforms, with their red, white and blue costumes beneath.

Drakoft smiled, his leather mask creaking. "Oh, good. You're awake in time to witness your own deaths."

Kid Sentry groaned. "Jim, I can't move."

"I can't have you fall off, before you arrive at your destination. You stole my face, Sentry, but I intend to steal your very life." Drakoft pontificated. James Adams' vision cleared and he realized they were chained to the drone airplane.

Drakoft continued. "Did your Allied Intelligence truly think I would be stupid enough to send this drone to Berlin, without studying it first? They must have intercepted and deciphered Black Skull's radio transmissions. The bomb housed in the belly of this craft would have destroyed half of Berlin."

Sentry stalled for time. "So you disarmed it and planned on sending the drone, and Kid Sentry and I, to Berlin?"

"I don't think so." Kid Sentry announced loudly.

Cody had pretended to be helpless for the last few minutes. He had slowly worked on the lock that held the chains in place. It now fell away and the chains were loosened. Sentry and Kid Sentry leapt at Count Drakoft. Kid Sentry pummeled the leather-faced villain. The androids approached, preparing to defend their master. Adams tore a high voltage line from the wall and tossed the raw wires at the first robot. It caught the live wires and began convulsing as the massive current ran through its metal frame. The androids were linked together, sharing a common man-made brain. Seconds later, all three lifeless metal-men fell to the floor with a loud crash.

The instant the giant androids struck the floor, Kid Sentry looked toward the loud noise. As he was distracted by the sound, Drakoft struck him from behind and stepped to a control console. He pushed a small red button and the drone engine rockets ignited, accelerating down the short runway.

Kid Sentry rose to one knee. "Guess your master plan is kaput now, Nazi. We have a prison cell with your name on it."

Drakoft smiled evilly. "Is it, child? Who said I disarmed the drone?"

Kid Sentry's eyes became large. "You're sending it back to Berlin armed? You're crazier than a bedbug."

Drakoft laughed loudly. "Who said I programmed it for Berlin?"

Sentry was looking at the control console. "Kid Sentry, he set the coordinates for here, in England."

"British Parliament to be precise. I believe your Allied Forces are meeting there tonight. You have a choice, Sentry, stay here and take me prisoner or stop the rocket and save the leaders of your Allied Forces." Drakoft explained.

Sentry's eyes narrowed. "Damn you, Drakoft."

Without saying another word, Sentry and Cody ran toward the unmanned rocket. It was picking up speed and would liftoff in seconds. Adams spotted a motorcycle, clambered aboard and quickly kicked it to life. Kid Sentry leapt onto the rear of the bike, as it was throttled into high gear. They were catching up quickly, but in two hundred feet the edge of the military base ended abruptly at a sheer cliff. One hundred feet below, the strong current of the North Atlantic Ocean pounded the cliff face relentlessly.

Adams gunned the engine and it whined in protest, and then rocketed forward. They were only twenty feet behind the drone. Ten. Five. Both men leapt as one and threw themselves at the unmanned craft. Suddenly, it was a manned flight.

Kid Sentry was able to grab the front guidance fin and hang on as the rocket accelerated. James Adams slid down the length of the smooth, metallic surface, seeking a handhold. Three fingers slid into a rear intake port and he held on. The temperature was near forty degrees Fahrenheit and as the craft cut through the air, the wind chill factor plummeted below freezing.

Sentry shouted, "Cody, hang on, but lean to your right. We can guide this drone away from its destination, using our bodies as rudders."

The craft banked north and leveled out as its passengers changed the programmed flight pattern. It was moving at an amazing speed now. The view below was the frigid waters of the North Atlantic as the shores of England were disappearing in the horizon behind them.

"Cody, we have to get off this rocket." Sentry directed his young friend.

Kid Sentry disagreed. "If we do, it will self-correct its course and head back to London. I can disarm the trigger, Jim. The control panel is right below here."

"Cody … Chris, no. Drakoft would have booby-trapped …" Sentry began.

From that second everything seemed to move in slow motion. The control panel cover was a small metallic piece of metal. When Kid Sentry opened it, the wind sheer threw it back and tore it off the hinges. The corner of the plate struck Adams on the forehead. His vision darkened for a brief second. Suddenly, he realized that his grip had relaxed and he was falling. He watched as Kid Sentry and the rocket left him behind.

Christopher 'Cody' Sawyer looked down and saw the control panel grow brighter. There was a tiny click noise. His eyes met Sentry's. The pregnant second of time slowed to a crawl.

Kid Sentry's body was enveloped in the bright flash of light. From forty feet away, Adams felt the punch of the blast and he was stunned almost senseless. His weightless body drifted through the atmosphere. He saw the sun peak its first ray of light over the horizon. He was floating in a world without pain, without feeling.

He slammed into the frigid, merciless waters with such intensity it forced the air from his lungs. His velocity drove him fifty feet below the icy surface. Reflexively, he drew in a deep breath and his lungs filled with the below-zero temperature ocean waters. Hypothermia seized his body and his stiffening limbs became enormous weights, too heavy to move. His eyes closed and Adams could feel them freeze shut, ice forming on the surface of his lids. His body stopped functioning but his mind continued working for several more seconds.

His last thoughts were of his friend, and partner, Cody Sawyer.

Chapter Sixty
The Plunge of the Seablade

April 13, 1945   10:00 am

Above an uncharted island, the enormous zeppelin christened Windjammer hovered easily in the soft morning breeze. The stabilizers kept the ship from bouncing or swaying, as it stood stationary in the soft clouds. The giant aircraft floated twenty thousand feet over the crystal blue ocean. Thirteen people gathered around a rather unique table and planned their invasion. Doc Titan, Preston Stockbridge, Luthor Gibson, Simon Blake, Pam Titan, Kong Larson, Bart Blackwell, Mick McGrath, Wall Walker, Gibs Maddox, Megan Meriwether, Cassie Greyson, and J. W. Campbell. Campbell had volunteered to accompany the group and stay aboard the cigar-shaped airship when the invasion started.

The plat table was a recent invention, designed by Doc and Gibs, created strictly for military surveillance. It was a combination camera and radar system that projected a full-scale, three-dimensional photo onto the surface of the table. The group was studying the layout of the entire length and breadth of Skull Island. This aero reconnaissance had another very distinct advantage over conventional photos. The group was able to see what was currently happening on the island, as it occurred.

The entire land mass was roughly one mile wide and eight miles long, about half the size of Manhattan Island. At the south end of the island was a half-moon cove. Anchored in this clear-water lagoon were two large German battleships. Guns were fully prepared and men were at their stations at all times. In seconds, they could be prepared to defend the island from invasion. The large guns mounted on the decks could easily fire shells to the other end of the small island.

Almost hidden from view were the entrances to a concealed airplane hanger. The hanger had been carved completely through the stone mountain that stood in the center of the island. Below the north entrance of the hanger was a large, deep-blue lake. Doc remembered swimming there as a child. Close to the high cliffs, at the opposite end of the land mass from the ships, were a gathering of ancient ruins and a small temple. The lake was between the ruins and the mountain. Between the South Entrance of the mountain hanger and the cove were the barracks, Totenkopf's headquarters, and the laboratory.

The laboratory and main headquarters were housed in an older building, a huge brick and stone monstrosity built over one hundred years ago. This sprawling labyrinth was built by an eccentric multi-millionaire, who had bought the island in the early 1800's. Parts of the foundation rested on an old prison complex built two hundred years prior. The wealthy millionaire had secret passages and hidden rooms built throughout the entire structure. This is the building Doc Titan had lived in for the first sixteen years of his life.

Doc, with his past familiarity of the island, was recommending a strategy to attack Wilder Island, now renamed Skull Island. Once more, he was proving himself as a capable leader of any gathering.

Doc indicated the west cliff face. "Pam, Cassie, and Megan. In this small depression on the west side of the island is a cliff of rock. At its base is an underwater entrance into a system of abandoned caves. The mouth of the cave is roughly thirty feet below the ocean's surface, so chances are good that it has not been discovered. Follow the tunnel upward and you should find a rock wall blocking the way. This was built when the plague started on the island, blocking off the tunnel route to the sea. This is where we've been told they are holding the prisoners."

"How do we reach the ocean from up here?" Pam asked.

Doc thumbed over his shoulder. "We have blue and white parachutes in that first cabin. They have a special coating that reflects surrounding light waves and color. While in the air, they should make you completely invisible from the island. When you reach the water, release the parachutes immediately. They are designed to disintegrate in water, so they can't be spotted floating on the surface."

Megan whispered to Cassie. "Hope it doesn't rain on the way down."

"Snorkels and diving gear are also in that cabin," Doc added.

Pam smiled. "Gotcha, Doc."

The three women left to change into their gear. Kong leaned close to Doc Titan and whispered.

"Doc, are you sure that the women should go down there? We could be facing some serious odds."

Doc shrugged. "The women have proven themselves capable and this is the least dangerous part of the invasion. Besides, if I try to leave Pam behind, she'll go anyway. That could spoil other carefully laid plans. We don't need any surprises."

Bart snorted. "Good point, Doc. What do you want us to do?"

"You men need to eliminate the threat of those two destroyers."

Kong elbowed Bart. "No problem. Bart you take the one on the right, I'll take the one on the left."

Bart laughed. "My left or your left?"

"We should have brought Monstro, your English mastiff. He'd just chew 'em up and spit 'em out."

"Nah. I've taught Duke to not eat garbage."

Doc ignored the tomfoolery. "Kong, Bart, Gibs, Wall, and Mick. We brought the Seablade for this part of the mission. Kong and I brewed up a little surprise for the crews of those two ships."

Gibs raised an eyebrow. "What's that?"

Kong flashed a huge smile. "Heck, that would spoil the surprise. We merely fixed up something that will help even the odds a bit. Let's get'er done, boys."

Doc indicated the thirteenth volunteer, with a nod of his forehead. "Campbell here has agreed to monitor the radios. Any problems, let him know."

"No problem, we'll give a shout if we run into trouble." Pam responded as she rejoined the men.

Bart and Kong, admitted skirt chasers, oggled the women as they re-entered the room. They were clad in skin-tight rubber suits that left very little to the imagination.

Pam sneered at the two men. "Eyes back in your heads, boys. Doc, when do we take off?"

"We give the Seablade crew a fifteen minute head start."

Gibs, Mick, and Wall had already climbed down into the submarine, bolted to the underside of the Windjammer. It was a tight fit for Wall, the huge electrical wizard. Kong and Bart prepared to follow. Simon Blake and Doc Titan were adjusting and tightening the straps to rather odd-looking backpacks. They were three feet long, metallic in appearance, tapered to a point at one end and with an exhaust port at the other.

Kong tapped one of the canisters. "Hey Doc. Isn't that one of those experimental jet packs you designed, like the one that Cliff Secord kid swiped from us? What'd he call hisself? Rocket-man or something. I didn't think they worked."

Blake looked a little concerned as he examined the metallic rocket pack. "What was wrong with them?"

Bart chuckled. "Not much. They had a tendency to explode, is all."

"And with all of that rocket fuel, it usually made one hell of a big bang." Kong made a booming noise and made motions with his hands, indicating a huge explosion.

Guardian looked questioningly at Doc Titan. Doc smiled and shrugged his shoulders. "I think I have all of the bugs worked out. The palm control has three speeds …"

Kong interrupted with more sarcasm. "Yeah, fast, faster, and 'Oh my god, I'm gonna die'."

Doc ignored Kong and continued. "Press a fourth time and the engine shuts off. Use your arms and body to steer your flight path."

Megan gave Luthor Gibson a firm embrace.

"I'll see you later, Luthor. Right?"

Luthor gave his agent a friendly smile. "Of course, darling. Be careful."

"Kong, is the Seablade prepped and ready to go?" Doc asked.

Kong gave him a thumbs-up. "You betcha, Doc."

Bart and Kong slid down the ladder and slammed the port shut, screwing it down tight. A few seconds later, Bart's voice came over the intercom.

"Ready when you are, Doc."

"Hang onto your hats, brothers." Doc warned. He pulled on a large lever and released the locking mechanism that docked the Seablade to the underside of the Windjammer. The Seablade hung suspended in space for half a second, then dropped like a stone. The Windjammer, relieved of its heavy cargo, weighing several tons, suddenly shot up a hundred feet higher in the air. Doc looked over the support rail and watched the Seablade vanish into the soft clouds.

Kong, Bart, Gibs, Wall, and Mick were strapped into seats bolted down to the deck. The G-forces of the freefall flight pushed them backwards. Gibs looked ill, more so than normal. Mick had his eyes squeezed shut and was saying a prayer. Bart simply and silently endured. Kong and Wall were having the time of their lives.

Kong was laughing hysterically. "Look, Ma, no hands."

Wall was grinning from ear to ear. "Most fun I've had since that Hell-Rocket thing back at your offices. When we get back to New York, you and I will have to wear that thing out."

"Heck you haven't even tried the freefall elevator we have, it's a blast," Kong hooted.

Wall shouted loudly, "Waahoo!!"

Gibs was turning green. "I'm too old for this. I think I'm going to be ill. How soon before we stop?"

"We'll be crashing into the water in five … four … three …" Kong counted down.

Bart crossed his arms in front of his face. "Shhiii …"

The Seablade had free-fallen from twenty thousand feet and struck the water at terminal velocity, around two hundred miles per hour. Even though the bow of the ship was designed to neatly cleave the water with minimum resistance, all five men were thrown forward against their harnesses with the greatly reduced forward momentum. It took several seconds to catch their breath.

Bart looked as white as a sheet. "Remind me to never do that again."

Gibs groaned miserably. "If I survive, I'll do just that."

Mick still had his eyes closed. "Is it over? Have we landed?"

Kong checked the dials and levers in front of him. "Yep, all systems are working and we can get under way. This ol' mudbucket can take anything we throw at her."

"That's good, because I'm about to throw my lunch at her." Gibs said weakly.

Kong chuckled. "Wonder how the girls are doing? Pam would have loved this ride!"

Chapter Sixty-One
War Clouds

April 13, 1945   10:30 am

Fifteen minutes had passed. Preston Stockbridge had been pacing the floor, anxious to see action, and more than a little worried about his friends.

Doc pointed at the three-dimensional image of the mountain hanger. "Stockbridge, when the Nazis discover they are being attacked, they will send every plane they have into the skies. You and Gibson were crack pilots years ago. Can you try to keep the airplanes from taking off? And can you still hold your own against a dozen veteran fliers, if they do get airborne?"

Scorpion sneered confidently. "It'll be no problem. And when I'm working, call me Scorpion."

Doc turned to Gibson. "When Scorpion begins his attack, Pam, Cassie, and Megan will begin their descent. Gibson, you need to take out the radio towers on both ships, so they can't call for assistance. And then assist Stock … Scorpion with the fighter planes. When you receive the signal from Kong, you need to drop your surprise on the two ships."

Gibson nodded. "Understood, Doc." He started to walk away and then turned back to Doc. "Just so you know, I've seen combat in the past. I've worked under the command of many brilliant men in battle. I've been hoping to return to combat since this war started. I've worked solo for a long time, John, and I suppose at times I don't play as well with others as I should. The main reason I'm taking orders from you now is because you are the best damn field commander I've ever known."

Doc was touched by Gibson's words of confidence. "Thank you."

"Oh, yeah, and thanks for the new goggles," he said, tapping the tighter-fitting glasses that Doc had cobbled together during their stop in New York.

"Scorpion, how soon will you be ready? Scorpion? Where did …" Guardian glanced around, searching.

The sound of plane engines firing came from below the zeppelin. With a pull of a lever, the small plane disconnected from the Windjammer. Scorpion flew forward half a mile then dove straight down toward the island, aiming directly for the stone mountain.

Guardian yelled into the radio. "Scorpion, what are you doing?"

Scorpion's laughter came over the airwaves. "Having fun, Simon."

Pam yelled into the transmitter. "You're going to kill yourself."

"Nah, I'm going to take care of that hanger in one sweep. I've always wanted to try this. I once saw my old pal G-8 try a similar maneuver. Darkness, get ready to attack the ships." Scorpion replied calmly.

Pam gave Doc a concerned look. "I really don't like the sounds of that."

The sound of a second plane engine firing up could be heard beneath the Windjammer.

Darkness' voice announced from the speaker. "Already on my way, Scorpion. You could have waited to hear the rest of the plan, you know."

Scorpion chuckled. "I'm not a planner, I merely follow my impulses."

The Scorpion's plane dove straight down, the engine whining heavily as it amplified the natural pull of gravity. Scorpion could feel the wings straining to resist the wind pressure. Downward and accelerating. The barometric altimeter counted down as the dial spun rapidly counterclockwise. Fifteen hundred, twelve hundred, nine hundred feet. The ground was approaching quickly.

Doc studied the three dimensional projection of Scorpion's plane. "The wings can't handle that much stress. You're going too fast! She'll break up!'"

"What are you doing, pull up or you'll crash!" Darkness warned him.

"That's the idea, old chum. Oh, by the way, Doc, sorry about the plane."

"What!?" Doc exclaimed loudly.

Scorpion's signal broke off and a morbid silence filled the large cabin of the Windjammer.

The cockpit cover was raised and the wind velocity sheared it off instantly. The Scorpion un-strapped his safety belt and crouched down on the ejector seat. As he pulled the lever, the seat sprang upward with bone-jarring force and propelled him high into the air. At this low altitude, the parachute would barely slow his speed before he hit the ground. It did manage to mushroom and for an instant he believed it would be sufficient. Then the silk fabric tore and the chute split in half. Scorpion jettisoned the white silk and flailing cords before he could become entangled.

The ejector seat crashed into the side of the cliff face at nearly two hundred miles an hour and disintegrated into minute pieces. He was only a hundred feet from the ground, and his cape was helping reduce his speed. Directly beneath the entrance to the hidden airplane hanger was a small lake. At the last possible second, he tucked his legs in and formed a ball shape with his body. Scorpion struck the water at nearly sixty miles an hour. At that speed, it was like hitting a concrete wall. There was a huge cascade of water marking his entry. A minute passed as the ripples lessened and then the lake surface was motionless.

At the very instant his body was striking the water, Stockbridge's plane crashed onto the tarmac of the runway. It hit at an angle and bounced several times, skipped across the surface like a stone thrown in a still lake. It skidded for fifty feet with a cascade of sparks, before coming to a rest in the middle of the cave. Scorpion's plane had narrowly missed every aircraft in the hanger. In a few minutes, the flight crews could have his craft dragged off of the field and would soon be airborne.

The nearest crewman walked close to the airplane. The fuel had not caught fire and there were no flames. He smiled to himself and muttered under his breath. "Stupid Americaner." On tiptoes, he was able to glance into the ruined cockpit. He was surprised to find no pilot in the downed craft. A small clock resting atop the dashboard attracted his attention. It was ticking and, as his eyes focused on it, a realization dawned. Three. Two. One.

The thunderous explosion seemed to rock the entire island. It was followed by several more, as the other planes caught fire and fuel storage containers joined the conflagrance. Scorpion's face had broken the surface of the pool of water the instant of the first explosion, as it threw a tongue of flame several hundred feet outward. It made him think of a dragon's breath. The ground began rumbling and the entire mountain collapsed under it own weight. A cloud of dust and smoke billowed out. The rock face that once resembled a skull was now only a pile of rubble. The airplane hanger was buried beneath a million tons of stone. A mischievous smile crossed Stockbridge's lips, even though it was obvious he was in pain. "Mission accomplished, folks. I took care of the airplane hanger and all of the planes. Consider my signal given."

Guardian shook his head in disbelief. "You are a madman."

Scorpion chuckled. "Yeah, but I finally got to blow something up. By the way, tell Kong I used most of the C-4 explosives." Scorpion laughed loudly and began swimming to shore. "God, I love this job."

Luthor Gibson, known to the underworld of crime as the Darkness, was a master pilot. In the Great War, he flew hundreds of dangerous missions, shooting down a record number of enemy planes. He went by the name Max Grant back then, but nobody ever knew if that was his true identity either. He tipped the nose of the plane toward the small cove at the southern end of Skull Island. In the half-moon cove were two large, dark objects. German battleships. Reputed to be the most disciplined and most dangerous crews on the seas. It had only been twenty seconds since Scorpion attacked the hidden airbase. Men were scurrying about the ships decks, preparing to repel attackers. They were confident in their skills. Their bluster would have faded slightly if they had been witness to Scorpion's kamikaze attack on the airbase.

The battleship commanders ordered the men to prepare to repel an attack from the center of the island or from the open outlet of the cove. While guns were trained in both directions, Darkness attacked in the center. He approached the island ten feet above the surface of the water, only increasing his elevation in time to miss the treetops that lined the shore. The powerful guns mounted to the front of his plane roared and the antennae of the first ship exploded into a shower of fragments. Seconds later, the antennae on the second ship followed suit.

A red light flashed on the console and Kong's voice came through the loudspeaker. "Luthor, we're set to go. Copy?"

Darkness pressed the transmitter button. "Understood. Beginning my strafing attack now."

Men scattered about the deck, trying to turn their defenses toward the attacker. A cheer rose from them as they saw gray-white smoke billowing from the tail of the aircraft. Someone must have shot the plane. The cheer was short-lived when the smoke reached them. Men began choking and coughing. Then they fell to the hard steel decks. The smoke was poison gas! Panic ensued. Those closest to the doorways bolted for the protection of the interior of the ship. Several men jumped overboard. The plane returned once more, spraying another cloud of quick death.

Scorpion was just reaching the edge of the cove when he saw Gibson start his third pass over the ships. He was close enough to see Gibson was looking out of the window, facing away from the island. Preston's eyes were drawn to a movement on the beach, three hundred feet away. A man was walking to the edge of the water with a tube in one hand. A rocket launcher. Stockbridge had only two rounds left in one of his automatics. He had met a great deal of opposition after leaving the lake. From this distance he couldn't be certain of killing the man before the rocket was launched. Then he did an odd thing. He aimed for a larger target, the Darkness' airplane.

The bullet struck the body of the plane, four feet behind the Darkness. Gibson turned and spotted Stockbridge immediately. Stockbridge was pointing his gun toward the beach. Gibson saw the man aiming the rocket launcher at his plane. Scorpion shot and half a second later the man collapsed. But the soldier had managed to pull the trigger first. The rocket shot away from the beach with lightning speed. Stockbridge screamed in frustration as he helplessly watched it climb toward the aircraft.

Gibson saw the approaching airborne death. "Oh, damn!"

The morning sky exploded with blinding force and Scorpion watched as fragments of the plane fell earthbound. Fiery comets of flame and debris struck the far side of the cove. Trees ignited as the high octane fuel splashed everywhere. Stockbridge stood in silent shock as he tried to grasp what had just occurred. He simply couldn't believe it.

Luthor Gibson, the Darkness, had been killed!

Chapter Sixty-Two
Attack on Skull Island

April 13, 1945   11:00 am

Doc Titan slipped on the compact rocket pack and adjusted the straps, pulling them tight around his large frame. He strapped a leather aviator's helmet over his shaved scalp.

"Campbell, any problems give a yell on the radio." Doc shook hands with the man. "And thanks for helping us today."

Campbell simply nodded. "No problem, old friend. And you're welcome."

"Guess it's our turn. You ready?" Doc asked Simon Blake.

Guardian's pale eyes reflected the large smile that his impassive face failed to display. "Adventure of a lifetime, right? Certain danger and possible death? Wouldn't miss it for the world. Can't let Stockbridge and Gibson have all of the fun. Let's do this."

Without any hesitation, the two men leapt from the open door and dropped into empty space. For several seconds of freefall, Blake enjoyed the blast of air on his face. Then he thumbed the throttle control button once. Instantly, he was propelled forward as the rocket pack ignited. Carefully moving the position of his arms, he turned to the right and climbed higher. He experimented for several seconds until he was comfortable with his flying abilities. The sensation was incredible, soaring through the clouds, weightless. Maneuvering required almost no effort at all. He was curious, so he thumbed the button twice more. After returning to the first speed, a moment later, he had to agree with Kong. Way too fast.

Doc Titan maneuvered close and they flew side by side. Simon Blake gave him a thumbs-up motion and they started down toward the island. With the sound of rushing air it was difficult to hear one another, so they used hand signals to relay information. They were descending toward the ocean on the west side of the island and leveled out approximately eighty feet from the blue waves.

As they passed over the roof of the main building, Doc Titan dropped a dozen thin-walled gas grenades at the feet of a score of soldiers on the left. Blake did the same with the soldiers on the right. Before the Nazis could react to their presence, the flying men were gone. The defenders had expected a ground attack, not a strafing from above. As the soldiers succumbed to the gas attack, Titan and Blake had already passed over the eastern shore of the narrow island.

In the time it took the two rocket-men to return to the rooftop, all of the soldiers were unconscious. They would wake up in three hours, none the worse for wear. Hopefully, the fighting would be over by then. A gigantic explosion came from the direction of the cove.

"Sounds like the Darkness is having fun." Blake motioned in the direction of the explosion. He removed his rocket-pack and flying gear and prepared to open the door leading down from the roof. Doc Titan placed one hand on his arm and motioned to him.

"There's a better way. This structure is honeycombed with secret passages and hidden rooms. If the Nazis haven't discovered them, we can avoid detection and a lengthy battle with the soldiers."

Doc approached a massive brick and stone chimney jutting through the roof's surface. He pushed hard against one wall and a doorway appeared in the pattern of the brick. A sturdy, steel ladder was bolted to the far wall of the interior of the chimney. Blake started down the ladder and Doc followed, closing the opening behind him. Once more the wall appeared to be quite solid, not even a minute crack showed where the door opening had been seconds earlier.

Doc whispered to Blake below him, "I often played in these tunnels and passages as a child. My father hated it, but never sealed them up."

Guardian descended into the core of the structure. "Why are they here?"

"This building was designed and built in the early 1800's by an eccentric, old millionaire. Designs were based on an ancient castle in Romania. He thought the rumor of the island being haunted was merely superstitious mumbo jumbo. What Percy calls Long Ju Ju." Doc explained.

"What happened to him?"

"Soon after the castle was completed, they found him dead, here on the island. Actually, the rumor was that they found him dead, all over the island. Something had ripped him into very small pieces."

"Sounds like the Wildman Curse I solved a few years ago. Turned out to be large rats." After a seconds pause, Blake added. "I'm certain those Wilders were no relation to you."

They finally reached the bottom rung. Doc thumbed his small flashlight to life.

"Looks like I spoke too soon," Doc whispered.

The steel ladder led down to a stone passageway. Across the corridor were twenty vertical iron bars, spaced every four inches, set into the floor and ceiling. Doc grabbed one of the bars and pulled, testing its strength. The inch and a half diameter bar moved slightly. He removed his long-sleeve shirt, folded it and tucked it into a pocket in his bullet-proof, utility vest.

Doc smiled. "No reason to ruin another shirt."

He grabbed the shaft again and applied leverage. With one arm he pulled toward himself, with the other he pulled down. The iron rod bowed slightly in the middle, making a grinding noise, as it pulled free from the ceiling. Doc's arm muscles bunched, the tendons resembling heavy piano wire. The average man would not have been able to budge the pole, much less bend it. However, Doc Titan was much more than the average man. With a final yank, he pulled the thick, iron bar free from its moorings. It was bent nearly double. He took several deep breaths and held up one hand.

"Guess I'm getting old. Give me a second and I'll pull out another."

"Let me give it a try." Blake removed his heavy jacket and placed it aside. He was also wearing a utility vest, much like Doc's. The white skin of his arms and shoulders were the same colorless hue as his undershirt.

Simon Blake had always been stronger than the average man. Much stronger. Now that the secrets of his unique physiology had been revealed, he understood why. He grabbed the next bar and braced himself. The shaft of iron bent and seconds later it lay on the ground next to the one Doc had removed.

Doc stared at Blake for a moment, amazed. "Okay, I'm impressed."

Blake picked up his jacket. They squeezed between the remaining bars and continued down the stone corridor. Doc held up his hand and motioned for silence. He slowly pushed against what appeared to be a solid stone wall. With a tiny click sound, it moved slightly. He pulled and a section of wall, as large as a man, swung inward. The room beyond was quite dark at first. After several seconds, as their eyes adjusted, they could make out a light entering from the far end of the room. It was rectangular in shape, three feet wide and five feet high. Doc flipped on the switch to a tiny flashlight and played it on the filthy, stone floor. They stepped over the bleached bones of a long-dead rat, around a steel lab stool, and toward the light. A small, flimsy curtain hung in front of the opening. Simon Blake drew it back and stared in amazement.

The rectangular opening was actually the back surface of a one-way mirror. The room beyond offered a perspective neither man had expected. It was like something from a science-fiction pulp novel. The room was thirty feet wide, sixty feet deep and twelve-foot tall ceilings. The main great room was beyond and was roughly twice as large.

Doc studied the layout. "This was the dining chamber. There is a large, open balcony above, overlooking the great room."

Blake continued staring at the contents of the connecting room.

Cylindrical glass containers, three feet in diameter and perhaps eight feet tall, filled the entire room. Brass straps circled and reinforced the glass at top, middle, and bottom. Hundreds of tubes and wires entered and exited the cylinders from every side. A thick, blue-green fluid undulated and swirled, completely filling each container. Faint lights swayed through the viscous material, making it difficult to clearly see the figures floating in each tank. Doc wiped dust and cobwebs from the surface of the mirror, improving the clarity. Blake sucked in a breath and held it. Infants, perhaps the age of a newborn child, hung suspended in each container. They were all perfectly developed males.

Guardian whispered. "What the hell ..."

Doc replied softly. "The Danner Journals. This is why they needed them. The Nazis and Black Skull are trying to breed an army of super-soldiers. And Kaine had the Journals."

"There are fifty of these ... incubators, Doc. Can you imagine an army of men, injected with the formula Danner created? They would be unstoppable."

He stepped away from the opening and stared into the darkness surrounding them. Doc was still studying every detail of the next room, through the mirror. Doc could not see Blake but he sensed something was wrong.

"Blake? What is it?"

Guardian spoke softly from the shadows. "Cover the mirror and flash your light over here."

Doc did as Blake instructed and found he was holding his breath. Obviously, Blake had discovered something important. The light played across the surface of a glass cylinder, similar to the ones in the next room. The technology was not as advanced. The materials were coated with years of dust and neglect. Blake leaned forward and stared through the filthy glass surface. He closed his eyes and a single tear ran down his cheek.

"They were telling the truth. This was the glass and steel womb I emerged from in 1938." Blake said softly.

He turned his back to the cylinder and looked about the room. His gaze rested on a rectangular object on a nearby lab table. Dust and cobwebs covered it. Blake wiped his palm across the glass surface, revealing a picture frame beneath the grime. A woman's face returned his wide-eyed stare. The woman's face from his dreams. The face he thought belonged to his wife, until he discovered she was a fictitious memory. But then, who was she?

"That's a photograph of my mother." Doc whispered. "She died the night I was born, January 1, 1900. The schooner, Prometheus, had docked in the southeast cove of Hydra Island, in the Aegean Sea off the coast of Greece. There was a terrible storm, the worst in a century. The boat smashed into a reef and was destroyed. Father found me and swam to shore. My mother's body was swept out to sea and never found."

Blake was numb. He blinked back a tear. "Doc, we don't have time for all of this. We need to finish our mission."

"You're right, Simon. Let's go."

They retraced their steps back to the stone doorway and re-entered the secret corridor. They had only gone thirty feet, about even with the room filled with cylindrical incubators, when they saw the wooden shipping crates. The flashlight played from box to box. These crates were relatively new, placed here only weeks ago. Minute quantities of a fine, light-colored powder dusted the stone floor. Doc pressed the end of his index finger into a small pile and sniffed. He sniffed again. He rubbed the finger with his thumb, testing the powder. Then he placed the finger to his tongue.

Doc looked at Blake. "Gelatin. Processed from a collagen of cattle or swine tissues and bone."

Blake began to question Doc's analysis, when something interesting caught his eye. He stooped behind one of the wooden crates. When he rose up again he was holding a broken child's doll. He looked past the doll's crushed body and at Doc, a realization playing in both of their eyes.

"Are you thinking what I'm thinking?" Blake asked.

"Yes. We might be too late. By now Pam should already be at the prison cells."

"Do you know how to get to Black Skull's quarters, Doc?"

"Follow me."

The men moved quickly but silently through the dark, hidden rooms and corridors. There wasn't much time. The path twisted and turned, but they knew speed was of utmost importance.

Kong opened the steel hatch to the Seablade and drew in a deep breath of air. Ten minutes ago, and half a mile away, the Darkness had been shot down and plunged comet-like to the earth. But Kong and the men aboard the Seablade were unaware of these details. Kong heard the distinct click of a large deck gun and slowly raised his massively muscled arms overhead.

"Don't you move, fella." came a voice. The nasally twang of a Boston New Englander was evident in the man's voice.

Kong shouted over his shoulder. "I'm American, don't shoot!"

Bart shouted from below, in the bowels of the submarine. "Who the heck are you talking to, bullet-head?"

Kong shouted back at Bart. "Your fans, why don't you come up and wave at them?' He smiled and added. "Bring your gun, Bart."

Another voice spoke behind Kong. "You must be Major Larson. And your friend down below must be Major Blackwell."

"What's happening up there, Kong?" Gibs said at Kong's feet.

Kong shrugged his wide shoulders. "I think we've traveled back in time … and to another war."

Kong slowly turned around, with his arms still raised high. A pleasantly gruff-looking young man was smiling and motioning for his men to lower their firearms. An unlit cigar was clenched tightly between his teeth. Several other young men were gathered at the front of the little PT boat. The PT boats were small, fast vessels known as motor torpedo boats or Patrol Torpedo - PT's for short. They were fairly unknown craft until one torpedo boat, designated PT-109, was cut in half by a Japanese destroyer *Amagiri* on August 2, 1943. Lieutenant John Fitzgerald Kennedy and eleven other sailors served on board. Their story became legend.

"Sergeant Richard Gunn, at your service, sir. These guys are nicknamed *'The Mosquito Fleet.'* I think it's 'cause they bite and flee."

Kong stared at the grinning man curiously. "How do you know us?"

Gunn beamed brightly. "Heck. My old man served with you fellas in the Great War. As a young man, I read about your exploits in his journals." Kong wasn't certain if he should be flattered or insulted. "Are you guys the reason the destroyers are dead in the water?" Kong stepped out on the small deck of the sub and allowed the other men to emerge from below. The young soldiers aboard the PT boat gawked openly when Wall squeezed his gargantuan frame through the small hole. "It's like a circus clown car. How many of you guys are in that little bathtub?"

Bart held up his hand. "One question at a time, son. Yes, we are the reason the battleships are silent. One of our men flew over the ships and strafed them with a knockout gas. They probably thought it was some kind of poison."

Mick added. "When they ran inside the ships they encountered the knockout gas we had pressure-pumped in through the lower bilge pumps. They'll all be sleeping peacefully for the next two days."

Gunn stomped one foot. "Hot Damn! That should make the clean-up a lot easier. And it looks like the big boys just arrived."

An enormous gray ship appeared at the entrance to the island cove. An American battleship.

Wall shaded his eyes and addressed Gunn. "Great, you brought back-up. Will one battleship be enough?"

Gunn laughed loudly. "You're thinking too small, big fella. We have half of the American and English fleet parked around this island."

Kong accepted Gunn's extended hand and boarded the PT boat. "How about giving us a ride to shore then? There are probably a couple hundred Nazis on the island we should say hello to."

Gunn saluted him. "No problem, Major Larson. Mind if I go with you guys? It'd be a great honor to fight alongside you men."

"Just don't ask for my autograph, kid." Kong replied gruffly.

Cassie's head surfaced in the dark waters of the dank cavern. Sunlight filtered into the large natural cathedral from the cave opening behind her. Pam and Megan surfaced next to her, treading water quietly. She slowly made her way to a rusty ladder attached to an ancient walkway next to the water's edge. At one time this was all part of a prison complex. The convicted men would be brought in through the tunnel and led to this location, where they would leave the world of sunlight, perhaps forever. From all appearances, this entire island prison had been abandoned for nearly three hundred years. Several cave-ins had occurred and blocked natural passages through the mountainside.

According to Doc, there was still a hidden tunnel that would lead them to the cells. Unless there had been other cave-ins, leading to more structural damage. Or if the Nazis had already discovered the hidden passageways and blocked them. Doc, had, against his father's wishes, snuck away occasionally and explored these caves and tunnels. Perhaps he had studied the confined cells and horrible conditions that the prisoners had to endure and this was one of his reasons to finance the Titan Rehabilitation Institute and Clinic.

Pam whispered, but her voice still carried further than anticipated. "Looks abandoned, still. Doc was right."

Cassie nodded in agreement. "We just need to find the passageway up to where they are keeping the prisoners."

The three women removed their swimming gear and changed into the dry clothes that they removed from sealed backpacks. In separately sealed bags, they retrieved their various firearms. Now they were prepared to infiltrate the enemy's lair. Several tunnels led to dead ends and they were forced to backtrack. The dust on the floor confirmed that nobody, except perhaps Doc as a young man, had used these tunnels for over a hundred years. Several cells had barred entrances that were rusted off their hinges, doubtlessly caused by the salty moisture from the underground cavern. The doors hung askew or were lying on the floor. Megan gasped when she found she had stepped on the brittle wrist of a skeleton, extending through the bars as though grasping for freedom. The bones crunched dryly under her boot heel. In several more dark cells, skeletons lay on their beds, resting eternally.

"Poor souls. Think they were abandoned here to die?" Megan asked.

Pam nodded. "According to Doc, an epidemic broke out and the entire complex was evacuated almost overnight. Hundreds of sick men were left behind."

"Without any medical assistance, that probably didn't take long." Cassie added.

Megan wiped cobwebs from her fingers. "And the prison was never reopened?"

Pam stepped past the cells. "France and England were at war and the entire island was more or less forgotten. The few seafarers who had it marked on their charts, knew about the plague and avoided the place at all costs."

Megan repeated herself, "Poor souls."

They pressed on and soon found a light, filtering in from a distant wall. As stealthily as possible, they advanced. The illumination was coming from between the joints of several stones. One smaller block, about knee-high, was loose and the weak mortar was soft and pliable. Grasping the edges, Pam was able to remove the stone without making noise. She knelt down and peered through the empty hole, Megan and Cassie close beside her. Their view was perfect. They were on the farthest end of the cellblock, where illumination was almost non-existent.

Close to their position was the door leading to the room where Black Skull had tortured Big Tom and Percy, and killed Gabe Robinson, however, they did not know of this situation yet. At the far end of the room was the only exit, guarded by two large men, in full Nazi dress uniform. These men stood unflinchingly at attention. To fail at guarding the prisoners meant certain death; a great motivation for doing their duty correctly.

As the women whispered in the dark recesses, a plan was agreed upon. A few more blocks were removed from the wall, creating a larger opening. Cassie squeezed through and crouched low to the ground. In the darkness, she was invisible. She gave a thumbs-up and entered the doorway to the dark room. Her eyes adjusted to the dismal lighting as she narrowly avoided running into a darkly stained chair. She took her place along the wall, next to the door.

Thump. Thump. Thump. The two guards looked at one another and then looked to the far end of the room. As they both moved forward, it became obvious the noise was coming from the last room in the cell block. They un-slung their rifles and approached cautiously, uncertain what to expect. Nobody had entered the cell block past them, so what could be making that noise? *Thump. Thump. Thump.* As they passed the cells, one guard noticed Isabelle in the shadows of her cell, glaring at them with death in her eyes. Her husband's dead body was still covered by a simple coat, two cells away. Ruthlessly murdered by Totenkopf. At least she had stopped those infernal crying and moaning noises, the guard thought to himself.

He reached in and flipped on the light switch. Cassie grabbed the first man and yanked him forward, off balance. Her boot struck the temple of the second man and he dropped to his knees. Several blows later and he fell unconscious. Before she could return her attention to the first guard, the butt of his rifle struck the back of her head. She went to her knees, her senses swimming. She knew he was about to strike her again, but her body failed to move. The sound of electricity filled the air for several seconds and the guard fell to the ground next to Cassie. The back of his coat was smoking and the smell of ozone filled the air. She slowly turned and saw Megan standing behind her with a large grin on her face and one of Gibs' electrical guns clutched in her hand.

"I like these guns. I wonder if Gibs would let me keep one, after this is all over? I know a few social octopuses I would like to use this thing on. You know the type, one drink and they're all hands."

"I'll make sure it happens." Cassie's skull ached. "Geez, I HATE getting hit on the head. I'm glad I have a thick skull. If I didn't, I would be falling out of chairs and putting my dresses on backwards by now."

Pam helped her to her feet. "Sorry I didn't make it sooner, I got stuck in the hole for a second."

Cassie rubbed her skull and roughly kicked the offending guard in the head. "Hope you wake up with a nasty headache, jerk!" With the lights on she noticed the fresh blood stains on the chair and shivered.

As they exited the room, after binding the unconscious guards, Cassie saw that the hole in the wall was much bigger now, to accommodate Pam's larger frame. Cassie carried the keys to the cell block and unlocked Isabelle's cell first. Her friend ran into her arms and seized her in a firm grip. The ebony hands were shaking and tears poured down Isabelle's face. Finally, she was able to speak.

Isabelle sobbed to the pretty blonde. "Oh, Cassie. My Gabe, they … kil …" She was unable to finish her sentence.

Megan had already taken the keys and unlocked the next cell, containing Whitney Van Pelt and Rav Chandra. Whitney finished Isabelle's incomplete sentence.

"They killed him. Black Skull shot him. His body is in the next cell." Whitney said reverently.

Cassie's eyes teared up and she held her friend. Any words of comfort that she could speak would be meaningless to the grieving woman at this time, so she simply rocked Isabelle in her arms. Pam unlocked the next cell as Whitney continued explaining the events of the last few days. In the last cell was the quiet man, who simply watched without comment.

"They tortured Big Tom and Percy for information. When they refused to answer, Black Skull threatened to kill Gabe. And then he did."

Pam had unlocked the chains holding the first man hanging from the prison bars and she lowered him gently to the ground. He was either unconscious, or worse. She wanted to remove the hood but was afraid of what she would see. She stood back up and started unbinding the other man. Megan knelt next to the covered body of Gabe Robinson. She pulled back the blood-caked coat that was draped over his still form. Isabelle stepped forward and lovingly cradled the dead man's cold hand in hers. Something was wrong. She pulled away and the palm of her hand was painted a darker umber. Makeup. The man beneath the coat was not a black man. Not her husband. Her face showed surprise, then realization.

"Pam, don't … !" Isabelle shouted.

Her warning came an instant too late. The second bound man had already fallen forward into her strong arms. As she supported him, his hand drifted out and grasped her large revolver. He shoved her away hard and held the gun pointed directly at her beautiful face. He raised his other hand and yanked the hood away, dramatically revealing his obsidian countenance. Black Skull stood glaring at them.

Chapter Sixty-Three
Final Reckoning (Project Gladiator Revealed)

April 13, 1945   12:15 pm

The fireplace mantle moved silently, swinging into the dimly lit room. Simon Blake and Doc Titan entered the private quarters of Black Skull, with weapons drawn and safety triggers off. Totenkopf was standing before a large window overlooking the island and the burning airplane hanger built into the side of the mountain. The stone cliff face had fractured and crumbled, no longer resembling a skull. Fryderyk Chopin's famous Piano Sonata No. 2, sometimes known as the Funeral March, was playing loudly in the background. Totenkopf appeared to be totally oblivious to the danger lurking several feet behind him. His hands were crossed behind his back, locked together, and his stance was a relaxed military position. Blake stealthily crept upon the figure of Black Skull. He could hear Totenkopf breathing through the obsidian face mask. He placed the barrel of his gun against the back of Totenkopf's head and one hand on his back.

"Don't move a muscle." Guardian warned.

Black Skull tensed, but did exactly as he was instructed. Blake was impressed by Totenkopf's calm demeanor. Anyone else would have jumped reflexively.

Guardian continued. "Turn around slowly. Don't tempt me to save America the chance to try you for war crimes. I'd gladly put a bullet in the back of your head for all of the trouble you've caused. All of the people you've killed."

Black Skull spoke calmly. "Don't shoot. You'll regret it if you do. And so will I, Simon."

Doc Titan aimed his firearm at Totenkopf. "You're in no position to threaten …" He stopped speaking as he noticed Blake had holstered his pistol. Blake nodded at Doc to lower his weapon as well. "What are you doing? Do you know who this man is?"

A voice came from behind them, as the door swung open. In the opening stood … Black Skull! Behind Totenkopf stood fifteen men, armed with German-style machine guns. As he stepped forward, the soldiers filed into the room.

"I admit I am also curious to know who this man is. This imposter who has been masquerading as me for the last two days. Remove that mask. Now!" Black Skull commanded.

Black Skull had suffered much embarrassment, being chained in a cell, and having someone impersonating him. His usual calm manner was cracking and anger was welling up. Beneath his black death mask, Totenkopf's face was flushed bright red. Over the imposter's shoulder, Black Skull could see the dark smoke of burning fuel from the destroyed airfield. The skull-faced cliff that he had admired was buried under tons of rock and debris.

The imposter reached behind his head, pulling apart the seam at the rear of the mask, and removed the dark face covering. There were several shocked expressions in the room, but none more so than the true Black Skull. Gabe Robinson smiled mischievously as he taunted the Nazi mastermind.

"Bet it kinda gets your goat, knowing that a member of an 'inferior race' has been masquerading as you for the past six days and nobody could tell the difference. By the way, your taste in music stinks. If I had to listen to that damn funeral march one more time …" Gabe reached out and dragged the needle of the record player across the face of the spinning vinyl disk, scratching and marring the grooved surface, a loud grating sound issuing from the speaker.

Black Skull began to reach for his pistol, but regained control and spoke to his troops. "Bring in the other two prisoners."

Two large men were forced into the room. These were the silent giants who had posed as Totenkopf's personal bodyguards, Ernst and Orban, for the last two days. Both were clubbed with gun butts and knocked to their knees. Totenkopf reached out and removed the black leather masks that covered their faces. The large Australian Big Tom and the gaunt Percy smiled up at Doc.

"Hey Doc, Simon, it's good to see you guys." Big Tom waved.

"Glad you could join the party, Doc." Percy was perspiring heavily. He was wearing several layers of clothes to appear bulkier.

Black Skull slapped Percy hard across the face. "Silence." With a nod of his head, several men stepped forward and pointed the business end of their machine guns at Big Tom and Percy. "You will drop all of your weapons or these two men will die before your eyes."

Doc and Blake could tell by the look in his eyes that Black Skull was not bluffing. Their weapons clattered on the floor. "I don't know how you overpowered me in the prison, but I am in control again. First, I have some unfinished business." He pulled out his revolver and pointed it at Gabe Robinson. Before he could squeeze the trigger, Simon Blake stepped between them. As Totenkopf hesitated for a second, Doc stepped in front of Blake. The tension in the room was thick enough to cut with a knife. From the doorway came a hesitant voice.

"I beg your pardon, Herr Totenkopf, for this intrusion." Professor Schmidt said timidly. "You asked me to inform you when the final phase was ready." Schmidt looked round the room and his gaze fixed on Doc Titan. Doc was staring back at Schmidt but turned away before it became obvious. He had discovered a mind-boggling secret and it would prove disastrous if revealed.

Black Skull sheathed his pistol and addressed Doc and Blake. "Another time. There are more pressing matters." He addressed his men. "Bring them. Watch them carefully." Doc, Blake, and Gabe were searched for weapons. They were prodded by machine guns as they walked alongside Big Tom and Percy. Pam, Cassie and Megan were several steps ahead. Isabelle, Whitney and Rav Chandra had been locked back into their cells.

As Black Skull walked down the hallway with Schmidt, several yards ahead of the prisoners, he whispered to the professor. "I have been held captive for the last six days by those men. Did the man masquerading as me ask you to do anything? Anything I should know about?"

Schmidt nodded. "Nein, Mein Herr. He simply asked me to keep him updated on the progress of Project Gladiator."

Black Skull's eyes burned. "So Kaine was able to find the missing page of the Danner Journals?"

"Ja. Professor Walters and I have already checked the formula and all appears to be in perfect order."

"Good." Black Skull was quiet for a minute as if he was lost deep in thought. "How did they overpower us in the prison?"

Schmidt shrugged his shoulders. "I was knocked unconscious. Perhaps one of the men had a gas grenade hidden on their body. When I woke up, you were standing over me and asking if I was okay. The guards were dragging out the covered body of the man you shot. I assumed that the gas had not affected you. I did not know of the deception. Do you think Kaine was involved? He made quite a scene yesterday about visiting the prisoners."

Black Skull's eyes narrowed. "I think it's time to dissolve our relationship with Herr Kaine. He cannot be trusted." He was quiet for a few seconds and then added. "I am glad you are well, Schmidt." Professor Schmidt was touched by this comment. For a man like Totenkopf, this was not easy, admitting concern for another human being.

A man approached with a clipboard tucked beneath his uniformed arm. He saluted Totenkopf and clicked his heels together. "Heil, Black … "

Black Skull interrupted, "Do you have a message from the destroyers?"

"Jawohl, Mein Kommandant. I contacted the naval officers of the destroyers as you requested. They reported that all attackers have been destroyed. It was only a few airplanes and a single submarine. The legions of storm-troopers on the island are on full alert."

Totenkopf nodded at the good news. "Any message from Count Drakoft?"

"Jawohl. He reports that the mission was a complete success. And that Sentry and Kid Sentry were killed during the conflict."

Black Skull's eyes narrowed. "Very good. Excellent." He stroked the chin of his mask and pondered for a moment. "Just in case we are attacked again, send word to Count Drakoft to leave immediately. I want him, and all of the military forces that he can muster, to be here within 24 hours."

The radio operator left on his assigned mission. Totenkopf leaned toward Professor Schmidt and whispered. "I want him to bear witness to the success of Project Gladiator. He has always considered himself better than I, simply because of his family name. I wish to rub his smug, mongrel nose in it." Totenkopf turned his attention to his prisoners. "Your friends are dead, your cause is a lost one. With the success of Project Gladiator, the Third Reich will rule the world." Without waiting for a response Totenkopf turned and walked away.

Big Tom tensed, as though considering attacking his guards. Blake placed his hand on the large man's powerful shoulder. He motioned for Big Tom to wait.

Blake whispered. "Let this play out. Something is about to happen."

"What's going on chief?" Gabe asked.

"I can't explain now, you'll just have to trust me."

Big Tom looked at Doc, who nodded in agreement of Blake's assessment. The guards behind them shoved hard and demanded they start walking. For a brief instant, Doc's gaze met Professor Schmidt's once more.

Count Drakoft snatched the message from Schuster's hand. His hand shook with fury when he read the command sent by the arrogant Black Skull.

Leave for Skull Island immediately. Bring all available troops, naval and air support. Project Gladiator must be defended at all costs.

In his other hand, Drakoft held reports from military sources throughout Europe. Adolf Hitler had already moved to the Führerbunker, located fifty feet below the Chancellery buildings in Berlin. The Eastern Front had been relatively stable since the end of Operation Bagration in late 1944, however, the Germans had lost Budapest and most of Hungary. Romania and Hungary were forced to surrender and declare war on Germany. On March 30th the Russians had entered Austria. By April 1st, 1945, the Russians were outside Berlin and captured Vienna on April 13th.

American newspapers announced the death of U.S. President Franklin D. Roosevelt; and that he was succeeded by his Vice-president, General Harry S. Truman. Truman boldly announced that the war would be over in mere weeks. Count Drakoft could see that Berlin would soon be captured, and with that the Third Reich would fall. The thousand-year Reich imperium that Adolf Hitler prophesized had lasted for only twelve years, and fifty million people were dead.

Black Skull was a fool. An insane, mongrel-blooded fool. Did he seriously believe that after betraying him to the Allied forces, Drakoft would simply follow his new orders? Drakoft smiled, his dark, leather mask creaking with the movement.

"Schuster, send the following message. *'Message understood. Leaving immediately with massive military force. Will arrive within 24 hours.'* That's all."

Schuster began tapping out the short, coded message and minutes later he received a response.

"The message has been acknowledged, Herr Drakoft."

"Very good, Schuster."

Without any warning, Count Drakoft drew his C69 Broomhandle Mauser from its holster and aimed at the radio transmitter/receiver. He did not stop shooting the semi-automatic pistol until the clip was empty. Schuster watched with wide-eyed amazement. Sparks and flames issued from the ruined radio.

"Schuster, I believe its time to pack our belongings and visit my villa compound in South America."

"But Black Skull is expecting …"

"Expecting me to follow his orders. Well, I've had enough of Black Skull, Adolf Hitler, and the Third Reich. The First Reich (or Empire) was the Holy Roman Empire, which existed from the time of Charlemagne 800 to 1806, a thousand years. The Second Reich was the German Empire of 1871-1918, created by Otto von Bismarck and lasting only 47 years. This Third Reich has lasted a total of twelve, mostly thanks to Hitler and Black Skull. Perhaps it is time to look to the future, instead of the past. One day I will return here and the world will tremble in fear before me."

Count Drakoft's insane laughter filled the large, empty castle, reverberating from the cold stone walls.

৵❖❖৵

Victor Kaine stared at Xena and Hermia standing in the corridor outside of his quarters. The corner of his lip pulled up on one side into a smirk. Earlier, he had felt the ground shake from the attack on the airplane hanger. But he did not seem disturbed with the possibility that they were under possible invasion. He knew Black Skull had the defenses to hold off an attack from outside of the island. But could he defend it from within?

Victor clasped his hands behind his back and addressed his bodyguards. "Ladies, I believe the time has come to dissolve our relationship with Black Skull and his Third Reich. I have a surprise for our ebony-faced friend."

As if on cue, two Nazi soldiers appeared at the far end of the hallway. Black Skull had issued a summons for Kaine. He wished for Kaine to be present during the final phase of Project Gladiator. This was the moment Victor Kaine had been awaiting. He removed a small box from his shirt pocket. Under a protective glass cover was a red button. This was his secret weapon.

Kaine, Hermia, Xena and the two guards entered the large main room of the laboratories. Much to his surprise, Doc Titan, the Guardian and several of their compatriots were gathered at the center of the great room. At the edge of the balcony, above the great room, were Black Skull, Professor Schmidt, and fifty Nazi soldiers, armed with machine guns. The guns were aimed at the gathering below. He noticed Orban and Ernst were missing, but was completely unaware of the deception that had taken place for the last several days. Kaine began to approach the stairs leading to the balcony. Black Skull removed his Luger P08 pistol from its black leather holster and leveled it at Kaine.

"Kaine. Stay where you are, with the other prisoners."

Kaine's face reddened with indignity. "What?!"

"Your usefulness to the Third Reich and myself has come to an end. We now possess the complete Danner Formula and no longer need your pathetic help. Our partnership is at an end, Kaine."

"Bastard! You shall regret …" Black Skull pulled the trigger of his pistol and Kaine was thrown back as a bullet tore at the top of his shoulder. He appeared more upset than injured.

"Guards, if he says another word, kill him." Totenkopf stated calmly.

Black Skull turned his gaze away from the prisoners below and questioned Professor Schmidt, at the top of the stairs. "Are you prepared? Is everything ready?"

"Yes, Herr Totenkopf." Schmidt stated.

"Very good." Turning to his captives, Totenkopf leered viciously, and started down the stairway. "And now, ladies and gentlemen, you shall all be witness to one of the greatest advances in the history of mankind. I shall throw this main switch and a new race of superior men shall be born this day. Fifty soldiers, loyal only to the Third Reich and myself. Supermen. Supersoldiers. Each with the strength of twenty men. They will be a military force that cannot be halted. Europe and the Allied Forces will fall beneath their booted heels, followed by America. Within the year, Germany will control and dominate the entire world."

"And then what?" Doc solicited Skull.

Totenkopf frowned at the question. "Explain your inquiry, Herr Titan."

Doc took a step forward. "After you conquer every country in the world, what do you do with these supersoldiers? Can you simply turn them off? Do you enslave anyone you deem inferior? Or just use your 'ultimate solution' and kill millions of defenseless people? Mankind has never been content being shackled. There will always be revolts. You will never know peace, never be able to rest. Right through might always fails. The question would-be world conquerors always seem to ask is *can* I enslave, *can* I defeat, *can* I conquer. But the simple question they always seem to miss is, *should* I? You are walking a dangerous trail, Totenkopf. It will not end well. It never has and it never will."

Totenkopf stared at Doc Titan for a long moment, as if contemplating the words Doc had spoken. Then his eyes narrowed and he replied coldly. "You are a fool, Herr Titan. I will not debate this with you. You waste my time with such questions." His gaze turned to his soldiers on the balcony. "If Titan speaks again, shoot his friends."

Black Skull finished walking down the stairs, with Professor Schmidt beside him and approached the control panel. His dark mask seemed almost animated with life. "Professor Schmidt, is all ready?"

"Jawohl, Mein Herr. You simply need to pull the switch." Schmidt instructed.

"Totenkopf, don't throw that switch." Guardian warned.

Black Skull raised an eyebrow. "Are you threatening me, Herr Blake?"

Guardian replied coldly. "Consider it a final warning."

Big Tom leaned toward Gabe and whispered. "Bet he throws the switch."

Gabe smiled. "Don't they always? The chief always warns them and they *still* do it."

The main switches were thrown and beneath their feet the thrum of generators could be felt coming alive. Static electricity filled the air and the smell of ozone permeated the large room. The gaze of everyone in the room was drawn to the glass cylinders that lined one wall. Suspended in a thick green-blue liquid were small humanoid bodies, barely discernable through the fluid. Even though the images were distorted, they appeared to be infants. There were a total of fifty of the glass tubes. As the dynamos below reached top speeds, Black Skull grabbed the last switch and pulled it down. Instantly, the cylinders began glowing, as if infused with liquid effervescence. The dark fluid lightened to an ocean-water color and then to a bright yellow. The liquid grew brighter still until the intensity of the light hurt the eyes. Totenkopf's evil obsidian mask seemed to glow and madness showed in his eyes. The surface of the liquids began to bubble and boil as the temperatures and pressure rose.

The light spectrum reached ultraviolet wavelengths and sonoluminescence began occurring. Sonoluminescence is the emission of short bursts of light from imploding bubbles in a liquid when excited by sound. The temperatures continued to rise to the point where steam rose from the water. The shadowy, silhouetted figures in each container moved and danced in the rising bubbles. They began to grow noticeably larger in size. The limbs moved with what might be considered the beginnings of life. Black Skull laughed and rubbed his hands together, resembling the comical villains of black and white silent movies.

Doc Titan noticed a change in the nearest cylinder. The figure contained in its bowels began to appear translucent. It had discontinued much of its earlier movement. The yellowish-white clear fluid began to turn red. Totenkopf had reversed the switches at Schmidt's direction and the noise level in the room greatly diminished. The turbines below ceased the ominous rumbling sound. All eyes were focused on the glass cylinders. In the nearest one, the liquid had continued to change color. At first it looked like this was simply part of the scientific process. Puff! A delicate-sounding explosion occurred in the tube and suddenly it was filled with what appeared to be remains of a human body. The next container followed suite. And another. And another. The room was filled with this disgusting sound as one cylinder after another met with a similar fate. The small body parts seemed to melt and dissolve completely in the super-heated liquids.

Black Skull stood quietly for a long moment. His mouth hung open slightly, his countenance - a grinning skull. He had just witnessed the grand finale of what he thought would be his triumphant moment of greatness. Single-handedly, he could have provided the fighting force that might have turned the final outcome of World War II. His super-soldiers would have been unstoppable. He closed his mouth and breathed deeply. His features maintained their calm composure as he turned away from the cylinders. His expressionless voice was as dead as the mask he wore when he looked at Professor Schmidt. "What is this? What just happened?"

Professor Schmidt looked directly into Totenkopf's eyes and ... smiled! He showed absolutely no fear of this dangerous megalomaniac. Black Skull was completely taken aback, he had expected groveling and begging. "Off-hand, I would say this charade has come to an end." All indications of his German accent were gone. As were his stooped shoulders. He took one step forward and drove his fist deep into Totenkopf's midsection, then pulled back and punched him with the other fist. Totenkopf doubled over with the wind knocked out of his lungs. With all of his body behind the blow, Schmidt smashed his right fist to the underside of Totenkopf's jawbone. Totenkopf dropped like a lifeless stone to the floor and did not move. "Check and mate. You'll never believe how long I've wanted to do that. Very satisfying." Schmidt smiled widely and looked toward Doc Titan.

Before anything else could be said or done, the Nazis on the balcony recovered from their shock. Fifty machine guns were leveled at the men and women on the laboratory floor, prisoners once more. The commanding officer of the platoon warned, "If anyone moves, I will issue the command to open fire."

Simon Blake stepped forward and confidently replied. "I think not. If you do, everyone in this room will die horribly."

The officer sneered in contempt. "And how would that happen?"

An audible click was heard and sound of terrified gasps filled the room. The deaths head bombs, epoxied to the throats of each soldier, had been activated. The small flashing light blinked like a terrifying one-eyed creature. "I discovered the frequency that Black Skull used on the deaths head bombs. Every bomb in the room has been activated. All I need to do is push this small red button and every soldier here will suffer that ghastly death. You have five seconds to drop your weapons." Gabe Robinson had carefully slipped the activator control to Blake while they were still in Totenkopf's private quarters.

"You're bluffing." The officer stammered, but looking into those ice-cold eyes and expressionless face, he knew otherwise. "Men drop your weapons."

Victor Kaine had nearly been forgotten in all of the activity. Now he was a blur of movement. He grabbed the Luger pistol from Black Skull's waistband, turned and hit Blake hard, creasing the side of his skull and knocking him to the ground. He caught the activator with the red button in mid-air. As Guardian started rising to his knees, Kaine leveled the gun between Blake's eyes. Nearly everyone in the room jumped as the first shot struck him squarely in the forehead, followed rapidly by five more shots in the chest. Blake slumped to the ground and didn't move.

Cassie screamed in horror. "Simon!"

"Shut up! You gentlemen on the balcony. If you'll notice, now I have the control box. Pick up your guns and kill Doc Titan and all of his friends. Now!" As the soldiers retrieved their guns, Victor met Doc's gaze. "Sorry, but you are much too dangerous to be allowed to live. Aiieee!!" His eyes became huge as he dropped the automatic pistol and the small black box. His left hand reached down and grasped the handle of the knife buried in his thigh. He pulled but the point of the razor-sharp blade was deeply embedded and he could not remove it. The Guardian easily caught the black box before it hit the ground. Kaine stared down at Blake as if he were the devil himself. He had just shot this man point blank six times, once in the forehead! It was impossible for him to still be alive! Blake got to his feet and rubbed the dented, but undamaged, skin on his pale forehead. He glanced around and saw everyone staring at him in astonishment.

Guardian shrugged his shoulders. "Guess I'm bulletproof. Who knew? It's been a hell of a week."

Kong entered the great room and waved his smoking machine gun pistol around. He noticed the soldiers on the balcony had their hands raised overhead in surrender. "Heck, looks like I'm too late. We've been shooting it out with Nazi troops. The entire island was a battlefield. Rick Gunn and his boys are rounding up the last of them." His shirt was torn and hanging in pieces. His face was smeared with gunpowder and mud, making him look more savage than ever. Across his chest were ammunition belts and several grenades hung from his waistbelt. Kong looked very pleased with himself.

Big Tom and Kong grabbed Kaine by the arms and roughly hauled him to his feet. He was still staring in disbelief at Blake. Suddenly, his eyes narrowed and a deep growl came from his throat. Despite the fact that he had been shot and stabbed in the past few minutes, Kaine pulled loose from Kong's grasp. With his free hand, he clubbed Big Tom on the side of the skull, momentarily dazing him. He then managed to drive his sharp elbow to the back of Kong's thick neck. He struck with such brutal force, both large men fell to their knees. Before anyone else could react, Kaine vanished through an open doorway.

"I'll get him." Kong was on his feet and running after Kaine, when Doc placed his hand firmly on Kong's shoulder, stopping him.

"Look at your belt, Kong."

Kong stared at the two grenade pins hanging from his belt.

"Blazes, he's got two handgren … " The explosion drowned out the rest of Kong's words in mid-sentence.

Billowing smoke poured in through the collapsed doorway. One of the glass and metal cylinders toppled as a supporting leg gave way. It slammed against the next and began a domino effect. Half a dozen containers smashed together and hundreds of gallons of yellow-red liquid splashed across the floor of the room. The doorway was completely blocked.

Doc Titan turned to Kong. "I know where Kaine is heading. I can outrace him, cut him off. You guys stay here and watch the prisoners." Before Kong could reply, Doc took two bounding steps, leapt to the balcony fifteen feet overhead and was gone.

Chapter Sixty-Four
Shadow and Sunlight

April 13, 1945 1:00 pm

Doc Titan followed Victor Kaine's trail into the catacombs of the ancient ruins. These structures had been here for centuries, nobody knew exactly who had built them. The records from the old prison architects stated that they had been constructed nearly a thousand years ago. Percy, the groups treasure hunter, would give a year of his life to examine them. And since the island would no longer be a secret after this battle, there would be no reason he wouldn't be able to stay and excavate. Doc had been banned from playing here as a child, as the crumbling old buildings were hazardous. Doc smiled at this thought. With all of the perils and dangers he had faced in the last dozen years, decrepit buildings seemed rather boring, not dangerous.

He had followed Kaine to the entrance leading underground, but now couldn't decide how to pursue him. The caves produced false echoes and reverberations that distorted every sound. Doc cranked the small generator on the end of his miniature flashlight and played it around on the floor. Most of the surface was solid rock but occasionally he would spot a footprint in a patch of dust or dirt. Following the trail was a slow business because there were alternate routes throughout the labyrinth and Doc had to find some kind of mark or clue to decide which one to take. More than once he had to backtrack and take another route when he discovered he had chosen wrong. It quickly became obvious to him that Victor Kaine was not following a path to an escape. Instead, he was lost in the winding catacombs.

Six shots rang out behind Doc and, as he felt the impact of each bullet, he staggered forward. His head began spinning dizzily. Something wet and warm was flowing down his back where his shirt had torn and tattered. Then he was numb from the waist down. He looked up, expecting to see Kaine standing above him. This man who rarely showed surprise, was taken off guard completely. A silhouette of shadow separated from the cold cavern walls and took solid form. Luthor Gibson, the man called Darkness, stood above the reclining form of Doc Titan, whose legs would no longer respond to his thoughts.

"Gibson? Why?"

"I'm truly sorry about this, Doc. Don't be too concerned, I used your anesthetic bullets, not real ones. You'll be fine soon. You claimed these only knock out men for about half an hour. That's all the time I'll need to finish my business with Victor Kaine. Finish it in my way, permanently." Gibson pulled the clip out of the gun and tossed it next to Doc. He then reloaded his handguns with real ammunition. He was down to six rounds so he loaded one gun with five bullets and the other with one. He tossed the gun with one bullet down in front of Doc. Seeing the question in Doc's eyes, he smiled and said. "In case Kaine gets past me, stop him. I assume you'll only need one bullet."

Doc noticed Gibson was limping and his cloak and clothes had been burned and torn in several places.

"Gibson, give me a few minutes and I can help you." Doc still couldn't feel anything from his legs down and now his fingers were also becoming numb. Usually the anesthetic pellets would put down a full-grown man in seconds, but Doc was anything but normal. His endurance was incredible.

"No. This conflict is not yours, John. Victor Kaine is my responsibility."

"But you've never even met him before."

"That's not true, John. I killed his father in Russia 28 years ago, in 1916. I should never have saved the boy's life. Prince Felix Yusupov tried to warn me, the son is more of a madman than the father ever was."

"I thought I was …" Doc's voice trailed off, as the drugs overpowered him.

"In the back of your mind, you carried a burden that was never yours. Iriana Noviskovaah, the Countess Matryvonav, was indeed Victor Kaine's mother, but he was already eight years old when you met her at the prisoner of war camp in 1917. She had seduced you then, but Irina only had one child in her lifetime. She and her son had been exiled from Russia one year earlier by Tsar Nicholas II the last Emperor of Russia, after the death of Rasputin. The name Countess Matryvonav, Iriana Noviskovaah is an anagram for the woman once known as Maria Ivanovna Vishnyatkova, a royal governess to Anastasia Romanova - The Grand Duchess of Russia.

"Only a handful of people ever knew that in the spring of 1909, Maria stated that Rasputin had allegedly molested her. Victor Kaine, or Joachim Issur Danielovich Rasputin, was the illegitimate bastard son of the Russian madman, Grigori Yefimovich Rasputin. I killed his father before his eyes. I spared his life in a moment of compassion. I will not let that happen again. There's only one way to deal with mad dogs, John. You put them down. Permanently."

The Darkness vanished into the dark cavern and blackness closed in around Doc. He used every ounce of effort and scratched the back of one hand with a fingernail, drawing blood. His vision began to fail and he slowly sank to the floor. His breathing was strong and steady. The cave became deathly quiet. Doc's memories swept him into the past.

She wore an ankle-length white fur coat, white leather boots, and a Russian-type white fur hat … she gave Titan a small and exceptionally long-fingered hand in a black elbow-length glove … Her large, dark blue eyes were as dazzling as her smile … Her narrow hips became an unusually small waist … Her all-white gown was the most low-cut he had ever seen … taking an afternoon promenade in a beautiful pink dress and wide-brimmed sky-blue hat and holding a pink parasol … she waved a pink-gloved hand …

… these were his memories of the Countess Matryvonav, Iriana Noviskovaah. The first woman John Titan might have fallen in love with, had the circumstances been different.

Victor Kaine sought an exit from the labyrinth of catacombs. He was pleased when he finally discovered a large open cavern where daylight streamed in through the mouth of a cave. Unfortunately for him, it ended abruptly. The exit to the cavern was several hundred feet above the ocean level and the jagged rocks below speared the sky like hundreds of teeth. The roar and cascade of powerful waves beat against the face of the cliff and filtered through the teeth. The teeming water was a light blue-green phosphorus-flecked froth. He unconsciously growled at the barrier to his escape. He turned to retrace his steps in the hopes of finding another exit. Kaine faced Darkness. Gibson was blocking the path to Victor's retreat.

"There's no place to run, Victor Kaine." Darkness pointed the automatic at the thin man as he stepped into the light. Gibson staggered slightly. His injuries and burns had taxed him.

"I'm through running anyway. Wait, I recognize you now. Your face is forever burned into my memory. You are Max Grant, the man who murdered my father." Kaine's face began a terrible transfiguration, as he devolved into primal madness.

"No. I put down a mad dog. He was insane and dangerous." Gibson countered.

"And now you will shoot me? An unarmed man?"

Gibson foolishly tossed the handgun onto the dirty floor of the cave. "However we do this, you are through."

"Come then, let us embrace this final time." Victor growled.

Gibson felt the years burn away, and he was Max Grant once more.

Grant snarled at Kaine. "Let's finish this."

Kaine sprang forward and swung a bony fist at Grant's skull. Even as Max ducked beneath the blow, he realized his mistake. This was simply a feint, but it was too late. Kaine raised one knee and struck him hard under the chin. His jaw snapped shut hard and his teeth bit into the tip his tongue, neatly severing the last quarter inch. Blood flowed freely into his mouth. Victor wrapped his long fingers around Max's neck and easily lifted him off of the floor.

With all of his might, Max struck his opponent's face with his hard fist. Once. Twice. Kaine merely took the blows and kept squeezing. Grant tried to break the fingers loose from around his neck, but to no avail. The Russian had powerful fingers and they were determined to squeeze the life from Max. Blood from his partially opened mouth splashed to his chest and rained down onto Kaine, giving the man a nearly satanic appearance. His senses were starting to lose cohesion and sparkles of lights were flashing before his eyes. Seconds more and Grant would lose consciousness, and possibly his life. He felt the bones and muscles creak in his neck and thought it might break before he could be strangled.

Victor's face was pure evil as words poured from his mouth. *"'To the last, I grapple with thee; From Hell's heart, I stab at thee; For hate's sake, I spit my last breath at thee.'"*

Grant's foot brushed against something. What was that? A memory came to him. Simon Blake's knife was still deeply embedded in Kaine's thigh. Victor had tried to pull it out earlier and nearly passed out from the pain. Drawing on the remaining reserves of strength, Max raised his foot and brought it down hard onto the knife handle. Kaine bellowed like an injured beast and dropped Max to the ground. He clutched his wounded leg and hobbled in circles, the pain exposing his animal reactions to the wound. Grant crawled a dozen feet away, wheezing for breath. His senses were still swimming and his skull throbbed as blood began circulating again.

Kaine recovered first and lunged at Grant again. This time Max ducked and drove his fist deep into Kaine's abdomen, followed by a blow to the head. His fingers went numb from striking the hard skull. Victor staggered but it was evident that he had more fight in him. He backhanded Grant and bright sparks of light exploded in Max's head. Strictly by instinct, Max caught the offending arm between his before it could withdraw and snapped the elbow joint backwards. Kaine growled and reached out again. Grant ducked under the grasping deathly clawing fingers and grasped the hilt of the knife that still protruded from Kaine's thigh. In one fluid movement, the knife was yanked free and, spinning on the ball of his heel, Grant plunged the blade back into its human sheath. The razor sharp stiletto sunk deep between the shoulder blades of Victor's back, until only the handle could be seen.

Kaine dropped to his knees. His breath came in jagged gasps. Bubbling blood dribbled from the corner of his mouth. The knife had punctured one of his lungs. Slowly, he stood back up, balancing precariously on his wobbling legs. Blood poured from the leg wound, painting the cave floor crimson. Grant was standing with his back to Kaine at the mouth of the dark tunnel opening. He had picked up something from the ground before rising, but Kaine could not see the object. It was hidden from his vision, by Max's body.

Victor spit blood and wiped his lips. "I think it's time I took my leave, old friend. Someday we shall meet again. Perhaps, I will visit your friend, Megan."

Grant snarled. "No. I am *not* your friend, you bastard, and this is *over. Today you die!*"

Darkness turned to face Kaine and lifted the pistol that he had retrieved from the cave floor. Their gaze met and Victor realized that pity did not exist in those sightless orbs of the Darkness. Kaine had already spun away and was running for the mouth of the cave. A furious cavalcade of shots rang out. Victor had surprised Grant by fleeing. He had expected an attack. Grant's vision was still wavering from the torture his body had endured. The first several shots went wild. Kaine had almost made it to the cave entrance when two shots struck him square in the back, propelling him forward. Without hesitation, Victor Kaine staggered out into daylight and plunged below Max's sightline.

Grant slowly got to his feet and forced his body to move forward. He stared down into the torrent of pounding waves and the dangerous jagged rocks below. No body could be seen, but that was not truly a surprise. The waters would have swept it away immediately. But no one could have survived a fall into such a watery hell.

He stood there for a minute as he gathered his strength. Gibson sensed movement behind him in the cave. Doc Titan stepped farther into the room.

Gibson leaned against the cavern wall. "How long have you been standing there, Doc?"

"I saw Kaine ... leaving."

Gibson smiled. "I thought those anesthetic bullets would keep you out for another half hour."

"I carry an antidote on my fingernails, just in case someone does exactly what you did. I was out for less than five minutes."

The two men quietly watched the crashing waves one hundred feet below. A minute passed in silence.

"'*A man thinks that by mouthing hard words, he understands hard things.*'" Doc quoted. "Men like Kaine and Totenkopf will never comprehend what that means. So, do you think we've seen the last of Victor Kaine?"

Gibson coughed and winced in pain. "I would be a cynic to say that Kaine escaped, but I would be a fool to say that he's dead."

Doc supported Gibson with his shoulder. "Come on, Gibson, let's find you a doctor."

Simon Blake, Rick Gunn, Bart, Gibs, Kong, Big Tom, and Mick led a troop of Allied soldiers throughout the building, rounding up small groups of enemy forces. Wall had tried to join the others but Cassie clung to him fiercely and refused to let go. Preston Stockbridge staggered into the room and looked around. Pam placed her shoulder under his arm and helped support him.

"Whitney's okay, Preston. So is Rav Chandra. Black Skull locked them up when he escaped. I'll show you where they are." Pam said.

Stockbridge noticed Megan looking from one entrance to another, waiting for Gibson to appear. His head hung low, Preston looked into her eyes and simply shook his head from side to side.

"I'm sorry, Megan. I watched his plane go down. There was no way he could have survived."

Megan's face sagged and her eyes filled with tears. She was about to lose control of her emotions when Luthor's voice came from the far entrance.

"Takes more than an exploding plane to kill the Darkness."

Doc Titan and Luthor Gibson entered. Megan ran to Gibson and held him tightly for a long time. Gibson was burned and bloody, but managed a weak smile.

Megan stepped back and looked into his face. His black glass lenses were cracked and dark bruises circled his neck, where Kaine had strangled him. "You're a mess, and you're bleeding."

"It's nothing." He said. "It's a mere flesh wound. I'll be fine."

Stockbridge slapped Gibson hard on the back and smiled widely. "Lew, how on earth did you survive that airplane explosion?"

Gibson smiled knowingly. "Only the Darkness knows. And if you call me Lew one more time, I'll shoot you. Twice. In fact, if somebody brought me a gun and I'd do it right now."

Stockbridge chuckled. "Like that would stop me. Man, I thought you were dead for sure. I'm glad I was wrong."

"Oh ye of little faith. I simply …" Gibson began.

But Stockbridge was already gone, following Pam to the prison cells. They found Gabe already there. He and Isabelle were sharing a private moment, whispering sweet affections and holding each other closely. Stockbridge greeted Whitney and Rav Chandra briefly, but enthusiastically and then they all grabbed firearms and ran off to join the fighting. Pam unlocked the last cell and helped the brutalized prisoner to his unsteady feet. She spoke to him, but he seemed oblivious to her questions and statements. When she mentioned that his son, Doc Titan, was on the island, his confused eyes searched hers.

The prisoner whispered hoarsely. "My son? He's here?"

Pam nodded. "Yes, he came here to rescue you."

"Rescue me?"

"Yes, come with me. I'll take you to him."

Pam left Gabe and Isabelle to their privacy, helping the tortured, dazed man walk toward the great room. Kong and Big Tom were entering the great main room from one of the many entrances.

"So that was you guys, Kong? Claiming to be the commanders of the destroyers?" Big Tom asked, scratching his thick beard. Wearing the thick, leather mask had made his face itch.

"Yep, they're all sleeping soundly on board their ships, Big Tom. Rick Gunn, that young kid you met outside, brought about twenty ships with him. The entire island is surrounded by Allied Forces."

Doc Titan was listening to Big Tom and Kong as his attentive eyes scanned the large room. So many things were happening all at once, that everything seemed to be moving in slow motion. Five guards were escorting Black Skull out of the room. The six professors were grouped together and watched by several soldiers, under Doc's orders. He had explained that they were not to be harmed in any way. Professor Schmidt watched Totenkopf being led away and he started walking toward Doc. Titan motioned to the guard that it was okay. Pam entered into the room, helping a dirty, battered man to walk.

"Doc, we found your father." Pam exclaimed happily.

Black Skull's head turned at this phrase. He struggled with his captors, knocking over several and grabbing a pistol from one of them. Without hesitation, he leveled the gun at the man with Pam and began firing. All six rounds hit the haggard man center mass and he dropped without a word. The guards grabbed Totenkopf, but before he fell under their weight, six small crimson grenades were launched in Doc's direction. It was later discovered Totenkopf had a miniature cavity built into his shoe heel and it housed half a dozen of these bombs. They were automatically activated, blinking with tiny scarlet lights. If Doc dodged the deadly projectiles, his cousin Pam would have been the new target. And he knew only too well what would happen if he caught them. Certain death from the Death's-Head Virus. He was still contemplating the best course of action when another element interfered.

Professor Schmidt dashed quickly between Doc and the grenades. He managed to catch all six of them as he stumbled to a remote corner, away from other potential victims. The scarlet explosion of deadly dust enveloped the scientist. Doc started forward, to save the professor from certain death. Big Tom and Kong grabbed him and held him back.

"Doc, it's too late. You can't save him."

Doc's face was a painting of horror, an emotion none of his aides had ever witnessed from this stoic copper-hued statue. His emotions had always been held tightly in check. Now they were evident to all. He slowly slid to his knees and tears rolled down his face. Pam was holding the dead man in her arms and she was in shock.

"I'm still alive?" Schmidt coughed and glanced around incredulously.

Doc stared at the elderly man in disbelief. The old gray-haired professor raised himself to one knee and glanced around the room. Everyone was staring at him, unbelieving.

Schmidt smiled. "Guess I'm immune to the virus. Hell of a way to find out."

"How did you know the virus wouldn't kill you?" Doc asked the elder professor.

Schmidt shrugged. "I didn't, but I couldn't just stand by and watch you die."

Doc jumped to his feet and gave the professor a bear hug, spinning him around in circles.

Pam, indicating the man she held. "But, Doc, your father …?"

Doc smiled at Pam, indicating the professor. "*This* man is my father."

Pam frowned, completely confused. "Then who is this? We all thought this prisoner was your father."

Schmidt pointed at the dead man. "That is Cameron Smythe's father."

Big Tom frowned. "Who the heck is that?"

"Black Skull. Totenkopf. His real name is Cameron Smythe."

Pam mouth fell open in disbelief. "You mean he's not even German?"

"No."

The guards had bound Totenkopf thoroughly and stripped off his boots, gloves and the majority of his uniform. Professor Schmidt approached him and tore the Black Skull mask from his face. The exposed features were obviously a younger version of the dead man that Pam Titan still held. Totenkopf, sans mask, shouted threats and oaths at the elderly professor.

Schmidt tossed the skull mask on the floor. "Without the mask, Black Skull is simply another cruel, sadistic man who was tortured by his domineering father as a youth. Last year, he discovered the identity and location of his father and has been brutally torturing him since. I regretted not being able to help the poor man."

Pam lowered the head of the dead man and approached Professor Schmidt. "So you really are my Uncle Clarke?"

Schmidt smiled. "And you're little Pamela? I haven't seen you since you were nine years old."

As he spoke, the professor removed the spectacles that were perpetually perched on the tip of his nose. He straightened his hair, removed contact lenses from his eyes, stood completely erect, and was soon a completely different man. Pam wrapped her arms around her uncle and gave him a kiss on the cheek.

Professor Titan breathed deeply. "Once my hair grows back in and I stop bleaching the color out, I'll feel more like my old self. John, do you remember my old friend Robert Hubertson?" Clarke Titan waved his open palm toward the man known as Professor Walters.

"Of course, I do."

"Unfortunately, I really am gray and balding." Robert shook Doc's hand and gave him a hug.

Big Tom and Kong shook hands with Professor Titan, glad he was still alive. Then they scolded him harshly, for letting them think he was dead for the past fifteen years.

"I am sorry about that. But I didn't think you, any of you, were ready for the entire truth." Professor Titan apologized.

"You might have been correct in your assumption, father." Doc agreed.

Simon Blake had entered the room and heard the last part of the discussion. Professor Titan noticed him and walked forward with open arms, embracing Simon as a father would embrace his long-lost prodigal son.

Professor Titan held Blake at arm's length and looked him over, top to bottom. "I am glad you grew up to be such a fine young man. It was rather a surprise when it turned out you were bulletproof. Of course, so was Hugo Danner. Do you know who that was?"

Blake nodded. "Yes, we visited Sanctuary and met with the Illuminati. They explained … many mysteries. Revealed many secrets."

"Yes, I wish I had been there." Titan nodded and then continued. "Unfortunately, I was rather busy, here on the island."

Professor Titan noticed Stockbridge and Gibson enter the room. "And these two fine gentlemen unknowingly saved my life, by supplying the missing page of the Danner Journals. That was the 'treasure' you delivered to the Hidden Acropolis."

Gibson smirked at Stockbridge. "And you thought that the treasure was that little monk."

"You had removed one of the pages before you entrusted me with them?" Doc asked incredulously.

"Strictly as a precautionary measure. Turned out to be a smart move on my part." Professor Titan said, half to himself.

"But you then had the page brought here? To Victor Kaine and Black Skull?"

Professor Titan smiled knowingly. "Actually, I had the Brothers at the North Pole create a rather convincing counterfeit, completely useless, of course. Not that it was necessary, I'm the only one who can decipher Danner's notations."

Pam and Megan were staring at the pools of various colored liquid on the cold stone floor, feeling a little ill.

"But, that was horrible. Those ... little babies cooked and disintegrated in those tubes." Megan said, pointing at the pools on the floor.

Pam shook her head in disbelief and looked a little pale. "I've never seen anything like that."

"You need not cry for them, they were never truly alive." Professor Titan waved a dismissive hand.

Pam stared at her Uncle Clarke in disbelief. "How can you be so heartless about that? How do you know what they could feel? That sounds just like a man, to ..."

"Because they were never truly alive." Blake offered, interrupting Pam.

Megan frowned. "What do you mean?"

Professor Titan explained calmly. "They were children's dolls, nothing more. Merely plastic and wax. The final phase of Project Gladiator merely super-heated the fluids until the dolls completely dissolved."

"The clincher was the fluid they were in, it looked incredibly convincing." Blake admitted.

"Lime and blueberry Jell-O, I believe?" Doc asked his father.

"That's correct, son. Fortunately, neither Black Skull nor Victor Kaine had any real scientific knowledge. A simple light show and a smattering of stage magic impressed them. Slight of hand and misdirection. Actually, it was rather amusing, pushing their buttons and seeing what kind of response I would get."

"But what about the other scientists that worked here?" Kong indicated the other four professors.

"All old friends of mine and all completely loyal to the USA. They were some of Doc's instructors." Professor Titan admitted.

Megan shook her head in disbelief. "This is all too much for me. So you've been running some kind of scam on the Nazis? What would have happened if we didn't show? Or if we were a day late?"

"I had faith in my boys and their friends." Professor Titan looked at Doc and Blake. "And I had an ace or two hidden up my sleeve."

"But why did you do all of this?" Megan pointed at Project Gladiator.

Professor Titan's face became serious. "I wanted the Danner Journals back in safe hands again. And I forced the National Socialist Party to invest time and resources on a wasted effort. They squandered millions of dollars to create and protect ... nothing."

Doc frowned and turned to Stockbridge and Gibson. "Wait a second. You were at my private Hidden Acropolis?"

Stockbridge grabbed Whitney's small hand and began walking away. "Sure. But Kaine was the one who blew a hole in the skylight, not us. I need to leave now but I'm sure Gibson will tell you all about it."

Doc's mouth dropped open. "There's a hole in the roof of my Acropolis? Hey, come back here and explain that to me again, Stockbridge. Stockbridge?!"

Later, Doc confronted Xena and Hermia. "I want all of the weapons that Victor Kaine stole from my Hidden Acropolis in 1938."

Xena pouted and crossed her huge arms over her chest. "Why should we believe you? You're probably as evil as Victor Kaine was."

Without hesitation, Doc presented them an offer they could not refuse. "I will give you five million dollars, donated to your choice of charities, for the location of the weapons."

The large women balked for a second and looked at one another.

Doc added. "Each."

Hermia smiled broadly. "Who are we to judge you? Mother always said to believe in the goodness of people."

Xena agreed. "We'll gladly draw you a map to the icebreaker, *Oldendorf*. The weapons are all locked in the lower hold of the ship."

Bart laid a world map on the table and the women provided him with coordinates to the *Oldendorf*.

Kong whispered. "Hey, Doc. How come you're willing to give away ten million dollars?"

Doc smiled knowingly. "It's not my money. Victor Kaine extorted ten million dollars worth of diamonds from the Third Reich, in exchange for the Danner Formula. We found them locked in Black Skull's safe."

In the next few months, the entire sum of money was generously donated by the sisters to various orphanages and children's hospitals. Their little sister, Ariel, was hired as a candy striper at the Manhattan City Hospital Children's Wing. Xena and Hermia entertained the children every weekend.

Pam Titan casually strolled across the great room in the center of the castle. She had a quick meeting to attend. Kong, Wall, Mick, Bart, and Big Tom were playing poker and smoking fat cigars. The mood was casual and relaxed. Less than a day had passed since the conflict in this very room. Most people would need a week or more to feel at ease. But these men ate, breathed, and slept danger. They learned long ago to enjoy every minute of free time.

"Hey, Pam you want us to deal you in?" Kong asked loudly.

She smiled and patted his thick shoulder. "I've got some place I need to be. But I'll be back to steal your money later."

The men laughed boldly and went back to their game.

"Wonder what she's up to?" Wall eyed Pam as she walked away.

Kong waved his hairy hand dismissively. "Aww, the girls are probably just having a slumber party. You know, braiding each other's hair, painting their nails, and having pillow fights."

Big Tom stroked his bearded chin. "I don't know. Pam is a shrewd business-woman. I would love to be a fly on the wall in that room. She's up to something."

Bart remained silent but smiled knowingly. He knew exactly what Pam was doing. Last year, Pam had called him to arrange a small investment matter. Establishing the Hunter Island Holding Company.

Pam knocked on the door of the large room being shared by the four women. Whitney Van Pelt, Cassie Greyson and Megan Meriwether were already waiting there for her. They had found a bottle of champagne and were celebrating in style. Pam was offered a glass, accepted it, and offered each woman a small red book.

"Remember how you all entrusted me with your money after the Hunter Island adventure? How we became partners in the Hunter Island Holding Company and I mentioned some other financial investments? Well, I didn't want to show you these until we were all together." She nodded at Whitney, who was kidnapped before she could meet with the other three women at Pam's beauty parlor … er … salon.

Megan giggled. "So are we mourning our losses or celebrating our gains?" She was a little tipsy from the champagne.

"Well, remember when I warned you that businessmen spend years developing a decent portfolio and sometimes investments lose money?"

"Uh oh. This doesn't sound good." Whitney frowned.

"Oh well. Easy come, easy go, right?" Megan said, taking a mouthful of champagne.

"These are your passbook savings accounts at a large, security bank that Doc uses. Go ahead, take a look."

Cassie's eyes grew large. Megan spit out her champagne, coughed, and dropped her glass. She sobered up very quickly.

"I've never seen that many zeros behind a number before. Is this for real?" Whitney asked breathlessly.

Pam placed her hand on Whitney's knee and looked into her lavender eyes. "Sweetheart, this is only the profits. Your principle is still invested in several new ventures."

Cassie's mouth kept working, opening and closing. Finally, she was able to speak. "This means I'm richer than Simon Blake and Luthor Gibson and Preston Stockbridge, all rolled into one. I don't know what to say. Is it legal to have this much money?"

Pam laughed boldly. "Everything is completely legal and above board. Bart Blackwell is our investment representative. He might not be a lawyer, but he's the most legal-minded, law-abiding man I know. And he is only charging us three percent, instead of his usual rate."

"His firm probably makes more from the four of us, than all of his other clients together." Whitney calculated.

"True." Pam admitted. "But he's the best broker I know, and he's like family."

"But will he tell anyone? I'm not sure I want the others to know about this." Cassie voiced her concern. "Money changes the way people treat you."

"Bart strictly believes in the client/broker privilege. He will never tell anyone. In fact, he rarely mentions his own business investments to anyone else. And you never need to worry about cash. Bart set up a trust fund for each of us. Charge everything to your bank account and his firm will take care of all of the bills."

Megan bounced up and down with excitement. "I'm rich! I've never really had money before. I don't even know what to do with this much money."

Whitney hugged Megan. "No problem, honey. We'll show you how to live right. I'll be your personal shopper."

"But you warned us about the possibility of losing money …" Cassie started.

"Actually, I said other investors lose money. Not me."

Whitney was still calculating numbers. "This is three times what we invested. At this rate …"

Pam smiled. "If our latest investment pays off, we should each have twice this much next year."

Pam refilled their glasses and proposed a toast. "To success."

The other three raised their glasses and in unison said. "To the Hunter Island Holding Company."

"I hate to leave, but I promised the boys that I would join them for some poker." She left three very happy women behind to discuss their vast fortunes.

Kong saw Pam return from her meeting with the girls. He patted the seat next to his own. "Ready to lose some money, Pam?"

Pam snatched one of the cigars from the tabletop, bit off the tip and clamped it in her mouth. Bart offered her a light. "So boys, what kind of game are we playing?" She puffed hard and a billow of gray smoke surrounded her head.

Kong blew a series of smoke rings across the table. "Straight poker. A dime per point and a quarter per hand. Loser buys the beer. I'm winning by fifty dollars. Sure you can afford to pay with us high-rollers, kiddo?"

Pam cut the deck of cards and smiled. "If I go bust, I know some nice people I can borrow money from. Let's play."

Act IV: The Finale

Chapter Sixty-Five
Destination Known (The Departure)

April 26, 1945   10:00 am

Doc Titan stood at the end of the path leading to the lagoon. Several airplanes were floating in the clear blue water. The last two weeks had been very calm on the island. All of the Nazi soldiers had been captured and the prisoners were loaded aboard the two German naval vessels. The large ships were then escorted back to the nearest United States naval base. The virus-spewing death's-head bombs had been removed from Black Skull's soldiers and destroyed in accordance to Doc's directions. The island had been evacuated of all military forces within the week.

The only visitor after that time was Sergeant Richard Gunn. He brought news and a warning, Black Skull had escaped. Despite a twenty-four hour guard and the strictest security, he had managed to extradite himself from the custody of the military forces. It was doubtful that he would attempt to return to Germany, with the failure of such a high profile special operation like Project Gladiator. He would be in poor favor with many influential men in the Nazi order, including the Fuhrer, Adolf Hitler, himself.

The morning breeze brought a cascade of wonderful smells from the nearby fields of wild honeysuckle and dew flowers. Doc thought of Sanctuary. The scent also reminded him of the days of his youth on this island. Despite the strenuous years of study and intense physical conditioning, Doc had many fond memories of the island. He stared at the old pylons of the abandoned wharf, where he and Ned Land had often sat and discussed trivial things, such as clouds and women. He smiled at the ancient memories of his youth. He decided, at that very moment, his life had been a very good one.

Kong, Bart, Gibs, and Big Tom approached from the distance, talking happily as they walked down the trail. They had all survived another adventure together and were enjoying their lighthearted companionship and camaraderie. They saw Doc and waved.

"Well, Doc, we're ready to head back to the States. Too much of this island life will make us soft. We're looking for Percy. Have you seen him?" Big Tom asked.

Doc pointed to the far end of the island. "Percy got up early this morning and headed back to the ancient ruins. He has some hieroglyphics he wants to study before we left. He believes he might have discovered a lost civilization. He's flying back with me in a few days."

Kong chuckled. "Another lost civilization? That makes four this year, don't it?"

Bart leaned against his black cane. "This has been an interesting adventure. But it'll be nice to get back home and relax for a couple of days."

Kong teased playfully. "Bart misses his suits and fancy clothing. Besides, the tailors in New York will go bankrupt without him around."

Bart tapped Kong's shoulder with his black walking cane. "Lead on, you hairy mistake of nature."

Gibs pointed a thumb over his shoulder. "Hey, Doc, if you see Pam, let her know we're waiting for her at the airplane. She wanted to hitch a ride with us."

Doc watched as his old friends walked down the path and he smiled.

Pam approached. "You seem to be in a good mood this morning, John." She hugged her cousin fondly and kissed his cheek.

"I have enjoyed this short vacation, Pam. It has recharged my batteries."

"Now you know why normal folks take vacations, Doc."

They watched as Luthor Gibson and Megan Meriwether led a small group toward them. Preston Stockbridge and Whitney Van Pelt were locked arm in arm, followed by the faithful, silent man-servant Rav Chandra. Whitney was smiling broadly.

"So are you heading back to New York, also?" Doc asked.

Gibson surprised them with his response. "Actually, we are stopping for a few days in Florida. For a wedding."

Whitney bounced up and down excitedly. "Preston has agreed to marry me."

Gibson smiled. "And I've agreed to be the best man. We'll throw bullets instead of rice. And instead of a honeymoon, they're going to chase bank robbers."

Pam and Whitney hugged and the men shook hands in congratulations. Professor Clarke Titan and Simon Blake approached while this exchange was going on and joined in on the well-wishing. Doc's father no longer looked like an elderly man. His scalp had been shaved to maintain the illusion of balding, but now a fine crop of hair was coming in thick. The gray color was gone and now the follicles were a deep copper color. He no longer walked with a slight hunch. Professor Titan looked like a man in his mid-forties. He set down a paper-wrapped package as he greeted everyone.

Whitney announced excitedly. "That's not all. It's going to be a double wedding."

Cassie, Mick, and Wall had joined the gathering.

"That's right! Wall proposed to me last night and I've accepted." Cassie giggled.

Pam was starting to cry with happiness. "That's wonderful, Cassie."

The entire group talked for several minutes, pairing into smaller conversations. While this was going on, Gabe and Isabelle joined in.

Isabelle was glowing with happiness. "I guess it's our turn. Before this all started, Gabe and I were going to let everyone know we are leaving Unsolved Mysteries, Incorporated. We're going to have a baby."

Gabe mock-whispered. "I keep warning her that twins run in the family, so she had better be prepared."

This announcement started another round of happy discussions. At one point, Cassie noticed Simon Blake and slowly strolled over to him. She reached forward and stroked his face with one tiny hand. Tears were in her own eyes as she looked into his pale eyes.

"Chief, Simon … I hope you … that we …" Cassie choked.

Blake reached up and pushed the sides of his mouth up, the lifeless facial muscles staying in the form of a smile. And she could see happiness in his eyes.

"Oh, Cassie, I wish the best for you both. I really couldn't be happier."

"I was afraid this would be the end of Unsolved Mysteries, Inc., with Gabe and Isabelle leaving to have a family and Wall and I getting married." Cassie admitted.

"Actually, I'm leaving as well." Blake saw the questioning look in her eyes and continued. "I'm going back to Sanctuary with Doc's father. I feel I can contribute to their group. But if you and Wall are interested, Andrew Carter is willing to create a new detective agency in New York. And I would be willing to finance the rebuilding …"

Cassie applied a tiny finger to Simon's lips to stop him from speaking. "I think Wall and I are going to retire from the life of crime fighting." Her fingers straightened out the smile on his lips. "We're thinking of starting a new life together, away from gangsters and madmen." She stared into his eyes and gave him a passionate kiss on the lips. "I do love you, Mr. Simon Blake. And I shall miss you." She smiled broadly. "Besides, you know how much I hate getting hit on the head by the bad guys."

After she stepped away, Blake wiped a tear from his eye.

As Cassie turned to walk away, she nearly collided with the elder Titan. Their eyes met and his grew wide. He seemed taken aback.

"Your eyes. I've seen your eyes before. Beautiful, light-gray eyes." Professor Titan muttered.

Cassie smiled at him and replied. "They run in the family. Perhaps you've met one of my relatives."

Professor Titan smiled, knowingly. "Yes, perhaps I have." It wasn't until later that the thought finally occurred to Cassie. This man, this strange man who had lived for several lifetimes, had met both her father and her grandmother.

Mick placed a hand on Blake's shoulder. "Lad, if ye'll have me, I'd like to accompany you and Professor Titan back to Sanctuary. Looks like a nice place to retire."

Blake was heartfelt at the offer. "I would like that, Mick. Very much."

Stockbridge shook Doc's hand and smiled. "Thanks for inviting me on such a great adventure."

"Next time …" Doc began.

Stockbridge stopped him. "Actually I'm not only getting married, I'm retiring from the crime fighting business. Whitney has waited patiently for too many years for this moment. She deserves some quiet time. Maybe we'll also start a family. Have a bunch of little scorpions running around."

Doc asked Gibson, "When will you be back in New York?"

Gibson smiled and replied mysteriously, "Only the Darkness knows."

Megan grabbed his tie and pulled him close for a kiss. "He'll be back when I'm through with him."

Pam had her arms wrapped around Professor Titan. "It was nice meeting you, Uncle Clarke. Please visit us in New York sometime."

Gibson, Megan, Stockbridge, Rav Chandra, and Whitney left, followed by Cassie, Wall, Gabe and Isabelle. Pam hugged everyone and ran to the airplane where Kong and the others had been waiting patiently.

Doc and Blake looked at each other.

"You want to bet that Scorpion is back in action before the honeymoon is over, Doc?"

Doc simply smiled and shook his head. "No bet."

Professor Titan was holding the package he had brought, under one arm. He now presented the paper-wrapped box to his son.

"What's this, father?"

"The Danner Journals."

"Don't you think someone else should … " Doc started to protest.

"I can't think of anyone who could keep these safer than you."

"I didn't really do such a great job last time, father. Maybe you should keep them at Sanctuary … "

Professor lowered his head. "I have a history of using such things … I'd rather not have the temptation around me." He hesitated for a moment and then continued. "Son, I have done many questionable things in my lifetime. And I pushed you so very hard, John ..."

"Father, its okay. I understand. And, looking back on my life, I wouldn't have changed anything. Honestly and truly. I ... like who I am, what I can do. And I owe it all, everything, to you."

Professor Titan smiled broadly. "Thank you, my boy. I'm very proud of you ... of both of you boys. You've done great things ... more than I ever could have imagined."

Professor Titan, Doc Titan, and Simon Blake talked together for several minutes, sharing a lifetime of experiences in a short time.

"Are you sure you won't join Simon and myself?" Professor Titan asked.

"Perhaps someday, father. There's still a lot for me to do."

Blake shook John Titan's hand. "Until then, brother."

"Until then, brother."

Professor Clarke Titan and Simon Blake walked down to their plane, where Professor Robert Hubertson waited for them.

Doc Titan waved as each plane left and headed for various destinations. He stood on top of the hillside, alone once more. But he no longer felt lonely. He had many good and loyal friends and a real family. For the first time in his life he felt happy and truly fulfilled. He had a very good life.

Chapter Sixty-Six
Epilogue

May 7, 1945   8:00 am

From the ground level, the towering building appeared to reach the heavens. High above the streets, at the 116th floor of the Titan Tower, were the spacious offices of Doc Titan. Doc and Percy had returned from the island only a few days ago. Percy sported a new plaster cast on one leg. He had broken the leg recently, while on the newly renamed Wilder Island. Pam had come for a visit and they quietly talked, while Percy finished a bowl of warm chicken soup.

Pam leaned forward and whispered to Percy. "How long has he been staring out of the window?"

Percy was grumpy this morning. His broken leg itched. "He's been there for over an hour. I'm beginning to worry." The gaunt treasure hunter was in no mood for a mystery, so he broke the ice. "Hey, Doc, is everything okay?"

Doc Titan slowly turned to his friends and smiled. They had never seen him so relaxed and it really didn't seem to fit him. When he wasn't crossing the globe to right some wrong, or battling some criminal mastermind, he could always be found working in one of the labs. But not today. He was taking today off.

"Actually, I don't remember a day when I felt better, Percy. I feel like something good is going to happen today."

As if on cue, Kong burst into the large room. He was so excited, that he was panting heavily. As it turned out, he had jumped out of the elevator on the wrong floor and ran up the last three stories of the skyscraper. "It … happened." That was all he could get out, before resuming his heavy breathing.

Bart couldn't resist an opportunity to jibe his old friend. "What's that? They found a cure for ugly and they want to test it on you first?"

Kong was so excited, he completely ignored Bart's jab. He stepped forward and tossed a newspaper on the large table. The bold-faced headline covered most of the page. *WORLD WAR TWO IS OVER! GERMANY SURRENDERS!* There were shouts of excitement and Bart and Kong even gave each other a hug and danced a sort of jig.

"I guess Sentry succeeded in his secret mission. Wonder how he's celebrating?" Kong had a broad grin on his homely face.

Doc said quietly. "I received a message from Rick Gunn this morning. Sentry and Kid Sentry are still missing in action."

Bart reassured Doc. "Heck, they'll probably show up any minute now. He's probably celebrating with a navy nurse somewhere." Bart frowned and swiped a finger at Kong's cheek and studied the digit earnestly. "Is this lipstick?"

Kong looked at them with a dreamy glaze in his eyes. "Yeah, some cute little girl came up to me and gave me a huge smacker on the cheek. She was so excited and happy about hearing that the war was over."

Bart looked sad. "Poor girl." Pam looked at him questioningly. "Well, obviously she must be blind, to have kissed Kong."

Kong searched his coat pockets. "Oh, we also got a postcard from the Bahamas from Preston Stockbridge and Whitney Van Pelt … I mean Whitney Stockbridge. It's a photograph of them at the beach."

Everyone gathered around. Pam looked away in disgust. Kong simply stared with his large mouth hung open.

Bart said it best. "Anyone with that much scar tissue should never be allowed to wear a bathing suit. There ought to be a law. In fact, I'll start drafting one up today."

The beautiful sunshine flooded the rooms and everyone relaxed in the leather armchairs. Duke, Bart's pet Mastiff, lounged contently at Bart feet, in a beam of sunlight, enjoying the sun's warming rays. The small bandit-eyed ferret name BJ hopped up on the arm of Kong's chair, wearing three pocket watches. Leaning over the snoring Duke, he removed the watch chains from around his neck and offered the baubles to Bart. After Bart accepted the gifts, BJ hopped into Kong's lap, curled up and fell fast asleep.

"Whatever possessed the little fella to do that, Kong?" Bart asked, astounded.

"I had a little talk with him earlier. Of course, he'll probably steal them again later." Kong chuckled.

"Undoubtedly." Bart agreed, smiling.

The air in the room was light and happy. Things were right with the world.

Percy had finished his soup. "Pam, I meant to thank you for bringing that hot chicken soup for me. I feel much better now."

Pam waved him away. "Don't look at me. I never cook anything. One of the girls at my beauty salon has the hots for you and asked me to deliver it for her."

Percy, ever the confirmed bachelor, scoffed. "Bah, I have no time in my life for a woman." He waited until Bart and Kong were discussing something and he turned back to Pam. "So, is she cute?"

Pam smiled attractively. "Don't ask me, you old scarecrow. I'll have her give you a ring on the phone. She's a sucker for a bird with a broken wing. She'll nurse you back to health." Pam frowned and continued. "By the way, how did you break your leg?"

Percy blushed and looked down, embarrassed. "I was examining the ruins on Doc's island and jotting down notes. I wasn't watching where I was going and stepped into a dang gopher hole."

Pam covered her mouth and smiled, not wanting to embarrass Percy any further. A squawk of noise came over the loud speaker mounted to the wall. Big Tom's deep voice pounded into the room. He was obviously distressed and seemed to be shouting over a battle raging in the background.

"Doc? Fellas? If you can hear me, Gibs and I need help. Right now. We're at the Global Navigator Consortium warehouse and we're under attack."

Doc flipped the switch and replied. "What is happening, Big Tom?"

"About twenty guys broke in here and they're trying to steal the Windjammer. Gibs and I are holding them off, but we're running out of ammo. We need backup, Doc."

"We're on our way, Big Tom. Hang in there."

Kong and Bart were already making a beeline for the Slip Stream in the next room, with Doc trailing right behind them. Pam and Percy looked at one another.

"Guess it's just you and me, ol' pal." Pam said solemnly.

Doc Titan stepped back into the doorway.

"C'mon, Pam. Grab your antique pistol. You don't want to miss out on the adventure, do you?"

If Pam were the type to cry at such moments, she would have teared up. She started to say something but Doc interrupted.

"Hey, you were right, Pam. You are as good as any of these men and you've proven you can take care of yourself a dozen times over."

Kong shouted from the other room. "C'mon Doc, we've got the Hell-Rocket ready to go."

Pam gave Percy a sympathetic look, being left behind with his broken leg. Then she grabbed her gun and followed Doc out of the room. "Hot dog! It's been a whole month since I had someone shoot at me. I was starting to get depressed."

Percy smiled. "Ah, go on. I'll be fine here by myself … " He stopped talking when he realized Pam had already bolted from the room. He sighed and picked up the newspaper. After a minute he stared outside the window and pondered thoughtfully. "I wonder what happened to Sentry."

If Percy could have flown several hundred miles north, he would have found the answer to his question. In the frigid Arctic waters, a large block of frozen ice drifted in the eddies and currents. It bobbed this way and that, seemingly to travel with no particular destination. The solid water was surprisingly clear and within its core could be seen the figure of a man. A man dressed in military clothing. But visible through the open collar of the shirt was a red, white and blue chain-mail costume. The costume of The Sentry.

The End.

References and Inspirations

The following is a short list of the world's greatest pulps, novels, trades, graphic novels, and comic books ever written and illustrated. If you enjoyed reading this action-adventure book, I would highly recommend these fine publications for your reading pleasure.   - Wayne

Lord of the Trees, *Mad Goblin*, *Feast Unknown*, *Ironcastle*,
Tarzan Alive, and *Doc Savage's Apocalyptical Life*
Written by Philip Jose Farmer and others

The Wold-Newton Universe
by Philip Jose Farmer and many others

Doc Savage Pulps, Novels and Comics
by Lester Dent (Kenneth Robeson) and others

Shadow Pulps, Novels and Comics
by Walter Gibson (Maxwell Grant) and others

Spider Pulps, Novels and Comics
by Norvell Page (Grant Stockbridge) and others

Avenger Pulps, Novels and Comics
by Paul Ernst (Kenneth Robeson) and others

Captain Hazzard Pulps
by Chester Hawks and Ron Fortier and others

Angel Detective Pulp
by Edward S. Ronns

Captain Satan Pulps
by William O'Sullivan

Frankenstein, the Modern Prometheus
by Mary Wollencraft Shelly

Sherlock Holmes and *Professor Challenger*
by Sir Conan Arthur Doyle

20,000 Leagues Under the Sea and *Around the World in 80 Days*
by Jules Verne

The Savage Gentleman and *The Gladiator*
by Philip Wylie

Tarzan
by Edgar Rice Burroughs

Planetary
Written by Warren Ellis and Illustrated by John Cassidy

Black as the Pit, from Pole to Pole
Written by Steven Utley and Howard Waldrop

The Bronze Gazette
editor Howard Wright, published by Green Eagle Publications

The League of Extraordinary Gentlemen
Written by Alan Moore and illustrated by Kevin O'Neill

Who goes there? aka *Thing from Another World*
by John W. Campbell, Junior

Fu Manchu
by Sax Rohmer

The Musings and Reviews of Dr. Hermes
The Dr. Hermes Reviews Website

A special thanks to the fine folks at
Wikipedia
The Free Internet Encyclopedia

To *IPC Graphics* - the printers of this novel.

To Marvel Comics, DC Comics, Dark Horse, Image,
and all of the others, for providing the fans with years of
incredible art, fantastic stories and wonderful entertainment.

And lastly, to my family, friends and wife who supported my
meager writing and artistic talents with kinds words and advice.

The Historical Timeline of

Spoiler warning!! It is highly recommended that you read *Pulp Heroes - More Than Mortal* before reading this Historical Timeline!! On the following pages, important information is revealed about both the characters and the main story.

1772 - Victor Frankenstein is born in Geneva, Switzerland.

1790 - The events of Mary Wollstonecraft Shelly's novel *Frankenstein* or *The Modern Prometheus* take place, in which Victor Frankenstein creates the first artificial life, called simply, the Creature or Frankenstein's Monster. This 'Monster' is a patchwork man, created from various corpses found in dissecting rooms and slaughterhouses, and stands nearly eight feet tall. In creating the creature, Victor triggered a series of events, which would lead to the deaths of his youngest brother, his bride, his father, and his best friend. Victor would hound his creation around the globe for ten years before dying in the Arctic in the arms of Robert Walton, who brought the story of Victor Frankenstein to the world. Victor's creature would apparently spend several years in the hollow interior of the earth, as told in *Black as the Pit, From Pole to Pole* by Steven Utley & Howard Waldrop.

1799 - Victor Frankenstein and his creature discover Sanctuary.

1808, July 18 - Birth of Prince Dakkar of India. Later in his life, Prince Dakkar calls himself 'Captain Nemo,' as told by Jules Verne in *20,000 Leagues Under the Sea* and *Mysterious Island*.

1817 - Birth of Allan Quatermain in England, exact date and location are unknown. Professional big game hunter, trader and expert marksman, Quatermain lived the majority of his life on the African continent.

1832 - Birth of Phileas Fogg. Other than his globe-spanning adventure in 1872, very little is known about this mysterious and eccentric individual.

1836 - Frankenstein monster creates first Illuminati group at the North Pole.

1846, June 12 - Birth of Colonel Simon Titan aka Colonel Richard Henry Savage in Utica, New York. Titan graduated from West Point in 1868 and was commissioned a second lieutenant in the U.S. Army Corps of Engineers. He joined the Egyptian army as a major in 1871. He subsequently served as U.S. vice consul in Marseilles and Rome. On January 2, 1873, he married Anna Josephine Scheible of Berlin, Germany.

Later, Simon Titan served on the Texas-Mexico frontier and as a chief engineer on a railroad in California, retiring in 1884. Following his retirement in 1884, Titan traveled extensively, visiting Turkey, Japan, China, Russia, Asia Minor, Korea, and Honduras.

Returning to the United States in 1891, and a confidant of President Ulysses S. Grant, Titan was given several diplomatic appointments around the world. Titan could talk of all the wild spots in the world that he had visited and had many personal mementos of his strange life.

Simon Titan, using the pen name Richard Henry Savage, wrote his first novel, My Official Wife (1891), which proved to be his most famous. Titan wrote over 40 books, including Our Mysterious Passenger and Other Stories.

Titan became senior Captain of the 27th U.S. Volunteer Infantry and was appointed Brigadier General and Chief Engineer of Spanish War Veterans in 1900.

After living such an adventurous life, Simon Titan was run over by a horse-drawn wagon while crossing Sixth Avenue in New York City, on October 3, 1903, dying eight days later at the age of 57.

1852, August 7 - Birth of Doctor John Hamish Watson From 1881 until his death in 1939, Watson chronicled the adventures and investigations of the great detective Sherlock Holmes. Married Constance Adams in 1886. She died the following year, in December of 1887. His brother Henry Watson died soon afterward. Married twenty-seven year old Mary Morstan in April of 1889. Tragically, only months after the 'death' of Sherlock Holmes in 1891, Mary became deathly ill and passed away. In 1894, when he discovered that his friend was still alive, he sold his medical practice in Kensington and returned to 221B Baker Street, where he remained with Holmes throughout the rest of his career.

1854, January 6 - Birth of William Sherlock Scott Holmes at a farmstead in the North Riding of Yorkshire. His first adventure, *A Study in Scarlet*, takes place in 1881 but is not published until 1887 in Beeton's Christmas Annual.

1859, May 22 - Birth of Sir Arthur Ignatius Conan Doyle, Scottish author and physician, best known for chronicling the adventures of detective Sherlock Holmes and Professor Challenger.

1861 - Birth of Mary Morstan, second wife of Doctor John Watson.

1863 - Birth of Professor George Edward Challenger in Largs, a village in Strathclyde, Scotland.

1866 - Birth of Arronaxe Land, daughter of Ned Land, mother of Arronaxe Larson, grandmother of John Titan.

1869, January 10 - Birth of Grigori Yefimovich Rasputin, a Russian mystic who is perceived as having influenced the later days of the Russian Tsar Nicholas II, his wife the Tsaritsa Alexandra, and their only son the Tsarevich Alexei. It has been argued that Rasputin, often called the 'Mad Monk,' was an unordained Russian mystic and holy man, and helped discredit the tsarist government, leading to the fall of the Romanov dynasty in 1917. Contemporary opinions variously labeled Rasputin a saintly mystic, visionary, healer, and prophet, or a debauched religious charlatan. Historians can find both to be true, but there is still much uncertainty. Accounts of his life have often been based on dubious memoirs, hearsay, and legend.

1871 - Second Reich begins. The new German government exists from 1871-1918. The Second Reich lasted till the end of World War I, when the Kaiser abdicates his rule, and Germany becomes a democracy.

1872, 8:45 on Wednesday October 2 - Enigmatic Englishman Phileas Fogg and his French valet, Jean Passepartout, depart Dover and begin their eighty-day trip around the world. His wager with the other distinguished members of the London Reform Club is for 20,000 English Pounds.

1872, 8:45 on Saturday December 21 - Phileas Fogg completes his trip around the world as chronicled by Jules Verne in *Around the World in Eighty Days*.

1872 - Professor Henry Jones, Senior is born in Scotland. A professor of medieval history, his obsessive search for the legendary Holy Grail will span decades of his life.

1883 - Arronaxe Larsen, Doc Titan's mother, is born. She is the daughter of Wolf Larsen and Arronaxe Land.

1884 - James Clarke Wilder meets Colonel Simon Titan aka Colonel Richard Henry Savage (A pen-name for his publications.) They become close friends and often travel together posing as brothers. Wilder assumes the pseudonym 'James Titan' during these trips.

1886 - Birth of Lieutenant Colonel Randolph Garnett 'Big Tom' Thompson. Enlisted in WWI in 1914, at age 28. Hailing from Botany Bay, Australia, he became one of the greatest pilots of the war, flying hundreds of successful military missions. Although shot down and captured several times, he always managed to escape and rejoin the battle. While still in his mid-twenties, it was discovered that he suffered from rare hormonal disorder called acromegaly, an enlarging of the extremities, specifically the hands, feet and jawbone. Doctor Clarke Titan was able to surgically remove a tumorous mass on his pituitary gland to prevent further damage.

1886 - Strange Case of Dr Jekyll and Mr Hyde is a novella written by the Scottish author Robert Louis Stevenson regarding the thoughts of the duality of man's nature, and how to incorporate the interplay of good and evil. Stevenson never says exactly what Hyde takes pleasure in on his nightly forays, saying generally that it is something of an evil and lustful nature; thus it is in the context of the times, abhorrent to Victorian religious morality. However, scientists in the closing decades of the 19th century, within a post-Darwinian perspective, were also beginning to examine various biological influences on human morality, including drug and alcohol addiction, homosexuality, multiple personality disorder, and regressive animality. The formula is turned over to James Clarke Wildman.

1888 - Birth of Major Bartholomew 'Bart' J. Blackwell. He was born and raised in Whitechapel, England. Father was shot dead by street thugs when he was 2 years old and mother was stabbed to death when he was only 4. He lived for a year in an orphanage, until an uncle living in USA adopted him. Enrolled at Princeton in 1908, he graduated at top of the class in Mathematical Sciences and Theories. Enlisted in WWI in 1914, at age 26.

Bart carries a simple black walking cane as a reminder of a wound he received during the Great War, although the injury left no permanent damage. One night, during a drunken brawl, Bart was shot through the gluteus maximus. He is resolute in the belief that Kong was somehow responsible for the embarrassing wound. Nearly thirty years later, Kong steadfastly swears he did not shoot Bart, but teases that he should have. For drunken and disorderly conduct, Bart was demoted to the rank of Major.

1888, August 31 - Jack the Ripper continues to terrorize Whitechapel, England. James Clarke Wildman begins murdering the prostitutes that he has been experimenting on. Quite by accident, he meets Alice Rutherton-Claybourne and injects her with his experimental formula. She and her husband leave England for the African continent within the week.

1888, November 10 - James Clarke Wildman murders his last victim. Anna Marie Blake gives birth to a son. The child suffers major birth defects, mostly due to mother imbibing in alcohol and narcotics during her pregnancy. Infant is placed in cryogenic suspension. Wildman spends next tens years at Sanctuary.

1888, November 10 - The true birth date of Simon Blake aka The Guardian. Named after prostitute mother, Anna Marie Blake and Colonel Simon Titan aka Colonel Richard Henry Savage. Also see 1909 and 1938.

1888, November 22 - Kan-Tar, Lord Greyson, aka Kevin Claybourne is born after his parents, Alice (Rutherton) and John Claybourne are stranded in the western coastal jungles of French Equatorial Africa.

1888 - Founding of the New Illuminati. Members include Sherlock Holmes, Professor George Challenger, Allan Quatermain, Hareton Ironcastle, Robert Hubertson, Professor Clarke Titan, and the man known only as Adam.

1891 - Birth of Preston Stockbridge II aka The Scorpion.

1891, May 4 - Sherlock Holmes and Professor James Moriarty wrestle at the edge of the abyss called Reichenbach Falls and appear to plummet to their deaths, locked in each other's arms. Story is told in *The Adventure of the Final Problem*. Three years later, Sherlock miraculously returns from the dead.

1892 - Birth of Prince Rav Chandra, christened Ghoshdashtidar Raviprakash Chandramouleeswaran Dakkar, in Afghanistan. He is the great-grandson of Prince Dakkar of India. (See 1808 – '*Captain Nemo*.')

1892 - Birth of Max Grant aka Luthor Gibson aka The Darkness.

1894 - Birth of Kenneth Xavier Percival 'Percy' Pierce in New Orleans, Louisiana. Enlisted in WWI in 1915, at age 21. He attained the rank of Corporal with Military Intelligence, before receiving a special request to transfer into the American Secret Service.

1894 - Birth of Major Henry Marmaduke 'Kong' Larson in Oklahoma. Nephew of Professor George Edward Challenger. Enlisted in WWI in 1916, at age 22. During the Great War, he met another brilliant young man named Blackwell and together they quickly rose through the ranks of the military. They found themselves competing for a promotion to the rank of Brigadier General. Several days later, after being reported AWOL, the MP's discovered a drunken Kong in a rundown brothel, with the twin daughters of a French General. An English commander intervened and saved Kong from a possible firing squad. He was, however, demoted to the rank of Major. Kong swears that Bart drugged him and set him up. Bart, of course, denies it.

1894 - Scientist Abednego Danner creates a serum designed to give great strength to human beings, and tests it on his unborn son as told in Philip Wylie's *Gladiator*. Danner's son, Hugo, grows up to have powers similar to those of Clark Kent; however, eventually Danner becomes a social outcast, turning to crime, going into seclusion, and finally meets his death after being struck by a bolt of lightning in South America.

1895 - Birth of Gilbert 'Gibs' Elliot Maddox in St. Louis, Missouri. He tries to enlist in WWI in 1915, at age 20. Due to his height, he is rejected. However, he soon becomes a leading member of the Military Intelligence.

1895 - Birth of Conall 'Mick' McGrath, member of Unsolved Mysteries.

1898, August - Birth of Henry Stone aka The Savage Gentleman.

1898, November 3 - Stephen Stone and infant son, Henry, are marooned on an uncharted island, as told in *The Savage Gentleman* by Philip Wylie. A Scotsman named David McCobb and a large Negro, known only as Jack, were also aboard the schooner Falcon. They will remain on this island until 1931. Stephen Stone and Clarke Wilder are old friends and business partners.

1899, July - First recorded gathering of the new *League of Extraordinary Gentlemen* in London. Mr. Hyde and Quatermain are members of the new League.

1899, July 1 - Birth of Henry 'Indiana' Jones, Junior in Princeton, New Jersey.

1899 - 1900 - The events of *The First Men in the Moon*, as told by H.G. Wells.

1899, September 12 - Clarke Wilder discovers Kan-Tar living in the western coastal jungles of French Equatorial Africa. He removes a blood sample, after bandaging the eleven-year-old boys' wounds.

1899, November 12 - Clarke Wilder injects his wife with a formula that contains DNA from Kan-Tar, to prevent her death from malaria. Wilder changes his last name to Titan.

1900, January 1 - Johnathon 'Doc' Titan is born on the schooner *Prometheus* in the southeast cove of Hydra Island, in the Aegean Sea off the coast of Greece. John's parents are Clarke Titan and Arronaxe Larsen. John's maternal grandparents are the notorious Wolf Larsen of *The Sea Wolf* and Arronaxe Land, who is the daughter of Canadian Ned Land of *20,000 Leagues Under the Sea*. A storm brews up, and as it does, Arronaxe goes into labor. Working hard, Clarke Titan and Robert Hubertson, led by the old sailor Ned Land, steer into the secluded cove where she is to bear her child. As the thunder crashes outside, a son is born ... John Titan. The *Prometheus* runs into a reef and sinks, apparently taking Arronaxe and her grandfather with it. By sheerest luck, Titan, his best friend, and son are the only survivors of the wreck.

1901 - Maple White discovers a plateau, a mysterious lost sliver from the past, inhabited by dinosaurs. White was a poet/artist from Detroit, Michigan who happened almost accidentally upon a plateau teeming with various prehistoric creatures. He managed to escape the summit, but died of a strange fever a year later. His miraculous discovery would have gone unnoticed, if Professor George Edward Challenger hadn't come upon the scene, discovered his notes, and led a new expedition back to the plateau.

1901 - Professor Clarke Titan relocates to Wilder Island and begins John Titan's vigorous training, at age 14 months. John Titan will not leave the island for the next 15 years.

1903 - Colonel Simon Titan aka Colonel Richard Henry Savage is run over by a wagon in Utica, New York on October 3, 1903 and dies in the hospital eight days later. He was 57 years old.

1903 - Professor Challenger's and Lord John Roxton's expedition to *The Lost World*, as related by Edward Malone (edited by Arthur Conan Doyle). Canonical books in the Professor Challenger series are: *The Poison Belt, The Land of Mist, The Disintegration Machine*, and *When the World Screamed*.

1904 - Professor Clarke Titan returns to John Hopkins to finish his medical degree and does post-graduate training in Neurosurgery. He develops a taste for big game hunting and travels around the world looking for sport. On one of his trips to Africa, he meets and befriends Hareton Ironcastle, a French adventurer.

1908 - Victor Kaine (Joachim Issur Danielovich Rasputin) is born to Iriana Noviskovaah, the Countess Matryvonav. He is the illegitimate bastard son of the Russian madman, Grigori Yefimovich Rasputin.

1909 - Recorded birth of Simon Blake. Blake will become The Guardian and found Unsolved Mysteries, Incorporated in the late 1930s. See 1888 for his true date of birth. See 1938 for his release from cryogenic freeze.

1912, January - Kan-tar receives an immortality treatment from an ancient witch doctor. He is 24 years old.

1912, May 7 - Births of Megan Meriwether and Whitney Van Pelt.

1914 - Birth of Pamela Titan, cousin of John 'Doc' Titan.

1914, June 28 - Archduke Franz Ferdinand of Austria and his wife are assassinated and the event lights a fuse that explodes into World War I.

1914 - Danner and fellow U.S. citizen Thomas Matthew Shayne join the French Foreign Legion upon the outbreak of World War I. Discovering his body could withstand gunfire, Danner unleashes his power against the

Germans, fighting dozens of Second Reich soldiers single-handedly. Especially enraged after Shayne's death, Danner has to be treated for psychological stress.

1914 - Birth of Barnaby Cornelius Roland 'Wall' Walker in Gokstad, Norway, aide to Simon Blake aka The Guardian. He marries Cassie Greyson, also of the Unsolved Mysteries, Incorporated group, in 1946.

1916 - John Titan leaves the Wilder Island and escapes to Europe. He meets Bart, Big Tom, Gibs, Percy, and Kong and enlists in the fighting of World War I. His father sends men around the world in search of his son. John also meets Frank Gunn, Max Grant, Preston Stockbridge, and Hugo Danner.

1916 - Professor Clarke Titan discovers Mayan gold in an abandoned city in a hidden valley in the country of Anacortes. He smuggles the ancient hoard from Mexico and returns to New York City. A small fortune is generously donated to hospitals, colleges and other facilities. The last of the gold bullion is used to build Titan Towers.

1916, December 16 - Victor Kaine (Joachim Issur Danielovich Rasputin) is witness to Max Grant killing his father, the Russian madman, Grigori Rasputin.

1916 - 1918 - Max Grant begins using the name Colonel Grantov aka The Dark Eagle. He becomes known as one of the greatest World War I aviators and spies, in the service of the Russian Czar.

1917 - Doctor Clarke Titan and Hareton Ironcastle mount a second expedition to The Lost World, discovered by Professor Challenger and Lord John Roxton. During the explosion that completely destroys Maple White Land, they lose all of the creatures they captured, but they escape with several million dollars worth of diamonds. (According to Philip Jose Farmer's *Ironcastle*, the retelling of J. H. Rosny's *L'etonnante Aventure de Hareton Ironcastle*.)

1918, July 4 - Birth of American patriot James Ethan Adams, the future Sentry, the Sentinel of Justice.

1918, July 4 - Birth of Totenkopf aka The Black Skull, Sentry's Nazi counterpart. Totenkopf's history, before being codenamed the Black Skull by Adolf Hitler, is unknown.

1918, November 11 - Germany's unconditional surrender is announced on the 11th hour of the 11th day of the 11th month. World War I ends abruptly. Hugo Danner wanders the globe aimlessly, in search of his true destiny.

1918 - John Titan reunites with father, introduces his military buddies and begins college.

1919 - John Titan graduates with three Masters Degrees from NYU.

1919 - Birth of future Unsolved Mysteries, Inc. agent Cassandra 'Cassie' Allison Greyson (Claybourne), the daughter of Kan-tar and Jane.

1920 - 21 - *Ironcastle* chronicles explorer Hareton Ironcastle's expedition to the African continent.

1921 - More than a decade of research pays off, as Sherlock Holmes perfects his Royal Jelly bee pollen elixir.

1920 - After crash-landing his plane, Max Grant is mortally injured and very near death. Stumbling blindly through the dense jungle, he collapses at the outskirts of an ancient, hidden city. His face and body are branded with unexplained symbols, as he is subjected to an arcane ritual that restores his eyesight, but only in the darkness of the night. During the day, he is completely blind. He is also unknowingly gifted with an age-delaying elixir used by the inhabitants of that city.

Two months later, Grant is found wandering aimlessly and with no memories of where he has been or what was done to him. Later, Doc Titan will develop glasses with specially tinted lenses that allow will him to see during the day.

1925 - Who Goes There? aka *The Thing from Another World* - MacReady, 'a bronze giant of a man,' joins an Antarctic expedition as meteorologist and second-in-command. He and the other members of the expedition must fight for their lives when they discover a Thing (from another world). Novella by John W. Campbell, Jr.

1926 - Hugo Danner, despondent over his inability to find a place outside of the military, fakes his own death. Doctor Clarke Titan, using the name Professor Hardin, meets Danner in Central America. Hugo gives Titan the notebooks containing his father's formulas. Hugo 'dies' the next day. He begins a period of aimless wandering that will bring him into contact with Max Grant, John Titan and others.

1929 - The Titan's, father and son, design the Titan Tower skyscraper and construction starts same year. Construction is completed in 1931, two months after the completion of the Empire State Building. The completed structure is 124 stories tall, 22 stories taller than the ESB.

1930 - For the safety of mankind, and to remove personal temptation, Clarke Titan surrenders the Danner Journals to his son, to be hidden away. More than any other living soul, Doc understands the dangerous contents of the six Journals. When Doc returns from the Hidden Acropolis near the Arctic Circle, he discovers that his father has passed away. In reality, Clarke has returned to Wilder Island with an old friend, Robert Hubertson. They begin subjecting the infant Simon Blake to a series of injections, using a variation of the Danner formula.

1930, July 7 - Sir Arthur Conan Doyle suffers heart attack and passes away at age seventy-one. The epitaph on his gravestone reads: Steel True, Blade Straight, Arthur Conan Doyle - Knight, Patriot, Physician, and Man of Letters.

1931 - Henry Stone, now 33 years old, is finally rescued from the uncharted island. His father's empire now includes twenty-two newspapers and eleven banks. He has never seen a woman. He meets Doc Titan and they become close friends.

1931 - Max Grant changes his name to Luthor Gibson and returns to America. The multi-millionaire creates the world's largest private investigation organization, with headquarters in Chicago, Los Angeles and New York. Darkness begins his quest for justice soon afterward.

1931 - Preston Stockbridge begins his one-man-war against crime as Scorpion.

1931 - Doc Titan and his friends begin their fight against the forces of evil.

1932 - Doc Titan meets his 18-year old cousin, Pamela Titan, for the first time.

1937 - Captain Rex Hazzard's only recorded adventure, *Python Men of the Lost City*, as told by Chester Hawks. In 1948, he will marry Pam Titan.

1937 - Doc Titan's first encounter with the dangerous villain named Victor Kaine. At the end of the adventure, Kaine is believed to be dead. Much to Doc's surprise, only months after the first conflict, Kaine returns from the grave.

1938 - In an unrecorded adventure, Doc Titan crosses paths with Victor Kaine for the third time.

1938 - Captain Lucifer (Lewis Afar) begins adventures with agents nicknamed the Satan's Angels. These include Irish, Lank, Shyster, Sad Sack, Ape, Prof, Dusty and Johnnie English.

1938 - Events of *Pulp Heroes - The Khan Dynasty*.

1938 - Simon Blake, The Guardian, begins gathering agents and establishes Unsolved Mysteries, Incorporated. Also see 1888 and 1909.

1939 - Death of John Hamish Watson, the exact date is unknown.

1945 - Events of *Pulp Heroes – More Than Mortal*.

1945 - Sentry aka James Ethan Adams is thrown into suspended animation in the North Atlantic. Death of Kid Sentry aka Christopher 'Cody' Sawyer.

1945, May 7 - World War II ends.

1948 - Marriage of Pam Titan and Captain Rex Hazzard.

1949 - Birth of Rex Hazzard, Jr., son of Rex Hazzard and Pam Titan.

1949 - Events of *Pulp Heroes - Sanctuary Falls*.

1961, May 7 - Birth of Wayne Reinagel. And the world will never be the same.

Note: Above information was compiled utilizing a combination of ginormous amounts of personal research, input from various pulp and novel fans, and Philip Jose Farmer's Wold-Newton Universe, edited by Win Scott Eckert.

An Introduction to Book Two of the Pulp Heroes Trilogy

The Khan Dynasty

Doctor Hunan Sun relaxed on his luxurious couch, surrounded by pillows and five nearly-naked women. In one hand, he held a smoking hookah pipe. The smell of shisha - a mixture of tobacco, molasses and fruit flavors, could not completely hide the odor of an opiate in the air. He leisurely turned his gaze towards his visitor. Their eyes met and locked.

Doctor Hunan Sun was an older man than ShangXia Khan, but it seemed impossible to determine his true age. And he was much older than he appeared. Rumors persisted that he measured his actual age in decades or centuries, depending on the person spreading the rumor. He was tall, lean and had a slightly feline appearance. He had a brow like Shakespeare and a face like Satan. His skull was closely shaven, with a thick braid of dark hair cascading past his waist. The most striking feature were his eyes, long, magnetic eyes of a true cat-green.

Doctor Sun smiled slightly and waved one hand at a nearby couch. His fingers were quite long, as were the nails on each digit.

"Welcome to my home, ShangXia Khan. I sincerely hope my little friends gave you a warm greeting." Sun spoke quietly.

Khan raised one eyebrow in surprise. "You know of me? Very good. And I received a very warm welcome, indeed. By the way, you'll need more spiders. They all met with a rather … bad ending."

"I've got a new breed hatching in the laboratory right now. Those last ones were too … tame." Doctor Sun clapped his hands and one of the silent women left his side and brought ShangXia Khan a tall goblet of dark liquid. She knelt beside him and stroked his thigh affectionately, offering him the drink. Khan stared into her pale green eyes for a long moment. She lowered the glass to her own lips and drank deeply. The glass was dropped from her frail fingertips, still half full. Without a sound, she sank to the thick carpet and didn't move. She was no longer breathing.

Hunan Sun nodded towards the dead woman. "A shame. She was one of my favorites."

Khan sneered. "I have never trusted women. At best, they are deceitful, lying creatures. I know you're a busy man, so I won't waste your time. How would you like to rule half of the world?"

"Am I correct to assume that you would rule the other half?" Sun drew a puff of smoke from the hookah pipe.

ShangXia Khan waved his long-fingered hands in the air. "But, of course."

Doctor Hunan Sun's eyes narrowed as he studied the other man. "You've piqued my interest. Please, continue."

An Introduction to Book Three of the Pulp Heroes Trilogy

Sanctuary Falls

The lone man was squatted down in front of the small fuel can. J. W. Campbell motioned for his men to surround the single stranger. In the glow of the flickering flame, Campbell glanced around the campsite. The intruder had no tent, no shelter of any kind, and apparently no food or other provisions. How did he expect to survive up here, within twenty miles of the North Pole? The Arctic winds had died down to ten miles an hour, but the temperature was still nearly twenty-five below zero Fahrenheit.

The man's hood was pulled up, concealing his face completely. But he was not wearing gloves, despite the freezing conditions. Campbell noticed the man's hands, twice as big as his own, with long tapered fingers. The man must have incredible will power, not to shiver in this incredibly cold climate. Campbell noticed something else that was a little odd. The man was dressed completely in black. Black knee-high boots, black khaki pants, black hooded coat.

The man spoke softly, but his voice carried easily on the cold, night breeze.

"Are you the Guardians of Sanctuary?"

This question caught Campbell off-guard. No one was even supposed to know about Sanctuary, much less what Campbell and his men were doing here. In the past ten years that he had volunteered for this duty, no one ever approached this desolate part of the world, unless they had been summoned. That's why this location had been selected. Far, far away from the prying eyes of mankind.

Campbell addressed the dark stranger. "What are you doing out here alone? What is your name?"

The man stood. He was tall, about six and a half feet, and thin. His movements were fluid and displayed cat-like strength and agility. He lowered the hood to his dark coat. His face was also thin, slightly pale, but still quite handsome. The features of a poet. He had a Marque De Sade scar, traveling from his forehead, through the eyebrow and several inches down the colorless cheek. The knife that caused the scar must have missed the eyeball by a fraction of an inch. His snow-white hair cascaded down onto his shoulders, a sharp contrast to the black clothes he wore.

The men with Campbell stepped back a pace but did not reach for their firearms. They were a well-trained unit. And besides, what kind of threat was one lone man in the middle of this icy wasteland?

"My name is Victor Kaine." Campbell noticed an evil glint in the stranger's eye. "And who says I've come here alone?"

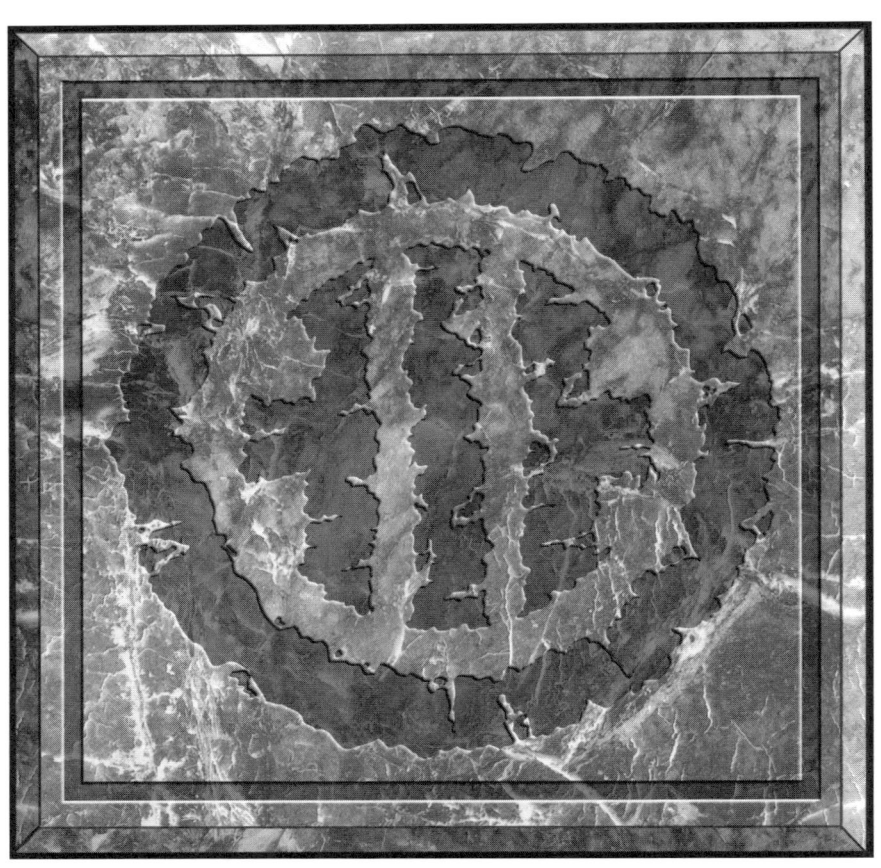

HAVE YOU SEEN THIS LUNATIC?

Writer/Artist

WAYNE

**APPROACH WITH EXTREME CAUTION!!
DO NOT TRY TO USE
LOGIC AGAINST THIS MAN!!**

Wayne Reinagel is a short, hairy gnome-like creature who dwells in dimly illuminated Hobbit burrows and cackles madly to himself as he pecks away at his computer keyboard. Raised on a steady diet of paperback novels, Mountain Dew, comic books, Snickers, and adventure movies, he churns out a steady flow of poetry, paintings, novels and other silly stuff. Warning: If sighted, approach with extreme caution!

WHO IS KNIGHTRAVEN STUDIOS?

ONCE A MONTH, IN A DESOLATE FOREST, WHEN THE SOFT LIGHT
OF THE FULL MOON BEGINS TO DRIFT AND SETTLE,
AN ANCIENT CULT OF OMINOUSLY ROBED AND HOODED FIGURES
GATHER SILENTLY TOGETHER IN A SECLUDED MEADOW.

USING THE ANCIENT DIALECT OF AN ELDER CIVILIZATION,
THEY BEGIN TO RHYTHMICALLY CHANT AND CROAK,
AND THE COOL NIGHT BREEZE WHISTLES AN EERIE MELODY
THROUGH THE BARE BRANCHES OF A LONG-DECEASED OAK.

BLOOD-RED ROBES ARE REMOVED AND CARELESSLY DISCARDED,
AS THE MANTA BECOMES MORE FRENZIED AND LOUDER,
ONLY TO REVEAL INHUMAN LEATHERY CREATURES AS ELUSIVE
AND FLEET-FOOTED AS QUICKSILVER AND MAGIC POWDER.

THE PALE, MIDNIGHT MOON SUDDENLY DARKENS, AS THOUGH
ECLIPSED BY A HUGE, UNSEEN SCARLET WINGED BIRD.
AND A DEEP, UNEARTHLY POWERFUL VOICE, THRUSTING UP
FROM THE DIRT AND MUD CAN NOW BE CLEARLY HEARD.

SHORT SHACKLES RISE ON THE BACK OF YOUR BARE NECK,
AS LOUDER GROWS THE FRIGHTFUL SHRIEKS AND MOANS,
DESPITE THE WARM NIGHT, GOOSEBUMPS APPEAR, A SUPER-
NATURAL COLD CHILLS THE VERY MARROW OF YOUR BONES.

STAGGERING BLINDLY THROUGH THE DARK WOODS,
REMEMBERING LONG-FORGOTTEN CHILDHOOD NIGHTMARES AND FEARS.
TREE BRANCHES GRASP AND SCRATCH LIKE DEATH'S CLAW-LIKE FINGERS,
WEARY HEARTBEATS THROBBING IN YOUR EARS.

THEN, SUDDENLY...

Huh?
What does this have to do with **Knightraven Studios**?
Absolutely nothing!
But it kept your attention, didn't it?

Thanks for visiting and hope you enjoyed the book!

And don't forget!
Coming soon from Knightraven Studios!
Doc Titan, **Darkness**, **Scorpion**, and **Guardian**
return in these two fabulous, action-packed novels!

Pulp Heroes - Khan Dynasty
Pulp Heroes - Sanctuary Falls

Don't miss the excitement and adventure!!